THE
CLOC

DATE DUE			
AUG 0 5 2015			
JUL 0 6			

D0980712

Sensitive

BURTON & SWINBURNE IN

THE CURIOUS CASE OF THE
CLOCKWORK MAN

Presented by

MARK HODDER

PYR

an imprint of **Prometheus Books**
Amherst, NY

Published 2011 by Pyr®, an imprint of Prometheus Books

Inquiries should be addressed to
Pyr
59 John Glenn Drive
Amherst, New York 14228–2119
VOICE: 716–691–0133
FAX: 716–691–0137
WWW.PYRSF.COM

15 14 13 12 11   5 4 3 2 1

Library of Congress Cataloging-in-Publication Data

Hodder, Mark, 1962–
    The curious case of the clockwork man : Burton & Swinburne, book 2 / by Mark Hodder.
        p. cm.
    ISBN 978–1–61614–359–6 (pbk.)
    1. Burton, Richard Francis, Sir, 1821–1890—Fiction. 2. Swinburne, Algernon Charles, 1837–1909—Fiction. 3. Criminal investigation—England—London—Fiction. 4. London (England)—Social conditions—19th century—Fiction. I. Title.

PR6108.O28C87 2011
823'.92—dc22

                                                                2010047322

Printed in the United States of America

Dedicated to

YOLANDA LERMA

One man's wickedness may easily become all men's curse.
—PUBLILIUS SYRUS

ACKNOWLEDGMENTS

My thanks to Rohan McWilliam, whose excellent *The Tichborne Claimant: A Victorian Sensation* (Hambledon Continuum, 2007) provided a wealth of background material, song lyrics, and quotes for this story.

George Mann, Lou Anders, and Emma Barnes, you are legends. Mike Moorcock, there's simply no way to adequately thank you.

As in the previous Burton and Swinburne tale, I have taken great liberties with respected (and some not so respected) famous names from the Victorian era. To any descendants of those whose reputations I have toyed with, I offer my apologies and an assurance that this is intended as speculative fiction and very definitely not biography. The alternative history imagined within these pages is a place where the inhabitants of Victorian England encountered different challenges and opportunities from those they met in real life, and have thus developed into very, very different people. They are quite unlike their historical counterparts and should not be in any way regarded as accurate depictions of the people who really lived.

In particular, I would like to offer respect and admiration to the current generation of the Tichborne/Doughty family. They still live in, and struggle to maintain, Tichborne House, which is a massively expensive undertaking, especially in these economically troubled times. They also continue the tradition of the Tichborne Dole, donating flour every year during the Feast of the Annunciation.

IN WHICH A GHOST
DESIRES DIAMONDS

Sir Roger Tichborne is my name,
I'm seeking now for wealth and fame,
They say that I was lost at sea,
But I tell them, "Oh dear, no, not me."

THE MAN OF BRASS

A handsome reward will be given to any person who can furnish such information as will discover the fate of Roger Charles Tichborne. He sailed from Rio de Janeiro on the 20th of April 1854 in the ship *La Bella*, and has never been heard of since, but a report reached England to the effect that a portion of the crew and passengers of a vessel of that name was picked up by a vessel bound to Australia, Melbourne it is believed. It is not known whether the said Roger Charles Tichborne was among the drowned or saved. He would at the present time be about thirty-two years of age, is of a delicate constitution, rather tall, with very light-brown hair, and blue eyes. Mr. Tichborne is the son of Sir James Tichborne, now deceased, and is heir to all his estates.

—Advertisement, newspapers worldwide, 1861

Sir Richard Francis Burton was dead.

He was lying on his back in the lobby of the Royal Geographical Society, sprawled at the bottom of the grand staircase with a diminutive red-haired poet slumped across his chest.

Algernon Charles Swinburne, tears streaming down his cheeks, his senses befuddled with alcohol, quickly composed an elegy. It was, after all, best to strike while the iron was hot.

He raised his head, his hair fiery in the flickering gas light, and, in his high-pitched voice, proclaimed:

> Wouldst thou not know whom England, whom the world,
>
> Mourns? For the world whose wildest ways he trod,
>
> And smiled their dangers down that coiled and curled
>
> Against him, knows him now less man than god.

He hiccupped.

Beneath his hand, in Burton's jacket, he felt a flask-shaped lump. Surreptitiously, he began to wiggle his fingers into the pocket.

"Our demigod of daring, keenest-eyed," he continued, with a sniff. "To read and deepest—"

"Atrocious!" a voice thundered from the top of the stairs.

Swinburne looked up.

Sir Roderick Murchison stood imperiously on the landing.

"Keep your hands to yourself, Algy," came a whisper.

Swinburne looked down.

Burton's eyes were open.

"Atrocious behaviour!" Murchison boomed again.

The president of the Royal Geographical Society descended with dignity and poise. His back was ramrod straight. His bald head was shining. He passed portraits of the great explorers: James Cook, Sir Walter Raleigh, John Franklin, Sir Francis Drake—this latter painting was hanging askew, having been struck by Burton's passing foot—William Hovell, Mungo Park, and others.

"I'll not brook such conduct, Burton! This is a respectable scientific establishment, not a confounded East End tavern!"

Swinburne fell back as his friend, the former soldier, explorer, and spy—the linguist, scholar, author, swordsman, geographer, and king's agent—staggered to his feet and stood swaying, glowering at Murchison, his one-time sponsor.

"Alive, then?" the poet muttered, gazing bemusedly at his friend.

At five foot eleven, Burton appeared taller, due to the breadth of his shoulders, depth of his chest, and slim athletic build. As inebriated as he was, he radiated power. His eyes were black and mesmeric, his cheekbones prominent, his mouth set aggressively. He had short black hair, which he wore swept backward, and a fierce mustache and beard, forked and devilish. A deep scar disfigured his left cheek, tugging slightly at his bottom eyelid, and there was a smaller one on the right, each marking the path of a Somali spear that had been thrust through his face during a disastrous expedition to Berbera.

"You're a damnable drunkard!" Murchison barked as he reached the bottom step. His narrow features suddenly softened. "Are you hurt?"

Burton snarled his response: "It'll take more than a tumble down the bloody stairs to break me!"

Swinburne scrambled up from the floor. He was tiny, just five foot two, and slope-shouldered. His head, perched on such a diminutive body, and with its mop of carroty hair, seemed perfectly enormous. He had pale-green eyes and was clean shaven. He appeared much younger than his twenty-four years.

"Confound it," he squeaked. "Now I'll have to use the elegy for somebody else. Who died recently? Anyone noteworthy? Did you like it, Richard? The bit about 'For the world whose wildest ways he trod' was especially appropriate, I thought."

"Be quiet, Swinburne!" Murchison snapped. "Burton, I'm not trying to break you, if that's what you're implying. Henry Stanley was better financed to settle the Nile question than you. I had little choice but to add the Society's backing to that which he received from his newspaper."

"And now he's disappeared!" Burton growled. "How many flying machines have to vanish over Africa's Lake Regions before you realise that the only way in is on foot?"

"I'm well aware of the problem, sir, and I'll have you know that I warned Stanley. It was his newspaper that insisted he take rotorchairs!"

"Pah! I know the area better than any man in the entire British Empire, but you saw fit to send a damn fool journalist. Who next, Murchison? Perhaps a dance troupe from the music halls?"

Sir Roderick stiffened. He crossed his arms over his chest and replied, icily: "Samuel Baker wants to mount a rescue mission, as does John Petherick, but whomever I send, it shan't be you, of that you can be certain. Your days as a geographer are over. It appears, however, that your days as a drinker are not!"

Burton clenched his teeth, tugged at his jacket, took a deep breath, paused, sighed it out, and all of a sudden the fight left him. He said, in a subdued tone: "Sam and John are good men. Accomplished. They know how to handle the natives. My apologies, Sir Roderick, I find it difficult to let go. I still think of the Nile question as mine to answer, though, in truth, I have a new and entirely different role to play now."

"Ah, yes. I heard a rumour that Palmerston has employed you. Is it true?"

Burton nodded. "It is."

"As what?"

"In truth, it's hard to say. I'm titled the 'king's agent.' It's something of an investigative role."

"Then I would think you're well suited to it."

"Perhaps. But I still take an interest in—well—sir, if you hear anything—"

"I'll get word to you," Murchison interrupted curtly. "Now go. Get some coffee. Sober up. Have some self-respect, man!"

The president turned and stamped back up the stairs, straightening Drake's portrait as he passed it.

A valet fetched Burton and Swinburne their coats, hats, and canes, and the two men walked unsteadily across the lobby and out through the double doors.

The evening was dark and damp, glistening with reflections after the day's showers. A chill wind tugged at their clothes.

"Coffee at the Venetia Hotel?" Burton suggested, buttoning his black overcoat.

"Or another brandy and a bit of slap and tickle?" Swinburne countered. "Verbena Lodge isn't far from here."

"Verbena Lodge?"

"It's a house of ill repute where the birchings are—"

"Coffee!" Burton said.

They walked along Whitehall Place and turned right into Northumberland Avenue, heading toward Trafalgar Square. Swinburne began to sing a song of his own composition:

> If you were queen of pleasure,
> And I were king of pain,
> We'd hunt down love together,
> Pluck out his flying-feather,
> And teach his feet a measure,
> And find his mouth a rein;
> If you were queen of pleasure,
> And I were king of pain.

His tremulous piping attracted disapproving glances from passersby. Despite the bad weather and the late hour, there were plenty of people about, mainly gentlemen strolling to and fro between the city's restaurants and clubs.

"Oh, bugger it," the poet cursed. "I think I just sang the last verse first. Now I'll have to start again."

"Please don't trouble yourself on my account," Burton murmured.

A velocipede—or "penny-farthing," as some wag had christened the vehicles—chugged past, pumping steam from its tall funnel into the already dense atmosphere of London.

"Hal-lo!" the rider exclaimed as he passed them, his voice rendered jittery as the vehicle's huge rubber-banded front wheel communicated every bump of the cobbled street to his spine. "W-what's g-going on in the s-square?"

Burton peered ahead, struggling to focus his eyes. There was, indeed, some sort of commotion. A crowd had gathered, and he could see the cockscomb helmets of police constables moving among the top hats.

He took Swinburne by the arm. "Come along," he urged. "Let's see what the hullabaloo is all about."

"For pity's sake slow down, will you!" complained his companion, who had to match Burton's every stride with two of his own. "You'll render me horrendously sober at this pace!"

"Incidentally, Algy, in the event of my demise, perhaps you'd show a little more restraint with the god and demigod references," Burton grumbled.

"Ha! What a contrary fellow you are! On the one hand you seem obsessed by religions; on the other, repelled by them!"

"Humph! These days, I'm more interested in the underlying motivation— in the reasons why a man is willing to be guided by a god whose existence is, at best, impossible to prove and, at worst, an obvious fabrication. It seems to me that in these times of rapid scientific and industrial advancement, the pro- curement of knowledge has become too intimidating a prospect for the average man, so he's shunning it entirely in favour of faith. Faith requires nothing but blind adherence, whereas knowledge demands the continual apprehension of an ever-expanding body of information. With faith, one can at least claim knowl- edge without having to do the hard work of acquiring it!"

"I say!" Swinburne cried. "Well said, old chap! Well said! You hardly slurred a single word! You're eminently reprehensible!"

"You mean *comprehensible*."

"I know what I mean. But Richard, surely Darwin's natural evolution has rendered God undeniably defunct?"

"Indubitably. Which begs the question: to what falsehood will the une- ducated masses willingly devote themselves next?"

They paced along, swinging their canes, their hats set at a jaunty angle. Despite the revitalising nip in the air, Burton was developing a headache. He decided to take a brandy with his coffee; perhaps it would numb the faint throbbing.

When they reached Trafalgar Square, the famous explorer plunged into the crowd and shouldered his way through it with Swinburne trailing in his wake. A constable stepped into their path, his hand raised.

"Stay back, please, gents."

Burton pulled out his wallet and withdrew from it a printed card. He showed it to the policeman who instantly saluted and stepped back.

"Beggin' your pardon, sir."

"Over here, Captain!" a deep, slightly husky voice called. Burton saw his friend Detective Inspector William Trounce of Scotland Yard standing at the base of Nelson's Column. Two people were with him: a young dark-skinned constable and, curiously, someone who was standing absolutely still, concealed from head to toe by a blanket.

Trounce met them with a hearty handshake. He was a bulky but amiable-looking individual, short but broad, with thick limbs and a barrel chest, bright twinkling blue eyes, and a large upward-curling brown mustache. His heavy square chin accurately hinted at a streak of stubbornness. He was wearing a dark worsted suit and a bowler hat.

"Hallo, chaps!" he said cheerfully. "Been drinking, have you?"

"Is it that obvious?" Burton mumbled.

"You didn't exactly cross the square as the crow flies."

"We're on our way to the Venetia for coffee."

"Very wise. Strong, black, with plenty of sugar. This is Constable Bhatti."

The policeman standing at Trounce's side saluted smartly. He was slender, youthful, and rather handsome.

"I've heard a lot about you, sir," he effused, with a slight Indian accent. "My cousin, Commander Krishnamurthy, was with you during the Old Ford affair."

He was referring to the recent battle that Burton, Swinburne, and a great many Scotland Yard men had fought against the Technologists and Rakes. Those two normally opposed groups—the one dedicated to scientific advancement, the other to anarchistic revolution—had banded together to try to capture a man from the future who'd become known as Spring Heeled Jack. Burton had defeated them and killed their quarry.

"Krishnamurthy's a thoroughly good egg," Swinburne noted. "But commander? Has he been promoted?"

"Yes, sir. It's a new rank in the force."

Trounce added: "They've made him head of the newly formed Flying Squad, and deservedly so. I don't know anyone who can handle a rotorchair the way Krishnamurthy does."

Burton nodded his approval and looked curiously at the silent, motionless blanket.

"So what's happening here, Trounce?"

The detective inspector turned to his subordinate. "Would you explain, please, Constable?"

"Certainly, sir." The young policeman looked at Burton and Swinburne and his dark eyes shone with excitement. "It's marvellous! An absolute wonder! Practically a work of art! I've never seen anything so intricate or—"

"Just the facts, please, lad," Trounce interjected.

"Yes, sir. Sorry, sir. This is my beat, you see, Captain Burton, and I pass through the square every fifty minutes or so. Tonight has been a quiet one. I've been making the rounds as usual, with nothing much to report aside from the customary prostitutes and drunkards—er—that is to say—"

He stopped, cleared his throat, cleared it again, and cast a pleading glance at his superior.

William Trounce laughed. "Don't worry, son, Captain Burton and Mr. Swinburne have been celebrating, that's all. Isn't that right, gents?"

"Quite so," Burton confirmed, self-consciously.

"And I wouldn't mind celebrating some more!" Swinburne announced.

Burton rolled his eyes.

Trounce addressed Bhatti: "So it was business as usual?"

The constable nodded. "Yes. I came on duty this evening at seven o'clock and passed this way three times without incident. On the fourth occasion, I noticed a crowd gathering here, where we're standing. I came over to investigate and found this—" He gestured at the concealed figure.

Trounce reached out and pulled the blanket away.

Burton and Swinburne gasped.

"Beautiful, isn't it!" Bhatti exclaimed.

A mechanical man stood before them. It was constructed from polished brass, slender, and about five feet five inches tall. The head was canister-shaped, flat at the top and bottom, and featureless but for three raised circular areas set vertically in the front. The top one was like a tiny ship's porthole, through which a great many motionless gears could be glimpsed, as small, complex, and finely crafted as the workings of a pocket watch. The middle circle held a mesh grille, and the bottom one was simply a hole out of which three very fine five-inch-long wires projected. They were straight and vibrated slightly in the breeze.

The neck consisted of thin shafts and cables, swivel joints and hinges. A slim cylinder formed the mechanical man's trunk. Panels were cut out of it, revealing cogwheels and springs, delicate little crankshafts, gyroscopes, flywheels, and a pendulum. The thin but sturdy arms ended in three-fingered hands. The legs were sturdy and tubular; the feet oval-shaped and slightly domed.

"It's a beauty, isn't it?" Constable Bhatti breathed. "Look here, in the small of the back. You see this hole? That's where the key goes."

"The key?" Burton asked.

"Yes! To wind it up! It's clockwork!"

"Bhatti, here," Detective Inspector Trounce put in, "is the Yard's amateur Technologist. Of all the policemen in London, he's certainly the right chap to have found this contraption."

"A happy coincidence for the constable," Swinburne observed glibly.

"It's my hobby," the young policeman enthused. "I attend a social club where we tinker with devices—trying to make them go faster or adapting them in various ways. Great heavens, the fellows would be beside themselves if I turned up with this specimen!"

Burton, who'd started to examine the brass figure with a magnifying glass, absently asked the policeman what he'd done after discovering it.

"The crowd was swelling—you know how Londoners flock around anything or anyone unusual—so I whistled for help. After a few constables had arrived, I gave the mechanism a thorough examination. I must admit, I got a little absorbed, so I probably didn't alert the Yard as quickly as I should have." He looked at Trounce. "Sorry about that, sir."

"And what is our metal friend's story, do you think?" asked Burton.

"Like I said, Captain, it's clockwork. My guess is that it's wound down. Why it was out walking the streets, I couldn't venture to guess."

"Surely if it was walking the streets, it would have attracted attention before it got here? Did anyone see it coming?"

"We've been making enquiries," Trounce said. "So far we've found fourteen who spotted it crossing the square but no one who saw it before then."

"So it's possible—maybe even probable—that it was delivered to the edge of the square in a vehicle," Burton suggested.

"Why, yes, Captain. I should say that's highly likely," the detective inspector agreed.

"It could have made its way through the streets, though," Bhatti said. "I'm not suggesting it did—I simply mean that the device is capable of that sort of navigation. You see this through here?" He tapped a finger on the top porthole at the front of the machine's head. "That's a babbage in there. Can you believe it? I never thought I'd live to see one! Imagine the cost of this thing!"

"A cabbage, Constable?" Trounce asked.

"Babbage," Bhatti repeated. "A device of extraordinary complexity. They calculate probability and act on the results. They're the closest things to a human brain ever created, but the secret of their construction is known only to one man—their inventor, Sir Charles Babbage."

"He's a recluse, isn't he?" Swinburne asked.

"Yes, sir, and an eccentric misanthrope. He has an aversion to what he terms 'the common hordes' and, in particular, to the noise they make, so he prefers to keep himself to himself. He hand-builds each of these calculators and booby-traps them to prevent anyone from discovering how they operate. Any attempt to dismantle one will result in an explosion."

"There should be a law against that sort of thing!" Trounce grumbled.

"My point is that when wound up, this brass man almost certainly has the ability to make basic decisions. And this here—" Bhatti indicated the middle opening on the thing's head "—is, in my opinion, a mechanical ear. I think you could give this contraption voice commands. And these—" he flicked the projecting wires "—are some sort of sensing device, I'd wager, along the lines of a moth's antennae."

Trounce pulled off his bowler hat and scratched his head.

"So let's get this straight: someone drops this clockwork man at the edge of the square. The device walks as far as Nelson's Column, then its spring winds down and it comes to a halt. A crowd gathers. According to the people we've spoken to, the machine got here just five minutes or so before you arrived on the scene, Constable. And you've been here—?"

"About an hour now, sir."

"About an hour. My question, then, is why hasn't the owner come forward to claim his property?"

"Exactly!" Bhatti agreed. "A babbage alone is worth hundreds of pounds. Why has it been left here?"

"An experiment gone wrong?" Swinburne offered. "Perhaps the owner was testing its homing instinct. He dropped it here, went back to his house or workshop or laboratory or whatever, and is waiting there for it to make its way back. Only he didn't wind the blessed thing up properly!"

Burton snorted. "Ridiculous! If you owned—or had invented—something as expensive as this, you wouldn't abandon it, hoping it'll find you, when there's even the remotest chance that it might not!"

Spots of rain began to fall.

Trounce glanced at the black, starless sky with impatience.

"Constable Hoare!" he shouted, and a bushy-browed, heavily mustached policeman emerged from the crowd and strode over.

"Sir?"

"Go to Saint Martin's Station and hitch a horse to a wagon. Bring it back here. On the double, mind!"

"Yes, sir!"

The constable departed and Trounce turned back to Burton.

"I'm going to have it carted over to the Yard. You'll have complete access to it, of course."

The king's agent pulled his collar tightly around his neck. The temperature was dropping and he was shivering.

"Thank you, Detective Inspector," he said, "but we were just passing. I don't think there's anything here we need to take a hand in. It's curious, though, I'll admit. Will you let me know if someone claims the thing?"

"Certainly."

"See you later, then. Come on, Algy, let's leg it to the Venetia. I need that coffee!"

The powerfully built explorer and undersized poet left the policemen, pushed through the throng, and headed across to the end of the Strand. As they entered the famous thoroughfare, the drizzle became a downpour. It hammered a tattoo against their top hats and dribbled from the brims.

Burton's headache was worsening and he was starting to feel tired and out of sorts.

A velocipede went past, hissing loudly as the rain hit its furnace.

Somewhere in the distance a siren wailed—a litter-crab warning that it was about to disinfect a road with blasts of scalding steam. It was a waste of time in this weather, but the crabs were automated and clanked around London every night, whatever the conditions.

"It's a good job brass doesn't rust," Swinburne observed, "or this weather would be the death of the clockwork man!"

Burton stopped.

"What is it?" his assistant asked.

"You're right!"

"Of course I am. It's an alloy of copper and zinc."

"No, no! About it being a coincidence!"

Swinburne hopped up and down. "What? What? Richard, can we please get out of this blasted rain?"

"Too much of a coincidence!"

Burton turned and took off back in the direction of Trafalgar Square.

"We're already too late!" he yelled over his shoulder.

Swinburne scampered along behind him, losing ground rapidly.

"What do you mean? Too late for what?"

He received no answer.

They raced into Trafalgar Square and rejoined Trounce and Bhatti. The latter had managed to open the uppermost portal in the machine's head and was peering in at the babbage.

"Oh, you're back! Look at this, Captain!" he said, as Burton reached his side. "There are eight tiny switches along the inside edge of this opening. Maybe they adjust the machine's behaviour in some manner? Each one has an up or down position, so how many combinations would—?"

"Never mind that!" the king's agent snapped. "Tell me the route of your beat, Constable!"

"My beat?" Bhatti looked puzzled.

"What's happening?" Trounce asked.

Burton ignored the detective inspector. His eyes blazed intently.

"Your beat, man! Spit it out!"

The constable pushed his helmet back from his eyes. Rainwater trickled down the back of his uniform. "All right," he said. "From here I proceed along Cockspur Street and around into Whitcomb Street. I walk up as far as the junction with Orange Street then turn right and keep on until I reach Mildew Street. I turn right again, at the works where they're shoring up the underground river, enter Saint Martin's, and foot-slog it back down to the square."

"And that takes fifty minutes?" Burton demanded.

"When you figure in all the alleyways that I poke my nose into, the shop doors that need checking, and so forth, yes."

"And places of note on the route? Places you check with the greatest diligence?"

"What's this about, Captain Burton?"

"Just answer the confounded question, man!"

"Do as he says, lad," Trounce ordered.

"Very well. There's the main branch of the Bright Empire Bank on the corner of Cockspur; the Satyagraha Bank is on Whitcomb; Treadwell's Post Office is on Orange Street, with SPARTA just opposite—"

"Sparta?"

"The Swan, Parakeet, and Runner Training Academy."

"Ah. Continue, please."

"The League of Enochians Gentlemen's Club is at the corner of Mildew, with the works on the other side; then going down Saint Martin's, there's Scrannington Bank, Brundleweed the diamond dealer's, the Pride-Manushi velocipede shop, Boyd's Antiques, and Goddard the art dealer. That's it. There are plenty of other places, of course, but those are the ones I make a special point of checking."

"Trounce, take Bhatti and follow the route from the Cockspur end," Burton directed. "Algy and I will take the opposite direction, along Saint Martin's."

Trounce frowned, held out his hands in a shrug, and asked: "But why? What are we looking for?"

"Can't you see?" Burton cried. "This bloody thing—" he struck the brass figure with his cane and it clanged loudly "—is nothing but a decoy! Whoever dropped it off in the square knew it would fascinate Bhatti, knew he'd pore over it obsessively before summoning help from the Yard, and knew that a fair amount of time would pass before he returned to his beat!"

"Hell's bells!" Trounce shouted. "You mean there's a crime in progress? Come on, Constable!"

He shoved bystanders aside, ordered a nearby police sergeant to guard the metal man, and raced away with Bhatti toward the end of Cockspur Street.

Sir Richard Francis Burton and Algernon Swinburne made their way to the edge of the square and pressed on through the rain to Saint Martin's.

Adrenalin had sobered them but Burton's headache was intensifying and a familiar ague—a remnant of Africa—was beginning to grip his limbs. It was an oncoming attack of malaria, and if he didn't get back to his apartment soon to quell it with a dose of quinine, he'd be immobilised for days to come.

They passed the police station and nodded to Constable Hoare, who was at the side of the road hitching a miserable-looking police horse to a wagon.

All along the street, gas lamps had fizzled out, their covers inadequate against the downpour. Only a few remained alight, and the deep shadows and streaming rain reduced visibility to just a few yards.

A little farther on, the two men came to Goddard's and peered through the night grille at the window behind.

"Good gracious!" Swinburne blurted excitedly. "There's a Rossetti in there and I modelled for it! I must tell Dante. He'll be over the moon!"

Dante Gabriel Rossetti was a founding member of the True Libertines—the most idealistic faction of the Libertine caste and a counterbalance to the notorious Rakes. He was also one of the "Pre-Raphaelite Brotherhood," a community of artists whose stated aim was to produce works that communicated at a "spiritual" level with the common man; a direct challenge to the current trend in propaganda. Few people admired them. Rossetti and his cohorts were mocked and ridiculed by the press, which claimed the artists were appealing to a void, since common men—the working classes—lacked anything resembling a well-developed sense of their own spirituality.

Swinburne often socialised with the group and had posed for their paintings on a number of occasions. He was surprised that Goddard dared display the small, medieval-themed canvas, which depicted the poet as a flame-haired knight with lance in hand, mounted on a sturdy horse. Admittedly, the picture was half hidden behind a more commercial portrait of the late Francis Galton, who was shown wielding a syringe and smiling broadly beneath the words: *Self-improvement! It doesn't hurt a bit!*

The premises was quiet and dark, its door secure, the windows intact.

"Let's move on," Burton said. "No one's going to steal a Rossetti."

An old-fashioned horse-drawn brougham—they were still common—came clattering alongside, splashed water onto their trouser legs, and disappeared into the gloom. Oddly, the sound of its horse's hooves thundered on, seeming quite out of proportion to the size of the animal.

"A mega-dray," Swinburne commented, and Burton realised that his assistant was right; the heavy clopping wasn't from the brougham's animal at all, it was from one of the huge dray horses developed by the Eugenicists, the biological branch of the Technologist caste. Obviously there was one nearby, though even as Burton thought this, the sound faded into the distance.

Boyd's Antiques, which was on the other side of the road, was, like Goddard's, locked up and undisturbed.

"Nothing happening here," Swinburne said as they walked on. "Great heavens, Richard, we're in desperate straits—we're both soaked, and not with alcohol!"

"Good!" Burton replied. "I thought I'd weaned you off the bottle."

"You had, but then you tempted me back! You've not been sober for more than two days since the Spring Heeled Jack hoo-ha!"

"For which I apologise. I think my frustrations over the Nile situation have been getting the better of me."

"Give it up, Richard. Africa's no longer your concern."

"I know, I know. It's just that . . . I regret the mistakes I made during my expedition. I wish I could go back and make amends."

A man hurried past them, spitting expletives as the strengthening wind turned his umbrella inside out.

Swinburne gave his friend a sideways glance. "Do you mean physically return to Africa or go back in time? What on earth's got into you? You've been like a bear with a sore head lately."

Burton pursed his lips, thrust his cane into the crook of his elbow, and pushed his hands into his pockets.

"Montague Penniforth."

"Who?"

"He was a cab driver—a salt-of-the-earth type. He knew his position in society, and despite it being tough and the rewards slight, he just got on with it, uncomplainingly."

"So?"

"So I dragged him out of his world and into mine. He got killed, and it was my fault." Burton looked at his companion, his eyes hard and his expression grim. "William Stroyan, 1854, Berbera. I underestimated the natives. I didn't think they'd attack our camp. They did. He was killed. John Hanning Speke. Last year, he shot himself in the head rather than confront me in a debate. Now half his brain is a machine and his thoughts aren't his own. Edward Oxford—"

"The man who leaped here from the future."

"Yes. And who accidentally changed the past. He was trying to put it right, and I killed him."

"He was Spring Heeled Jack. He was insane."

"My motives were selfish. He revealed to me where my life was going. I broke his neck to prevent any chance that he might succeed in his mission. I didn't want to be the man that his history recorded."

They trudged on through the sodden rubbish and animal waste. Unusually, this end of Saint Martin's Lane hadn't yet been visited by a litter-crab.

"If he'd lived, Richard," Swinburne said, "the Technologists and Rakes would have used him to manipulate time for their own ends. We would have lost control of our destinies."

"Does not Destiny, by its very nature, deny us control?" Burton countered.

Swinburne smiled. "Does it? Then if that's the case, responsibility for Mr. Penniforth's death—and the other misfortunes you mentioned—must rest with Destiny, not with you."

"Which would make me its tool. Bismillah! That's just what I need!"

Burton stopped and indicated a shopfront. "Here's Pride-Manushi, the velocipede place."

They examined the doors and windows of the establishment. No lights showed. Everything was secure. They squinted through the gaps in the metal shutter. There was no movement, nothing amiss.

"Brundleweed's next," Burton murmured.

"Gad! I don't blame you for wishing you were back on the Dark Continent!" Swinburne declared, pulling at his overcoat collar. "At least it's warm there. A thousand curses on this rain!"

They crossed the road again. As they mounted the pavement, a beggar stepped out of a shadowy doorway. He was ill kempt and wore disreputable clothes. A profusion of greying hair framed his face, and it was quite apparent that he was well acquainted with neither a comb nor a bar of soap.

"I lost me job, gents," he wheezed, raising his flat cap in greeting and revealing a bald scalp. "An' it serves me bloomin' well right, too. I ask you, why the heck did I choose to be a bleedin' philosopher when me mind's nearly always muddled? Can you spare thruppence?"

Swinburne fished a coin out of his pocket and flipped it to the vagrant. "Here you are, old chap. You were a philosopher?"

"Much obliged. Aye, I was, lad. An' here's a bit of advice in return for your coin: life is all about the survival of the fittest, an' the wise man must remember that, while he's a descendant of the past, he's also a parent of the bloomin' future. Anyways—" he bit the thruppence and slipped it into his pocket "—Spencer's the name, an' I'm right pleased to have made your acquaintance. Evenin', gents!"

He raised his cap again and retreated to his doorstep, where the rain couldn't reach him.

Burton and Swinburne continued their patrol.

"What an extraordinary fellow!" Swinburne reflected. "Here's Brundleweed's. It looks quiet."

It did, indeed, look quiet. The grille was down, the window display was intact, and the lights were off.

"I wonder how Trounce and Bhatti are getting on," Burton said. He tried the door. It didn't budge. "It looks all right. Let's foot it to Scrannington Bank."

The cold wind battered them and the deluge lanced into their faces. They pulled the brims of their hats down low and the collars of their coats up high, but it was a lost cause.

Burton was shivering uncontrollably. Tomorrow, he knew, he was going to be in a bad way.

The bank loomed ahead. It was a big, dirty, foreboding edifice. The water had cut grey rivulets into its sooty coat.

Swinburne hopped up its steps to check the doors. They were closed and barred. He came back down. All the windows were shuttered.

"This isn't very inspiring at all. I think we're on a wild goose chase," he complained. "What time is it?"

"Nigh on midnight, I should say."

"Look around you, Richard. Everyone has disappeared. We haven't even seen an automated animal. Man, woman, and beast are tucked up in their warm, dry beds! So are criminals!"

"You're probably right," Burton replied grumpily, "but we should press on until we reunite with Trounce."

"Fine! Fine! If you say so," Swinburne replied, throwing up his arms in exasperation. "But please remember that—should another occasion like this arise in the future—being wet to the bone and frozen to the marrow is definitely not the sort of pain I enjoy. The sting of a hard cane, yes! The sting of a hard rain, no! What's that?" He pointed across the road to a fenced area beside an intersection. Beyond the low barricade, there was pitch darkness.

"It's Mildew Street," Burton answered. "Let's take a look. Those are the works where they're shoring up the underground river."

They crossed Saint Martin's again and leaned over the waist-high wooden barrier. They couldn't see a thing.

Burton pulled a clockwork hand-lantern from his pocket, shook it open, and gave it a twist. The sides of the device spilled light into the rain. He held it up over the fence, illuminating a muddy pit. The saturated ground angled down to the mouth of a well, from which the top of a ladder projected. Streams of water gurgled over the slope and disappeared into the wide shaft.

"Look!" he exclaimed, pointing to a patch of mud at the top of the slope, just beneath a collapsed segment of fencing on the Mildew Street side.

"You mean the footprints?" Swinburne shrugged. "So what?"

"Don't be a blessed fool!" Burton growled. "How long are muddy foot-prints going to last in this weather?"

"My hat! I see what you mean!"

"They're recent. Some of them haven't even filled with water yet."

The two men moved around the barrier to the broken section. Burton squatted and examined the footprints closely.

"Remind you of anything?" he asked.

"It looks like someone's been pressing flat irons into the mud," the poet observed. "My goodness, those are deep prints. Whoever made them must have been very heavy. Ovals, not shoe-shaped. I say! The clockwork man!"

"Not the one in Trafalgar Square," Burton corrected. "It had clean feet and these prints were made while it's been standing beside the column. There were other clockwork men here—three of them—and less than fifteen min-utes ago, I should think. Look who was with them!"

Burton moved his lantern. The circle of light swept across the mud and settled on a line of big, widely spaced, very deep oblong prints. Who- or whatever had made them obviously possessed three legs.

Swinburne recognised them at once. "Brunel!" he cried. "Isambard Kingdom Brunel! The Steam Man!"

"Yes. See how deep his prints are by the well? He obviously waited there while the brass men went down. I wonder what they were up to?"

Burton stepped over the fence's fallen planks and turned to his assistant. "I'm going to have a look. You run back to that Spencer fellow. Give him another thruppence and ask him if he saw anything unusual around here, then come back and wait for Trounce and Constable Bhatti. Go! We mustn't waste any more time!"

Swinburne raced off.

Burton crouched, lowering his centre of gravity to improve his balance on the slippery surface. He began to inch downward, bracing himself with his cane, holding the lantern high. The rain hissed around him. He wondered whether he was doing the right thing. Brunel and his clockwork companions were getting away—but from what? What had they been up to?

He'd covered half the short distance to the well when his feet shot out from under him. He slapped down onto his back and went slithering uncon-trollably toward the mouth of the shaft, slewing sideways until his hip thudded against the top of the ladder which, thankfully, was bolted to the side of the well. He felt his shoulders swerving over the sodden clay and was propelled headfirst into the opening. Without thinking, he let go of his cane and threw out a hand. It closed over a rung and he gripped hard as his body turned in the air, swung down, and slammed against the ladder. The force of the impact knocked the wind out of him and loosened his hold. He fell before catching another rung. Pain lanced through his shoulder. His cane clacked onto a solid surface somewhere below.

He scrambled for a foothold, secured himself, and hung on, shaking. An involuntary groan issued from his lips.

He felt weak and ill. Despite the cold weather, beads of sweat were gathering on his forehead.

The lantern went out.

Shifting to better secure himself, he gave the device a twist. It spluttered back into life and he lowered it past his knee, revealing a brick walkway not far below. A river flowed beside it, the brown surface heaving and frothing as it sped past.

Burton descended with water pouring around him from the pit above. He stepped off the ladder and flexed his arm, winced, then picked up his cane and flashed the light around, finding himself in a small section of newly built brick-lined tunnel. Farther down in both directions, it gave way to a soft-walled, insecure-looking passage which, for as far as he could see—which wasn't very far—had been shored up with timber.

The walkway ran alongside the river and disappeared into the darkness. On it, three sets of muddy oval-shaped footprints trailed back and forth.

He followed them.

The course of the river was by no means straight but the explorer felt certain that it remained more or less beneath Saint Martin's on its way to the Thames.

Moments later, he came to a hole cut into the wall on his left. Big lumps of stone were scattered around it and a pile of rubble blocked the path beyond. A glance at the ground assured him that the three mechanical men had passed this way, so he entered and stepped through a short stretch of roughly cut tunnel.

It broke through into the unlit and damp basement of a building, empty but for broken pieces of packing crates, a rusty iron bedstead, and an old chest of drawers. Smeared mud cut a channel across the dusty floor to an open door and up the stairs beyond.

Treading softly, the king's agent ascended. There was another door at the top of the stairs, which he opened carefully. His lantern illuminated what appeared to be a workshop. There was a large safe in the corner. Its door had been wrenched off and lay, warped out of shape, on the floor nearby. The safe was empty.

He passed through to a hallway and entered the next room, which he found was at the front of the building. He recognised it at once. He'd seen it through a security grille. It was Brundleweed's—the diamond dealer's shop.

He returned to the safe and examined it.

"Emptied out!" he said, softly. "But why would Brunel—the most lauded engineer in the Empire—steal diamonds? It doesn't make sense!"

The public believed that Isambard Kingdom Brunel had died from a stroke in 1859. They regarded him as one of the greatest Englishmen ever to have lived. Little did they know that he'd actually retreated into a mobile life-maintaining mechanism, and, from it, still directed the Technologists' various projects.

"What the devil is he playing at?" Burton muttered.

There was nothing further he could do here—and the longer he remained, the farther away the Steam Man and his three clockwork assistants would get.

He turned and ran back the way he'd come. It took but a few moments to reach the ladder and climb it.

Someone called to him as he poked his head out into the rain: "Burton! Burton! Hurry up, man!"

"Trounce? Is that you? Give me a hand, will you?"

"Wait there!"

He squinted through the downpour, saw figures milling about, sliding down the slope toward him, and was surprised when Spencer the philosopher emerged from the rain.

"Hallo, Boss! Reach up an' we'll 'ave you out in a jiffy!"

"Hello, Mr. Spencer! Here, grab the end of my cane!"

He extended his stick toward the vagrant, who clutched it tightly.

Burton clambered up and gripped Spencer's wrist. He saw that the beggar was held by Trounce, who in turn was held by Bhatti.

Swinburne, who wasn't holding anybody, was jumping up and down on the other side of the fence, screeching: "Don't let go of him! Don't let go!"

The chain of men pulled Burton up out of the pit, over the fallen fence, and onto the pavement.

"By Jove!" Trounce observed. "You're a sight!"

Burton looked down at himself. He was caked with mud from top to toe. He felt as bad as he looked, but, ignoring the ache burrowing through his bones, he twisted off the lantern, thrust it into his pocket, and reported his discovery: "It's a diamond robbery. They tunnelled into Brundleweed's from the side of the underground river."

"Strewth!" Constable Bhatti gasped. "Old Brundleweed took a big delivery a couple of days ago. The crooks must have made off with a fortune!"

"And they're heading west!" Trounce declared.

"How do you know that?" Burton asked.

"Mr. Spencer saw them!" Swinburne revealed.

Burton turned to the vagrant. "Explain!"

"There were one of 'em whoppin' great pantechnicons parked here, Boss. One of the ones what's drawn by the jumbo dray horses. I didn't see nothin' goin' on, but it galloped off at a rare old pace just a few moments afore you arrived."

"We heard it!" Burton confirmed.

"And it passed us on Orange Street!" Trounce said. "Heaven knows where it is now. We'll never catch up with it!"

"Are you joking?" Burton cried. "How can we miss a horse that size? It's a veritable mountain!"

"True, but a fast-moving one that might have headed off in any direction by now!"

The king's agent turned suddenly and started to race away along Mildew Street.

"Follow me!"

"What? Hey! Captain Burton!" the detective inspector shouted after the retreating figure. "Damn it! Come on, Bhatti!"

The two policemen took off after the king's agent. Swinburne followed, and behind him came Spencer, who'd decided to stick with the group in the hope that another thruppence might be forthcoming.

They dashed into Orange Street, and Trounce hadn't gone far before he spotted Burton ahead, hammering on a door and bellowing, "Open up in the name of the king!"

The detective inspector recognised the building. He'd checked it just a few minutes before: SPARTA, the automated animal training centre.

In a flash, he realised what Burton was up to.

"This is the police!" he hollered officiously. "Open the door!"

He heard a bolt being drawn back.

Swinburne and Spencer arrived, panting.

The portal opened slightly and an eye was put to the crack.

"I was asleep!" a female voice protested.

"Madam, I'm Detective Inspector William Trounce of Scotland Yard. These are my associates and we need your help!"

The door opened wider, revealing a young woman clad in dressing gown, nightcap, and slippers. Her face was strong, oval-shaped, brown-eyed.

"What do you mean?"

"Have you any trained swans on the premises?" Burton asked brusquely.

"Yes. No. That is to say, not fully but six are close enough. Trained, I mean."

"Then I'm afraid we must commandeer four of them."

"Five," Spencer corrected.

The woman looked astonished, her eyes flicking from Burton to Trounce and back again.

"Please, ma'am," Trounce said in a softer tone. "This is an emergency. You will be compensated."

She stepped back. "You'd better come in. My name is Mayson, Isabella Mayson."

They entered.

Miss Mayson lit an oil lamp and held it up.

"Merciful heavens! What happened to you!" she gasped upon noticing Burton's mud-encrusted clothing.

"Would you mind if I explained later, Miss Mayson? There really isn't any time to spare."

"Very well. This way, please." She lifted an umbrella from a stand and led them along the passage. "I'm afraid you'll have to pass the parakeets to get to the swans."

Bhatti grinned and said, "We policemen are used to a little abuse. I take it they've not found a solution to the problem yet?"

"Through this room, gentlemen. The cages are beyond. No, Constable—um—?"

"Bhatti, Miss."

"No, Constable Bhatti, they haven't. Wait a moment."

She stopped at a door, fiddled with a key ring, located the appropriate key, and fitted it into the lock.

"Brace yourselves," she advised, with a wry smile.

She opened the door and they all stepped through.

Insults exploded from the stacked cages encircling the room: "Piss-guzzlers! Cheese-brains! Stench-makers! Cross-eyed baboons! Drooling fumblers! Flush-faced sots! Blubberous flab-guts! Witless remnants! Boneheaded contortionists! Sheep-tickling louts! Maggotous duffers! Ugly buffoons! Slime-lickers!"

It was a deafening roar, and it didn't let up for a moment as they traversed the long chamber toward the door at its far end.

"I'm sorry!" Miss Mayson shouted at the top of her voice. "Take it on the chin!"

Swinburne giggled.

Messenger parakeets had been one of the first practical applications of the Eugenicists' science to be adopted by the British public. A person only had to visit a post office to give one of their birds a message, name, and address, and the parakeet would fly off to deliver the communication. No one but the Eugenicists knew how the colourful little creatures found the addresses, but they always did.

There was one problem.

The parakeets cursed and insulted everyone they encountered. Invariably, messages were liberally peppered with expletives not put there by the sender. Nevertheless, the system proved popular, especially as some of the birds displayed a rather amusing talent for creating totally meaningless words that, nevertheless, sounded insulting. These "new insults" were all the rage at Society events. Swinburne himself had recently been called a "blibbering chub-fluffer" by a parakeet delivering an invitation to a poetry reading at Lord Haverleigh's. He'd laughed about it for days. *You are cordially invited— you blibbering chub-fluffer—to an evening of stinking poetry and abysmal piss wine—*

The foul-mouthed birds demonstrated an issue that had troubled eugenics from the very start. Whatever modification the scientists bred into a species, it always brought with it an unexpected side effect. The giant dray horses, for example, had no control over their bladders or bowels and were overproductive in both departments. This had proven a serious problem in London's already filthy streets until the Engineering branch of the Technologists invented the automated mechanical cleaners, popularly known as "litter-crabs," to tackle the issue.

"Hag-kissers! Slack-jaws! Dirt-gobblers! Mumblebums! Dolts! Filthy blackguards! Bulging scumbags! Gusset-sniffers! Gibbering loonies! Puppy-munchers!"

Trailing behind Miss Mayson, the men reached the other side of the room. The young woman unlocked a door, threw it open, and ushered them through. The portal slammed shut behind them and she leaned against it, opening the umbrella. "That's quite enough of that, I think! My apologies, gentlemen."

They stood in a very spacious rain-swept yard beside a row of cages, each containing an upright wheel. In each wheel there was a dog—all greyhounds—sprinting at top speed. There must have been at least twenty of them, and the rumble of the spinning wheels drowned out even the noise of the rain.

The greyhounds were known as runners, and they formed the other half of the British Postal Service. Where the parakeets communicated spoken messages, the dogs delivered letters, racing from door to door with the missives held gently between their teeth. In fact, they were unable to *stop* running, and even when they arrived at a delivery destination they jogged on the spot until the letter they carried was taken. They were also voracious eaters, and any person using the service was obliged to feed them.

"They've just gone to sleep," Miss Mayson said, gesturing toward the animals.

"They run in their sleep?" Swinburne asked wonderingly.

"Yes, which is why I had the wheels put inside their cages. It's better than having them racing around the yard. The swans are over there."

She indicated the far end of the enclosure, where nine breathtakingly huge birds stood in high-roofed pens. Their heads were poised, about fifteen feet up, at the top of elegantly curved necks. Their beady eyes watched the group as it approached them.

"Don't worry. They're almost tame."

"Almost?" Trounce asked, doubtfully. "Somehow, I don't find that very comforting."

"If they were any wilder, they'd bite your head off before you could blink. They're aggressive by nature."

Trounce smoothed his mustache with his fingers.

"But four are tame enough to fly, yes?" Burton asked.

"Five," Spencer added.

"Yes, sir, though you might struggle a bit. They're a touch headstrong."

"Let's get them buckled up. We have to work fast."

Miss Mayson crossed to a shed from which she produced harnesses and big folded box kites. Then she picked up a long, thin wooden cane, returned to the pens, and used it to drive out five of the enormous white birds.

"Down!" she commanded, while slapping one of the swans on its side with the rod. It obligingly squatted, and, while Spencer held the umbrella over her, she showed the men how to attach the long reins to the base of the bird's neck, passing them over its back. Swinburne, who'd flown swans before, assisted her by buckling the ends of lengthy leather straps to its legs and clipping the other ends to one of the box kites which Burton and Trounce had unfolded.

While they worked, the king's agent instructed his companions: "Look out for litter-crabs."

"Why litter-crabs?" Trounce asked in a puzzled tone.

"I noticed that the end of Saint Martin's hadn't been cleaned," Burton responded. "Now I know why. The litter-crabs were tempted away from it by the mega-dray. You know how the contraptions tend to follow behind the horses, cleaning up the manure. I dare say they're still on its trail!"

"Good thinking, Captain!" the policeman exclaimed.

Miss Mayson helped Constable Bhatti into a kite. He sat on the canvas seat, slipped his boots through the stirrups, and took the reins. The woman showed him how to control the bird.

A few minutes later, all five men were in position.

Miss Mayson stepped back. "Half a mo!" she cried. "Wait there—I have an idea!"

She ran back along the yard and into the training centre.

"What's she up to?" Burton grumbled truculently, but even as he spoke she reappeared and hurried over to them.

She held a small blue and yellow parakeet in her hand.

"All messenger parakeets are identified by a postcode," she said. "This is POX JR5. She's one of the new breed. As long as she knows you, she'll be able to find you. She doesn't even need your address. You can use her to communicate between the kites. She'll keep up with the swans—she's the swiftest of all my birds. Tell her your names!" She held the parakeet out to each of the men in turn.

"Captain Richard Burton."

"Odorous thug!" the bird whistled.

"Detective Inspector William Trounce."

"Ponderous buffoon!" it cheeped.

"Algernon Charles Swinburne."

"Illiterate bum-pincher!" it cackled.

"Constable Shyamji Bhatti."

"Nurdle-thwacker!" it squawked.

"Herbert Spencer."

"Angel-faced beauty," it crooned.

"My goodness!" Miss Mayson exclaimed. "Was that a compliment?"

Burton blew out a breath. "Please," he said, "there's no time for this!"

She gave a small nod and placed the parakeet on Burton's shoulder. It hunkered down and he felt its little claws sinking into the soggy cloth of his overcoat.

"Good luck!" the young woman said, stepping back. "Constable, call in tomorrow and tell me all about it!"

Bhatti smiled and nodded. "Get yourself inside and dry off," he advised. "Your slippers are wet through!"

Sir Richard Francis Burton snapped his reins the way she'd shown him. His swan stretched out its wings, ran five steps forward, and, with a mighty flapping, soared into the air. The leather straps of the harness uncoiled, snaked up after it, jerked taut, and his kite shot upward.

Thrown violently back into his canvas seat, the king's agent found himself rising at phenomenal speed into the sodden atmosphere. The rain pelted against his face. His swan spiralled higher and, when he glanced back, he saw that his colleagues were following behind.

The chase was on!

A DESIGN FOR UTOPIA

Errors using inadequate data are much less than those using no data at all.

—SIR CHARLES BABBAGE

The water-laden air jabbed cold needles into Burton's face, but despite being hatless—for, like the others, he'd placed his headgear into a spacious pocket at the back of the kite—he actually felt unpleasantly warm; a sign that his malarial fever was developing rapidly. He tried to stay focused but a peculiar sense of disassociation was creeping over him.

"Bloody git-face," POX JR5 mumbled.

The five giant swans began to circle over the western end of Orange Street. Visibility was poor in the rain so the men flew them close to the rooftops, except for Swinburne, who, despite being the most experienced flier, was having problems controlling his unruly bird. He was currently somewhere overhead, inside the low blanket of cloud.

Tracking the mega-dray proved easier than Burton had anticipated.

It was Bhatti who spotted the trail. He steered his swan in beside Burton's, but the kites, at the end of their long tethers, were flying extremely erratically due to the wind and beating rain, making it impossible to shout across to one another.

Burton spoke to the parakeet: "Pox! Message for Constable Shyamji Bhatti. Message begins. What is it? Message ends. Go."

The brightly coloured bird launched itself from his shoulder. A few moments later, when the constable's kite tumbled upward past his own, Burton saw that the messenger was already squawking into the young policeman's ear.

The explorer shifted his hips, trying to stabilise his vehicle. It was foul weather for flying!

The parakeet returned. "Message from dribbling sponge-head Constable Shyamji Bhatti!" it whistled. "Message begins. Look off to the right, snot-picker—the bloody litter-crabs are all along Haymarket. Message ends."

Burton told Pox to take the message to Trounce, Swinburne, and Spencer. He then sent his swan wheeling to the right and along Haymarket. He passed over four of the large eight-legged, steam-driven street cleaners and spotted a fifth at the end of Piccadilly. Yanking at the reins, he veered to the left and followed the thoroughfare. He soared past a sixth crab, a seventh, an eighth, and Green Park hove into view. The ninth litter-crab was clearing up a mountain of steaming manure outside the exclusive Parthenon Hotel; after that, all the way to Hyde Park Corner, he didn't see a single one.

Pox returned to his shoulder.

He circled counterclockwise around the edge of Green Park, peering into the gloom.

There!

The massive pantechnicon was in the park, close to the Queen Victoria Memorial, with the mega-dray towering in front of it.

Looking back, he saw his colleagues following. Swinburne's bird suddenly plummeted from the clouds, honked loudly, and swooped downward to land in the park. Behind it, the box kite was dragged through treetops, splintering and ripping until nothing of it was left. Burton saw the tiny poet bounce from branch to branch and tumble from the trees to the ground.

With a heartfelt curse, he slowed his swan, pulled it around in a tight turn, and flew low over his friend.

"Are you hurt?" he bellowed as he flapped past.

He wheeled again; flew back.

"Yes!" came a small voice from below. "It was thrilling!"

Burton marvelled at his swan's manoeuvrability as he pivoted it through the air to fly over Swinburne once more.

"Round up some policemen!" he shouted. "Capture that pantechnicon!"

He increased altitude, wiping the rain from his eyes, and rejoined the others, who were circling above the massive vehicle. The bulky figure of Isambard Kingdom Brunel could be seen at the back of it. He was unloading four machines, aided by his three clockwork men.

As always, Burton felt awed by the sight of the Steam Man.

The most famous and successful engineer in the world stood on three multijointed mechanical legs. These were attached to a horizontal disk-shaped chassis affixed to the bottom of Brunel's body. The body was like a barrel lying on its side, with domed protrusions at either end. Each of these bore nine triple-jointed arms, and each arm ended in a different tool, ranging from delicate fingers to slashing blades, drills, hammers, spanners, and welders.

A further dome rose from the top of Brunel's body. From this, too, arms extended—six in all—though these were more like tentacles, long and flexible. Each ended in a clamplike hand.

At various places around the barrel-body, revolving cogwheels poked through slots, and on one shoulder a piston slowly rose and fell. On the other, something resembling a bellows pumped up and down and Burton knew from previous experience that it made a hideous wheezing noise.

This massive mechanism kept Brunel alive—but what of the man inside? How did he breathe or see or hear or eat? How much of his humanity did he retain?

The king's agent—along with Swinburne, Trounce, and two or three others—was aware that some of the engineer's recent activities were not only ethically dubious but had, perhaps, gone beyond the boundaries of the law. However, as Sir Richard Mayne, chief commissioner of police at Scotland Yard, said: "It would be unwise to arrest a national hero—a man who has done, and secretly continues to do, great good for the Empire—unless we have absolute and irrefutable proof of his crimes."

So far, that proof had not been forthcoming.

Burton gave a whistle of amazement. He'd just realised what Brunel and his assistants were doing. They were unpacking and unfolding ornithopters.

"Message for Detective Inspector Trounce," he said. "Message begins. They have ornithopters. I don't know how fast these swans are but they're about to be tested. Message ends. Go."

Pox plunged out of the kite.

Along with gas-filled airships and electrical engines, ornithopters were generally considered to be one of the Technologists' "dead-end" inventions— good in theory but not in practice. The winged machines possessed great speed and could cover enormous distances without refuelling, but they were also impossible for a person to control; human reactions simply weren't fast enough to compensate for their innate instability. It had been suggested that a babbage could fly them but, of course, babbages were rare and prohibitively expensive. Except, Burton thought, there were three of them down there right now, with Brunel, each housed in a clockwork body, each mounting an ornithopter's saddle.

The engineer's own flying machine was massive—the biggest of the type the explorer had ever seen—which it needed to be in order to carry Brunel's great weight.

The four swans swooped overhead as the ornithopters started to roll forward.

The parakeet returned to Burton's shoulder.

"Message from skunk-scented Detective Inspector Trounce!" it screeched. "Message begins. Use your gun. Shoot the blasted ornithopters, you sludge-brained nincompoop, but don't fire at bilious Brunel. Message ends."

Burton passed the right rein to his left hand and pulled a Smith and Wesson revolver from his coat pocket. It was difficult to steer the swan one-handed and the kite was swinging about wildly. What with that and the rain and the wind, making an accurate shot seemed impossible. His hand, too, was trembling with his oncoming fever. Hopelessly, he pointed the gun in the general direction of the ornithopters and pulled the trigger. Immediately, one of the machines disappeared in a ball of steam and a loud detonation echoed across the park. A brass head went spinning into the air, narrowly missing Herbert Spencer's swan.

"Lucky shot!" Burton mumbled. "Must have hit the pressure boiler!"

The three remaining ornithopters accelerated over the grass, belching vapour from their funnels, their wings flapping. A ratcheting noise reached Burton's ears as the machines angled into the air and picked up speed.

Gunshots sounded from Trounce and Bhatti's kites, and one of the flying contraptions suddenly slid sideways, turned over, and thumped back down to earth, crushing the clockwork driver beneath it. Burton caught a glimpse of a mangled and twitching figure as he flew past.

He fired another shot, pocketed his revolver, grabbed at the reins with both hands, and gave them a hefty flick, urging his swan to greater speed.

The ornithopters, with wings beating so fast they became nothing but a blur, leaned to the right and turned, heading northward. They increased altitude and disappeared into the clouds. The swans followed.

Burton was wretchedly wet. His teeth chattered and he shook uncontrollably.

He wiped his face in the crook of his elbow and when he looked up he found that he'd unexpectedly emerged into clear, dry, still air.

The layer of cloud had fallen away beneath him and a full moon glared down, turning the top of the billowing weather front a bright silvery grey. There was no rain and hardly a breeze at this altitude, and his box kite immediately settled into smooth flight, losing the sickening weaving and bobbing motion that had marked the pursuit so far.

Brunel's machine flapped ahead. Where was his companion?

Burton looked to his right and saw Bhatti and Spencer. He looked to his left and saw Trounce—and shouted a warning! Too late!

The surviving clockwork man's ornithopter plunged from above straight into Trounce's swan. A metal wing tore through the bird's neck, slicing its head clean off.

The ornithopter arced away as the bird's decapitated corpse plummeted down into the cloud, dragging the kite behind it. In the instant before Trounce vanished into the thick mist, Burton saw him yank his emergency strap, separating the kite from the bird.

He breathed a sigh of relief. His friend would float safely to earth, though the landing might leave him shaken and bruised.

He steered closer to his two remaining companions. Here, above the bad weather, his voice carried: "Where did it go?"

"I don't know!" Bhatti yelled, peering up and around.

"Down into the cloud!" Spencer shouted. "It went right under your bloomin' kite, Boss! It—*aaah!*"

The ornithopter shot up from below, passing straight through the harness that attached the vagrant philosopher to his bird. Spencer tumbled away in his kite while the swan, with no one to guide it, turned and flew back the way it had come.

Burton snatched at his revolver, fumbled, and dropped it out of the kite. He cursed and glanced across at the constable, hoping his moment of weakness hadn't been witnessed. It hadn't. Bhatti was looking this way and that, scanning the sky for their attacker.

"Coming down at you!" the policeman screamed, pointing upward.

The king's agent yanked fiercely at his reins, sending his bird, with a honk of protest, swerving sharply to the left. Bhatti's revolver barked twice as the ornithopter plunged past, narrowly missing a collision with Burton's kite. The enemy vehicle twisted in the air and rose up beside the constable's swan. The driver, mounted on the ornithopter's saddle, turned to look at the giant bird. The frightened swan responded with its species' characteristic belligerence. It whipped its neck sideways, gripped the brass head in its beak, and ripped it from the mechanical shoulders.

Bhatti cheered, but his delight was short-lived. With nothing to steer it, the ornithopter slid into his bird. Metal and fleshy wings clashed and a stream of blood showered back over the constable. The swan shrieked and started to fall, the ornithopter spinning down beside it, trailing a spiral of steam.

"Good luck, Captain!" Bhatti shouted, yanking at his release strap. He disappeared behind and below Burton's kite.

Ahead, the Steam Man had gained some distance and was bearing slightly to the east.

A violent tremor ran through Burton's body. He gritted his teeth.

"All right, Brunel," he ground out harshly. "Now it's just you and me."

He cracked the reins.

The chase continued over the clouds and across rain-swept London.

Burton struggled to keep his mind from drifting. He wondered where his onetime travelling companion John Hanning Speke was, and thought about the time they'd spent together in Africa. It turned into a hallucination; the canvas seat of the box kite became a canvas stretcher, swaying beneath him as natives bore him along. He saw Speke bending over him, sprinkling water from a flask onto his burning, fevered brow.

"Not long now, Dick," Speke said. "We'll reach Ujiji before sundown. We can lay up there awhile and get ourselves shipshape before we explore the lake more thoroughly. It's easy going for the rest of the afternoon, old thing. Flat savannah. No more swamps. There's lots of wildlife. I shot three gazelles and five vultures this morning!"

Shooting. Always shooting! God, how Speke loved to kill!

The water continued to sprinkle onto his face.

Enough!

Speke didn't stop. The droplets fell with greater force, drenching him.

He snapped awake.

Bismillah! Where's Brunel?

Looking this way and that, furious with himself, he found that he'd dropped back into the clouds. He tugged angrily at the reins, guiding his bird back upward.

Emerging into the clear air, he spotted the ornithopter ahead and to the left. It was descending. He followed and the vapour swallowed him again. Moments later he was being tossed around by the wind and rain. Looking down at the streets below, he recognised nothing until he saw the familiar landmarks of Muswell Hill and Alexandra Park. He watched as Brunel steered his ornithopter in a wide arc and settled in Priory Park, a lesser patch of greenery to the southeast.

After flying a slow circuit around it, the king's agent swooped in low above the bordering trees and, as they fell away behind him, tugged his release strap. The world somersaulted wildly as he tumbled away from the swan, then the ground swelled up and a terrific impact knocked his senses from him.

Burton opened his eyes.

Why was he lying in the rain? Why was he tangled in material? Why—?

Memory returned.

He stirred, rolled over, pushed canvas and broken spars away, got to his knees, and vomited. His whole body was shaking.

He groped around until he found the kite's pocket, pulled his silver-topped, panther-headed cane free, and, leaning heavily upon it, hauled himself to his feet.

POX JR5 fluttered onto his shoulder.

Burton fished a handkerchief from his pocket and wiped his mouth. As he pulled it away, he saw rain-diluted blood on the square of cotton. He felt his face and discovered a deep gash on the bridge of his nose. Holding the cloth to it, he stumbled across the boggy grass into a nearby thicket.

He leaned against the bole of a tree. His head ached abominably.

"Pox. Message for Detective Inspector Trounce," he croaked. "Message begins. Brunel landed in Priory Park, Crouch End. He is inside the priory. Get here fast. Bring men. Message ends. Go."

The parakeet blew a raspberry and departed.

Burton, concealed in the shadows beneath the huddle of trees, looked out over the lawn at the forbidding old building. The big ornithopter stood in front of its large double doors. The rain drummed loudly on the contraption's metal fuselage, and tendrils of steam coiled from the funnel.

Drawing on the remarkable reservoir of strength that had seen him through so many adventures, the king's agent took off across the lawn and skidded into cover behind the machine. He moved along its side, ducked under a folded wing, and leaned out to look past it at the front of the priory.

The front doors had opened and light shone from within. The Steam Man clanked into view. Bells chimed: Brunel's odd and almost incomprehensible mechanical voice. Burton, with his extraordinary ear for languages, was able to discern the words: "Come in out of the rain, Captain."

"So much for concealment," he grunted.

Straightening, he trudged across to the entrance. With a puff of exhaust fumes, Brunel stood aside.

"Do not be concerned for your safety," the engineer rang as Burton stepped in. "Come and warm yourself by the fire. There is someone I want you to meet."

The interior of the building had been completely refurbished to accommodate Brunel's size. Originally, it had been a three-floored property. Now only the upper level survived. The bottom two had been knocked into one enormous space, punctuated by tall iron braces that replaced the supporting walls. A narrow staircase, lacking a banister, ran up the wall to Burton's left.

Off to his right, behind wooden screens of Indian design, he could see items of ornate furniture standing on patterned rugs, and a big inglenook fireplace in which flames flickered invitingly. It was to this area that one of the Steam Man's multijointed arms gestured.

"Where are the diamonds, Brunel?" Burton demanded.

There came a whir of gears and another arm lifted. The clamp at its end held a number of flat jewel cases.

"Here. An explanation awaits you by the fire. I insist that you go and dry yourself, Sir Richard. If you refuse, you'll catch your death."

The threat was unmistakable.

Burton turned and walked unsteadily to the furnished area, passing benches strewn with small items of machinery, tools, drills, brass fittings, gears, and springs. He stepped around the screens and looked down at an elderly man seated in a leather armchair. Bald, shrunken, hollow-eyed, and with pale liver-spotted skin, he was unmistakably Sir Charles Babbage.

"By the Lord Harry!" the old inventor exclaimed in a cracked and raspy voice. "Are you ill? You look all in! And you're sopping wet, man! For heaven's sake, sit down! Pull the chair closer to the fire. Brunel! Brunel! Come here!"

Burton placed his cane to the side of the hearth and collapsed into an armchair.

The Steam Man thudded over and lifted a couple of the screens away. He loomed above the two men.

"Where are your manners?" said Babbage. "Get Sir Richard a brandy!"

Brunel moved to a cabinet and, with astonishing delicacy considering his great bulk, withdrew from it two glasses and a crystal decanter. He poured generous measures, returned, and held them out—one to each man. Burton and Babbage accepted them, and Brunel took a few paces back. With a hiss of escaping steam, he lowered into a squat and became entirely motionless but for the rhythmic wheezing of his bellows.

"Creak creak! Creak creak!" Babbage observed. "Abysmal racket! On and on it goes. And all evening, the rain on the windows! Pitter-patter! Pitter-patter! How is a man supposed to think? I say, drink up, Burton! What on earth's the matter with you?"

Burton gulped at his brandy. The edge of the glass rattled against his teeth. He pulled the stained handkerchief from his pocket and used it to wipe the blood from his face, dabbing at the cut on his nose.

He sighed, threw the reddened square of cotton into the fire, and muttered: "Malaria."

"My dear fellow, I'm so sorry! Is there anything I can do?" Babbage asked.

"You could explain, sir."

"I *can* explain, Sir Richard, and when I do, I'm afraid you'll find that your pursuit of Brunel and your wanton destruction of three of my probability calculators was a grave misjudgement."

"My actions were prompted by the fact that Brunel, the great engineer, seems to have stooped to common burglary."

"I can assure you there was nothing common about it; that I was willing to sacrifice one of my calculators as a decoy is indication enough of that, don't you think? Let me ask you a question: does the theft of diamonds qualify as a crime when millions of people—in fact, the entire Empire—will benefit from it? Before you answer, may I remind you that a similar question is frequently employed by the British government to justify the pillaging of entire countries?"

Burton held up a hand. "Stop. I myself have argued that the spread of so-called civilisation is little more than invasion and suppression, looting and enslavement, but for the life of me I can't see how it relates to the squalid burglarising of a diamond dealer's shop!"

Babbage chuckled. "There you go again. Two men crowbarring a door and coshing a policeman, that I will accept as squalid, but a mechanised genius leading three clockwork probability instruments? Tut-tut, Sir Richard! Tut-tut!"

"Answer the—" Burton stopped and groaned as a tremor overwhelmed him. The glass dropped from his hand and shattered on the edge of the hearth. Babbage flinched at the noise, then recovered himself and made to get up. Burton stopped him with a wave of a hand.

"Don't! I'm all right! So tell me, how does the good of the Empire relate to tonight's burglary?"

The Steam Man clanked into action, moving back to the drinks cabinet.

"I must share with you a vision of the future," Babbage said. "I want to tell you what is possible—the kind of world we can start building immediately, providing I survive."

"The diamonds have something to do with your survival? I don't understand."

"You will."

Burton took the replacement drink offered by Brunel.

The Steam Man resumed his former position. A small hatch flipped open in the front of his body and a pliers-like appendage reached in and pulled out a long, thick cigar. The hatch closed and the roll of tobacco was fitted into a small hole located a few inches beneath the bellows. Another arm rose and the blowtorch at its end ignited and lit the cigar. The bellows rose and fell. The cigar pumped blue smoke into the air.

Old habits die hard.

Burton sipped at his drink. It was gin. Good choice.

Babbage leaned forward. "Burton, what if there was no longer a requirement for the working classes?"

The king's agent looked down at his shoes, which were steaming before the fire.

"Keep talking," he said. He felt weirdly disjointed, as if the world he inhabited were something he might awaken from.

"Imagine this: from one end of the Empire to the other, mechanical brains control the day-to-day necessities of human life. They cook our food. They clean our homes. They sweep our chimneys. They work in our factories. They deliver our goods. They monitor and maintain our infrastructure. They serve us absolutely, unquestioningly, uncomplainingly—and require absolutely nothing in return!"

"You mean the babbage devices?" Burton queried, his voice thick and slurring.

"Pah! The probability devices are mere prototypes. They are nothing compared to what I can achieve—if I live!"

"If you live," Burton echoed. "And how do you propose to do that, old man?"

"Come with me."

Babbage pushed himself out of the chair, took a walking stick from beside it, and shuffled out beyond the screens.

Weakly, Burton retrieved his cane and followed.

With a whir, a clank, and a plume of steam, Brunel fell into pace behind them.

They crossed to the centre of the workshop, where a plinth stood, draped with a thin cloth.

"Please," Babbage said to Brunel.

The Steam Man extended an arm and pulled the material away.

Burton looked bemusedly at an intricate contraption of brass; a fantastic array of cogwheels, springs, and lenses, all contained within a brain-shaped case. It was delicate, confusing, and strangely beautiful.

"A babbage?" he asked.

"Much more than that. It is my future," the scientist responded. "And thus, also the future of the British Empire."

Burton leaned on his cane and wished Detective Inspector Trounce and his men would hurry up.

"How so?"

The elderly scientist gently brushed his hand over the device.

"This is my latest creation," he said. "A probability calculator designed to employ information held in an electrical field."

"What information?"

"Everything in here," Babbage replied, tapping the side of his cranium with a bony forefinger.

The king's agent shook his head. "No. The brain's electrical activity is so subtle as to be immeasurable," he said. "Furthermore, the brain is mortal, not mechanical—when it dies, so does the field."

"As far as measurement goes, you are wrong. With regard to death, you are right. However, there's something you haven't taken into consideration. Would you show us, please, Brunel?"

Isambard Kingdom Brunel lowered himself and placed the jewel cases on the floor. There were six of them, all removed from Brundleweed's safe. The Steam Man's arms flexed. Clamps held the cases steady while fine saw blades slid through their locks. Gripping devices took hold and pulled the containers open. Five of them were pushed aside. Pincers moved forward into the sixth. One by one, five large black stones were separated from the rest.

"The Cambodian Choir Stones!" Babbage announced.

"What about them?" asked Burton, impatiently. His eyelids felt heavy and his legs weak.

"My greatest technical challenge, Sir Richard, has not been the gathering, processing, and dissemination of information, but the storage of it. It is relatively easy to make a machine that thinks, but to make a machine that *remembers*—that is quite another thing. Pass the gemstones to our guest, Brunel."

The famous engineer obeyed, dropping the black diamonds one by one into Burton's extended palm. The king's agent looked at them closely, struggling to keep his eyes focused.

"You are holding in your hand the solution to the problem," Babbage said. "These diamonds were retrieved from a temple in Cambodia by a Frenchman, Lieutenant Marie Joseph François Garnier. There were seven in total. They've been known in that country as the Choir Stones since their discovery in 1837 on account of the fact that they occasionally emit a faint musical hum.

"François Garnier gave two of the diamonds to his colleague, Jean Pelletier, and kept the remaining five for himself. Pelletier happened to be a committed Technologist. He knew we were on the lookout for such stones. We'd heard that something of the sort existed and suspected they might possess unique qualities. When he brought his two to my attention, I experimented with them and was intrigued by the possibilities offered by their rather unusual crystalline structure. I made a prototype device into which to fit them. Unfortunately, before I finished my work, Pelletier suffered a heart attack, and when his body was found there was no sign of the stones. No doubt a member of his household staff made off with them. You can't trust these lowly types. My prototype was useless to me without them, so I gave it to Darwin, who had it fitted to a man I believe you are acquainted with— John Speke."

Burton gave a gasp of surprise.

"Without the two diamonds fitted into it, the device didn't function as I had intended but it enabled Darwin to gain some measure of control over the poor fellow," Babbage continued. "Though why he should want it, I don't know. Nor do I care."

"But surely he gave some indication why Speke was important to him?" Burton asked.

"Maybe. I forget. It's beside the point. What matters is that the Pelletier diamonds were just two of seven, and the remaining five recently appeared in London. Obviously, by hook or by crook, I had to have them—the François Garnier Collection."

"So you chose *by crook*."

"I selected the most efficient and immediate method," Babbage answered. "These black diamonds, you see, Sir Richard, can contain and maintain an electrical field, no matter how slight it may be. Do you understand the significance?"

"Not really."

"Then I shall put it into simple terms. At death, there is a surge of electrical activity in the human brain—a transmission, if you will. The Choir Stones are so sensitive that, if they are close enough, they will receive and store that transmission. Memories, sir—they hold memories. I intend to die in their presence. My intellect will be imprinted upon them. Brunel will then set them into the machinery of this probability calculator, which, like its predecessor, is designed to process the information recorded in their structure. In other words, the essence of Charles Babbage will live on—or, rather, *think* on—in this device."

Burton laughed mirthlessly. "You mean to achieve immortality?"

"I mean for my intellect to survive."

"And your soul?"

Babbage clucked with irritation. "Pshaw! I no more believe in that superstitious claptrap than you do! I refer to my thought processes! The quintessence of myself!"

"Nonsense! A human being adds up to far more than the electrical field generated by, or contained within, the spongy matter of his brain. What about the heart, sir? What about emotion? What about how he *feels* about his memories—his triumphs and regrets?"

Now it was the elderly scientist's turn to laugh. "Firstly, there is absolutely no empirical evidence that emotion is housed in the heart," he said scornfully. "And secondly, even if it was, it is eminently disposable! What good has emotion ever done except to wound and anger and weaken and give rise to humanity's most primitive and animalistic urges? Surely you're not going to lecture me about the majesty of love?"

"No, I'm not. I do say, though, that there are certain decisions a man is called upon to make which transcend the dictates of reason."

"Balderdash! Those are simply occasions where a lesser intellect struggles; where intelligence gives up and submits to emotional impulses. I design machines that decide the best course of action based upon *logic*."

Burton fought to keep his mind focused, his head from nodding. His fever was raging now. The room was spinning and Babbage's voice seemed to echo from a long way off. He was aware of Brunel's bulky presence a few paces behind him.

"No, Sir Charles, it won't do," he rasped. "You have overlooked the fact that a mind separated from the heart entirely eliminates ethics and morality. Look at what you and Brunel have done tonight. You have stolen! You've performed what to you is merely an act of logical necessity—but did you for one minute consider the consequences for Mr. Brundleweed? In a few hours from now he'll awaken to find his business in ruins. His reputation will suffer. His income will be devastated. He and his family will be penalised for your actions."

"Irrelevant!" Babbage jerked. "The man is nothing but a common merchant."

"And what of his son or his daughter? Do you know their destiny?"

Babbage licked his lips. "What are you talking about? I don't even know whether he *has* a son or daughter. I know nothing about the man!"

"Exactly! You know nothing about him, yet you judge him dispensable. What if one of his children was destined to discover a cure for influenza, or the secret of perpetual motion, or a system by which poverty could be eliminated? What might you have deprived us of?"

The old man looked disconcerted. "None of that is certain," he protested. "And since they are a lower class of people, it is highly unlikely."

"Your disdain for the working classes is well known, Sir Charles. Perhaps that is why you seek to replace them with thinking machines. But your contempt does not eliminate the possibility that someone in the Brundleweed family might one day play a crucial role in our social evolution."

The king's agent fought the impulse to vomit. An unbearable hammering assaulted the inner walls of his skull.

"It's a very simple equation," Babbage grumbled. "A matter of probability. We can state that *maybe* Brundleweed's children will become an important influence to future generations, but we can also state that I, Charles Babbage, am *already* an important influence and will continue to be so."

"Conceit!"

"Fact! I can certainly make the world a more efficient place!"

"But maybe," Burton whispered, "efficiency isn't all it's held up to be. Maybe it's the inefficiencies and mistakes that give us the best impetus to change and grow and improve!"

"No! Miscalculations slow us down! I don't make them. I deal only with the proven and the certain, yet who can dispute that I am evolved? Hand me the diamonds!"

Burton passed the five black gemstones to the old man.

"You can kill me now," Babbage said.

"I beg your pardon?"

"Kill me, Sir Richard. Brunel will do the rest."

With a shaking hand, Burton pulled the blade from his swordstick.

"Are you sure? You really want me to kill you?"

"Of course I do. Get on with it, man! I have work to do!"

"You are absolutely certain that your memories will be transferred to the diamonds?"

"Yes!"

"Then you illustrate my argument admirably. Nothing in life is certain, Sir Charles. The diamonds are fakes." He stepped forward and plunged his rapier into the scientist's heart. "Do you now get my point?"

Babbage whispered: "Fakes?"

He died. His corpse slid from Burton's sword and crumpled to the floor.

The king's agent turned and faced the Steam Man.

The hulking machine stood motionless but for the bellows on its shoulder, which scraped up and down incessantly. Little more than an inch of the cigar remained.

Bells chimed: "The François Garnier Collection is not genuine?"

"The stones are onyx crystals."

"Impossible."

"Look for yourself."

Burton stepped back. Brunel lumbered past him and retrieved a stone from Babbage's hand, holding it up with a pincer while another arm held a magnifying tool in front of it.

Burton had no idea what the engineer used for eyes.

"You are correct," Brunel rang. "Then Babbage is dead and his device is useless."

The king's agent felt his knees giving way. He sheathed his sword.

"I can't fight you, Brunel. I'm not sure I can even stand up for much longer. The best I can do is offer some advice."

"Advice?"

"Stop associating with insane scientists. The authorities are already concerned about you after your involvement with Darwin and his cronies. This latest caper will do your reputation no good at all. Redeem yourself, Isambard. Redeem yourself."

Even as the words left his lips, the room began to reel and Burton staggered to one side and collapsed onto the floor.

The massive engineer loomed over him. "Sir Richard, there are those in my faction who would have me kill you."

"I don't doubt it," Burton whispered, as darkness pushed in at the periphery of his vision. "And I bet John Speke is foremost among them."

"You are wrong. Lieutenant Speke is no longer affiliated with the Technologists. He and a small group of Eugenicists absconded to Prussia some weeks ago."

Burton's eyes began to close. "Do your worst," he said sleepily. "I'm at your mercy."

"I would rather make a request of you."

"A request? What—what is it?"

"My fiancée, nurse Florence Nightingale, is missing. She has not been seen or heard of for slightly over a month. Find her for me."

"You want me to—"

"Find her. Will you try?"

Burton managed to nod. The room tumbled.

Distant bells: "I shall take Sir Charles and locate a quiet graveyard for him. He so abhorred noise. We will meet again, Sir Richard."

Oblivion.

Shouts.

Gunshots.

War cries.

Orange light flickered across the canvas roof.

John Speke stumbled in. His eyes were wild.

"They knocked my tent down around my ears!" he gasped. "I almost took a beating! Is there shooting to be done?"

"I rather suppose there is," Burton replied. "Be sharp, and arm to defend the camp!"

A voice came from behind: "There's a lot of the blighters and our confounded guards have taken to their heels!" It was Lieutenant Herne, returning from a scouting mission. "I took a couple of potshots at the mob but then got tangled in the tent ropes. A big Somali took a swipe at me with a bloody great club. I put a bullet into the bastard. Stroyan's either out cold or done for. I couldn't get near him."

Have they killed William Stroyan? God! I'm sorry, William. It's my fault! I'm so sorry!

A barrage of blows pounded against the canvas. Ululating war cries sounded. Javelins were thrust through the opening. Daggers ripped at the material.

"Bismillah!" Burton cursed. "We're going to have to fight our way to the supplies and get ourselves more guns. Herne, there are spears tied to the tent pole at the back. Get 'em!"

"Yes, sir!" Herne responded. He turned, then cried: "They're breaking through the canvas!"

Burton spat expletives. "If this blasted thing comes down on us we'll be caught up good and proper. Get out! Come on! Now!"

He hurled himself through the tent flaps and into a crowd of twenty or so Somali natives, setting about them with his sabre, slicing right and left, yelling fiercely.

Clubs and spear shafts thudded against his flesh, bruising and cutting him, drawing blood. He glanced to the rear, toward the tent, and saw a thrown stone crack against Speke's knee. The lieutenant stumbled backward.

"Don't step back!" Burton shouted. "They'll think that we're retiring!"

Speke looked at him with an expression of utter dismay.

A club struck Burton on the shoulder. He twisted and swiped his blade at its owner. The crush of men jostled him back and forth. Someone shoved him from behind and he turned angrily, raising his sword, only recognising El Balyuz, the expedition's guide, at the very last moment.

His arm froze in midswing.

White-hot pain tore through his head.

He stumbled and fell onto the sandy earth.

A weight pulled him sideways.

He reached up.

A javelin had pierced his face, in one side of his mouth and out the other, dislodging teeth and cracking his palate.

He fought to stay conscious.

The pain!

Damn it, Speke—help me! Help me!

A damp cloth on his brow.

Dry sheets beneath him.

He opened his eyes.

Algernon Swinburne smiled down at him.

"You were having a nightmare, Richard. *The* nightmare."

Burton moved his tongue about in his mouth. It was dry, not bloody.

"Water," he croaked.

Swinburne reached to the bedside table. "Here you are."

Burton pushed himself into a sitting position, took the proffered glass, and drank greedily.

His friend plumped the pillows behind him and he leaned back, feeling comfortable, warm, and unbelievably weak. He was in his own bedroom at 14 Montagu Place.

"It was a bad attack," Swinburne advised. "I refer to the malaria, not to the Berbera incident," he added, with a grin.

"Always the same bloody dream!" Burton grumbled.

"It's not surprising, really," the poet noted. "Any man who had a spear shoved through his ugly mug would probably have nightmares about it."

"How long?"

"The spear?"

"Was I unconscious for, you blessed clown."

"You were in a high fever for five days then slept almost solidly for three more. Doctor Steinhaueser has been popping in every few hours to keep you dosed up with quinine. We forced chicken broth into you twice daily, though I doubt you remember any of that."

"I don't. The last thing I recollect is talking with Brunel in the priory. Eight days! What happened? Last time I saw you, you'd just taken a tumble through some trees."

"Yes, that confounded swan was an unmanageable blighter! I rounded up a little squadron of constables and we drove the pantechnicon to Scotland Yard. Of course, it was an utter waste of time; there were neither fingerprints nor any other admissible evidence to connect it either with the Brundleweed robbery or with Brunel and his clockwork men.

"Anyway, while I was having my cuts and bruises attended to by the Yard physician, William Trounce, Herbert Spencer, and Constable Bhatti all came limping in for the same treatment. We knew you'd get word to us, so after we'd been bandaged, soothed, patted on our heads, and sent on our merry way, we regrouped in Trounce's office, sat steaming by the fire, and waited. When the parakeet arrived and delivered your message, we gathered a force together and raced to Crouch End on velocipedes. You were unconscious inside the priory with the diamonds at your side. There was no sign of Isambard Kingdom Brunel."

"Did you find one of Babbage's devices? On a plinth?"

"Yes. Trounce took it in as evidence. The diamonds were returned to

Brundleweed. He's not happy, though. It turns out that Brunel made off with a select few and left fakes in their place."

"The black ones? François Garnier's Choir Stones?"

"Yes. How did you know?"

"I'll tell you later, Algy. But you're wrong. It wasn't Brunel who took the originals. I need to sleep now. I'll write up a full report when my strength is back. Oh, by the way, what became of Herbert Spencer?"

"He got a little reward from Scotland Yard for helping us out. Miss Mayson has given him an occasional job, too. He cleans out the parakeet cages at the automated animal academy."

"He must have a thick skin!"

"He doesn't need one. Apparently the birds have taken a shine to him and barrage him with compliments!" Swinburne stood. "I'm staying in the spare bedroom. Just ring if you need anything."

"Thank you," Burton replied sleepily as his friend departed.

He lay back with his hands behind his head and stared at the ceiling.

Two weeks passed.

Burton worked on an expanded edition of his book *The Lake Regions of Central Africa*.

He slowly regained his strength. His long-suffering housekeeper, Mrs. Iris Angell, cooked him magnificent meals and despaired when he sent them back barely touched. His appetite had always been slight, but now—as she told him every single morning and every single evening—he needed sustenance.

She underestimated his iron constitution.

Little by little, the gaunt hollows beneath his scarred cheekbones filled out; the dark shadows around his eyes faded; his hands steadied.

Algernon Swinburne, now living back in his own apartment on Grafton Street, Fitzroy Square, was a frequent visitor and observed with satisfaction the normal swarthiness returning to his friend's jaundiced countenance.

Burton eventually got around to writing a report detailing his confrontation with Sir Charles Babbage. He held nothing back.

Rolling the document, he placed it in a canister, which he slotted into an odd-looking copper and glass contraption on his desk. He dialed the number 222 and pressed a button. There came a gasp, a plume of steam, a rattle, and the canister shot away down a tube, en route to the prime minister's office.

He was just settling in his armchair and reaching for a cigar when there came a knock and Mrs. Angell entered.

"There's a Countess Sabina to see you, sir."

"Is there, by James!? Send her up, please!"

"Should I chaperone?"

"There's no need, Mrs. Angell. The countess and I are acquainted."

Moments later, a woman stepped into the study. She was tall and may once have possessed an angular beauty, but now looked careworn; her face was lined, her chestnut hair shot through with grey, her fingernails bitten and unpainted. Her eyes, though, were extraordinary—large, slightly slanted, and of the darkest brown.

She was London's foremost cheiromantist and prognosticator, and had given Burton much to think about during the Spring Heeled Jack case.

"Countess!" he exclaimed. "This is an unexpected pleasure! Please sit down. Can I get you anything?"

"Just water, please, Captain Burton," she answered, in a musical, slightly accented voice.

He crossed to the bureau and poured her a glass while she sat and patted down her black crinoline skirt and straightened her bonnet.

"I'm sorry to intrude," she said as he handed her the drink and sat opposite. "My goodness, you look ill!"

"Recovering, Countess, and I assure you, your visit is very welcome and no intrusion at all. Can I be of some service?"

"Yes—no—yes—I don't know—maybe the other way around. I—I have been having visions, Captain."

"And they concern me in some way?"

She nodded and took a sip of water. "When you came to me last year," she continued, "I saw that you had embarked upon a course never meant for you, yet one that would lead to greater contentment."

"I remember. You said that for me the wrong path is the right path."

"Yes. But in recent days, I have been increasingly aware of the alternative, Captain, by which I mean the original path. Not just yours, but that which we were all destined to tread until the stilt-man drove us from it."

"Edward Oxford. He was a meddler with time."

"With time," she echoed, softly. Her eyes seemed to be focused on the far distance. "I'm sorry," she whispered. "I had intended to talk to you first but it is overwhelming me. I cannot stop it. I have to—I have to—"

Burton lunged forward and caught the glass as it dropped from her loose fingers. Her eyes rolled up into her head and she began to rock slightly in her chair. She started to speak in a voice that sounded weirdly different from her own, as if she was far away and talking to him through a length of pipe.

"I will speak. I will speak. It is all wrong. No one is as they should be. Nothing is as intended. The storm will break early and you shall witness the end of a great cycle and the horrifying birth pains of another; the past and the future locked together in a terrible conflict."

A coldness gripped Burton.

"Beware, Captain, for a finger of the storm reaches back to touch you. There are layers upon layers, one deception concealing another—and that one but a veil over yet another. Do not believe what you see. The little ones are not as they appear. The puppeteer is herself a puppet and the sorcerer is not yet born. The dead shall believe themselves living."

Her head fell back and a horribly tormented groan escaped her.

"No," she whispered. "No. No. No. I can hear the song but it should not be sung! It should not be sung! The stilt-man broke the silence of the ages and the sorcerer hears; and the puppeteer hears; and the dead hear; and, oh, God help me—" her voice suddenly rose to a shriek "—I hear, too! I hear, too!"

She clapped her hands to her ears, arched her back, thrashed in her seat, and slumped into a dead faint.

"My God!" Burton gasped. He took her by the shoulders and straightened her; pushed his handkerchief into the glass of water and folded it over her brow; went to a drawer and retrieved a bottle of smelling salts. Moments later she was blinking and coughing.

He poured her a small brandy. "Here, take this."

She gulped it, spluttered, breathed heavily, and slowly calmed.

"My apologies. Did I fall into a trance?"

"You did."

"I suspected something of the sort might happen, though I hoped I might have more control over it. For two weeks I've felt the urge to see you, to transmit a message to you, but I did not know what it was, so I didn't come."

Burton repeated what she had told him.

"Do you know what it means?" he asked.

"I never know. When I'm spellbound, I'm unaware of what I say, and it seldom makes sense to me afterward."

Burton gazed at her thoughtfully. "Is there something else, Countess? Even though the message has been delivered, you seem uneasy."

The prognosticator suddenly stood and paced back and forth, wringing her gloved hands.

"It's—it's—it's that I can't trust that the message is valid, Captain."

"Why do you say that?"

"Because—I know it sounds strange—but *this*, what I do, my ability to glimpse not only the future, but *futures*—plural—should not be possible!"

"I'm not sure I understand what you mean. You have a reputation for accuracy and I've seen it demonstrated. Plainly, it is not only possible but also actual."

"Yes, and that's the problem! Prognostication, cheiromancy, spiritualism—these things are spoken of in the other history, but *they do not work there*, and those who claim such powers are regarded as nothing but charlatans and swindlers."

Burton got to his feet, took his visitor by the upper arms, and turned her to face him.

"Countess, you and I are privy to a fact that very, very few people know: namely, that the natural course of time has been interfered with. The history we are living is different from what would otherwise have been. People are being exposed to opportunities and challenges they perhaps should not experience, and it is changing them entirely. Future mechanisms, hinted at in conversations between Edward Oxford's companion, Henry Beresford, and Isambard Kingdom Brunel, are being developed according to current knowledge, giving us a glut of contraptions that, in all probability, should never have existed at all. Yet, amid all this chaos and confusion, there is one thing we can be certain of: changing time cannot possibly alter natural laws. I don't know whether spiritualist powers belong to the science of physics or to the science of biology; I know only that they are real. You are the living evidence."

Countess Sabina's eyes met his, and in them he saw utter conviction as she said: "And yet, in the world that should have been, they are not real. *They are not real.* Somehow, Captain Burton, I feel this is the key!"

"The key to what?"

"To—to the survival of the British Empire!"

Later that same day, Burton was standing by one of his study windows smoking a Manila cheroot, filling the room with its pungent scent and staring sightlessly at the street below, when a messenger parakeet landed on the sill. Raising the window, he received: "Message from that dung-squeezer, Detective Inspector Trounce. Message begins. Word has reached me that you're back on your feet, you dirty shunt-knobbler. I'll call round at eight this evening. Message ends."

Burton chuckled. Dirty shunt-knobbler. He must tell Algy that one.

He did, later, when Swinburne visited, and the poet roared with laughter, which was cut short when Fidget, Burton's basset hound, bit his ankle.

"Yow! Damn and blast the confounded dog! Why does he always do that?" he screeched.

"It's just his way of showing affection."

"Can't you train him to be a little less expressive?"

They sat and chatted, relaxing in each other's company, enjoying their easy though unlikely friendship. Perhaps no stranger pair could be found in the whole of London than the brutal-faced, hard-bitten explorer and the delicate, rather effeminate-looking poet. Yet there was an intellectual—and perhaps spiritual—bond between them, which had begun with a shared love for the work of the Portuguese poet Camoens; had been sustained by a mutual need to know where their own limits lay—if, indeed, they had any; and was now strengthened by the challenges and dangers they faced together in the service of the king.

On the dot of eight, there came a hammering at the front door, followed by footsteps on the stairs and a tapping at the study door.

"Come!" Burton called.

The portal swung open and Mrs. Angell crossed the threshold. She stood nervously wrapping her hands in her pinafore.

"Detective Inspector T-Trounce and a young con-constable to see you, sir," she stammered. "And—and—goodness gracious me!"

"Mrs. Angell? Are you quite all right?"

Trounce stepped into the room behind her. Constable Bhatti followed.

"Hallo, Captain! Hallo, Swinburne!" the Scotland Yard man cried cheerfully. "Mrs. Angell, my dear woman, don't worry yourself! I promise you, it's absolutely harmless!"

"B-but—bless my soul!" the old dame stuttered. She threw up her hands and bustled out of the room.

"What's harmless?" Burton asked.

"You look like your old self again!" Trounce exclaimed, ignoring the question. "But never mind! Worse things happen at sea!"

Swinburne gave a screech of laughter.

"Come in, gentlemen; help yourself to a drink and cigar," Burton invited, indicating the decanter and the cigar box.

They did so, pulled over a couple of armchairs, and settled around the fireplace with the king's agent and the poet. Fidget sprawled on the hearthrug at their feet.

"We have a gift for you, Captain," Trounce declared with a mischievous twinkle.

"Really? Why?"

"Oh, for services rendered and whatnot! Besides, I noticed that your shoes are never polished, your cuffs are frayed, and your collars need starching!"

"Ever the detective. What on earth has my personal grooming got to do with anything?"

"I'm suggesting, Captain Burton, that you're in dire need of a gentleman's gentleman—a valet!"

"I have a housekeeper and a maid. Any more staff and I'll be managing a 'household!'"

"Only those that need managing," Trounce said. He winked at Bhatti.

The young constable smiled and called: "Enter!"

A figure of gleaming brass walked in, closed the door, and stood, whirring softly.

Fidget yelped and dived behind a chair.

"My hat!" Swinburne exclaimed. "Is that the clockwork man of Trafalgar Square?"

"The very same!" Trounce answered. "Constable Bhatti has been studying him for the past three weeks."

"We found a key that fitted him in the priory," the constable added. "Then it was just a matter of experimentation. As I suspected, the little switches at the front of the babbage dictate his behaviour. He can be rendered more aggressive, subservient, independent; you can set him to respond to any voice, specific voices, or just your own. What do think, Captain Burton?"

Burton looked at each of his guests, then turned his gaze to the brass man.

"Frankly, gentlemen," he said, "I'm at a complete loss. You mean me to keep this mechanism as a valet?"

"Yes," Trounce said. "It will do whatever you tell it!"

Bhatti nodded and added: "It has enough independence to perform tasks without needing to be told all the time. For example, if you order it to ensure that your shoes are polished by six o'clock each morning, then it will never need telling again."

"I wish I could say the same about my missus!" Trounce muttered.

"Wait, Captain!" Bhatti said, jumping up. He strode to the brass man and stood in front of it. "Everybody remain silent, please. Captain Burton, would you say a few words when I nod at you?"

"Words? What words?"

"Any! It doesn't matter!"

The constable took a small screwdriver from his pocket, turned to the clockwork figure, unscrewed the small porthole in its "forehead," and used the tool to click down one of the small switches inside.

"The next voice you hear," he told the device, "will be the only voice you obey unless it instructs you otherwise."

He turned and nodded to Burton.

Rather self-consciously, the famous explorer cleared his throat: "I—er—I am Richard Burton and, apparently, you are now my valet."

The brass man turned its head slightly until it appeared to be looking straight at Burton.

It saluted.

"That's its way of acknowledging your command," said Bhatti. He reached into the porthole and flipped the switch back, then closed the little glass door and started to screw it into place.

"One moment, Constable!" Burton interrupted. "If you are all agreeable, I'd like the device set to accept commands from everyone present, and Mrs. Angell, too."

"You're sure?" Trounce asked.

Burton nodded and pulled a cord that hung beside the fireplace. It rang a bell in the basement, summoning the housekeeper.

When she arrived, he told her about the new valet, and Bhatti went through the process again with her, with Trounce, and with Swinburne.

Mrs. Angell left the study, a bewildered expression on her face, while Bhatti joined the others around the fireplace and lit a pipe. He watched, smiling, as Burton moved over to the mechanism, looked it up and down, tapped its chest, and examined the little cogs that revolved in its head.

"Useful!" the king's agent muttered. "Very useful! Might I train it as a fencing partner?"

"Certainly!" Bhatti answered. "Though you'll probably find it too fast an opponent!"

Burton raised his eyebrows.

"Incidentally," the constable added, "it'll need winding once a day, and, if I may suggest, you should name it. A name will make it easier to issue orders."

"Ah, yes, I see what you mean."

Burton stood in front of his new valet and addressed it: "Do you recognise my voice?"

The brass man saluted.

"Your name is—Admiral Lord Nelson!"

Another salute.

Burton's guests laughed.

"Bravo!" Swinburne cheered.

The king's agent turned to the policemen. "Thank you, Detective Inspector Trounce, Constable Bhatti—it's a magnificent gift! And now I propose that we bring the case of the clockwork man of Trafalgar Square to a close by giving my valet his first order."

Trounce nodded encouragement.

"Admiral Nelson!" Sir Richard Francis Burton commanded. "Serve the drinks!"

The drinks were duly served.

Later that night, the king's agent found himself unable to sleep. A question was bothering him. He offered it to the darkness: "Whatever became of the genuine Choir Stones?"

CHAPTER 3

THE EYES AND THE CURSE

MY DEAR MOTHER,

The delay which has taken place since my last Letter, Dated 22nd April, 54, Makes it very difficult to Commence this Letter. I deeply regret the truble and anxsity I must have cause you by not writing before. But they are known to my attorney and the more private details I will keep for your own Ear. Of one thing rest Assured that although I have been in A humble condition of Life I have never let any act disgrace you or my Family. I have been A poor Man and nothing worse. Mr. Gibbes suggest to me as essential That I should recall to your memory things which can only be known to you and me to convince you of my Identity. I don't think it needful My Dear Mother. Although I send them. Namely the Brown Mark on my side. And the Card Case at Brighton. I can assure you My Dear Mother I have keep your promice ever since. In writing to me please enclose your letter to Mr. Gibbes to prevent unnesersery enquiry as I do not wish any person to know me in this country. When I take my proper position and title. Having therefore made up my mind to return and face the sea once more I must request to send me the Means of doing so and pajing a fue outstanding debts. I would return by the overland Mail. The passage Money and other expences would be over two Hundred pound, for I propose Sailing from Victoria not this Colonly And to sail from Melbourne in my own Name. Now to annable me to do this my dear Mother you must send me at least £400.

—LETTER FROM THE TICHBORNE CLAIMANT

I t was the first Monday of April, 1862. Five weeks after the death of Sir Charles Babbage.

A hiss, a clatter, and a sound like a large bung being pulled from a jar announced the arrival of a canister in the device on Sir Richard Francis Burton's desk.

Fidget raised his head from the hearthrug, barked, whimpered, then went back to sleep.

The maid, fifteen-year-old Elsie Carpenter, put down her broom, left the study, ran up the stairs, past the bedrooms, up the next staircase, and knocked on the library door.

Exotic music was coming from the room beyond.

"Come!" a voice called.

She entered and curtseyed.

Burton, wrapped in his *jubbah*—the loose robe he'd worn during his famed pilgrimage to Mecca—sat cross-legged on the floor amid a pile of books. He had a turban wound around his head and was smoking a hookah. The ends of his slippers curled to points.

He'd shaved off his forked beard some days ago and now sported long, exotic mustachios, which drooped to either side of his mouth. The new style made him appear younger and, in Elsie's opinion, rather more dashing.

There was another man in the library, squatting in a corner, who was a good deal less prepossessing than her master. Elderly, brown, and skinny, he wore a voluminous white and yellow striped robe and a tall fez. He was playing a *nay*—the long Arabian flute—the tones of which were hauntingly liquid and melodic.

Burton nodded at the man, who responded by laying down his instrument.

"Thank you, al-Masloub. Your talent shines ever more brightly as the years pass. Take what you need from the sideboard, and blessings be upon you."

The old man stood, bowed, and murmured: *"Barak Allahu feekem."*

He moved to a heavy piece of furniture to the right of the door and opened the small, intricately carved wooden box that stood upon it. From this he extracted a few coins, before silently slipping past Elsie and out of the room.

"What is it, Miss Elsie?" Burton asked.

"Excuse me, sir," she said, curtseying for a second time. "Sorry to dis— disperupt your music, but a message just arrived in the thingamajig."

"Thank you. And you mean *disrupt*."

"That's right, sir. Disperupt."

The maid bobbed again, backed out of the room, ran down the stairs, retrieved her broom, and was out of the study before Burton got there. She descended to the basement and entered the kitchen.

"All swept clean as a whistle, ma'am," she told Mrs. Angell.

"Did you dust the bookshelves?"

"Yes, ma'am."

"And the mantelpiece?"

"Yes, ma'am."

"And that big old African spear?"

"Yes, ma'am."

"And did you polish the swords?"

"Yes, ma'am."

"And beat the cushions?"

"Yes, ma'am."

"And what about the doorknobs?"

"You can see your face in 'em, ma'am."

"Good girl. Take a piece of fruitcake from the tin and have a rest. You've earned it."

"Thank you, ma'am."

Elsie took her slice of cake, put it on a plate, and settled on a stool.

"By the way, ma'am, the musical shriek has left and the master's got a message in the thingamajig."

"Sheik," the housekeeper corrected. She sighed. "Oh dear. I'm convinced that contraption only ever delivers trouble!"

She turned to the clockwork man, who was standing at the table, peeling potatoes. "Attend Sir Richard, please, Lord Nelson."

The valet laid down his knife and saluted, wiped his fingers on a cloth, and marched out of the kitchen and up the stairs to the study. He entered and moved to the bureau between the windows, standing motionless beside it, awaiting orders.

Burton was by the fireplace.

"Listen to this," he said, absently. "It's from Palmerston."

He read from the note in his hand:

Investigate the claimant to the Tichborne title.

The king's agent sighed. "I was hoping to avoid all that blessed nonsense!"

He looked up, saw his valet, and said: "Oh, it's you. Lay out my day suit, would you? I think I'll drop in on old Pouncer Trounce, see what he knows about the affair."

Half an hour later, Burton stepped out of 14 Montagu Place and strolled in the direction of Whitehall. He'd not gone more than three paces when a voice hailed him: "What ho, Cap'n! Fit as a fiddle, I see!"

It was Mr. Grub, the street vendor, who supplied chestnuts from a Dutch oven in the winter, and whelks, winkles, and jellied eels from a barrow in the summer.

"Yes, Mr. Grub, I'm much improved, thank you. How's business?"

"Rotten!"

"Why so?"

"Dunno, Cap'n. I think it's me pitch."

"But you always pitch your barrow here. If it's so bad, why not move?"

Grub pushed his cloth cap back from his brow. "Move? Phew! Dunno about that! I've been here for years, an' me father afore me! Fancy a bag o' whelks? They're fresh out o' the Thames this morning!"

"No thank you, Mr. Grub. I'm on my way to Scotland Yard."

Burton wondered how anything from the Thames could possibly be classified as "fresh."

"Well, you ain't the only one what don't want nuffink." Mr. Grub sighed. "Cheerio, Cap'n!"

"Good day, Mr. Grub!"

Burton tipped his hat at the vendor and continued on his way.

It was a fine spring day. The sky was blue and the air still. All across the city, thin pillars of smoke rose vertically, eventually dissipating at a high altitude. Rotorchairs left trails of steam between them, a white cross-hatching that made an irregular grid of the sky. Swans, too, swooped among the columns like insects flying through a forest.

The king's agent swung along at a steady pace, with the hustle and bustle of the streets churning around him. Hawkers hollered, prostitutes wheedled and mocked, ragamuffins yelled, traders laughed and argued and haggled, street performers sang and juggled and danced, pedestrians brandished their canes and parasols and doffed their hats and bobbed their bonnets, horses *clip-clopped*, velocipedes hissed and chugged, steam-horses growled and rumbled, carriages rattled, wheels crunched over cobbles, dogs barked. It was an absolute cacophony. It was London.

He spotted a familiar face.

"Hi! Quips!" he called, waving his cane.

Oscar Wilde, nine years old, orphaned by the never-ending Irish famine and earning his daily crust by selling newspapers, was loitering outside a sweet shop.

"Top o' the morning to you, Captain!" He smiled, revealing crooked teeth. "Help me to choose, would you? Bullseyes or barley sugars? I'm after thinking barley sugars."

"Then I agree, lad."

Oscar pulled off his battered top hat and scratched his head.

"Ah, well now, whenever people agree with me I always feel I must be wrong. So I suppose it'd better be bullseyes!" He sighed. "Or maybe both. It seems to me that the only way to get rid of a temptation is to yield to it. Don't you think so, Captain Burton?"

The explorer chuckled. Young Oscar had a remarkable way with words—thus his nickname.

"Are you flush, young 'un?"

"Aye, I am that. My pockets are heavy with coins, so they are. I sold out in less than an hour. It seems everyone in London is after having a newspaper this morning. Have you seen the news yourself, sir?"

"Not yet. I've had my nose in books."

"Then you must be the exception that proves the rule, for I have it in mind that the difference between literature and journalism is that journalism is unreadable and literature is not read!"

"I suppose the Tichborne business is still making the headlines?"

A nearby organ grinder started to squeeze out something approximating a tune on his tatty machine. Oscar winced and raised his voice: "I'll say! It has all the classes gossiping—from high lords to low layabouts! Everyone has an opinion!"

"What's the latest?" Burton shouted above the unmelodious groans, squeaks, wails, and whistles.

"The Claimant arrived in Paris and his mother has recognised him!"

"By James! Is that so?"

The Tichborne affair was a huge sensation—and one that touched a sensitive area of Burton's life, for the family was connected by marriage to the Arundells, to whom Isabel, his ex-fiancée, belonged.

The Tichbornes were one of the oldest families in the southern counties, but the estate's fortunes had dwindled considerably over the past two or three generations—due, it was rumoured, to an ancient curse. In recent years, the continuation of the line had depended upon two heirs. The eldest, Roger, was a fairly typical example of an ill-educated aristocrat, while his younger brother, Alfred, was even more vacuous, and a gambler, too. Roger had offered the greatest hope for the family until, disastrously, he was lost at sea in 1854, while sailing back from South America to claim the baronetcy after the death of his father. So it was Alfred who became the latest in the long line of Tichborne baronets, and he almost ran the estate—near Winchester in

Hampshire—into the ground. Money trickled through his fingers like water. His mother, Lady Henriette-Felicité, was French. She'd not enjoyed a happy marriage and had retreated to Paris long before her husband died. From a distance, she kept a close eye on the diminishing Tichborne coffers, and when the situation became so dire that she feared Sir Alfred would make a pauper of her, she sent a family friend, Colonel Franklin Lushington, to live at Tichborne House and take control of the estate's finances. Lushington had managed to curb her son's worst excesses, but what he couldn't do was turn the young baronet into a good prospect for marriage.

Sir Alfred would almost certainly be the last Tichborne.

Then something totally unexpected happened.

A year ago, while the Dowager Lady Henriette-Felicité was visiting Tichborne House, a down-on-his-luck Russian sailor came begging for alms. The old lady, by this time frail and feeble-minded, asked him if he'd ever heard of *La Bella*, the ship that took her eldest to the bottom of the ocean. The sailor had not only heard of it but also knew that a small group of survivors had been rescued from a longboat bearing its name. They'd been landed in Australia.

Lady Henriette-Felicité immediately placed advertisements in the *Empire* and a number of Australian newspapers.

A month ago, she'd received a response in the form of a badly written and misspelled letter.

It was from Roger.

He was alive.

He told her he'd been living under the name "Tomas Castro," and was working as a butcher in Wagga Wagga, New South Wales, about halfway between Sydney and Melbourne.

He asked his mother to send him money so he could come home, and, as evidence that he—the author of the letter—truly was her son, he referred to a brown birthmark upon his side. The dowager remembered the blemish and sent the money.

Now, it seemed, the man the newspapers had dubbed "the Claimant" had met the old woman and she'd confirmed his identity.

The long-lost Roger Tichborne had returned!

As Oscar explained to Burton, the upper classes were delighted that an ancient family was restored, while the lower classes were celebrating the fact that an aristocrat had been living as a common labourer.

Dowager Lady Henriette-Felicité was bursting with joy. The rest of the Tichborne family—the cousins and assorted relatives, most of whom bore the surnames Doughty or Arundell—were not.

They didn't believe a word of it.

"He'll be over to assert ownership of the estate soon!" Oscar shouted, as the barrel organ screamed and belched.

Burton nodded thoughtfully, pulled a sixpence from his pocket, and pushed it into the urchin's palm.

"I'll see you later, Quips," he said. "Here's a coin for a pie. You can't live on sweets alone!"

"I can get plump trying! Thank you, Captain!"

Oscar disappeared into the shop, and Burton walked on, relieved to hear the organ music fading into the background.

On the corner of Baker Street, he waved down a hansom, which, pulled by a puffing steam-horse—like a smaller version of the famous Stevenson's Rocket—took him along Wigmore Street and halfway down Regent Street before jolting to a halt when its crankshaft snapped and punched a hole in the boiler. Dismissing the driver's apologies, he hailed another and continued on through Haymarket to Whitehall and Scotland Yard.

Mounting the steps of the forbidding old edifice, he was encountered going up by Detective Inspector Trounce, who happened to be on his way down.

"Well met!" the policeman declared.

"I was just coming to pick your brains," said Burton, shaking his friend's hand.

"I'm off to put the wind up Freddy Blue, the pawnbroker. Care to tag along?"

"Rightio. Why? What's he done?"

They descended the steps and set off toward Trafalgar Square.

"A little bird told me he's started to fence stolen property again."

"A parakeet?"

Trounce shook his head. "No, Cock Sparrow, the child pickpocket. What was it you wanted to jiggle my grey matter about?"

They skirted around the edge of the square and entered Northumberland Avenue, which was clogged with traffic as delivery wagons trundled up from riverside, heading into the centre of the capital.

"I was wondering what you might know about the Tichborne Claimant."

"Only what I've read in the papers."

"That's all? You mean Scotland Yard isn't looking into it?"

"Why should we? No charges have been brought against anyone. What's your interest, Captain?"

"To be frank, I haven't any. It's little more than newspaper sensationalism, as far as I can see. Pam, unfortunately, has other ideas."

"Palmerston? Why would it concern the prime minister?"

"Who knows? The man's brain is as unfathomable as one of those babbage devices."

Trounce made a sound of agreement. "Incidentally," he said, "you should have seen the men he sent to collect the babbage we found at the priory on the night of the Brundleweed raid. They were like a couple of blessed morticians!"

"Ah. That'll be Damien Burke and Gregory Hare. They're his odd-job men."

"*Odd* is right. I've never seen odder. And speaking of oddities, how's young Swinburne?"

"He's working on a new batch of poems. And pursuing his hobby, of course."

Trounce snorted. Both men knew that Swinburne's "hobby" involved frequent visits to brothels where he enjoyed being flogged by willing madams.

"He has strange tastes, that one," the detective muttered. "Why anyone would enjoy being birched, I can't imagine. I suffered the rod once or twice at school, and didn't like it one little bit!"

"The more I learn about him," Burton replied, "the more I believe Swinburne has a genuine physiological condition that causes him to feel pain as pleasure. He's a fascinating study!"

"And a thorough pervert. Though a damned courageous one, I'll give him that. Absolutely fearless! Here's Mr. Blue's shop. I'll do this alone, if you don't mind. Will you wait here?"

"Certainly. Don't pummel him too hard."

"A verbal dressing-down, that's all, Captain!" Trounce smiled. He cracked his knuckles and vanished into the pawnbroker's.

Sir Richard Francis Burton leaned on his cane and watched the traffic pass by. The traders' vehicles were mostly horse-drawn. There weren't many who could afford a steam-horse. The men on the carts were tough and wiry individuals. Their shirtsleeves were rolled up to their elbows and Burton could see the knotted muscles of their forearms, the thickness of their bones, and the leathery quality of their skin. There wasn't an ounce of fat on any of them, nor was there even a hint of pretension—nary a whiff of self-consciousness. They were stripped down to the basics of existence. They toiled, they ate, they slept, they toiled again, and they never imagined anything different. He admired them, and, in a strange way, he envied them.

A couple of minutes later, he heard a footstep behind him and turned.

Detective Inspector Trounce had emerged from the shop.

"He started blubbing like a baby before I'd said more than two words," the policeman announced. "I expect he'll stay on the straight and narrow for a while. It's his second warning. He'll not get another. I'll have the bracelets on him. What say you we drop in at Brundleweed's? It's just around the corner."

"Good idea."

They set off.

"Has there been no clue to the Choir Stones' whereabouts?" Burton asked.

"Not a whisper, unless Brundleweed's heard something through the grapevine since I last spoke to him. He maintains that he locked the genuine articles in the safe that evening. Yet we know that Isambard Kingdom Brunel removed fakes. So either Brundleweed is lying—which I find hard to believe; his reputation is absolutely spotless—or an extremely accomplished cracksman got there first and left no trace."

They passed back into Trafalgar Square, weaving through the crowds, and on into Charing Cross Road, heading toward Saint Martin's.

"Do you have a suspect?"

Trounce removed his bowler, slapped it, and placed it back on his head.

"The obvious man would be—" he began, then interrupted himself: "By Jove! Look at that!"

A bizarre vehicle had snaked into view from around the next corner and was thundering toward them at high speed. It was a millipede—an actual insect—grown to stupendous proportions by the Eugenicists. When it had reached the required size, they'd killed it and handed the carcass over to their Engineering colleagues, who'd sliced off the top half of its long, segmented, tubular body. They'd removed the innards until only the tough outer carapace remained, and into this they'd fitted steam-driven machinery via which the many legs could be operated. Platforms had been bolted across the top of each segment and upon them seats were affixed, over which canopies arched, echoing the shape of the missing top half of the body. A driver sat at the front of the vehicle in a chair carved from the shell of the head. He skillfully manipulated a set of long levers to control the astonishing machine.

It was a new type of omnibus, and it was packed solid with passengers, with three people to every seat and a fair number standing and hanging on for dear life as it hurtled along. They cheered and hooted with delight as hansoms and growlers, carts and velocipedes, horses and pedestrians hurriedly moved to the side of the road, out of the oncoming vehicle's path. Dense clouds of steam boiled from pipes along its sides and, as it came alongside Burton and Trounce and careened into the narrow gap that opened up through the centre of the traffic, hot vapour rolled over the two men, obscuring the scene. Impassioned curses and profanities came from within the cloud; there was a crash, a scream, and the shuddery whinny of a panicked horse.

"Damned freakish monstrosity!" Trounce yelled. He took a handkerchief from his pocket and wiped the moisture from his face.

"That's one of the most extraordinary things I've ever seen!" Burton exclaimed. "I'd read that the Technologists were experimenting with insect shells but I had no idea they'd progressed so far!"

"You regard that as progress?" Trounce objected. He waved his hat at the milieu that was slowly emerging from the thinning haze. "Look! It's utter bloody chaos! We can't have horses and steam-horses and penny-farthings and now steam-bloody-insects as well, all on the streets at the same time! People are going to get hurt!"

"Humph!" Burton agreed. "We certainly seem to be entangled in a profusion of mismatched machineries."

"A profusion? Call it whatever you will, Captain Burton, but the fact of the matter is that if the dashed scientists don't slow down and plan ahead with something at least resembling foresight and responsibility, London is going to grind to a complete standstill, mark my words!"

"I don't disagree. Come on. Let's move along. What was it you were saying? About the suspect?"

"Suspect? Oh, Brundleweed. Yes. Well, the obvious safecracker to look at would be Marcus Dexter—there's no strongbox he can't open and he's as cunning as a fox—but he's operating in Cape Town at the moment, that's for certain. Cyril 'the Fly' Brady is locked up in Pentonville, and Tobias Fletcher is consumptive and out of action. There's no one else I know of who could have opened Brundleweed's safe without dynamite."

A one-legged beggar swung himself on crutches directly into Trounce's path. He pleaded in a throaty voice for a ha'penny: "Jest fr'a cuppa tea, me ol' china."

The detective glowered at him, told him to move along, but pressed a penny into his palm as he went.

"I'm almost inclined to run with the diamond merchant's theory," he muttered.

"Brundleweed has a theory?"

"Of sorts. He believes a ghost took the diamonds."

Burton stopped and stared at his companion in amazement.

"A ghost?"

"Yes. He's fooled himself into believing that he saw a phantom woman that night."

"You don't believe him, surely?"

"No, of course not. He probably dozed off and dreamt it. Except—"

"What?"

"The friend of François Garnier; the one he gave two of the black diamonds to—"

"Jean Pelletier."

"Yes. I contacted the Sûreté in Paris. They confirmed that he died from a heart attack."

"So?"

"So he was found in his lodgings, the room was locked from the inside, and the windows were closed. Yet, for some reason, his face was frozen into an expression of sheer terror. The detective I spoke to actually used the words *'like he'd seen a ghost.'*"

"Intriguing."

"Hmm. Anyway, let's hear what Brundleweed has to say. C'mon, shake a leg."

They arrived at the shop a few moments later and entered.

Edwin Brundleweed looked up from his counter, which was secured behind metal bars. He was a stooped, middle-aged gentleman, with a long brown pointed beard drooping from his narrow chin. His head was prematurely bald, his lips thin, and thick-lensed spectacles were perched on the bridge of his hooked nose.

"Why, Detective Inspector! How very nice to see you! Is there news?"

"I'm afraid not, Mr. Brundleweed. This is Captain Sir Richard Burton. He's the gentleman who discovered the robbery here."

"Then I'm very much in your debt, sir," the dealer said to Burton. "If it weren't for you, the rest of the diamonds would have been lost too and I'd have been put out of business. Pray, come in, gentlemen."

Brundleweed moved to a door set in the bars at the side of the counter, unlocked it, and stepped back to allow his visitors through. He relocked it behind them.

"I have a fresh pot of tea just brewed and a new tin of custard creams. Would you care to join me?"

Burton and Trounce answered in the affirmative. A few minutes later, they were seated with their host around a table.

"Mr. Brundleweed," Burton said, "I'm puzzled. Why would the mystery person who replaced the Choir Stones with fakes take only those gems and not the others you had in your safe?"

The king's agent knew from Babbage that the missing gems possessed special qualities but he wondered who else might be aware of the fact.

"Good question!" came the reply. "I believe the culprit must be a specialist, a collector, a man who has interest in diamonds only for their history rather than for their financial worth. Do you know their background?"

"Only that they were discovered after they started 'singing' in 1837, were recently taken from a temple in Cambodia by Lieutenant François

Garnier, and there were originally seven of them, but he gave two away. Those two subsequently went missing after the death of their owner."

"That's correct. However, there's much more to the tale, and it's this that makes the remaining gems so eminently collectable. Black diamonds aren't the same as the white variety; they're not found in diamond fields, such as we have in South Africa and Canada. Current thinking posits that they fall from the sky as aerolites."

"Yes, I've come across that theory."

"According to an obscure occult manuscript—dating from the sixteenth century, if I remember rightly—which is quoted in Schuyler's *De Mythen van Verloren Halfedelstenen*, a large aerolite that fell in prehistoric times broke into three pieces. One piece landed in the West, another in Africa, and the third in the Far East. They are known as the Eyes of Nāga."

"Three eyes?"

"Yes. Three eyes. Peculiar, isn't it? I'm afraid I have no understanding of the Dutch language and wasn't able to read the Schuyler volume myself—my information came from a summary in *Legendary Gemstones* by Jerrold Wilson—but I believe the author goes on to recount two myths: a South American one which tells how the Amazon sprang into being when a large black diamond fell from the sky; and a Cambodian one about a lost continent in which a great river flowed from the spot where a black stone fell. He speculates that a similar story probably exists in the African interior concerning the source of the Nile."

"It does!" Burton exclaimed. "While I was in the central Lake Regions, in a town named Kazeh, I was told that the fabled Mountains of the Moon supposedly mark the outer rim of a crater where an aerolite fell, giving rise to that river."

"It can't be a coincidence, can it?" Brundleweed said. "I suppose the mythical shooting star really did fall. Anyway, the Choir Stones are supposedly the fragments of the Far Eastern Eye. If that's true, then the original diamond must have been considerably larger than the Koh-i-noor."

"Hmm," Burton grunted. "The Nāga. I've encountered references to them. They equate to the Devanagari of Hindu mythology; seven-headed reptilian beings who established an underground civilisation long before Darwin's apes learned how to walk upright."

"Ah, well, there you are," Brundleweed commented, noncommittally.

"I shall have to look into that," Burton murmured thoughtfully. "What of the African and South American diamonds?"

"Not a trace," the dealer answered. "Although there are vague suggestions that, seventy years or so ago, an English aristocrat discovered an enormous black diamond in Chile. However, I very much doubt the veracity of the claim, for no such diamond has ever been seen, let alone cut and placed on the market."

"The aristocrat's name?"

"I have no idea, Captain. As I said, it's the vaguest of rumours."

"Hmm. And what of François Garnier? Why did he decide to sell his collection?"

Brundleweed snorted scornfully: "Believe it or not, he claimed that they emanate a deleterious influence. Tosh and piffle, of course!"

"Did you have any prospective buyers?"

"No, but my advertisement in the trade newspaper was only published a couple of days before the robbery. I received just a single enquiry, from a chap who came into the shop to confirm that I was putting the stones on the market, but he was one of those dandified Rake-ish sorts, and though he expressed an interest, he didn't leave a name or address, and I haven't heard from him since."

"I followed that up," Detective Inspector Trounce put in, "but it's been impossible to trace the fellow."

Burton sipped his tea and gazed at the biscuit tin, his mind working.

He looked up. "Is there any explanation for the sound the diamonds are reputed to make?"

"Not that I know of. The sound is real, though. I heard it myself—the faintest of drones. I believe there's a Schuyler in the British Library, if you want to consult it. Maybe the author makes mention of the phenomenon."

"Thank you, Mr. Brundleweed. One final question. You reported a ghost?"

The diamond dealer looked embarrassed. He coughed and scratched his chin through his beard.

"Um, to be frank, Captain Burton, I think I must have nodded off and dreamed it."

"Tell me, anyway."

"Very well, but please bear in mind that I was strangely out of sorts that afternoon. I don't know why. I developed a migraine and felt oddly nervous and jumpy. For some reason, I imagined that my lot in life was very unsatisfactory and I grew rather morose. I inherited this little business from my father and have never before or since considered that I might do anything else in life but run it. However, that afternoon I was suddenly filled with resentment toward it, feeling that it had prevented me from doing something more important."

"What, precisely?"

"That's the thing of it! I have no idea! The suggestion that I might abandon the family business is absurd in the extreme! Anyway, I was in a thoroughly bad temper and, at four o'clock—I remember the time because the clock suddenly stopped ticking and I couldn't get it started again—I decided to pack it in for the day. The François Garnier Collection was already locked in my safe but, before leaving, I went to double check it. As I passed through into the workshop, the figure of a woman caught my eye. It made me jump out of my skin, I can tell you. She was standing in the corner, white and transparent. Then I blinked and she was gone. Believe me, after that I had a thorough case of the jitters and left the shop in a hurry, though not before locking up carefully. On the way home, the fresh air seemed to do me good and the migraine left me. I began to feel more like my old self. By the time I stepped through my front door, I was perfectly fine. I went to bed early and slept heavily. I didn't awake until the police knocked the next morning."

Burton looked at Trounce. "Some sort of gas?" he suggested. "Causing hallucinations?"

"That was my thought," the detective replied. "But we checked every inch of the floors, walls, and ceilings and found no residue and no indication of how gas might have been introduced. Certainly it didn't come up from the cellar. The tunnel from the underground river wasn't dug until hours later."

There was a long pause, then Burton said: "I apologise for imposing upon you, Mr. Brundleweed. Thank you for the tea and biscuits. I hope the diamonds are recovered."

"I suppose they'll surface eventually, Captain."

"And when they do," Trounce offered, "I'll hear about it!"

The men stood, exchanged handshakes, and Burton and Trounce took their leave.

"What next?" the detective asked as they stepped out onto the street.

"Well, Trounce old chap, this has piqued my curiosity, so I think I'm going to bury my head in books for the rest of the day to see what more I can dig up about the Nāga, then on Wednesday I shall take my rotorchair out for a spin."

"Where to?"

"Tichborne House. Much as I'd rather pursue this diamond affair, orders are orders, so I ought to have a chat with the soon-to-be-deposed baronet."

Burton spent an uncomfortable afternoon at the British Library consulting Matthijs Schuyler's *De Mythen van Verloren Halfedelstenen*, along with a number of other books and manuscripts.

He became increasingly ill.

Malaria is like an earthquake; after the initial devastating attack, a series of lesser aftershocks follow, and one of them crept over the king's agent as he studied.

It began with difficulty focusing his right eye. Then he began to perspire. By five o'clock he was trembling and feeling nauseous.

He decided to go home to sleep it off.

Sitting in a hansom, being bumped and jerked toward Montagu Place, he considered what he'd read.

According to the occult text consulted by Schuyler, a continent named Kumari Kandam once existed in the Indian Ocean. It was home to the Nāga kingdom, whose capital city spanned a great river, the Pahruli, which sprang from the spot where a black diamond had fallen from the sky.

The Nāga were reptilian, and were constantly warring with the land's human inhabitants, enslaving them, sacrificing them, and, it was hinted, eating them.

However, the humans were growing in numbers, while the Nāga were diminishing, so there came a time when the reptilian people had little choice but to seek a peaceful coexistence.

The humans sent an emissary, a Brahmin named Kaundinya, and as a symbol of the peace accord, he was married to the Nāga monarch's daughter.

However, Kaundinya was not just an ambassador, he was also a spy. He discovered that while the Nāga were a multitude, they were also one, for their minds were joined together through means of the black diamond.

After a year living with the reptilian race, during which time he convincingly acted the loving husband, Kaundinya was granted the right to add his own presence to the great fusion of minds.

He was taken before the gemstone, and watched without protest as a human slave was sacrificed to it. Then, with great ritual, pomp, and ceremony, he was sent into a trance and his mind was projected into the stone.

What a mind he possessed!

Trained since early childhood, Brahmin Kaundinya had achieved the absolute pinnacle of intellectual order and emotional discipline. For a year, the Nāga had been covertly projecting their thoughts into his, and for a year, despite feeling them crawling around inside his skull, he'd appeared to be nothing but a simple goodwill ambassador when, in truth, he was a living weapon—and their nemesis.

As his awareness sank into the crystalline structure of the stone, Kaundinya was able to position some aspect of himself in its every angle, every line, and every facet. He filled it until no part of it was free from his consciousness. Then he turned inward, delved into the depths of his own brain, and purposely burst a major blood vessel.

The massive haemorrhage killed him instantly, as he'd known it would, and, because he'd infiltrated the entire stone, his death caused it to shatter, tearing apart the minds of every single Nāga on the continent of Kumari Kandam.

It was genocide.

Many generations later, the land itself was destroyed when the Earth gave one of its occasional cataclysmic shrugs.

Now, in 1862, little evidence remained of the prehistoric lizard race. They were depicted in carvings in a few Cambodian temples, such as Angkor Wat, but whether these representations were accurate could never be established.

What fascinated Sir Richard Francis Burton, though, was that this myth of a lost reptilian civilisation existed not only in Cambodia but also in South America, where the lizard men—known as *Cherufe*—were also overthrown by the expanding human race. Their kingdom had been invaded, there had been mass slaughter, and just a few of them had escaped. This small group, carrying their sacred black diamond, had been pursued almost the entire length of the continent, far south to Chile, where they had vanished and were never heard of again.

In Africa, too, there were the *Chitahuri* of the Zulus, called the *Shayturáy* by the tribes in the central Lake Regions.

It was, of course, surplus information that didn't, as far as he could see, have much bearing on the unsolved theft of the François Garnier Collection, but Burton possessed a self-confessed "mania for discovery" which drove him to peel away layer after layer of whatever subject he studied. It at least enabled him to establish a wider and, to him, more interesting context.

There was one more thing.

The Cambodian fragments had been discovered in 1837, when a priest became aware of a low humming while meditating in his quarters. He'd lived in that room for forty-seven years and had never heard the low musical tone before. He traced it to the base of a wall, and a loose brick. The five diamonds were behind it.

1837.

It was to that year Edward Oxford, the man from the far future, had been thrown after his arrival in 1840, where he'd accidentally caused the assassination of Queen Victoria.

A coincidence, surely.

At around six o'clock, Burton got home and was hanging up his hat and coat when Mrs. Angell came down the stairs, looked at him askance, and said: "There's a nasty sheen on your brow, Sir Richard. A relapse?"

"It seems so," he replied. "I just need to sleep it off. I'll take a dose of quinine and work on my books awhile."

"You'll take a dose of quinine and go straight to bed!" she corrected.

He didn't have the strength to argue.

Ten minutes later, she brought him up a jug of water and a cup of tea.

He was already asleep.

His afternoon of study invaded his dreams.

He became aware of a fierce light, which burned through his eyelids. He opened them expecting to see firelight flickering on a canvas roof. Instead, he squinted up at a blazing blue desert sky.

Turning his head, he found that he was on his back, with limbs spread out, and wrists and ankles bound with cord to wooden stakes, which were driven deeply into the ground.

Dunes rose up on either side of him. From beyond them came the sound of voices, arguing in one of the languages of the Arabian Peninsula. He couldn't make out the words but one of the voices belonged to a woman.

He opened his mouth to shout for help but only a croak came out. His throat was dry and his skin was burning. The sun had sucked every particle of moisture from the air.

Grains of sand, riding a hot, slow breeze, blew against the side of his face.

He couldn't move.

Something nudged his left hand. He looked. There was a fairy standing by his wrist; a tiny female figure with transparent butterfly wings fluttering from her shoulder blades. She had a colourful mark painted on her forehead—like a *bindi*, though designed to more resemble an actual third eye.

Burton blinked rapidly. He had the sense that he wasn't bringing the little creature into full focus, despite being able to see her clearly. She seemed only partially present, as if imposed onto something else by his own mind, and he struggled, but failed, to pierce the illusion.

The strange being regarded him with golden-coloured eyes, then turned, bared her tiny pointed teeth, and started to chew at his bonds.

A second fairy appeared, also female, and clamped her jaws around the cord binding his right arm.

Movement at his ankles told him there were fairies at work there, too.

A fifth fluttered onto his stomach and ran up onto his chest. She put her hands on her hips and looked down at his face.

Burton felt his mind manipulated until words emerged from it, and he heard, in his own voice: "The long slow cycle of the ages turns, turns, and turns, O human. Thou art one of the few who knowest how an individual of thy strange kind didst spring from the next level of the spiral into that which thou currently inhabits, into that which thou callest thine own time. This action marked a dividing. Yet the path thou treadst echoes the one that is lost, and upon both a transition begins—a melting of one great cycle into another. Be warned!—tumultuous the change that comes! The storm shall wipe many of thy soft-skinned kinsfolk from the Earth, and thou shall be present when the thunder sounds, for the time allotted to thee is filled with paradox. There is a role assigned to thee, and thou must play the part out to its end. Thy kind infest a world in which there is only dark because there is light, there is only death because there is life, there is only evil because there is good. Be thou aware that a world conceived in opposites only creates cycles and ceaseless recurrence. Only equivalence can lead to destruction or a final transcendence. Remember that, Richard Francis Burton. Do not forget it. Only equivalence can lead to destruction."

Or a final transcendence, he wanted to add.

The bonds fell from his ankles and wrists.

The five fairies backed away from him, floated into the air, landed on the sand, fell onto all fours, scampered like lizards, and burrowed into it. They vanished from sight.

He lifted his arms and rubbed his wrists.

A figure strode into view and looked down at him from the top of a dune. It was Isabel Arundell, dressed in flowing white robes and looking radiantly beautiful.

She opened her mouth to speak.

He sat up.

Light was filtering through his bedroom curtains.

It was late on Tuesday morning.

He stretched, reached for the bell cord that hung beside his bed, and gave it a tug. Moments later, the door opened and his valet stepped in.

"The usual, please, Nelson."

The clockwork man saluted and departed.

Only equivalence can lead to destruction.

Meaningless nonsense. As for the rest of it, obviously Countess Sabina's words had become jumbled with his research, populating his nocturnal imaginings with little people and gobbledygook about vast cycles of time.

The little ones are not as they appear.

The king's agent sat and pondered until his valet delivered a basin of hot water and a breakfast tray. He got out of bed, took a small bottle from a drawer, and poured five drops from it into a glass of water, which he swallowed in a single gulp. Dr. Steinhaueser had instructed him to use quinine and nothing else when his attacks came on, but, secretly, Burton had also been dosing himself with Saltzmann's Tincture, which Steinhaueser scorned on the basis that its manufacturer had never disclosed the medicine's full ingredients. He'd warned that it almost certainly contained cocaine, which could lead to dependency.

Burton washed and shaved at the basin. A warm vitality soaked into his flesh as the tincture took effect—honey and sunlight oozing through his arteries. Nevertheless, he was still feeling weak and decided to spend the rest of this Tuesday wrapped in his *jubbah*, dedicating himself to driving out the last vestiges of malaria with strong tobacco and perhaps a brandy or two.

After finishing his toilet and winding the brass man's key, he repaired to the study, lit a Manila, and began to leaf through the morning newspapers. A great many of their pages were devoted to the Tichborne case, and he quickly realised that he was still lacking sufficient background information about the affair. It was time, he decided, to start earning his salary.

A little later, when Mrs. Angell brought him a coffee, he asked her to take a note:

> *To Mr. Henry Arundell,*
>   *My dear sir, though, to my deep regret, relations continue to be strained between us, I hope I can go some way to repairing them by doing you a service with regard to the Tichborne situation. The prime minister has commissioned me to look into the matter, and I would greatly appreciate the advice of one who has greater knowledge of the family than I. To that end, may I extend to you an invitation to dine with me at the Venetia Royal Hotel at seven o'clock this evening?*
>   *Ever yours sincerely,*
>   *Rich'd F. Burton*

"Send that by runner, please. Mr. Arundell is currently residing at the family's town house, 32 Oxford Square."

"A nice area for those that can afford it," the old lady opined. "If you don't mind me asking, has there been any word from Miss Isabel?"

"The last I heard, her parents had received two letters. It seems my former fiancée is running around with the notorious Jane Digby, the bandit queen of Damascus. I believe they've gathered quite a force of brigands and are currently raiding caravans on the Arabian Peninsula."

"My stars!" Mrs. Angel exclaimed. "Who'd have thought?"

"The Arundells still consider that my breaking the engagement caused her to run off to Arabia in the first place. I expect to receive a frosty response from her father."

His housekeeper left the room, went downstairs, lifted a whistle from a hook, opened the front door, and blew three quick blasts. Moments later, a runner arrived on the doorstep. It jogged, turned in circles, and whined restlessly until she produced a tin from beneath a hall table. She took a chunk of roast beef from it and fed it to the ravenous hound. Then she placed the waxed envelope between its teeth and stated the delivery address. The dog turned and sped away.

In his study, Burton had settled at his main desk and was writing in his journal, copying out the notes he'd taken at the British Library and adding copious annotations and cross references. An hour later, he moved to a different desk and began work on a tale from *The Book of the Thousand Nights and a Night*. He employed a unique device for this: a mechanical contraption invented by Mrs. Angell's late husband. It was the only one of its kind, an "autoscribe," which Burton played rather like a piano. Each of its keys corresponded to a letter of the alphabet or an item of punctuation and printed it onto a sheet of paper when pressed. It had taken the king's agent two weeks to master the machine but, having done so, he was now able to write at a phenomenal speed.

At four o'clock, a runner brought a reply from Henry Arundell:

Sir Richard,
  The Venetia is booked solid by a large private party. I have reserved a table for us at the Athenaeum Club instead. I will see you there at seven.
  H. Arundell

"To the point but satisfactory," Burton muttered.

He abandoned the desk, flopped into his armchair, and contemplated the case at hand.

Burton met his former prospective father-in-law at the appointed time and place. As they shook hands, the elder man exclaimed: "You look positively skeletal!"

"A bout of malaria," Burton explained.

"Still bothering you, eh?"

"Yes, though the attacks come less frequently. Have you heard from Isabel?"

"I don't want to discuss my daughter, let's have that clear from the outset."

"Very well, sir," Burton replied. He noticed that Arundell's face was haggard and careworn, and felt a pang of guilt as they made their way into the club's dining room.

The Athenaeum was crowded as usual, but in keeping with its reputation as one of the bastions of British Society, the members restricted their voices to a civilised murmur. A low buzz of conversation enveloped the two men as they passed into the opulent dining room and were escorted to their table by the maître d'. They ordered a bottle of wine, deciding to take a glass before commencing their meal.

Arundell wasted no time with niceties. "Why has Lord Palmerston taken an interest?" he asked.

"I really don't know."

"You haven't enquired?"

"Have you ever met Palmerston?"

"Yes."

"Then you know how blasted tight-lipped he is, and I don't mean the surgery!"

Burton was referring to the Eugenicist treatments the prime minister had received in an attempt to maintain his youth. His lifespan had been extended to, it was estimated, about a hundred and ten years, and his body had been stretched and smoothed until he resembled an expressionless waxwork.

"He's evasive, that's true," Arundell mused. "As are all politicians. Goes with the territory. But I'd have thought he'd at least give you something to go on."

Burton shook his head. "When he offered me my first commission, last year, it was simply a case of 'look into this,' then he left me to it. This is the same. Perhaps he doesn't want to plant any preconceptions."

"Maybe so. Very well, how can I help?"

"By telling me about the Tichborne family curse and their prodigal son."

Henry Arundell tapped his forefinger on the table, gazed at his wine glass, and looked thoughtful for a few moments. He raised his eyes to Burton and gave a curt nod.

"Tichborne House sits on a hundred-and-sixteen-acre estate near the village of Alresford, not far from Winchester. The Bishop of Winchester granted it to Walter de Tichborne in 1135, and it was, just a few years later, inherited by his son, Roger de Tichborne, a soldier, a womaniser, and a brute. It was his treatment of his wife as she lay dying from a wasting disease that brought about the curse."

"Tell me what happened."

"What sayest thou, Physician Jankyn? Shall the bitch die this night?"

Squire Roger de Tichborne threw his riding crop onto a table and dropped into a chair, which creaked beneath his considerable bulk. There was a sheen of sweat on his brow. He'd been riding with the hounds, but the one fox he and his colleagues had flushed out had been a mangy little thing with no fight in it. The dogs had brought it down in a matter of minutes. He and the men had vented their frustration in a tavern. He was now drunk and in a foul mood.

He yelled at his valet, though the man was less than fifteen feet away: "Hobson! Dost thou stand there a doltish idler? Get these accursed boots off me, man!"

The valet, a short and meek individual, hurried to his master's feet, knelt, and started to tug at a boot.

"Well, Jankyn? Answer me! Am I to be free at last, or wouldst the filthy harridan dally?"

Physician Jankyn, tall, bony, and gloomy in aspect, wrung his large hands nervously, his mouth twitching.

"The Lady Mabella be sore stricken, my lord," he announced. "Yet she may bide awhile."

Hobson, gripping de Tichborne's left calf, looked up and said: "My Lady doth wish to see thee anon, sire."

De Tichborne pulled back his right leg and, with a vicious grunt, sent his heel thudding into his valet's face. Hobson yelped and tumbled backward onto the floor, blood spurting from his nose.

"Pardieux! That's the case, is it?" de Tichborne snarled. "Get thee upstairs, thou whimpering dog, and tell the harpy that I'll see her at my own convenience and not at hers, the hell-spawned witch! Get out of my sight!"

The valet clambered to his feet and staggered away across the opulent parlour, knocked into the corner of a table, almost fell, and stumbled out of the room.

"So thinkest thou she'll tarry, hey?" de Tichborne enquired of the medical man. He bent and started to yank at his boots. "For how long, pray? Hours? Days? Weeks, may God preserve me?"

"Weeks? Nay, my lord. Not a week—nary a day. I have it that she'll live but the night through and will be taken by sunup."

Finally liberating his right leg, de Tichborne flung the riding boot across the room. It hit a wall and dropped to the floor.

"Praise be! Fetch me a draught, wouldst thou, Master Physician? And take one for thyself."

Jankyn nodded and moved from the fireplace to a bureau upon which

decanters of wine stood. He filled two goblets and took one over to de Tichborne, placing it on an occasional table beside his host's chair.

The squire's second boot came free and followed the first through the air.
It crashed into a vase atop a cabinet, shattered the ornament, and fell to the
floor amid the fragments.

"Fortune grant me a single boon: to be free of that damnable nag by the
morn!" the aristocrat muttered.

He took the wine and downed it in a single gulp, then jumped to his
stockinged feet, pushed past the doctor, and crossed to the bureau to pour
himself another.

"Prithee, repair to the library awhile, Physician. I shall take me up to see
the whore."

"But my lord!" Jankyn protested. "The Lady Mabella is in no fit condition to receive!"

"She'll receive her damned husband, and if the effort should kill her, thou
canst aid me in quaffing by way of celebration!"

Jankyn moistened his lips, hesitated, nodded unhappily, and, with
goblet in hand, shuffled out of the parlour through the door that led to the
library.

Casting a sneer at the elderly physician's back, de Tichborne turned and
also left the room. He paced to the reception hall, retrieved his shoes, buckled
them on, and stamped up the broad, sweeping staircase to the gallery above.
Here he stopped and emptied his goblet. He tossed it over the balustrade and
wiped his mouth as the tin vessel clattered on the tiled floor below. He proceeded along a corridor to his wife's bedchamber.

One of her nurses, sitting outside the room, stood as he approached the
door. She curtseyed and moved aside.

He ran his eyes appreciatively over the girl then pushed open the portal
and entered the dimly lit room without announcement.

"Art thou living, wife?"

There came movement from the large four-poster bed, and a tremulous
voice, directed at the two nurses who sat beside it, said: "Leave us."

"Yes, ma'am," they chorused, and bobbing at the squire as they passed
him, they hurried out to join their colleague in the hallway.

De Tichborne closed the door after them.

"Come thou here," the Lady Mabella whispered.

He paced over to her and looked down in disgust at her wrinkled face,
sunken cheeks, and long white hair.

The eyes that looked back at him were of the blackest jet.

"I have but a short time," she said.

"Hallelujah!" he responded.

"Drunken sot!" she exclaimed. "Hast thou no mercy in thy soul? Art thou in truth so barren of feeling? There were times—distant, aye—when thou held me close to thy bosom!"

"Ancient history, old woman."

"'Tis so. I shall be well rid of thee, Roger, when I pass, for thou art a brute and a whoremonger!"

"Say what thou wilt. I care not. So long as thou go to judgement by morn!"

The woman struggled to push herself into a sitting position. De Tichborne watched coldly, not raising a finger to help. Finally, she managed to drag herself up a little and rested back on her pillow.

"The final judgement troubles me little, husband, for have I not given to the poor of this parish through every sad year that I abided here? It is my final wish that thou shalt do the same."

"Ha! I'll be damned!"

"Of that I am certain. Nevertheless, I would have the de Tichbornes donate, during the Feast of the Annunciation every year, produce of the fields to the people."

"The blazes they will!"

"Payest thou this dole, husband, or I avow, with my very last breath I shall curse thee and thy offspring forevermore!"

Sir Roger blanched. "Have I not suffered thy evil eye sufficiently?" he muttered uneasily.

"For all thou hast inflicted upon me? Nay, there can be naught sufficient for that!" the old woman croaked. "Wilt thou concede?"

The squire looked down at his dying wife. His mouth was twisted with hatred and his eyes glinted horribly in the faint candlelight.

"I shall do as thou command me," he growled, after a long pause. "But with one provision: it shall be thou who sets the levy!"

The old woman regarded her husband, blinking in puzzlement.

"What is this?" she exclaimed. "Thou biddest me to choose the amount of the annual donation?"

"In a manner! I bid thee traverse the borders of the fields from which the wheat must be taken. I shall dedicate to the poor of the parish the produce of whatever land thou encircles. Thou hast the time it takes for a torch to burn its full length to thus mark the extent of the charity."

Lady Mabella gasped in horror. "What sayest thou? Surely to God thou cannot expect me to walk?"

"Then crawl," de Tichborne snarled. "Crawl!"

He strode to the door, yanked it open, and bellowed: "Nurses! Take thy mistress from the bed and dress her! At once!"

The three young women, waiting outside the bedroom, looked at each other in confusion.

"My lord?" stuttered one. "What—what—?"

"Question me not, wench! Have her clothed and on the steps of the house good and prompt, or by God's teeth you'll suffer!"

He shoved them aside and stamped away, calling for Hobson, who met him at the bottom of the stairs. The valet had a twisted and bloodied handkerchief hanging from his left nostril.

"Bringest thou two bottles of Bordeaux up from the cellar, and be brisk about it!" de Tichborne ordered. "I shall be outside, at the front of the house!"

He then paced down the hall, joined Physician Jankyn in the library, and cried: "Here, Jankyn! Follow! We are to be right entertained!"

He led the mystified physician out, and to the lobby.

"Assist me. I would take this bench outside."

He indicated an oak bench beside the wall near the entrance. Together, they lifted it and took it through the big double doors, across the portico, down the steps, and over the carriageway to the border of the wheat fields.

"Sit, man!"

Jankyn sat. He shivered. The sky was clear and the full moon radiated a penetrating chill.

Squire Roger de Tichborne settled beside him and chuckled to himself.

Hobson emerged from the mansion and brought over the wine bottles. De Tichborne took them and handed one to Jankyn.

"Now," he snapped at the valet, "I require three brands and a flint to light them. Hurry, fool!"

Hobson scuttled away.

De Tichborne used his teeth to pull the cork, and took a swig from his bottle.

"Drink!" he ordered Jankyn.

"My lord, I—"

"Drink!"

Jankyn raised the bottle to his mouth, extracted the cork, and took a sip.

They sat in silence until the valet returned. De Tichborne stuck a brand in the earth at either end of the bench and lit them. He saved the third, holding it in his hand. He dismissed Hobson.

"Ah!" he breathed, moments later, looking back at the house.

Physician Jankyn turned and let out a cry of dismay at what he saw.

Lady Mabella, held upright by her nurses, had tottered out of the door and was descending the steps, a frail old woman, seemingly little more than a shroud-wrapped skeleton. In truth, she was barely clothed, having pulled a gown around her night garments, draped a shawl over the top of it, and pushed her feet into slippers.

"Blessed Mary, mother of God!" Jankyn exclaimed. "What means this?"

"Do not thou interfere, Physician, I caution thee!"

Jankyn raised the bottle to his lips again, and this time he took a large gulp.

They waited, while slowly, painfully, the dying woman tottered closer.

"Hail to thee, wife!" de Tichborne bellowed. "It is a merry night, if a little chilly!" He laughed.

The woman, who would have fallen at his feet were it not for the strength of her nurses, stood trembling before him.

"Thou art bent on this course?" she wheezed.

"Thou it was who demanded the dole," he answered, "so the charge for the levy falls upon thy shoulders. Wouldst thou retract thy final wish?"

"Nay."

"Then take this brand. Yonder lay the wheat fields."

He turned to the physician. "My dear Jankyn, the Lady Mabella hath commanded that I do make an annual donation to the poor of this parish. I have agreed. The good lady will now set the amount by encircling the land whose crop she deems sufficient for the purpose."

Jankyn, who had stood at the lady's arrival, now fell back upon the bench in shock.

"She can barely walk, my lord!" he gasped.

De Tichborne ignored him and lit the brand. He held it out to his wife.

"Take it. Order thy nurses away. Show thou to me what I must set aside for charity. Thou hast until the brand is done."

A bony hand reached forth and took the guttering torch. Bottomless black eyes held de Tichborne's for a moment. A toothless mouth muttered: "Leave me!"

The nurses stepped away.

Lady Mabella swayed for a moment. With her joints cracking, she then turned and hobbled to the edge of the field.

The squire laughed wickedly and swigged his wine. He sat down.

Speechless, helpless, Physician Jankyn watched as the old woman fell to her knees and began to crawl, supporting herself with one hand while holding the brand with the other.

"See, Master Physician," de Tichborne chuckled. "We have fine sport this night, hey? Dost thou care to make a wager? I reckon she'll set the levy at maybe half a sack o' grain afore the devil takes her unto his breast!"

"I cannot be party to this!" Jankyn cried. He made to stand but de Tichborne's hand clamped down hard on his arm.

"Hold! If thou makest to leave, as God is my witness, I'll run thee through with my sword!"

Jankyn fell back. He pulled a handkerchief from his pocket and wiped it across his brow.

The old woman crawled on.

And on.

And on.

Squire Roger de Tichborne became increasingly uneasy as his wife traversed the border of the lengthy field before him and passed beyond it to the next, pulling herself up the long sloping side, across the far end, and now back down toward him. By the orange glow of her torch, he could see that her knees were bleeding and tears streamed down her face.

"Fie! From whence doth the crone's strength come?" he muttered. "The devil himself, I'll warrant! The damned enchantress!"

"By the saints, my lord," the physician said, slurring his words slightly. "How many acres hath the Lady Mabella encompassed?"

"If she returneth to us before the brand is extinguished, nigh on twenty-three!"

Painful inch after painful inch, the dying woman crawled the remaining length of the border until, finally, she dragged herself across the carriageway and collapsed onto her face at de Tichborne's feet. The torch crackled, guttered, and died.

The squire poured the last dregs of wine down his throat then threw the bottle aside with savage force.

He looked down at the woman, his lips curling back from his teeth.

"Attend her!"

The physician crouched and pulled Lady Mabella over onto her back. Her eyes rolled then fixed intently on her husband. Her lips moved.

"What?" de Tichborne snapped. "Doth she speak?"

"Aye, my lord. She biddeth thee bend closer."

The aristocrat snorted but, nevertheless, squatted on his haunches.

The old woman whispered: "Two fields of wheat, sir. Two fields!"

Her husband hissed vehemently.

"Thinkest thou that I would honour my word to a slattern and sorceress? Foul necromancer! Scold! Shrew! Two fields of wheat to the poor? Never! They shall receive naught from me!"

"Then listen thou to my final words, O husband," Lady Mabella whispered. "From my heart, I curse thee and thine, and this curse shall hold true through all the ages. Should the allotted dole fail for e'en a single year, there shall be seven sons born to this house, aye, and nary a one shall sire a man-child. Seven daughters shall follow, and the name of de Tichborne will thus be lost for all time. And the house itself shall fall into ruin, until naught but wind-borne dust remains of thy family!"

Her eyes closed and a rattle sounded from her throat.

The physician looked up.

"The Lady Mabella is dead, my lord."

"And may the devil have her eyes!" The squire looked across the wheat fields. "Hang it! Twenty-three acres, Jankyn!"

"Wilt thou accede to the lady's wish, then?"

"I have but little choice. The witch's curse is upon the family now."

He looked up at the stars and muttered: "Heaven grant mercy upon those who follow!"

Sir Richard Francis Burton sat with his mouth open, his wine glass held inches from it. He blinked, took a breath, and gasped: "Good God! The man was an animal!"

Henry Arundell agreed: "A cad of the first order, and his brutality has had a lasting influence, for every year since he killed his wife—let us not pretend he did otherwise—the Tichbornes have paid the dole, with the exception of a short period that began in 1796."

"What happened then?"

"The seventh baronet, Sir Henry, who'd been travelling overseas for some considerable time, returned to Tichborne House, stopped the dole, and declared the estate off-limits to all. For the next few years, he lived as a recluse, not emerging from his self-imposed isolation until the Napoleonic Wars. By this time, the eldest of his seven sons had produced only daughters and the others were childless. When a large part of the manor fell down, Sir Henry realised that the curse was upon him. He immediately restored the annual contribution, had the rest of the house demolished, and built the current manor on its foundations."

"You say he travelled," Burton interjected. "Do you know where?"

"Mainly in the Americas, I believe. Anyway, despite the resurrection of the dole, the Tichbornes' misfortunes weren't quite over. While fighting in France, Sir Henry's third son, James, married an ill-tempered girl named Henriette-Felicité. Though she bore a male heir to the estate—Roger Charles Doughty Tichborne, born in January of 1829—her marriage to James soon faltered."

Arundell broke off as a waiter approached. "Shall we order?" he asked Burton.

The king's agent, who'd been absorbed in the other man's tale, waved his hand distractedly and said: "Yes, yes, of course, please do."

Henry Arundell requested a chicken vindaloo and Burton, hardly caring what he ate, asked for the same.

"So this Roger Tichborne is the prodigal who's lately been the preoccupation of all the journalists?"

"Yes. He was doted on by his mother and raised as a Frenchman. He didn't learn to speak English until he was about twelve years old, and always spoke it with a strong French accent.

"A second son was born, too. A surprise, really, considering that James and his wife grew to hate each other. This one, Alfred, was a weak-willed lad, and was all but ignored by Henriette-Felicité, who remained devoted to her firstborn.

"To return for a moment to the grandfather, Sir Henry; when he died, one of his other sons, James's elder brother Edward, became the eighth baronet. Edward had changed his surname to Doughty as a condition of an inheritance. This is where my family comes into it, for after becoming Sir Edward Doughty, he married my aunt, Katherine Arundell, and they had a child, 'Kattie' Doughty, in 1834. She became romantically involved with young Roger Tichborne, who had, after being educated at Stonyhurst Jesuit School, joined the Sixth Dragoon Guards, and was spending his furloughs at Tichborne House. My aunt objected strongly to this romance on the grounds that Roger lacked prospects and didn't act in a sufficiently English manner. Plus, of course, he and the girl were cousins.

"Having been banned from seeing Kattie for at least three years, Roger determined to prove himself. Typically, he followed a flight of fancy. According to a family legend, Sir Henry had discovered a fabulous diamond in South America—"

"*What?*" Burton cried, causing an outbreak of tut-tutting from the surrounding tables.

Arundell looked at him in astonishment then shook his head. "No, no, Burton," he said. "It's just a fancy. There's never been anything to substantiate it—certainly no such gem has ever been seen, and, considering the family's current finances, it obviously doesn't exist."

"Frankly, I hardly know what to think!" Burton revealed.

"Why so?"

"Because the—the—well, it doesn't matter—suffice it to say that I've experienced rather a profound coincidence!"

"Anything I should know about?"

"No. Yes. No. Um—my apologies, sir, I'm somewhat at a loss. A few weeks ago there was a rather daring diamond robbery—"

"I don't remember that."

"It wasn't reported. Scotland Yard has been keeping it quiet while the investigation proceeds. I had some involvement with the affair, and my subsequent inquiries suggest that the missing diamonds are connected with one that is rumoured to have been discovered in Chile by an English aristocrat."

"Ah."

"I wasn't told the aristocrat's name."

"So now you're thinking it was Sir Henry Tichborne? I'm sorry to disappoint you but, really, the whole thing is nothing but a fairy tale."

Burton cleared his throat at the mention of fairies.

"An enticing one, to be sure," Arundell continued. "Certainly young Roger fell under its spell, and decided to visit all the places where his grandfather had travelled in the hope that he, too, would stumble upon untold wealth. A quite ridiculous endeavour, and it would have been an utter waste of time had he gone through with it—but no sooner did he step ashore at Valparaiso than word reached him that his uncle, Sir Edward Doughty, had passed away."

"So the baronetcy passed to his father, James?"

"Quite so—until, seven days later, Sir James dropped dead from heart failure. Our prodigal was now the new baronet, entitled to all the wealth and estates of the Tichbornes. Rather eagerly, I imagine, he hopped aboard a ship—*La Bella*—to make his way home. On the 20th of April, 1854, it sank without a trace, and the third baronet in less than a fortnight was lost. His young brother, Alfred, inherited the estate instead, and would have bankrupted it in no time at all had his mother not sent her friend Colonel Lushington to Tichborne House to take him in hand."

Henry Arundell paused to sip his wine and to nod a greeting to an acquaintance seated at a nearby table.

Burton asked: "If Sir Alfred is such a liability, why are the Arundell and Doughty families so concerned that his elder brother has shown up alive and well? Why contest Roger Tichborne's claims to the baronetcy?"

The older man blew out an exasperated breath and said in a sharp tone: "Simply because the man currently in Paris is most definitely not Roger Tichborne."

The king's agent looked surprised. "He isn't? That's not what Lady Henriette-Felicité says. Surely you don't doubt a mother's recognition of her own son?"

"I do, absolutely!"

"On what grounds?"

"On grounds that the dowager is on death's doorstep and is desperate for her lost son's return; on grounds that she's almost entirely deaf and blind; on grounds that Roger Tichborne always, without exception, wrote to his mother in French, yet the man currently posing as him wrote to her in English—and very, very bad English to boot—and on grounds that his handwriting is entirely different."

"A man's handwriting can change over the course of a decade."

"Can a man forget how to spell?"

"Hmm," Burton grunted.

The waiter arrived with their food and for a few minutes the men ate in silence.

"So Sir Roger Tichborne—" Burton began.

"The Claimant," Arundell snapped. "I'll not honour him with the name Tichborne until he's demonstrated beyond a shadow of a doubt that he is who he says he is."

"Very well then, the Claimant—he's still in Paris?"

"Yes. Apparently he has a scalp infection and is being treated by a doctor, though he's expected at Tichborne House during the course of the coming week. I fear he means to eject Colonel Lushington."

"I would like to be there when he arrives. Could you arrange it?"

Arundell looked Burton in the eye. "If you go as representative of the Arundell and Doughty families, yes. My question is: can I depend on you to act in our interests? You and I don't have a good history, Burton, and my wife would have a hysterical fit if she found out I'd drawn you into the affair."

"It was the prime minister who drew me into the affair, sir, and what you can depend on is that I will do my utmost to get to the truth of the matter, whatever it may be."

Arundell pushed the food on his plate around with his fork, then sighed and said: "Fair enough. I'll get a message to Lushington. He's a dependable sort, if a little long-winded in manner, and will give you whatever assistance you need. When do you intend to go?"

"Tomorrow afternoon."

"Good. You'll definitely be there before the Claimant arrives. In addition to the colonel and Sir Alfred, there are a couple of other people at the house you should be aware of. The first is Doctor Jankyn, the family physician. He belongs to an unbroken line of medical practitioners who've been associated with the Tichbornes since the year dot, and he's currently nursing Sir Alfred through some sort of nervous complaint."

"Related to his brother's return?"

"I don't know. The second person is Andrew Bogle, an old Jamaican who served as butler to Sir Edward Doughty and who now works in that same capacity for Sir Alfred. Both men knew Roger Tichborne before he left for South America."

With that, Henry Arundell had little more to tell Burton, so the two men finished their meal and Isabel's father took his leave.

The king's agent retired to the smoking room and there fell in with Samuel Baker and John Petherick from the Royal Geographical Society. They were bluff, hearty, bushy-bearded men, whose plan to go in search of Henry Morton Stanley by following the course of the Nile from Cairo to its source struck Burton as naïve and overly ambitious. The warring tribes around the upper reaches of the great river had so far prevented any such penetration into the heart of Africa.

"It can't be done," he told them.

"We'll see, Sir Richard. We'll see!" Baker replied, with a smile and a slap to Burton's shoulder.

The three of them discussed the matter for an hour or so before the two would-be rescuers took their leave of the more experienced man. Burton shook his head.

"The bloody fools are going to their deaths," he muttered.

He swallowed his drink and turned to leave only to find himself facing another member of the RGS. It was Richard Spruce, a botanist, author of *The Hepaticae of the Amazon and the Andes of Peru and Ecuador*; a man who knew South America extremely well.

"Ah, Spruce!" the king's agent enthused. "Just the man! Would you allow me to buy you a tipple? I have an ulterior motive, mind—I want to grill you about Brazil and Chile."

Spruce acceded, and, for half an hour, Burton questioned him about black diamonds and the mythical *Cherufe*. Spruce just shrugged and declared that there were no diamonds in that part of the world and he'd never heard of any prehistoric reptilian civilisation. He then turned the subject to his ongoing work with the Eugenicists to solve the great Irish famine, and talked with such obsessive zeal that Burton began to feel uncomfortable, sensing that he was in the presence of a fanatic.

"The seeds my fellows and I have developed are already growing!" Spruce raved. "You should see them! They've sprouted into massive plants! Huge, Burton, huge! And they're pollinating far earlier than we'd anticipated!"

He banged a fist onto the bar, causing glasses to rattle along its length.

"It's just the beginning! Soon we'll be cultivating plants that'll perform specific functions in society in much the same way as machines do! Imagine a factory that was actually a plant! Imagine if we could grow our industrial infrastructure from seeds!"

Burton, whose encounters with Charles Darwin and Francis Galton, and, more recently, with Sir Charles Babbage, had made him extremely wary of such propositions, gave an excuse and departed in haste. There was, he reflected, something quite unnerving about Richard Spruce.

GHOSTS

CATERPILLAR DUSTBIN

THE EASY WAY TO DISPOSE OF VEGETABLE WASTE.

There is nothing more offensive than the stench of an overflowing dustbin!

Mann-Voight Caterpillars solve the problem!

It may look like a normal tin dustbin but inside are our eugenically enhanced caterpillars! Whatever vegetable matter you throw away, they will consume in a matter of minutes!

NEVER NEEDS REPLACING!

When each caterpillar matures into a beautiful butterfly, it will breed only with other Mann-Voight butterflies and it will lay its eggs nowhere except in a Mann-Voight dustbin. You will thus maintain a constant stock of waste-consuming caterpillars!

Why open your dustbin lid to the foul stench of rubbish when you can open it to a colourful cloud of butterflies?

The Mann-Voight Refuse System.

2/- Monthly Subscription.

Apply Mann-Voight, 6 Nibbins Road, Rye.

The next morning, Algernon Swinburne called at 14 Montagu Place and was ushered through the house by Mrs. Angell, into the yard, and to the garage beyond. Inside, he found Sir Richard Francis Burton, who was applying oil to his rotorchair's many moving parts.

"I say! What happened to your beard?" the diminutive poet enquired.

"Vanity happened," Burton admitted. "I got tired of seeing that forked bird's nest in the mirror."

"You look younger, but no less barbaric. Are you feeling better? You're still skinny and yellowish."

"I'm through the worst of it, Algy, and feeling stronger by the day. What have you been up to? Here, hold this."

"What is it?"

"The flywheel. I want to lubricate the bearings."

"Ah." Swinburne sighed. "I know a rather fetching young doxy who does something similar. You'd like her."

Burton clicked his tongue disapprovingly and said: "Then my question is answered. It's quite apparent what you've been up to."

The poet adopted a wounded expression and objected: "I've been writing, too! As a matter of fact, my latest efforts have caused quite a stir."

"So I read. The *Empire* is calling you a genius."

"Yes, but the *Times* is calling me a deviant."

"It's hardly surprising. Your poetry is somewhat—shall we say—*florid*? Here, give me that back."

Swinburne handed over the flywheel and watched as his friend fitted it into its housing.

"*Filthy* was the word the *Times* used. Are you preparing it for a flight or just tinkering?"

"I'm flying out to Hampshire this afternoon."

"What's there?"

"Tichborne House."

"What! What!" Swinburne cried, twitching and jerking like a maniac. "Surely you haven't got yourself mixed up in *that* business!"

Burton picked up a cloth and wiped oil from his hands.

"I'm afraid so. There's a remote possibility that the François Garnier Collection is involved, too."

"Eh? The Fra—What? How? You mean Brunel—? What?"

"Really, Algy, you're the most incomprehensible poet I've ever met! But to answer the question you haven't managed to ask: no, I don't think the Steam Man has anything to do with the Tichborne case. However, I do suspect that whoever stole the diamonds from right under his mechanical nose might have some connection with the returning heir."

"Ah ha! So there's a safe cracker among the Tichborne clan!"

"It's not impossible. All I know thus far is—"

Burton went on to recount the legends concerning the three Eyes of Nāga. He then told the history of the Tichborne family.

"So you see," he concluded, "I'm working on the premise that perhaps Sir Henry found the South American Eye—even though Henry Arundell poohpoohs the suggestion—and that someone in or connected in some way with the family might now have possession of the Choir Stones, too."

"Which just leaves the African diamond," Swinburne commented.

"Indeed."

"Which strikes me as peculiar."

"Peculiar?"

"It gave rise to the Nile."

"According to myth, yes. What are you getting at?"

"Just that you and Speke went hunting for the source of that river, then Henry Stanley did, and now his expedition has disappeared."

Burton frowned. "His expedition has disappeared because he was stupid enough to fly over the region in these—" He rapped his knuckles against the side of his rotorchair. "Not a single flying machine that's entered the region has ever come out again. He knew that, but still he flew."

"Yes, but that's not what I meant."

"What, then?"

"Come into the house with me. Have a cigar. I want you to tell me a story."

The king's agent considered his friend for a moment, then shrugged, nodded, put away his tools, and led Swinburne from the garage.

Minutes later, they were relaxing in the study.

Burton took a sip of port and said: "What do you want to know?"

"About your expedition with Speke. If I remember rightly, you reached Lake Tanganyika by March of '58. What happened next?"

"Illness, mainly. We'd heard there was a port town named Ujiji on the eastern shore of the lake where we could establish a base camp, but when we got there we found that it consisted of nothing but a few decrepit beehive-shaped huts and a pitiful market—"

Captain Richard Francis Burton was blind.

Lieutenant John Hanning Speke's face had become paralysed down one side.

Both men were too weak to walk more than a few paces.

For two weeks, they rested in a half-derelict domed hut and ate the boiled rice brought to them by their guide, Sidi Bombay. They lay limply on their cots, crushed by the oppressive heat, and suffered and slept and moaned and vomited and lapsed in and out of consciousness.

"Mary, mother of God, is it worth it, Dick?" Speke whispered.

"It has to be. We're almost there, I'm sure of it. You heard what Bombay told me this morning."

"No, I didn't. I was out of my mind with fever."

"The locals claim a river flows northward out of the lake. If we can get a dhow onto her, I'm certain we'll find ourselves floating down the Nile, straight past the warring tribes, and all the way to Cairo."

Burton clung on to that conviction and used it to slowly haul himself out of the pit of ill health. Infuriatingly, Speke, who was far less driven than his commanding officer, nevertheless made a much speedier recovery, and was soon strolling around during the short spells of cool morning and evening air, bathing in the lake, and shopping in the little market, where he would appear with a native holding an umbrella over him, with strings of trading beads slung over his arm, and with smoked-glass spectacles protecting his eyes.

He was a strange, restless, self-conscious man. Tall and thin, long-bearded and watery-eyed, hesitant in manner and stuttering in conversation, he only ever seemed at peace with himself when he was hunting.

Lieutenant Speke shot at everything. He put bullets into hippos and antelope, giraffes and lions, elephants and rhinos. He killed gleefully and indiscriminately, and had left a seven-hundred-mile-long trail of corpses all the way back to Zanzibar.

Even so, as the days dragged on in Ujiji, he became maddened by the shimmering landscape, the unending profusion of dried-out grass and trees, the hard, dusty, cracked earth.

"Brown! Nothing but blasted brown! Not a spot of green anywhere! I can't bear it. Even hunting is tedious in this damned hellhole. Can't we move on? I feel like I'm losing my mind!"

"Soon, John, but I need a little more time," answered Burton, whose sight was still impaired, his legs still paralysed.

Speke groaned. "Will you at least permit me to take a canoe across the lake with Sidi Bombay? We know Sheikh Hamed is over there and he has a dhow. Maybe I can talk him into hiring it out to us? And he might know something about the northern river."

"It's too dangerous. The rainy season is due. They say it causes violent storms on the water."

Speke, though, became fixated upon the idea and eventually persuaded Burton to allow the excursion. He departed on the 3rd of March and was gone almost a month, during which time Burton dosed himself morning, noon, and night with Saltzmann's Tincture and gave himself up to what he would later describe as *dreaming of things past, visioning things present.*

By the time the lieutenant returned, Burton was feeling a little better. His ophthalmia had cleared and he was able to totter around unassisted.

"The river?" he asked, eagerly.

"It's called the Rusizi. Hamed gave me an absolute assurance that it flows out of the lake. The tribes in the region are friendly and will guide us to it."

Burton punched a fist into the air. "Allah be praised! Did you secure the dhow?"

"He'll loan it to us three months from now at a cost of five hundred dollars."

"What? That's ridiculous! Didn't you barter?"

"I lack the language skills, Dick."

Burton seethed. What a waste of time and resources! Damn Speke's incompetence!

The lieutenant should have been mortified by his failure to get the dhow, yet he wasn't. Instead, his manner became odd, distant—almost furtive.

A few days later, he approached Burton and said: "I say, old chap, would you mind helping me to put my diaries into order? You know how confounded amateurish I am when it comes to writing."

"Certainly," answered Burton, and the two men settled at a makeshift table with Speke's journals open before them.

They went through the notebooks, and Burton pointed out where a more extensive description would be beneficial, where cross references could be inserted, and, very frequently, where spelling mistakes and grammatical errors required correction.

Then he turned a page and found a map sketched out.

"What's this?"

"It's the northern shore of the lake."

"You mean this lake? Tanganyika?"

"Yes."

"But John—what's this horseshoe of mountains in the north?"

"In my opinion, they're the Mountains of the Moon."

"That's not possible. All the natives say the Mountains of the Moon are far away to the northeast of here."

"Sheik Hamed's people say otherwise. They've been to the northern shore, in the shadow of that range."

"And the Rusizi? Do you mean to suggest that it flows out of Tanganyika and up into the mountains?"

Speke shifted in his seat. "I don't know," he muttered.

"Besides, if they're as big as legend suggests, surely we'd be able to see the distant peaks from here?"

"Maybe the land slopes down beyond the northern shore, so the peaks are actually below the horizon?"

Burton could barely believe his ears. What on earth was his companion babbling about?

He turned the page and they continued to work, but Speke rapidly lost interest and said: "That's enough for now. I'm going for a walk."

He left the hut and, some minutes later, Burton heard rifle shots—more animals falling to his companion's bloodlust.

The increasingly humid, sweaty days passed.

With his health continuing to improve, Burton decided to risk a foray onto the lake. He borrowed two large canoes from the Ujiji natives and instructed Sidi Bombay to have them loaded with supplies and crewed by the strongest oarsmen.

"Aren't you too sick for this?" Speke asked.

"I'm fine. And we must establish for certain which way the Rusizi flows. Hearsay is not enough. I have to see it with my own eyes."

"I think we should wait until you're stronger."

Burton ground his teeth in vexation. "Dash it all, John! Why are you suddenly so reluctant to see this expedition through?"

"I'm not!" Speke protested. His attitude, though, remained surly as the two canoes were launched, with Burton in the first and him in the second.

On choppy water, the crew paddled northward.

The weather broke. They were by turns soaked by torrential rain, baked by ferocious sun, and battered by downpours again.

They put ashore at a village named Uvira, where the oarsmen from Ujiji mutinied.

"They have much fear," Sidi Bombay explained. "People in village say we be killed if we go more north. Tribes there very bad. Always make war."

Then came a terrible blow: "Boss man here say Rusizi come in lake, not go out."

"Sheikh Hamed claimed otherwise!" Burton cried.

Sidi Bombay shook his head. "No, no. Mr. Speke he no understand what Sheikh Hamed say."

Despondency settled over Burton.

The lieutenant avoided him.

The explorers turned around and returned to Ujiji. From there, they trudged back inland to a village named Kawele.

Burton rallied. He felt sure that with the evidence he'd so far collected, he could raise sponsorship for a second, more fully equipped expedition—and, by God, he'd bring a better travelling companion!

"I'd like to circumnavigate Tanganyika," he told Speke, "but we should save what's left of our supplies for the trek back to Zanzibar. If our furlough ends before we report to the RGS, we'll lose our commissions."

"Agreed," the lieutenant answered stiffly.

So, on the 26th of May, they began the long march eastward, reaching Unyanyembe in mid-June, where a mailbag awaited them. One of its letters revealed to Burton that his father had died ten months previously, and another that his brother, Edward, had been savagely beaten in India and had suffered severe head injuries.

His despondency deepened into depression.

They slogged on over the endless savannah until they reached the Arab trading town of Kazeh. Here they rested.

Speke encouraged Burton to take Saltzmann's Tincture to drive away the last vestiges of malarial fever. He even mixed the doses himself. No amount of medicine, though, could fully protect the Englishmen from Africa's insidious maladies, and in addition to all their other ailments, they now both suffered from constant, eye-watering headaches.

Death hung oppressively over this part of Africa—and it wanted them.

One day, Speke came to Burton and told him that the locals were hinting that there was a huge body of water fifteen or sixteen marches to the north.

"We should explore it," he said.

"I'm not well enough," came the reply. "I'm short of breath and can't think straight. My mind is all over the place. I don't even trust myself to take accurate readings. Besides, we don't have the supplies."

"How about if I take a small party? I can travel fast and light, while you rest here and get your strength back."

Burton, who was lying on a cot, tried to sit up and failed.

"Where's your medicine?" Speke asked. "I'll prepare you a dose."

"Thank you, John. Do you really think you can get there and back without eating into our provisions too much?"

"I'm certain of it."

"Very well. Organize it and go."

Secretly, Burton was relieved at the prospect of time apart from his colleague. Speke had been a thorn in his side ever since the visit to Sheikh Hamed, and while they'd been in Kazeh, the lieutenant hadn't made a single concession to Eastern customs and etiquette, repeatedly offending their Arabian hosts and leaving Burton to explain and apologise.

His departure lifted a weight from Burton's shoulders. The explorer put aside his medicine and started compiling a vocabulary of the local dialects for use by future travellers. As scholarly pursuits usually did, this activity revived his spirits.

Six weeks later, Lieutenant John Hanning Speke returned.

"There's an inland sea!" he declared, triumphantly. "They call it Nyanza or Nassa or Ziwa or Ukerewe or something—"

"*Nyanza* is the Bantu word for *lake*, John."

"Yes, yes—it doesn't matter; I named it after the king! I swear to God, Dick, I've discovered the source of the Nile!"

Burton asked his companion to describe all he'd seen.

It turned out that Speke had seen very little. His evidence was more guesswork than science. He'd been within sight of the water for only three days, hadn't sailed upon it, and had, in fact, observed only a small stretch of the southeastern shore.

"So how do you know its size? How do you justify calling it an inland sea? How do you know the Nile flows out of it?"

"I spoke to a local man, a great traveller."

"Spoke?"

"Through gestures."

Burton looked at the map his companion had sketched.

"Great heavens, man! You've set the far shore at four degrees latitude north! Is this based on nothing more than the wave of a native's hand?"

Speke clammed up. He became increasingly cantankerous, caused arguments among the porters, and barely spoke a word to Burton.

It quickly became apparent that he'd used up more of their supplies than predicted. There was no way they could afford to make a diversion northward. However big the lake was, however likely the source of the Nile, it was going to have to wait.

September arrived, and they departed Kazeh and began the long march back to Africa's east coast.

The ensuing weeks were unpleasant in the extreme. There were fights, disputes, thefts, accidents, and desertions. Burton was forced to punish some of the porters and to pay off others. They drove him into a fury, and, on one occasion, he used a leather belt to thrash a man, then stood panting over him, confused and disoriented, his head throbbing, hardly realizing what he had done.

He had to push the expedition every step of the way homeward and

Speke did nothing to help. If anything, his attitude toward the natives just made the situation worse.

The two explorers exchanged barely a word until, a month later, Speke fell seriously ill. They halted and Burton nursed him as a high temperature erupted into a life-threatening fever. The lieutenant, lying in a cot, ranted and raved. He was obviously in the grip of terrifying hallucinations.

"They have their claws in my legs!" he howled. "Dear God, save me! I can hear it in the room above but they won't let me approach! I can't get near! My legs! My legs!"

Burton mopped Speke's brow, feeling the heat radiating from his skin.

"It's all right, John," he soothed.

"They aren't human! They are crawling into my head! Oh, Jesus, get them out of me, Dick! Get them out! They are putting their claws into me! Dragging me away from it, across the cavern, by the legs!"

Away from what? Burton wondered.

Speke's body arched and he shook violently, gripped by an epileptic fit. Burton called Sidi Bombay over and they forced a leather knife sheath between the lieutenant's teeth to prevent him from biting his tongue. They held him down as spasms twisted and contorted him.

Eventually, Speke fell into a stupor and lay semiconscious, muttering to himself.

"Hobgoblins," he whispered. "Great crowds of them spilling from the temple. Heaven help me, I have them inside my soul! They are setting loose their dragons!"

His face was suddenly wrenched out of shape by a ferocious cramp, his eyes became glassy, and he began to bark like a dog. He was almost entirely unrecognisable, and Sidi Bombay backed away hastily, wearing an expression of superstitious dread.

"It is *kichyomachyoma*," he said. "He attack by bad spirits! He die!"

Speke screamed. He screamed ceaselessly for an entire day—but he didn't die. Eventually he quieted, lapsed in and out of consciousness, and finally slept.

Another week slipped by.

John Speke was sitting up, sipping at a cup of tea, when Burton entered the tent.

"How are you feeling, John?"

"Better, Dick. I think we'll be able to move on soon. Maybe in a couple of days."

"When you're ready, but not before."

Speke put down his cup and looked Burton squarely in the eyes. "You shouldn't have said it."

Burton frowned, puzzled. "Said what?"

"At Berbera. When we were attacked. You said: 'Don't step back or they'll think we're retiring.' I'm not a coward."

"A coward? What are you talking about? Berbera was three years ago!"

"You thought I was retreating in fear."

Burton's eyebrows rose. He was amazed, shocked. "I—what? I didn't—"

"You accused me."

"John! You have it all wrong! I did no such thing! I have never, not for a single moment, considered you anything other than courageous in the face of danger!"

Speke shook his head. "I know what you think."

"John—" Burton began, but Speke interrupted: "I'll rest now."

He lay down and turned his face away. Burton stood looking at him, then quietly left the tent.

After a further three days, the safari got moving again, with the lieutenant being carried on a stretcher. The long line of men—the two explorers and their porters—wound like a snake through the undulating landscape. They seemed to make no progress, seeing only sun-baked grass for mile after mile after mile.

In fact, they were wending their way up onto higher ground, and the gradual change of air did Burton and Speke a world of good, driving the fevers, diseases, pains, and infections from their ravaged bodies, though they continued to suffer from terrible headaches.

Christmas Day came and went. By this time, they were maintaining a polite but cold relationship. Speke's excursion to the great lake was never spoken of.

Desertions and disobedience among the porters halted them for another fortnight. Burton warned the men that they'd forfeit their pay if they didn't pick up their packs and start moving. They refused. He rounded up the troublemakers and dismissed them, hiring nine new men from a passing caravan.

They moved on.

Walking, walking, walking! Would it never end?

It did.

On the 2nd of February, 1859, they climbed to the top of a hill and saw the blue sea scintillating in the far distance.

They threw their caps into the air and cheered.

"Hip, hip, hurrah!" John Speke hollered. "Let's get ourselves off this filthy damned continent, and I pray to God that my blasted headache stays behind!"

"We reached Zanzibar and from there sailed to Aden, where I decided to lay up awhile to recover my strength. John, meanwhile, jumped onto the first available Europe-bound ship. He promised to await my arrival in London, so we could report our findings to the Royal Geographical Society together. In any event, he went there alone and claimed sole credit for the discovery of the source of the Nile."

Burton flicked his cigar stub into the hearth.

"It was a terrible betrayal," Swinburne said.

"The worst. I was his commanding officer. It was my expedition. His evidence was so incompetent that he made an embarrassment of the entire endeavour."

A short silence settled over the two men.

Burton ran the tip of his right index finger along the scar on his cheek, as if reminded of that old, mind-numbing pain.

"Of course," he continued, "in going to the RGS, he wasn't acting entirely of his own volition. He'd been mesmerised during the voyage home by the leader of the Rakes, Laurence Oliphant."

He stood, crossed to the window, and looked down at the traffic that clanked and steamed and rolled and rumbled along Montagu Place. Almost inaudibly, he said: "You think John betrayed me even before we left Africa, don't you? At Tanganyika."

"Yes, I'm sorry, Richard, but it all adds up. I think Speke learned from Sheikh Hamed that the Mountains of the Moon were nowhere near, but far away to the northeast; that the tribes to the north of Ujiji were hostile; and that the Rusizi flows into, not out of, the lake. He then set about convincing you of the exact opposite, so that you'd waste time and resources and be forced to return to Zanzibar."

Burton sighed. "A lust for glory. He wanted to be *John Hanning Speke, the man who discovered the source of the Nile.*"

"It would seem so, and though his map didn't fool you—you're too good a geographer to be taken in by absurdly misplaced mountains—the rest of it worked. Your attempts to see the Rusizi precluded any further explorations."

The king's agent clenched his fists and leaned with his knuckles against the window frame and his forehead touching the glass.

"So," the poet continued, "you began the long journey back eastward and when you reached Kazeh, Speke dosed you up with Saltzmann's Tincture until you couldn't think straight. He then used rumours of a lake to justify his independent excursion north to where Hamed had told him the Mountains of the Moon were located. Whether he found them or not, something happened in that region that made the Nile question irrelevant to him."

Burton pushed himself back upright, turned, frowned, and said: "You're referring to his subsequent hallucinations?"

Swinburne nodded. "You said he ranted and raved about dragons dragging him away from something. Dragons, Richard—mythical reptiles, just like the *Shayturáy*, the African Nāga. Is that a coincidence, do you think?"

"And the Nāga are associated with a fabled black diamond that fell from the sky and gave rise to the Nile," Burton whispered. "Bloody hell, Algy, did he see the African stone?"

"It would certainly account for his subsequent actions."

Burton whistled and ran his fingers through his hair. He paced over to the fireplace, took another cigar from the box on the mantelpiece, and immediately forgot it, holding it unlit while he gazed thoughtfully at Swinburne.

"When Babbage said the Technologists had become aware of the black diamonds, I wondered how. Now we know: Speke told Oliphant and Oliphant told the Technologists."

"Yes, and that's when the whole game changed. Let me ask you a question: why did Speke receive Murchison's backing for a second expedition? He's an inept geographer, a terrible public speaker, a bad writer, and has proven himself thoroughly unreliable. Yet he was chosen over you. Why?"

Burton's jaw dropped. The cigar fell from his fingers.

"My God," he whispered. "My God. At last it's making sense. The Rakes and Technologists must have offered to fund him!"

"What still remains unclear is what actually *happened* during that second expedition. He took with him a young soldier named James Augustus Grant—I don't know if he was a Technologist or a Rake, but one or the other, I should think—and they used swans to fly to Kazeh. Speke failed to properly guard the birds and lions killed them. That was the first of a string of disasters that forced him to return to Zanzibar. When he arrived there, Grant was no longer with him. Speke claimed that his colleague had died of fever and was buried near the shore of the lake."

Burton dropped back into his armchair and said: "He also reaffirmed that he'd discovered the source of the Nile—but, again, his evidence was pathetically flawed."

Swinburne grunted his agreement. "He was scheduled to give a fuller account at the Bath Assembly Rooms last year. Instead, knowing that you were going to expose the scale of his ineptitude, he shot himself in the head. Oliphant abducted him from the hospital, and the Technologists replaced the damaged half of his brain with a clockwork mechanism."

"Babbage's prototype. I never understood why they did that until now. Bismillah! They still needed him to show them where the diamond was. But then the Spring Heeled Jack affair occurred, the Technologist and Rake alliance diverted their resources to capturing Edward Oxford, and Speke was left trailing about after them, awaiting further orders. When I defeated the alliance and killed Oliphant, he fled."

Swinburne twitched, jerked, and jumped to his feet.

"Where do you suppose he is now?"

"Brunel says he's in Prussia."

"Hmm," Swinburne hummed. "I wonder why there? Could he have arranged the Brundleweed theft?"

"Are you suggesting he's making a play for the Eyes?"

"Yes, I think it quite likely. If Darwin and his cronies implanted that device in his head to somehow impel him to retrieve the African Eye, is it not possible that it might also have driven him to acquire the Cambodian diamonds? If Speke or the alliance researched the matter, they will know that there were three Eyes and that the Choir Stones are the fragments of one of them."

"You're making a lot of sense, Algy. In which case, if the Tichbornes really do have the South American stone and Speke is aware of it, they'll be his next target."

"Then let's stop chinwagging and get ourselves to Tichborne House!"

Swinburne leaped to his feet and ran to the door. Burton followed.

"Really, Algy, there's no need for you to come."

They descended to the ground floor.

"There's every need! You know how trouble dogs your footsteps and you're obviously not at the peak of physical fitness. What better time to call on your faithful assistant for support? I say, speaking of dogs, where's that blasted basset hound of yours?"

"Fidget? I don't know. In the kitchen with Mrs. Angell, probably."

"Well, he can jolly well stay there, the brute! What say you?"

"I have no objection, and I'm certain he doesn't either, what with the scraps of food my esteemed housekeeper throws into his welcoming maw."

Swinburne screeched and clapped his hands together. "I mean about me coming to Tichborne House with you, you buffoon!"

Burton smiled, took his assistant's top hat from the stand, and pushed it down over the little poet's mop of red hair.

"Very well, Algy. In truth, I'll be glad of your help, though I must confess, I was looking forward to using the rotorchair. I like flying! It's a shame the contraptions are single-seaters. I suppose we'll have to resort to the train."

"No we won't." Swinburne grinned. "I have a much better idea."

"Why, it's Captain Burton and Mr. Swinburne!" Miss Isabella Mayson exclaimed. "How lovely to see you again. Come in! Come in!"

Doffing their hats, the two men stepped into the SPARTA building.

"I've just made some soup. Will you join us?"

"Thank you, that would be most welcome," said Burton. He and Swinburne followed her through to the kitchen. As they crossed the threshold, a heavenly aroma assailed their nostrils, and there came an exclamation: "Hallo, hallo! Welcome to the chamber of bloomin' miracles, gents!"

It was the voice rather than the face they recognised, for the vagrant philosopher Herbert Spencer had blossomed into something that might almost be called respectable. Above all, he looked cleaner; his beard had been shaved off, his large side-whiskers were combed, and the thin border of curly hair around his bald head was now short and neat, rather than wild and straggly. He'd filled out, too, losing the hungry gauntness that had marked him when they'd last met.

"I swears to you," he said, shaking their hands, "there's no woman what can cook like Miss Mayson in the whole blessed world!"

"Herbert!" Swinburne said. "You look a new man!"

"It's the grub! This young lady here is a blinkin' marvel with the dogs an' the birds, but I tells you, gents, in the kitchen she's somethin' else entirely! I ain't never indulged in victuals like it."

"Thank you, Herbert," said Miss Mayson. "Would you set a couple more places around the table, please? Our two friends will join us for lunch."

Moments later, the king's agent and his assistant were enjoying a thick vegetable soup served with freshly baked bread.

"This is utterly delicious!" Burton declared.

"*Utterly* utterly!" Swinburne added.

"Told you so!" said Spencer. "There ain't nothin' so nourishing!"

"And you're obviously flourishing!" Swinburne rhymed.

"On which note, have you been ill?" Miss Mayson asked of Burton. "You look a little jaundiced."

"I have been, yes. I suffer occasional bouts of malaria. The attacks are decreasing in frequency since my return from Africa but this latest was a bad one. Flying your swan through a rainstorm didn't help."

"That were a nasty night, Boss," Spencer observed. "I came down with the sniffles meself."

"As a matter of fact, Miss Mayson—"

"Isabella, please!"

"Isabella. Swans are the reason for us dropping by. I was hoping we could hire a couple."

"The last time you borrowed my swans, two were killed and one never came back," the young woman noted, with a wry smile.

Burton nodded in acknowledgement. "I trust Scotland Yard compensated you?"

"Very generously, as a matter of fact."

Spencer waved his spoon and announced: "That young Constable Bhatti has been here nearly every blinkin' day, the scallywag!"

"It's on his beat, Herbert," Miss Mayson protested.

"Ha! He's givin' you the glad eye, that's what it is!"

A faint blush coloured the woman's cheeks and she said: "Actually, I think that brain of yours is the attraction. Why, when the two of you start philosophising, I can barely get a word in!"

She turned to Burton. "I have a couple of new swans that are fairly well behaved. For how long will you need them?"

"Two, three, maybe four days. We'll be staying at a country house in Hampshire. I believe there's a large lake on the grounds, so they'll be quite comfortable."

"'Specially if I come along to look after 'em!" Spencer interjected.

"There's no need to trouble yourself, old fellow," said Burton.

"It ain't no trouble at all!"

Miss Mayson agreed. "It's an excellent idea. Swans can be a handful, gentlemen, but Herbert has the magic touch. Even the parakeets love him! I would feel far happier if he went with you. There's sure to be a local village where he can put up, or maybe your hosts will find room for him in the servants' quarters?"

Burton considered the vagrant, and asked him: "Would you object to rooming with the staff? It might be useful for me to have a man on the inside, as it were."

"Don't worry, Boss, I knows me proper station in life. Servants' quarters are a step up for the likes o' me!"

"Then I'll be very happy to have you accompany us to Tichborne House."

"Tichborne?" Spencer and Miss Mayson chorused.

"Yes, I'm investigating the matter."

"Cor blimey! Well, I never did in all me born days! That's a right turn up, an' no mistake!" Spencer mused, philosophically.

An hour later, the three men, sitting in box kites, bade Isabella Mayson goodbye and were jerked into the air.

They steered between vertical shafts of smoke as they crossed the great city, heading in a westerly direction with the dome of St. Paul's Cathedral glinting in the sunlight behind them.

It was mild and pleasant and Burton felt a thrill of freedom as the vista expanded around him. England's tight horizons had always given him a sense of claustrophobia. They were so unlike the vast distances of India, Africa, and Arabia, and it felt wonderfully liberating to see them drawing back as he gained altitude.

Soon, the crowded and dirty city dropped behind until only towns, villages, fields, forests, and rivers populated the landscape. It was densely green and possessed a warm cosiness quite different from any other country he'd ever visited.

"I suppose you're not so bad, old England," he murmured, and blew out a breath in surprise. That was a sentiment he'd never expressed before!

"Wheeee-oooo!" came a cry, and Swinburne shot past, a blur of white swan feathers and bright red poet's hair.

"Look alive, Boss! The race is on!" Spencer yelled, whipping past Burton on the other side.

The king's agent grinned savagely, snapped his bird's reins, and bellowed: "Hey! Hey! Hey!"

His swan responded magnificently, pumping its wings so hard that the sudden acceleration pushed Burton back in his canvas seat. In this still air, his kite glided along smoothly, with none of the gut-churning twisting and tumbling that had characterised his pursuit of Brunel.

The small town of Weybridge slid beneath as Burton's bird caught up with Spencer's and overtook it.

"Keep up, dawdler!"

As the philosopher fell behind, Burton set his sights on Swinburne, who was by now a considerable distance ahead. The poet's bird was undoubtedly the fastest of the three, but did it possess endurance enough to hold the lead all the way to Tichborne House?

Burton settled into the chase.

They soared over Woking, then Aldershot, and, as they passed Farnham, he finally caught up with his assistant.

"Your bird's slowing!" he shouted.

"We shouldn't push them too hard!" Swinburne yelled back. "I concede defeat! You've won. Let's rein them in a little."

They slowed, relaxed, flapped on. Herbert Spencer came abreast.

The sun was sagging lazily at the edge of the sky as Itchen Valley hove into view, the light golden on its pastures, the shadows long and darkly blue.

Burton led them onward, sinking down, flying low over patchwork fields and the rooftops of Bishop's Sutton to the village of Alresford. They veered in a southwesterly direction, passed over high hedges and rich water meadows, and arrived at the Tichborne estate.

Circling a willow-bordered lake, they flew low along its shore and yanked their release straps. The three box kites separated from the birds, drifted earthward, touched the grass, tumbled, and came to a standstill. The swans beat their wings and swept up over the willow trees and down onto the water beyond, landing with splashes and honks of delight. They paddled contentedly and watched through the drooping branches as the men clambered out of their wood and canvas carriages, each pulling a portmanteau from the large storage pockets at the rear of the kites.

"It's a precarious experience, landing these blinkin' things," Spencer commented.

"Exciting, though," said Swinburne.

"Yus, lad, that as well," the philosopher agreed. "I'll go an' remove the birds' harnesses."

While Spencer dealt with the swans, Burton and Swinburne dismantled and folded the kites.

A man approached. He was wearing a fustian shooting jacket and baggy corduroy trousers, and held a double-barrelled shotgun crooked over his elbow. With his short dark hair, drooping mustache, and swarthy skin, he bore a passing resemblance to the king's agent, though he was shorter and lacked the habitual frown.

"Here, what's this, then?" he demanded.

"Good afternoon. Don't worry yourself, my good man. We're expected. I'm Burton."

"Ah, yes, sir, sorry, sir. Colonel Lushington said you'd be arriving. I'm Guilfoyle, the groundsman."

"Pleased to meet you, Mr. Guilfoyle. Is it all right with you if we leave our swans on the lake?"

"Of course, sir. There's plenty for them to eat in there, so they won't go hungry."

Spencer rejoined them and was introduced: "This is Mr. Herbert Spencer, their keeper. He'll be down here from time to time to tend to them."

"Very well, sir," Guilfoyle answered, raising his cap to Spencer. "They're expecting you at the house, gentlemen. I'll walk you up. Leave your kites here. I'll find a place to store them."

"Thank you."

They followed the groundsman up the gently sloping lawn, which rose from the lake to the back of the house, skirted around the ivy-clad building, and arrived at its front. Beyond a carriageway, wheat fields stretched up to the brow of a distant low hill.

"Those are the famous Crawls," Guilfoyle remarked.

"Crawls?"

"Aye. The fields old Mabella de Tichborne encircled to set the dole. Do you know the legend?"

"Yes. Bismillah! What a distance! No wonder she dropped dead!"

"Aye, sir, and no wonder she cursed the place first!"

Guilfoyle nodded a farewell and made to depart, but then stopped and gave a slightly strangled cough.

"Is there something else, my man?" Burton asked.

The groundsman removed his cap and pulled it nervously through his fingers.

"Well, sir, it's just that—that—well, what I mean is—"

"Yes?"

"Please, gentlemen, if you don't mind me sayin' so, you should be careful at night. Stay in your rooms. That's all. Stay in your rooms."

He turned and walked away, not looking back.

"How extraordinary!" Swinburne exclaimed.

"Yes, very odd," Burton agreed. "Come on, let's go and announce ourselves."

Four white Tuscan columns framed the entrance to the grand house. The three men climbed the steps and passed between them, through the portico. Swinburne tugged at a bellpull. It felt loose in his hand.

"Humph! Seems like the spring's broken!" he grunted, and used the brass knocker instead.

After a minute or so, the door was opened and a small, elderly, white-haired, and pleasant-faced Jamaican greeted them. Andrew Bogle, the butler.

"Sir Richard Burton and associates to see Colonel Lushington," the king's agent announced.

"Yes, sir. Please come in. If you'd like to wait in the Reception Room, I'll inform the colonel that you have arrived."

They were escorted into a plush chamber, where the butler left them, and were joined a few minutes later by a tall, smartly dressed, broad-shouldered man of ramrod-straight military bearing. Bronzed by an outdoor life, he appeared to be in his early sixties. He wore his greying hair cut very short, but possessed extravagant muttonchop whiskers, which stood out horizontally, ending in carefully waxed thin points above the tips of his shoulders.

"Good afternoon," he barked. "Or evening. Which? No matter! Colonel Franklin Lushington is my name. Lushington will do. No formality required.

Colonel, if you prefer. I'm glad you're here, Sir Richard. Henry Arundell speaks very highly of you. You are Sir Richard, aren't you? No mistake?"

"None, sir. I'm Burton."

They shook hands, and Burton introduced his companions.

After arranging a room for Spencer—"below stairs" with the servants—to which he was escorted by Bogle, Burton and Swinburne followed Lushington to the library.

Supplied with the obligatory brandies and cigars, they settled into high-backed armchairs and got to business.

"Sir Alfred will join us for supper," Lushington advised. "Or perhaps not. The plain unvarnished fact of the matter is—let's not beat about the bush—he's been behaving erratically in recent days and isn't reliable. I tell you that in confidence, of course. He doesn't always make sense. Some sort of nervous breakdown, I fancy."

"I suppose the reappearance of his elder brother is to blame?" Burton suggested.

"Absolutely. Well, that's my theory, anyway. I should warn you that he'll tell you a cock-and-bull story about a ghost."

"A ghost, by Gad!" Burton exclaimed, startled by the occurrence of yet another coincidence. Tichborne and Brundleweed, both haunted?

"Absolute rot, of course," Lushington added. "Unless it's true. Who knows? I hear there's great enthusiasm for table-tapping in London these days, so maybe there's something in all that life-after-death nonsense, but I'm inclined to think otherwise. Have you ever been to a séance? I haven't. Don't see the need for them."

Burton leaned forward. "So you haven't witnessed anything yourself?"

Lushington hesitated, took a gulp from his glass, and answered: "I haven't seen anything, no. . . . Well, that is to say, not with my eyes. But I must admit, I might have spotted something with my ears. Spotted? No. Hah! Obviously a man doesn't see with his ears. Ahem! I mean I heard something. But then there's an awful lot to hear in a big old house like this, so it was probably nothing. Perhaps mice, except they don't knock, that's the thing of it."

"You heard knocking?" Burton was beginning to feel more than a little frustrated by the colonel's rambling manner of speech.

Lushington shook his head, coughed, and nodded. "That's right, I did. Knocking, these two nights past, as if someone were walking through the house banging on the walls. Not mice, then. I don't know why I said mice."

"Did you investigate?"

"Of course, military instinct. Seek out the enemy. On both occasions, as I approached the noise, it stopped."

"The enemy mice ran away?" put in Swinburne, mischievously.

"Quite so, if it was mice, which it obviously wasn't."

"So what was it then?" Burton asked.

"Not a clue. Haven't the remotest idea. Completely at a loss. The foundations settling as the day's heat dissipated, perhaps? Ah! There you have it! Mystery solved!"

Over the course of the next two hours, they reviewed the history of the Tichborne family and the circumstances leading up to the Claimant's imminent arrival. He was due at the house the day after tomorrow, and Lushington was eager to see the individual who'd caused such a furore.

"Bogle, the butler, the Jamaican fellow—at least I think he's Jamaican. West Indian, anyway—has been with the family for many years. He knew Roger Tichborne and will be sure to recognise him on sight. Then there's the resident physician, or doctor—what's the difference?—Jankyn, and the groundsman, er—er—er—"

"Guilfoyle," Swinburne offered.

"Ah!" Lushington responded. "Is he, indeed? And your name, sir?"

"Algernon Swinburne. We were introduced earlier, if you remember. Are you really in charge of the estate's finances?"

"What of Sir Alfred's opinion?" Burton interrupted hastily. "Surely you aren't discounting that? He is, after all, the brother."

"True, but he also has a vested interest. I'm sure he'd much rather this fellow was exposed as an outright crook. If not, he loses the estate."

Burton looked surprised. "Surely you don't mean to suggest that he might purposely deny his brother simply to keep hold of the title?"

"Good lord, of course not!"

A gong sounded and echoed through the house.

"That's the summons to supper or dinner or something similar. What time is it? Clocks don't work here. I never have the vaguest idea what the confounded hour is!"

The king's agent frowned and pulled out his pocket watch.

"It's half-past six. What do you mean, clocks don't work?"

"Simply that. Every timepiece in this house stopped a month or so ago. I daresay yours will, too, if you stay here long enough. Perhaps it's something to do with the position of the building and the Earth's magnetics. I wouldn't know. I'm a soldier, not a Technologist! Anyway, Bogle will take you and your luggage up to the guest rooms so you can change into your evening wear. Just a formality. Observing the rituals. The mark of civilisation. A man should always dress for whatever it is, don't you think? We'll reconvene in the dining room in fifteen minutes. You'll meet Sir Alfred there. If he comes. He may not."

A quarter of an hour later, wearing their formal attire, Burton and Swinburne descended the grand staircase. The poet giggled, remembering that his friend had, a few weeks ago, come down a similar staircase in a far less controlled fashion. He wondered whether Sir Roderick Murchison would ever forgive Burton.

They passed along the hall, in which polished suits of armour stood silent guard, and entered the long dining room. A grand table dominated its centre, and all around it the walls were hung with portraits.

Bogle bowed as they entered. Colonel Lushington greeted them.

"That's the young Roger Tichborne," he said, pointing at one of the paintings. "While that—" he turned and indicated another "—is his ancestor, the notorious Roger de Tichborne. The same name, you'll note, except for the *de*. It means *of*, I believe. Roger *of* Tichborne, on account of the fact that he was—"

He cleared his throat and fell silent.

"He was what?" Swinburne asked.

"Of Tichborne, man!"

"Ah. I see. Rather a nasty-looking cove!"

"Oh, I wouldn't say so," came a voice from the door. "But perhaps that's because I bear a distinct resemblance!"

They turned their heads and saw two men crossing the threshold.

"May I introduce Sir Alfred Tichborne?" the colonel said. "Sir Alfred, this is Sir Richard Burton and his assistant, um—um—um—"

"Algernon Swinburne," said Swinburne.

"Welcome, gentlemen, and thank God you're here!" Tichborne stepped forward with his hand outstretched. "You've got to help me!"

Burton was taken aback by Sir Alfred's appearance, for though the baronet was young, his hair was completely white and there were deep lines scoring the skin around his eyes.

Tichborne stood about five foot nine and was of a large build. He did, indeed, resemble the man in the portrait—facially, at least—but where his ancestor's features were cruel, Sir Alfred's were weak. His lips possessed an unpleasantly loose and damp appearance; his chin was too receded; his eyes too widely set. In attire, he was foppish to the point of effeminacy, and the hand that Burton shook felt boneless.

The baronet's eyes moved restlessly, fearfully.

Before he could say anything else, the second man interrupted: "I'm sure Sir Richard will do all he can to assist, Sir Alfred, but let's not ask him to do so on an empty stomach? What!"

"Gentlemen, this is Doctor Jankyn, our resident physician," said Lushington. "Or Physician Jankyn, our resident doctor. I don't know how it works. One way or the other, I would think."

"Pleased to meet you, what!" said Jankyn.

He was a tall and lanky fellow, with big hands and feet, and a long jaw. His grey hair was brushed back and fell in curls to the nape of his neck. His ears stuck out and his close-set eyes were of the palest blue.

The five men sat at the table, wine was served by Bogle, and maids brought platters of food.

Sir Alfred twitched and fidgeted, outdoing even Swinburne's habitual nervous agitation.

"So how may I be of service?" Burton asked him. "Do you seek my opinion of the Claimant?"

"Fiddlesticks!" Tichborne cried passionately. "He's nothing but a cheap swindler! No, Burton, I want you to get rid of the damned witch before she gets rid of me!"

"Witch?"

"The Lady Mabella! The foul sorceress who wishes me, the last of the Tichbornes, dead!"

Jankyn spoke: "Sir Alfred is under the impression that this house is being haunted by that man's—" he pointed at the portrait of Roger de Tichborne "—wife."

"You've actually seen the ghost, Sir Alfred?" Swinburne asked.

"Three times!"

"The human mind can play very convincing tricks when in a state of high anxiety," Doctor Jankyn offered.

"I didn't imagine it!" the baronet shouted.

There came a loud clang as one of the maids dropped a serving spoon onto the floor.

"Take care, young lady! Have some discipline!" Colonel Lushington snapped. "An accident, I should think. Never mind. Go and fetch a fresh spoon, there's a good girl."

"Wait!" Burton interrupted. "What's your name, miss?"

The maid turned beetroot red, curtseyed, and answered: "Christina Flowers, sir."

"Have you seen the spectre, too, Miss Flowers?"

She swallowed, licked her lips, and looked anxiously at each of the men. "I—I—"

"You can speak freely," Lushington advised. "I'm sorry I barked at you that way. Military training. What is it you've seen?"

The girl sniffed and said: "Beggin' your pardon, sirs, it—it were in the 'allway leading to the kitchen. Two nights past—in the early hours of the mornin'. I couldn't sleep an' I wanted a drink o' water. As I came along the 'all, I 'eard a knock-knock-knockin' an' I thought Mrs. Picklethorpe must be up and about."

"Mrs. Picklethorpe is the cook," Lushington explained to Burton and Swinburne. "So it wasn't mice, as I thought. Although I didn't. Think, that is."

"Aye, sir, the cook. So I goes toward the kitchen to see if anythin' was amiss and there—there in the 'allway—there was—was—"

The girl began to tremble violently and put her hands to her face.

"Oooh!" she moaned.

"What was it, Miss Flowers?" Burton asked gently.

She looked up. Her face had gone from red to stark white.

"It were like a mist, sir, but in the shape of a woman. She were a-knockin' on the walls, then she turned 'er 'ead an' looked straight at me."

"You could see her eyes?"

"Yes! Oh lor', terrible they were! Like black pebbles a-floatin' in the cloud. She stared at me all wicked, then disappeared. Just blew away, she did, like smoke in the wind."

"Yes!" Sir Alfred cried. "Those eyes! God in heaven, they're frightful!"

"Thank you, Miss—what-was-it?" said Lushington.

"Flowers, sir."

"Ah yes, very pretty name. Reminds me of—um—um—um—flowers. Well, continue with your duties, please."

The maid bobbed and ran out of the room.

Swinburne looked at Burton and raised an eyebrow.

Burton gave a slight shrug and turned to Tichborne: "And you, Sir Alfred—you saw the same?"

"Yes! I've been hearing that damnable knocking around the house for nigh on a month, always at night."

"A month? So it started around the same time as all the clocks stopped?"

"Ah, why yes, that's right. Each time I've heard the noise, I've gone to investigate only to have it fall silent as I approached. I didn't see anything until two weeks ago. It was, I'd guess, about three in the morning, and I was unable to sleep, so I went down to the library, smoked a few cigars, and read awhile. I was in one of the high-backed armchairs facing the fireplace. If you sit there and someone enters, they can't see you, but it works the other way, too, and unknown to me, someone did enter."

He shivered and wrapped his arms around himself, staring down at the food on his plate. He hadn't yet touched it. His companions weren't paying much attention to their supper either.

"A sudden knocking from the other side of the room made me jump out of my skin. It was the sound of knuckles on the wooden panelling of the far wall. Knock-knock. Knock-knock. Over and over, progressing across the wall. I leaned over the side of my chair, looked back, and saw the ghost."

"The same as Miss Flowers described?"

"In every respect. She was drifting alongside the wall, with an arm raised, banging on the panels. I watched, and I don't mind admitting that I was paralysed with fear. Perhaps half a minute passed, then something—I don't know what—alerted the phantom to my presence. She suddenly swirled around and a pair of ghastly eyes, blacker than pitch, glared at me with such malevolence that I screamed in terror. The thing then vanished, just as the maid said, as if blown away by a wind."

Sir Alfred looked up at the portrait of his ancestor.

"It was Lady Mabella," he whispered.

"What makes you think so?"

"The eyes were hers."

"But Mabella de Tichborne lived hundreds of years ago, man! How do you know what her eyes were like?"

Tichborne stood. "Wait," he said. "I'm going to get something."

He left the room.

"What do you think?" Lushington asked Burton, in a low voice.

"Were it only Sir Alfred who saw the apparition, I might consider him mentally disturbed," Burton answered. "But we have the girl's account, too. And you yourself have heard the knocking."

"I haven't heard a thing," Doctor Jankyn said, "and I'm a light sleeper, what!"

"I shall sit up tonight!" Swinburne declared. "I want to see this mysterious phantom for myself!"

"We can't discount the clocks, either," Burton added. "They provide empirical evidence that something very peculiar is happening in this house."

"In that case, you'd better add the gunroom to your list," said Lushington.

"What? Why?"

"All the guns have jammed. No explanation. In fact, the only shooters on the estate that work are those the groundsman keeps in his lodge."

"That's extraordinary! Would I be right to suppose that they stopped working at the same time as the clocks?"

"Not sure, but probably, yes."

The men gave their attention to the meal until, a few minutes later, Sir Alfred returned, holding a sheet of parchment. He sat and said: "Listen to this. It's been in the family for generations. A poem. No one knows what it signifies."

He began to read:

> "Hell's bane black, lamenting 'neath tears,
> That weep within My Lady's round,
> Under the weight of curséd years,
> By her damnéd charity bound.
>
> "One curse here enfolds another,
> Vexations in the poor enables,
> Consume if thou wouldst uncover
> Eye blacker than Lady Mabella's."

"My Aunt Agatha's blue feather hat!" Swinburne screeched. "But that's awful! Hideous doggerel! Who wrote it? A simpleton?"

Sir Alfred Tichborne cleared his throat and said: "According to family legend, it was written by Roger de Tichborne himself. It was passed to my father by my grandfather, just as it had been passed to him by his." He handed the parchment to Burton. "As you can see, it clearly suggests that the Lady Mabella had notably black eyes."

Burton looked at the paper, nodded, and said: "Could I borrow this? I'd like to examine it more closely."

"Be my guest."

"I say, Richard!" Swinburne said, excitedly. "That seems rather—"

He stopped, brought up short by a fierce glance from his friend.

Burton turned back to Tichborne. "Your second and third sightings of the ghost—what happened?"

"The second was three nights later. I was woken in the night by the knocking, which was coming from the upper landing at the top of the stairs. I left my bed and went to investigate. Lady Mabella was there, moving—floating, really—from the top of the staircase toward the bottom, rapping on the wall as she went. The instant I saw her, she turned, cut me through with those dreadful eyes, and vanished.

"Two nights ago, I saw her again. This time it was in the corridor that leads from the main drawing room to the billiard room. I'd come down to fetch my cigars. It was about half-past two in the morning."

"Another sleepless night?"

"Yes. I've been having a lot of them since this blasted Claimant affair began. Anyway, I was walking along the corridor when, all of a sudden, the air in front of me thickened, a mist formed, and it took the shape of Lady Mabella. She seemed to be facing the other way, for when I took a step backward, a board creaked beneath my feet and the mist whirled, bringing her eyes around to face me. They pierced me through, then suddenly the ghost rushed forward and wrapped me in such an intense chill that I passed out on the spot. When I awoke, perhaps thirty minutes later, I returned to my room, collapsed onto my bed, and passed out again. In the morning, I found that my hair had turned entirely white."

"Good lord!" Burton exclaimed. "You mean to say it turned white overnight?"

"Jankyn and the colonel will attest to it. The day before yesterday, my hair was dark brown in colour."

Burton looked at Jankyn and Lushington. They both nodded.

For a few moments, the men ate in silence. The maids had withdrawn, and only Bogle moved about the table, keeping the diners well supplied with wine and water.

"May I ask you about another matter?" Burton enquired of Tichborne.

"Of course, Sir Richard. Anything."

"Would you tell me about the family legend—the one concerning a fabulous diamond?"

"My goodness, how do you know about that?"

"Henry Arundell mentioned it. What's the story?"

"Oh, there's nothing much to it. It's whispered that my grandfather found a large black diamond in South America. It's utter nonsense."

"But how did it arise?"

"From idle gossip. When Sir Henry returned from his travels, he stopped the dole and became something of a hermit, banning everyone from the estate. In an attempt to explain this behaviour, the locals came up with idea that he'd brought a fabulous jewel back with him and was scared to let anyone near it. Utter bunkum, of course. There's no such diamond, of that I'm certain."

"Then how do you account for his actions?"

"It's all very prosaic, I'm afraid. The annual gift of free flour was attracting hordes of beggars to the area, which is why he stopped it. As for keeping people off the land, that's not entirely accurate, for he had a gang of builders coming back and forth. The truth is, the old house was falling down so he had it demolished and replaced with this one. Banning people from the estate was simply a safety precaution while the construction took place."

"Ah. I see. As you say, very humdrum."

"Yet by stopping the Dole," Swinburne commented, "he invoked the witch's curse."

"Yes, the old fool!"

After supper, they spent the rest of the evening in the main parlour, where they smoked, drank, and made plans. It was decided that Burton would patrol the house from midnight until three in the morning. Swinburne would then take over and patrol until dawn.

By ten o'clock, Sir Alfred, who'd been drinking without cease, was nodding off.

"I haven't slept well for days," he slurred. "Perhaps tonight the bloody spook will give me some peace!"

He made his apologies and stumbled off to bed.

At eleven, Bogle showed the two guests upstairs to their bedchambers, which faced each other across a narrow hallway. The king's agent and his assistant then convened for an hour in Burton's room.

Laying the Tichborne poem on a table, Burton took an eyeglass such as jewellers use from his pocket and peered through the lens at the parchment.

"As I suspected."

"It's not genuine, is it?"

"It certainly hasn't been handed down through generations of Tichbornes, Algy. As I'm sure you recognised, the language is entirely wrong for anything predating the current century. I can confirm that the paper and the ink are more recent than Sir Alfred thinks, too. In fact, I'd lay money on this having been written by his grandfather, Sir Henry."

"He should have been horsewhipped," Swinburne opined. "Such doggerel is a terrible crime."

"I can't disagree." Burton put aside the parchment and looked at his assistant. "Sir Alfred believes this poem is about the Lady Mabella, but it's obvious to you and me that it actually concerns the South American diamond. No matter how vociferously our host denies its existence, the Eye of Nāga is real. I suspect that when his grandfather stopped the dole and cut off the estate, it wasn't just to rebuild the house—it was to construct a hiding place."

He held the up parchment.

"And this is a treasure map!"

THE CLAIMANT

I think my poor, dear Roger confuses everything in his head, just as in a dream, and I believe him to be my son, though his statements differ from mine.
—DOWAGER LADY HENRIETTE-FÉLICITÉ TICHBORNE

Sir Richard Francis Burton, with a clockwork lantern in his hand, walked quietly through the chambers and passageways of Tichborne House, his ears alert for any sound, his eyes scanning every shadowy corner, nook, and cranny.

Having just inspected the smoking room, he entered a corridor and moved toward the ballroom.

He pondered the facts of the case. He was thinking about Sir Alfred's claim that he'd been hearing the knocking around the house for "nigh on a month." That meant the haunting began soon after the François Garnier Choir Stones vanished from Brundleweed's safe, and both those events occurred mere days before the emergence of the Tichborne Claimant.

He looked at his pocket watch. It was half-past two in the morning.

"Coincidences?" he muttered. "I wonder."

The ballroom was a big, empty, gloomy space, and his footsteps echoed as he crossed it and passed beneath a heavy chandelier. He opened an ornate double door and stepped into another hallway. It took him to the rear part of the house and the gunroom, which he examined with an ill-suppressed shudder, unnerved by the glass-eyed gazes of its wall-mounted trophies. There were stags, deer, and boar in profusion, a tiger and two lions, and above a row of gun cases, the massive head of a rhinoceros.

It occurred to Burton that John Speke would be in his element here.

A thick curtain hung over a glass-panelled door in the opposite wall. He went over, pushed it aside, and peered out past a paved patio to the lawn beyond. Beneath the light of a full moon, a white mist was flowing around the house and down the slope, clinging closely to the grass and accumulating in the lake's basin. The willow trees beside the water humped grotesquely out of it like shrouded monks huddled together in malignant contemplation. There was, thought Burton, something horribly sentient about them.

He sneered contemptuously. *Idiot! They're just trees!*

He turned away and traversed the length of the chamber to a door at its end. The portal creaked open onto a small parlour, through which he passed to the music room. This was long and rectangular in shape and, like the hunting room, had a curtained door that gave access to the patio.

As Burton entered, his lantern wound down and its light stuttered and died. Thankfully, he was not plunged into pitch darkness, for, through a chink in the curtains, a ray of moonlight angled across the chamber. Vaguely, in the faint radiance on either side of the bright shaft, Burton detected the outlines of violins, mandolins, and guitars hanging on the walls. A cello stood on a stand in one corner and, in the middle of the floor, there was a grand piano with a cloth draped over it and an elegant candelabrum on top. Jacobean armchairs stood around the sides of the room.

He rewound his lantern. Its glare threw everything into stark relief, the light somehow feeling like a terrible intrusion.

A full-length portrait of Sir Henry Tichborne hung over the wide fireplace. He was pictured with three hunting dogs at his feet, a riding crop in one hand, and a tricorn hat in the other. He wore a long beard and a severe and haughty expression.

Burton raised the lantern higher, looked at the hard, cold face, and stepped back.

Sir Henry's disapproving eyes seemed to follow him and the king's agent felt himself gripped by a curious sense of disquietude.

The back of his neck prickled.

"What events did you set in motion, you old goat?" he asked softly.

A reply came from behind: a low, quiet note from the piano, as if a string had been gently plucked.

Burton froze. The chord lingered in the air. Chill fingers tickled his spine as the sound faded with dreadful slowness.

He twisted to face the instrument and saw that he was alone in the room.

He breathed out. The expelled air clouded in front of his face.

To his left, there was a closed door. Something—he knew not what—drew his attention to it, and as he looked, he jumped, and his lantern swayed, causing shadows to jerk over the walls and ceiling. Nothing material had jolted him—just the sudden sense of a presence behind that door.

Sir Richard Francis Burton was undoubtedly a brave man but he was also superstitious and possessed a dread of darkness and the supernatural. Patrolling the gloomy house had, for him, been unsettling enough. Now, although he was faced with nothing tangible, he found himself trembling and the hairs on his head stood on end.

Taking a deep breath, suppressing the instinctive urge to run, he crept to the door and put his fingers around the brass handle. He pressed his ear against the wood. It was cold.

He could hear no movement from the other side, yet the idea that the room was occupied persisted. With great care, he squeezed the handle and began to turn it. Clenching his jaw, he braced himself and applied his shoulder to the door.

He stopped.

What was that?

Had he heard something? A voice?

"Help! Help!"

Cries from outside the house! Again they came: "Help! Help!"

The voice was familiar. Surely that was Herbert Spencer!

Releasing the handle, Burton turned away and strode rapidly across to the patio door, drew the curtain aside, opened the portal, and stepped out of the house into the still air of a clear-skied night.

Herbert was running up the slope, thick milky mist swirling around his calves.

"Is that you, Boss? Help me!"

Burton hurried forward. "Herbert! What is it? What's wrong?"

The vagrant philosopher reached him and clutched his arm. His eyes were round, his lips drawn tightly over his teeth. He was plainly terrified.

"There!" he cried, pointing back at the lake.

Burton looked and saw the vapour, glaringly white beneath the rays of the moon, crawling languidly between the boles of the hunched willows like a living, amoebic creature.

"There's nothing there!" he exclaimed. "Herbert, why—?"

"Can't you see 'em?"

"Them? Who? What?"

"There—there was figures," the philosopher stammered. "Not in the mist, but *of* the mist!"

"What the devil do you mean?"

"They was *wraiths*!" Spencer whispered, his voice quavering.

The king's agent backed away, dragging the philosopher with him.

"What are you talking about? Why are you out here at this time of night? Have you been sleepwalking?"

"No," Spencer croaked. "I came to—" He stopped and pointed, his eyes wide and panicked.

"*There!*"

Burton stared at the lake. Was that a figure moving, or just an opaque surge of vapour billowing through the cloud?

"Let's get inside," he said.

Spencer didn't need any further persuasion. They quickly made their way up to the house, crossed the patio, entered the music room, and closed the door behind them.

They looked at each other in terror, both suddenly overpowered by a sense that the chamber was already occupied. They pressed their backs against the door and looked this way and that, peering into the corners, seeing nothing but shadows.

"Mother of God!" Herbert wheezed, his eyes bulging. "Is the devil himself in here?"

Breathing was difficult. The room was frigid.

The light of Burton's lantern reeled across it and caught and lingered in the glimmering eyes of Sir Henry Tichborne. The portrait radiated evil, and for a moment, it appeared to the king's agent that the face in the painting had changed, that it was someone else entirely, someone gaunt and evil and filled with malicious intent.

The light sank down over the surface of the picture, and for a moment the eyes blazed through the shadow, then dimmed as the illumination retreated back across the room, slithering over the floor as if the clockwork lantern were sucking it in. It flickered and died, plunging them into darkness. Only a silvery parallelogram of moonlight remained, stretched across the floor, framing the two men's shadows.

Burton's heart hammered in his chest.

As his eyes adjusted, they were drawn to the door that he'd been about to open earlier.

Its handle began to turn.

Burton stood transfixed, unaware that Spencer, too, was staring at the door.

Agonisingly, little by little, the brass handle revolved.

From a great way off, the sound of the piano chord returned, coming closer and closer, filling the room.

The piano chimed.

The door opened.

A weird figure stepped in.

Burton and his companion yelled in fright.

"My hat! What on earth's the matter?" Swinburne shrilled, for the bizarre figure was his: small, slope-shouldered, his head framed by a corona of fiery red hair. He looked on bemused as his companions collapsed against each other, panting hard. "I say! Have you been drinking? And you didn't invite me? Blessed scoundrels!"

Burton let loose a peal of near hysterical laughter, turned to the patio door, then cried out and stepped back in horror as a demonic face glared at him from the darkness outside.

It was his reflection.

"*Bismillah!*"

"You're as white as a sheet!" Swinburne exclaimed.

"What—what are you playing at sneaking around at this time of night?" Burton demanded, failing to suppress the tremor in his voice.

"We agreed I'd take over at three."

"It's three already?"

"I think so. My watch has stopped."

Burton pulled his own pocket watch from his waistcoat and looked at it. It, too, had stopped. He shook it, wound it, and shook it again. It refused to work.

He twisted the clockwork lantern, only to find that it was also broken; there was no resistance in its spring.

"Herbert," he muttered, "what were you doing out there?"

The vagrant philosopher swallowed nervously, wiped a sleeve across his brow, and shrugged. "I—I could—couldn't get any kip on account o' Mrs. Picklethorpe's bloomin' snoring. Her bedchamber is next to the kitchen an' I'm two rooms away, but sound carries strangely in that part of the house an' I swear it sounded like her trumpetin' were a-comin' from the walls themselves. Anyways, I couldn't take another blasted minute of it, so I thought to go an' check on the swans. I hoped a spot o' night air might encourage a visit from what's-'is-name—Morpheus. I was just headin' back to the house when them wraiths surrounded me. Fair panicked, I did!"

"Wraiths?" Swinburne asked excitedly. "What? What?"

"Herbert thought he saw figures in the mist," Burton explained.

"*Of* the mist," the philosopher corrected.

"And the knocking?" the poet enquired. "Where was that coming from?"

"Knocking?"

"You didn't hear it? It was either from this room or the next, but it stopped when I came along the corridor."

"Hmm," Burton grunted. "Well, there was certainly a strange atmosphere in here and I haven't a notion how to explain it. It seems entirely normal now, though. Herbert, why don't you get yourself back to bed? There's no point in all of us losing sleep. Algy and I will have a poke around for a few minutes, then I think we'll call it a night."

"Right you are, Boss. Blimey! I'll take the bloomin' snorin' over this malarkey any day o' the week!"

An hour later, Burton was lying in his bed, trying to work out exactly what he'd experienced. Some form of mesmerism, perhaps? Or maybe an intoxicating gas, as he'd suspected at Brundleweed's? How, though, could either of those account for the sudden loss of elasticity in the springs of his watch and lantern?

Whatever the explanation, the room's malevolent aura had vanished upon Swinburne's arrival, and the two of them had encountered nothing more during their subsequent patrol.

He slept.

It wasn't until fairly late the next morning that Burton and his assistant made an appearance downstairs. They were informed by Bogle that Colonel Lushington was awaiting them in the library with the Tichborne family lawyer. Upon entering, they saw the two men standing near the fireplace and were immediately struck by the gravity of their host's expression.

"There's news," the colonel announced. "It's bad. The Dowager Lady Henriette-Felicité passed away last night at her apartment. The one in Paris."

"The cause of death?" Burton asked.

"Heart stopped. Failed. Old age, no doubt. She'd been ailing for a considerable period."

He looked from his two guests to the other man and back again.

"Forgive me, I should make introductions. Polite thing to do. Ahem! Forgot myself. This gentleman is Mr. Henry Hawkins. A lawyer. He'll be defending the family against the Claimant. Mr. Hawkins, may I present Sir Richard Burton and Mr.—um—um—um—"

"Algernon Swinburne." Swinburne sighed.

"A pleasure to meet you," said Hawkins, stepping forward to shake their hands. He was an average-sized and average-looking individual whose bland features were at odds with his reputation, for Burton had heard of "Hanging Hawkins," and knew him for a man whose cross-examinations in court were probing in the extreme—"savage," some might say. A hint of this came with Hawkins's next comment: "Of course, the dowager's death is more a blow to our opponent than it is to us. A mother's recognition would be virtually indestructible in court, were it demonstrated in person. Now, though, we can reduce it to the status of hearsay."

"Was the man who claims to be her son present at her death?" Burton enquired.

"No. He's already in London. He'll be arriving here tomorrow afternoon."

"What about Sir Alfred?" Swinburne put in. "Has he been informed?"

Colonel Lushington nodded. "About an hour ago. I'm afraid it didn't do much for his nerves. Jankyn is attending to him. How was your midnight patrol? Did you encounter the mice—that is to say, Lady Mabella?"

"Pardon me, what's this?" Hawkins interrupted.

"Oh, just some nonsense about the Tichborne family curse," Lushington answered. "Utter tosh and balderdash, without a doubt. Young Alfred has got it into his head that the house is haunted. By a ghost, be damned! A ghost!"

"My word! We mustn't let him mention it in court. He'll lose all credibility!"

"What if it's true?" Swinburne asked.

Burton jabbed his fingers into the poet's ribs.

"To answer your question, Colonel," said the king's agent, "no, I didn't see a ghostly woman floating about last night. Nor did I expect to. There was, however, a rather remarkable mist flowing past the house, down the slope, and into the lake."

"Ah, yes," said Lushington. "It's a fairly common occurrence. It's a mist, plain and simple. It arises in the Crawls and flows down into the hollow. Covers the lake."

"Intriguing!" Burton exclaimed. "It only forms over the Crawls? Not the other wheat fields?"

"That's so. Absolutely the case. Odd, now that I think about it. I don't know why. Something to do with the lie of the land, perhaps? Have you eaten?"

"No."

"Neither has Mr. Hawkins. Come to think of it, neither have I. I suggest we have a late breakfast. What do you say? A cup of tea, at least? Good for the stamina."

Later that day, while Lushington and Hawkins worked on their legal case in the library, Burton and Swinburne sat in the smoking room and considered the Tichborne poem.

"I'm pretty certain that *Eye blacker than Lady Mabella's* is a reference to the Eye of Nāga," Burton announced.

"I don't disagree," said Swinburne. He imitated Lushington: "Or do I? I don't know!"

"Shut up, Algy."

"Certainly. Or certainly not, as the case may be."

Burton sighed and shook his head despairingly, then continued: "And it seems that a considerable part of the first stanza might be a reference to the Crawls."

Swinburne nodded: "*My Lady's round* and *By her damnéd charity bound*. Do you think the *tears that weep* might be the mist?"

"I don't know. That doesn't feel quite right to me. What about this line: *One curse here enfolds another?*"

"Her curse was that the annual dole must continue in perpetuity or else the Tichborne family would find itself without an heir," Swinburne noted. "But you'll remember that the dole itself attracted hordes of beggars to the estate. Maybe that's one curse wrapped in another?"

"Possibly. But *Vexations in the poor enables?* Vexations? Why would the poor respond to a gift of free flour with vexation? No, Algy, it won't do."

The king's agent struck a lucifer and applied it to his third Manila cheroot of the day. Swinburne wrinkled his nose.

"If the diamond were buried beneath the Crawls," Burton mused, "then *Consume if thou wouldst uncover* becomes a directive: eat the wheat to uncover the treasure."

"Or burn it."

"Indeed. However, it's the beginning of the growing season and I doubt the family will give us permission to destroy their crop, not least because it would make it impossible to pay the dole. No harm in having a poke around out there, though. Besides, a breath of fresh air will do us good."

"For sure," Swinburne agreed, eyeing his friend's cigar.

Some thirty minutes later, the king's agent and his assistant met beneath the portico at the entrance to the house. They were wearing tweed suits, strong boots, and cloth caps, and each carried a cane. As they descended the steps, a voice hailed them from the doorway: "I say, you chaps, do you mind if I join you?"

It was Sir Alfred, his white hair stark against his dark mourning suit. His face was gaunt, his eyes red.

"Not at all," Burton answered. "My condolences, Sir Alfred. We heard the news earlier."

"My mother lived only for my brother," the baronet said as they stepped down to the carriageway and started across it. "When he was lost, she began to age very rapidly. The last time I saw her, she was extremely frail. If the bounder who claims to be Roger really is who he says he is, then I blame him for her demise. If he isn't—and I still maintain that he isn't—then I blame him doubly. I feel certain that she knew in her heart of hearts that the cad is nothing but a wicked imposter. She died of disappointment, I'm convinced of it."

"Yet she passed away maintaining that her eldest son had returned?"

"She did. The pitiful wish of a broken woman. Where are we going— just for a stroll?"

"I want to have a closer look at the Crawls. I'm curious as to why a mist arises from them but not from the adjoining fields."

"Ah, yes. Mysterious, isn't it? I've often wondered myself."

The three men reached the edge of the wheat field and started to skirt around its right-hand border, walking alongside a low hedgerow.

"A promising crop this year," said Tichborne. "Look how green it is!"

"Now that you mention it," Burton said, thoughtfully, "it appears that the Crawls are the greenest of all your fields."

"Yes, it's ironic, don't you think? The best wheat we grow, we have to give away!"

The king's agent stopped walking and looked around at the landscape.

"I don't see any obvious geographical explanation. All the fields on this incline are equally exposed to whatever weather conditions prevail. If the Crawls dipped down slightly, I might suspect an underground water source, but in fact, if anything, they appear to hump up somewhat."

Swinburne squatted, using his cane for balance, and peered at the horizon.

"You're right," he said. "It's barely noticeable, but this part of the slope is definitely a little bit higher. My goodness, what a geographer's eye you have, Richard!"

"Enough to know that something's not quite right here. At this low altitude, mist should form in hollows, not on the raised part of a slope. The only explanation for the vapour is that there's a warm spring beneath our feet. Yet, as I say, it should result in a slight dip in the incline, not the opposite. Let's walk on."

They hiked to the top of the field and continued on into the one beyond.

"My hat! The Lady Mabella crawled all this way!" Swinburne exclaimed.

"Driven by the devil." Tichborne shuddered. "Did you hear her knocking last night?"

"No," said Burton, quickly, before Swinburne could open his mouth. "Did you?"

"I'm afraid I rather overdid it at supper," the baronet answered. "I was oblivious to all from the moment my head hit the pillow—wasn't conscious of a thing until I awoke this morning."

"Something rather peculiar occurred in the music room. A note was struck at the piano—"

"—But no one was there," Tichborne finished. "I bet that put the wind up you."

"It did. It's happened before, then?"

"For as long as I can remember. Three or four nights a week—bong!—for no apparent reason. Always the same note, too."

"B below middle C."

"Really? I wouldn't know. It used to give Grandfather the heebie-jeebies, but my guess is it's nothing more than the piano stretching and contracting with changes of temperature."

They reached the top of the slope and Tichborne pointed to the surrounding land.

"All these wheat and barley fields are part of the estate, up to that line of trees, there. The houses yonder form the hamlet of Tichborne, which is mostly occupied by the families who work our land. As you can see, the estate is on a shallow slope that runs down into the Itchen Valley and the river. Over there—" he pointed northeastward "—is the village of Alresford."

They continued on along the top border of the Crawls then turned at the corner and started back down toward the mansion. When they passed into the bottom field, Burton stopped and walked out into the crop.

"What are you doing?" Tichborne asked.

"Wait a moment."

Burton pushed the end of his cane into the loamy soil then leaned on it with his full weight. It sank into the soft earth until the soil's resistance stopped it.

Swinburne said: "Anything?"

"No."

"What were you expecting?" asked Tichborne.

"I don't know. I'm convinced there's something under these two fields. I thought perhaps the end of my cane might encounter rock or brickwork."

"Wheat roots can reach a depth of almost four feet," the baronet said, "so the soil here is deep; too deep for your stick to touch the bottom, if there is one."

Burton withdrew his cane, wiped a handkerchief along its length, and returned to the edge of the field.

They made their way down to the carriageway.

"I'd like to see your swans," Tichborne said. "Would you care to stroll around to the lake with me?"

"Certainly," Burton agreed.

As they walked, the king's agent cast sidelong glances at the aristocrat. Sir Alfred's mood seemed strange; he was touring his estate with what appeared to be a sense of finality, as if he were saying goodbye to his ancestral home. Burton's intuition told him that this was more than the baronet's reaction to his supposed brother's imminent arrival—something else was bothering him.

"I expect you'll be somewhat relieved to see the Claimant tomorrow," he said. "After all these weeks, you'll finally set eyes on the man, and will, at least, know one way or the other."

"Yes, perhaps so," Tichborne answered, with a distracted air.

He fell into a self-absorbed silence

They circled the lake then returned to the house with barely another word spoken.

By suppertime, despite that the rooms were brightly lit with camphor lamps and mole candles, an ominous atmosphere had settled over the house. Sir Alfred sat at the dinner table with Burton and Swinburne, Colonel Lushington, Henry Hawkins, and Doctor Jankyn, and began to drink even more heavily than the night before.

Conversation was desultory and sporadic, and the men ate with little enthusiasm, though the food was excellent.

"Your Mrs. Picklethorpe works wonders," Swinburne commented after a long and uncomfortable silence.

"She does," Sir Alfred answered, with a slight slur. "The Tichborne pantries have always enjoyed the reputation of being the best stocked in all of Hampshire, and she certainly does justice to their contents."

Burton froze with a forkful of beef half raised to his mouth.

"Richard?" Swinburne enquired, puzzled by his friend's expression.

Burton lowered the fork. "Do you think I might see the kitchen and pantries at some point?" he asked.

"Of course," said Tichborne. "Why? Do you take an interest in cooking?"

"Not at all. It's the architecture of the house that fascinates me."

"The cook and her staff will be cleaning up now, after which it'll be a little late. What say you we go down there tomorrow morning before the Claimant shows up?"

"Thank you."

They finished eating.

Tichborne stood and swayed slightly.

"I'd much appreciate a few rounds of billiards," he said. "Will you gentlemen join me?"

"Sir Alfred—" Doctor Jankyn began, but the baronet stopped him with a sharp gesture.

"Don't fuss, Jankyn. I'm perfectly fine. Join us."

They repaired to the billiard room. Hawkins began a game with Swinburne and was surprised to find the poet a formidable opponent.

Bogle served port and sweet sherry.

Lushington put a flame to a meerschaum pipe, and Jankyn lit a briar, while Burton, Hawkins, and Tichborne all opted for cigars. Within minutes, the room was thick with a blue haze of tobacco smoke.

"By golly, it's a veritable drubbing!" the lawyer exclaimed as Swinburne potted three balls in quick succession.

"If only you were as accurate with a pistol!" Burton whispered to his friend.

"To be perfectly honest," Swinburne replied, grinning, "I'm not hitting the balls I'm aiming at. It's sheer luck that the ones I *am* hitting are going in!"

He won the game against Hawkins, then played Colonel Lushington and beat him, too.

Sir Alfred took up a cue. "I'll be the next lamb to the slaughter," he announced, and they began the game.

As Burton watched, he became aware that he was feeling oddly apprehensive, and when he looked at the others' faces, he could see they were experiencing the same sensation: the inexplicable presentiment that something was going to happen.

He shook himself and emptied his glass in a single swallow.

"Another port, please, Bogle."

"Certainly, sir."

"You might open the window a crack, too. It's like a London pea-souper in here."

"I would, sir, but it's worse outside."

"Worse? What do you mean?"

"It's the mist, sir. It's risen unusually high tonight—quite suddenly, too. Right up to the second storey of the house, and thicker than I've ever seen it."

Burton crossed to the window and drew aside the curtain. The room was brilliantly reflected in the glass, and he could make out nothing beyond. Twisting the catch open, he drew up the sash a little, bent over, and peered through the gap. A solid wall of white vapour collapsed inward and began to pour over the sill and into the room.

Hurriedly, he closed the window and pulled the curtain across it.

Behind him, the room fell silent.

A glass hit the floor and shattered.

He turned.

Swinburne, Lushington, Hawkins, Jankyn, Tichborne, and Bogle were all standing motionless. Even through the blue haze, he could see that the blood had drained from their faces. They were staring wide-eyed at a corner of the room.

Burton followed their gaze.

There was a woman there—or, rather, a column of denser tobacco smoke that had taken on the form of a thickset, heavy-hipped female.

She raised a nebulous arm and pointed a tendril-like finger at Sir Alfred Tichborne. Black eyes glared from her head.

Tichborne shrieked and backed away until he was pressed against the wall, banging into a rack of billiard cues which clattered noisily to the floor.

"Lady Mabella!" he moaned.

To either side of him, the haze suddenly congealed, forming two ghostly, indistinct, top-hatted figures. They wrapped transparent fingers around his arms.

"Bloody hell!" Hawkins breathed.

Bogle let loose a piercing scream, dropped to his knees, and covered his eyes.

"For God's sake, help me!" Tichborne wailed.

Before any of the men could move, the wraiths had dragged the baronet across the room. Lady Mabella surged forward, wrapped her swirling arms around him, and plunged through the door, taking him with her. The door didn't open, nor did it smash; the ghostly woman, wraiths, and man simply disappeared through the wood as if it were nothing but an illusion.

A muffled cry came from the corridor beyond: "Save me! Oh, Christ! They mean to kill me!"

"After him!" Burton barked, breaking the spell that had immobilised them all.

In three long strides, he reached the door and wrenched it open in time to see Tichborne being hauled through another at the far end of the passage. Again, the flesh-and-blood baronet passed straight through the portal without it opening or breaking.

Burton hurtled along the hallway with the others trailing behind, threw open the door, and ran into the drawing room.

Tichborne's terrified eyes fixed on him.

"Burton! Please! Please!"

Lady Mabella levelled her black eyes at the king's agent, and he heard in his mind an accented female voice command: "Do not interfere!"

He stumbled and clutched his head, feeling as if a spear had jabbed into his brain. The pain passed in an instant. When he looked up again, the ghost and Tichborne had vanished through the door leading to the main parlour.

"Are you all right?" Swinburne asked, catching up with him.

"Yes! Come on!"

They burst into the parlour, paced across it, and tumbled into the manor's entrance hall.

The two wraiths, led by Lady Mabella, were pulling Sir Alfred up the main staircase. He screamed and pleaded hysterically.

A gun boomed and plaster exploded from the wall beside him. Burton looked around and saw Lushington with a pistol in his raised hand.

"Don't shoot, you fool!" he shouted. "You'll hit the baronet!"

He started up the stairs.

Sir Alfred was dragged around a corner, his cries echoing through the house.

Burton, Swinburne, and the others followed the fast-moving wraiths down the hallway leading to the rear of the mansion, through the morning room, into a small sitting room, then to a dressing room, and into the large bedchamber beyond.

Burton stumbled into it just as Lady Mabella gripped Tichborne around the waist and disappeared with him through the closed window. His body passed through the glass without shattering it. A short scream of terror from outside ended abruptly.

The two wraiths hovered before the glass. One of them turned, reached up, and raised its phantom top hat. The figures dissipated.

Stepping to the window, Burton slid it up and looked out. About three feet below, swells of impenetrable white mist rose and fell like liquid.

"Jankyn!" he bellowed, spinning on his heel. "Follow me! The patio! Quickly, man!"

The physician, who'd been lagging behind the others and had only just entered the room, found himself being tugged along, back down the stairs, and through the house to its rear. The rest of them followed.

"What's happening?" Lushington demanded. "Where's Sir Alfred?"

"Come!" Burton called.

They entered the hunting room and the king's agent pulled open the door to the patio. Dense mist enveloped the men as they stepped outside.

"I can't see a thing!" said Jankyn.

"Over here."

Burton knelt beside Sir Alfred Tichborne, who lay broken upon the pavement, blood pooling from the back of his head.

Jankyn joined them.

"He was thrown from the window," Burton explained.

Tichborne looked up at them, blinked, coughed, and whispered: "It hurts, Doctor Jankyn."

"Lie still," the physician ordered.

Sir Alfred's eyes held Burton's. "There's something—" He winced and groaned. "There's something I want—I want you to—do."

"What is it, Sir Alfred?"

A tear slid from the baronet's eye. "No matter who claims this—this estate tomorrow, my brother—my *real* brother—he and I were the last Tichbornes. Don't allow anyone else to—to take the name."

He closed his eyes and emitted a deep sigh.

Jankyn leaned over him. He looked back at Burton.

"Sir Alfred has joined his mother."

Even though it was near enough midnight, Burton took a horse and trap and galloped to Alresford, where he hammered on the door of the post office until the inhabitants opened a window and demanded to know what in blue blazes he thought he was bally well doing. Displaying the credentials granted to him by the prime minister, he quickly gained access to the aviary and gave one of the parakeets a message for the attention of Scotland Yard.

Early the next morning, an irregular ribbon of steam appeared high over the eastern horizon and arced down toward the estate. It was generated by a rotorchair, which landed with a thump and a bounce and skidded over the gravel on the carriageway in front of Tichborne House.

A burly figure clambered out of it, pulled leather-bound goggles from his eyes, and was mounting the steps to the portico when the front door opened and Burton emerged.

"Hello, Trounce. Glad to see you!"

They shook hands.

"Captain, please tell me the parakeet was joking!"

"Joking?"

"It told me murder had been done—by ghosts!"

"As bizarre as it sounds, I'm afraid it's true; I saw it with my own eyes."

Trounce sighed and ran his fingers through his short, bristly hair.

"Ye gods, how the devil am I supposed to report that to Commissioner Mayne?"

"Come through to the parlour, I'll give you a full account."

Some little time later, Detective Inspector Trounce had been introduced to Colonel Lushington, Henry Hawkins, and Doctor Jankyn, and had taken a statement from each of them. He then examined Sir Alfred's body, which lay in a small bedroom, awaiting the arrival of the county coroner.

Trounce settled in the smoking room with Burton and Swinburne.

"It's plain enough that he was killed by the fall," he muttered. "But how am I to begin the investigation? Ghosts, by Jove! It's absurd! First Brundleweed and now Tichborne!"

"That's a very interesting point," Burton said. "We can at least establish that the two crimes are linked—beyond the presence of a ghost, I mean."

"How so?"

"We dismissed Brundleweed's spook as either imagination or a gas-induced hallucination. However, last night I witnessed ghosts pulling poor Sir Alfred straight through solid matter. It strikes me that if they can do that with a man, then they can certainly do it with diamonds."

"You mean to suggest that, some little time before Brunel's clockwork raiding party arrived, Brundleweed's ghost reached into his safe and pulled the François Garnier gems right out, replacing them with onyx stones, all without even opening the door?"

"Yes. Exactly that."

"And was it the Tichborne ghost, Captain? This Lady Mabella?"

"It would be fair to assume so. The motive appears to be the same; she has an interest in black diamonds. There's rumoured to be one, of the same variety as the Choir Stones, concealed somewhere on this estate. Lady Mabella has spent night after night knocking on the walls around the house. What does that suggest to you?"

"That she's been searching for a secret hiding place?"

"Precisely—although it's strange that she should knock on walls when she has the ability to walk right through them. That aside, we appear to have a diamond-hungry spook on our hands. I propose that our priority should be to discover the stone before she does; perhaps then we can find out why it's so important to her."

Trounce rubbed his hands over his face, his expression a picture of exasperation. "Fine! Fine! But it beats me why a diamond should be of *any* blessed use to a ghost!"

"As I say, my friend, that is the crux of the matter."

"And why murder Sir Alfred?"

"Perhaps to make way for the Claimant?"

Algernon Swinburne clapped his hands together. "Dastardly!" he cried. "The witch and the imposter are hand-in-glove!"

Trounce groaned. "I was the laughing stock of the Yard for decades because I believed in Spring Heeled Jack. Lord knows what mockery I'm letting myself in for now, but I suppose we'd better get on with it. Where do we start?"

"In the kitchen."

"The kitchen? Why the kitchen?"

"Of course!" Swinburne enthused, as realisation dawned. "Mrs. Picklethorpe's snoring!"

Trounce looked from the king's agent to the diminutive poet and back again.

"You know, I could easily grow to dislike you two. What in the devil's name are you jabbering about?"

"We have Herbert Spencer the vagrant philosopher with us," Burton explained. "He's staying down in the servants' quarters. He complained that the cook snores, and that the sound reverberates through the walls. Perhaps it's because the walls are hollow."

"And there's a dreadful old family poem," Swinburne added, "which says *Consume if thou wouldst uncover*. We think the diamond is hidden somewhere under the two wheat fields at the front of the house. Initially, we speculated that the doggerel was instructing whoever wanted to find it to get rid of the crop and dig, but perhaps there's an easier way."

"You mean a secret passage from the kitchen?" Trounce asked.

"Or, more specifically, from one of the famous pantries," Burton responded.

"Gad!" Trounce exclaimed. Then again: "Gad!"

"The Claimant is due here soon, so I suggest we have a poke around straightaway. I don't know how welcome we'll be in the manor once he sets foot in it."

Trounce jerked his head in agreement.

They left the smoking room and sought out Colonel Lushington, who they found pacing in the study, next to the library.

He looked up as they entered. "More news," he announced. "Bad. Maybe good. Not sure. Could be either. Depends how it goes. Hawkins is of the opinion that it'll be a civil trial: *Tichborne versus Lushington*."

"Why so?" Burton asked.

"The Claimant, under the name Roger Tichborne, will contest my right to act on the family's behalf. He'll try to have me removed from the house. Ejected. Out on my ear, so to speak. However, if he's not Roger Tichborne, we'll counter by suing for a criminal trial. Court. Jury. So forth. *King versus Claimant*."

"Good!" Trounce grunted. "That would bring Scotland Yard in on the matter."

Lushington agreed. "High time. I'd certainly like to know more about what the Claimant fellow got up to in Australia when he was calling himself Tomas Castro!"

"Rest assured, Colonel, the moment it becomes a criminal matter, the Yard will send someone to the colonies."

Burton interrupted: "Colonel, it may seem trivial and badly timed but, as I mentioned last night, I have good reason for wanting to examine the kitchens. I assure you it's relevant to this whole affair. Would you mind?"

Lushington looked puzzled but nodded. He summoned Bogle and told him to take Burton, Swinburne, and Trounce "below stairs."

They found that the basement of the manor was divided into a great many small rooms. There were the servants' sleeping quarters, sitting rooms, and washrooms, storerooms, coal cellars, sculleries, and a dining room. The kitchen was by far the largest chamber, and it opened onto three pantries, all stocked with cured meats, jars of preserved comestibles, sacks of flour, dried beans and sugars, cheeses, oils, and vinegars, vegetables, kegs of beer, and racks of wine.

"Let's take one each," Burton suggested. "Check the walls and floors. We're looking for a concealed door."

He stepped into the middle room and began to move sacks and jars aside, stretching over the piled goods to rap his knuckles against the plaster-coated back wall. He heard his colleagues doing the same in the rooms on either side.

As thorough as he was, he found nothing.

"I say, Captain, come and have a look at this!" Detective Inspector Trounce called.

Burton left his pantry and entered the one to the right.

"Got something?"

"Perhaps so. What do you make of that?"

The Scotland Yard man pointed to the top of the back wall, where it abutted the ceiling. Initially, Burton couldn't see anything unusual, but upon closer inspection he noticed a thin, dark line running along the joint.

"Hmm," he grunted, and heaved himself up onto a beer barrel.

Leaning against the wall, he reached up and ran his thumbnail along the line. Then he stepped down and said: "I'm not the slightest bit peckish, so I'd rather not eat and drink my way through this lot despite the poem's directive. Let's settle for clearing it out into the kitchen."

He called Swinburne.

"What?" came the poet's voice.

"Come here and lend some elbow grease!"

The three men quickly moved the contents of the pantry out, exposing every inch of the rear wall.

"The line extends down the sides and across the base of the wall," Burton observed.

"A door?" asked Swinburne.

"I can't see any other explanation. There's no sign of a handle, though."

Trounce placed both his hands against the wall and pushed.

"Nothing," he grunted, stepping back.

The three men spent the next few minutes pressing different parts of the barrier. They then examined the rest of the small room in the hope of finding a lever or switch of some sort.

"It's hopeless," the inspector grumbled. "If there's a way to get that blasted door open, it's not in here."

"Perhaps we've overlooked something in the poem," Swinburne mused.

"Possibly," answered Burton. "For the moment, we'd better get back upstairs. We don't want to miss the Claimant's grand entrance. We'll return later. Algy, go and track down Herbert and tell him what's what. He can be poking about down here while we're occupied. I'll ask the cook to leave this room as it is for the time being."

Some little time later, the king's agent and his companions joined Colonel Lushington, Hawkins, and Jankyn in the library. It was just past midday.

The colonel, twisting the points of his extravagant muttonchops, paced up and down nervously.

"Mr. Hawkins," he said, "tell me more about this Kenealy fellow."

"Who's Kenealy?" Burton asked.

"Doctor Edward Vaughan Hyde Kenealy," said Hawkins. "He's the Claimant's lawyer. He also considers himself a poet, literary critic, prophet, and would-be politician. He's a through-and-through Rake—a member of the inner circle thought to have gathered around the new leader, whoever that may be."

"Well now!" Burton exclaimed. "That's very interesting indeed!"

Laurence Oliphant and Henry "The Mad Marquess" Beresford had formerly led the Rakes, but both had been killed by Burton last year, and the faction had been in disarray for some months.

"Not John Speke, surely!" Burton muttered to himself. Recent events would make a lot more sense if Speke was guiding the Rakes and using them to get at the black diamonds, but, somehow, Burton just couldn't see it. His former partner didn't possess leadership qualities, and furthermore, he was extremely conservative and repressed in character—not at all representative of the Rake philosophy.

Burton wondered whether he'd be able to prise some information out of the Claimant's lawyer.

"*Interesting* is not a word I'd use to describe Edward Kenealy, Sir Richard," Henry Hawkins was saying. "*Barking mad* would be my choice. He's as nutty as a fruitcake, and a confounded brute, too. Ten years ago, he served a month in prison on a charge of aggravated assault against his six-year-old illegitimate son. The boy had been beaten half to death and almost strangled. Kenealy has since been accused—but not charged—with a number of assaults against prostitutes. He's a very active follower of the Marquis de Sade and adheres to the belief that inflicting pain weakens social constraints and liberates the spirit."

Detective Inspector Trounce eyed Algernon Swinburne, who frowned back and muttered: "Some are givers, some are takers, Inspector."

Hawkins continued: "He also subscribes to a rather incoherent theology which claims that a spiritual force is beginning to change the world—that we currently exist on the borderline between two great epochs, and the transformation from one to the other will cause a social apocalypse, overthrowing the world's ruling elite and passing power, instead, into the hands of the working classes."

Burton shifted uneasily, remembering Countess Sabina's prophecy and his subsequent strange dream.

Hawkins went on: "He's published a number of long-winded and non-sensical texts to promote this creed but, if you ask me, the only useful information one can draw from them is the fact that their author is an egomaniac, fanatic, and fantasist. All in all, gentlemen, a very dangerous and unpredictable fellow to have as our opponent."

"And one who's currently travelling down the carriageway, by the looks of it, what!" Jankyn noted from where he stood by the window. "There's a growler approaching."

Lushington blew out a breath and rubbed his hands on the sides of his trousers. "Well, Mr. Hawkins—ahem!—let's go and cast our eyes over, that is to say, have a look at, the man who says he's Roger Tichborne. Gentlemen, if you'd be good enough to wait here, I'll introduce the Claimant and his lunatic lawyer presently."

The two men left the room.

Swinburne crossed to the window just in time to see the horse-drawn carriage pass out of sight as it approached the portico.

"What do you think?" he asked Jankyn quietly. "Swindler or prodigal?"

"I'll reserve my judgement until I see him and he makes his case, what!"

Burton, who was standing beside one of the large bookcases with Detective Inspector Trounce, caught his assistant's eye.

With a nod to Jankyn, the poet left the window and walked over to the explorer, who pointed to a leather-bound volume. Swinburne read the spine: *De Mythen van Verloren Halfedelstenen* by Matthijs Schuyler.

"What of it?" he asked.

"This is the book that tells the myths of the three Eyes of Nāga."

"Humph!" the poet muttered. "Circumstantial evidence, I'll grant, but the ties between the Tichbornes and the black diamonds appear to be tightening!"

"They do!" Burton agreed.

Bogle entered carrying a decanter and some glasses. He put them on a sideboard and started to polish the glasses with a cloth, preparing to offer the men refreshment.

The door opened.

Colonel Lushington stepped in and stood to one side. His eyes were glazed and his jaw hung slackly.

Henry Hawkins followed. He wore an expression of shock, and was holding a hand to his head, as if experiencing pain.

"Gentlemen," the colonel croaked. "May I present to you Doctor Edward Kenealy and—and—and the—the Claimant to the—to the Tichborne estate!"

A man entered behind him.

Dr. Kenealy possessed the same build as William Trounce; he was short, thickset, and burly. However, where the Scotland Yard man was mostly brawn, the lawyer was soft and running to fat.

His head was extraordinary. An enormous bush of dark hair and a very generous beard framed his broad face. His upper lip was clean-shaven, his mouth was wide, and he wore small thick-lensed spectacles behind which tiny bloodshot eyes glittered. The overall effect was that of a wild man of the woods peeking out from dense undergrowth.

He jerked an abrupt nod of greeting to each of them in turn, then said, in an aggressive tone: "Good day, sirs. I present—"

He paused for dramatic effect.

"—Sir Roger Tichborne!"

A shadow darkened the doorway behind him. Kenealy moved aside.

A great mass of coarse cloth and swollen flesh filled the portal from side to side, top to bottom, and slowly squeezed through, before straightening and expanding to its full height and breadth, which was simply enormous.

The Tichborne Claimant was around six and a half feet tall, prodigiously fat, and absolutely hideous.

A towering, blubbery mass, he stood on short legs as thick as tree trunks, which were encased in rough brown canvas trousers. His colossal belly pushed over the top of them, straining his waistcoat to such an extent that the material around the buttons had ripped and frayed.

His right arm was long and corpulent, stretching the stitching of his black jacket, and it ended in a bloated, plump-fingered and hairy hand. The left arm, by contrast, seemed withered below the elbow. It was shorter, and the hand was that of a more refined man, smooth-skinned and with long, slender fingers.

The enormous round head that squatted necklessly on the wide shoulders was, thought Burton, like something straight out of a nightmare. The face, which certainly resembled that of Roger Tichborne, if the portrait in the dining room was anything to go by, appeared to have been roughly stitched onto the front of the skull by means of a thick cartilaginous thread. Its edges were pulled tautly over the flesh beneath, causing the features to distort somewhat, slitting the eyes, flaring the nostrils, and pulling the lips horribly tight over big, greenish, tombstone teeth.

From behind this grotesque mask, dark, blank, cretinous eyes slowly surveyed the room.

The head was hairless, the scalp a nasty spotted and blemished yellow, and around the skull, encircling it entirely like a crown, were seven irregular lumps, each cut through by a line of stitches.

There came a sudden crash as Bogle dropped a glass.

The butler clutched at his temples, grimaced, then, his eyes filling with tears, he said: "My, sir! But how much stouter you are!"

The creature grunted and attempted a smile, pulling its lips back over its decayed teeth and bleeding gums. A line of pinkish drool oozed from its bottom lip.

"Yaaas," it drawled in a slow, rumbling voice. "I—not—the boy—I was when I leave Tichborne!"

The statement was made hesitatingly, and dully, as if it came from someone mentally impaired.

"Then you recognise my client?" Kenealy demanded of Bogle.

"Oh, yes, sir! That's my master! That's Sir Roger Tichborne!"

"By thunder! What nonsense!" Hawkins objected. "That—that *person*—may possess a passing likeness in the face but he is blatantly not—not—"

He stopped suddenly and gasped, staggering backward.

"My head!" he groaned.

Colonel Lushington emitted a strangled laugh and dropped to his knees. Doctor Jankyn hurried forward and took the colonel by the shoulders.

"Are you unwell?" he asked.

"Yes. No. No. I think—I think I have a—I'm dizzy. It's just a migraine."

"Steady!" the doctor said, pulling the military man to his feet. "Why, you can barely stand!"

Lushington straightened, swayed, pushed the physician away, and cleared his throat.

"My—my apologies, gentlemen. I feel—a bit—a bit . . . If Sir Roger will permit it, I shall—retire to my room to—to lie down for an hour or so."

"Good idea!" Kenealy said.

"You go," the Claimant grunted, lumbering into the centre of the room. "You go—lie down now. Feel better. Yes."

To the other men's amazement, Colonel Lushington, who'd gone from calling the creature "the Claimant" to "Sir Roger" in less than a minute, stumbled from the room.

"What the deuce—?" Trounce muttered.

Doctor Jankyn announced: "He'll be all right after he rests awhile, what!" He turned to the Claimant and extended his hand. "Welcome home, Sir Roger! Welcome home! What a marvellous day this is! I never thought to see you again!"

The Claimant's meaty right hand enveloped the doctor's and shook it.

"So much for reserving judgement!" Swinburne whispered to Burton. "Although he might be right. Maybe this isn't an imposter at all!"

Burton gazed at his assistant in astonishment.

Hawkins shook his head, as if to clear it. He turned to Jankyn.

"You don't mean to suggest that you also recognise this—this—?"

"Why, of course I do!" Jankyn cried. "This is young Sir Roger!"

"It is—good to see you—Mr—Mr—?" the creature rumbled.

"Doctor Jankyn!" the physician supplied.

"Yes," came the reply. "I remember you."

Hawkins threw up his hands in exasperation and looked across at Burton, who shrugged noncommittally.

"And who might you gentlemen be, may I ask?" Kenealy enquired, in his brusque, belligerent manner.

"I am Henry Hawkins, acting on behalf of the relatives," the lawyer snapped, bristling.

"Ah ha! Then advise them to not oppose my client, sir! He has come to take possession of what's rightfully his and I mean to see that he gets it!"

"I think it best we save discussions of that nature for the courtroom, sir," Hawkins responded coldly. "For now, I'll restrict myself to that which courtesy demands and introduce Sir Richard Francis Burton, Mr. Algernon Swinburne, and Detective Inspector William Trounce of Scotland Yard."

"And, pray, why are they here?"

Trounce stepped forward and, in his most officious tone, said, "I am here, sir, to investigate the murder of Sir Alfred Tichborne, and I advise you not to interfere with my duties."

"I have no intention of interfering. Murder, is it? When did this occur? And how?"

Trounce shifted his weight from one foot to the other. "Last night. He fell from a window under mysterious circumstances."

"My—brother?" the Claimant uttered.

"That is correct, Sir Roger," said Kenealy, turning to the monstrous figure. "May I be the first to offer my condolences?"

"Yes," the Claimant grunted, meaninglessly.

Kenealy looked back at Trounce. "Why murder? Why not an accident or suicide?"

"The matter is under investigation. I'll not be drawn on it until I have gathered and examined the evidence."

"Very well. And you, Sir Richard—is there a reason for your presence?"

Burton glowered at the lawyer and said, slowly and clearly, "I don't think I like your tone, sir."

"Then I apologise," Kenealy said, sounding not one whit apologetic. "I remind you, however, that I'm acting on behalf of Sir Roger Tichborne, in whose house you currently stand."

Henry Hawkins interrupted: "That remains to be seen, Kenealy. And for your information, Sir Richard and Mr. Swinburne are here as guests of Colonel Lushington and at the behest of the Doughty and Arundell families, who have a stake in this property and whose identities are beyond question."

"Do you mean to imply that my client's identity *is* in question?" Kenealy growled.

"I absolutely do," Hawkins answered. "And I intend to have him prosecuted. It is blatantly obvious that this individual is an imposter!"

Doctor Jankyn stepped forward, shaking his head. "No, Mr. Hawkins," he said. "You're wrong. This is Sir Roger. I couldn't mistake him. I knew him for the first two decades of his life."

Hawkins rounded on the physician. "I don't know what you're playing at, sir, but if I find that you're a willing participant in this conspiracy, I'll see you behind bars!"

"The doctor and the butler have both acknowledged my client's identity," Kenealy snapped, "as has Colonel Lushington—"

"I dispute that!" said Hawkins. "The colonel made a slip of the tongue while feeling unwell, that's all."

"Be that as it may, two individuals who were in the service of the family before Sir Roger sailed for South America have confirmed that this man is who he says he is. Need I remind you that he was also recognised by his own mother?"

"Motherrrrr—" the Claimant moaned, gazing blankly at Hawkins.

"Those present who oppose my client never even knew Sir Roger," Kenealy continued. "It doesn't take a court of law to see where the power lies, does it?"

"By God! What kind of lawyer are you?" Hawkins cried.

"Mr. Hawkins," Kenealy snarled, "there is a certain degree of decorum demanded by the bar which, once we oppose each other before a judge, will prevent me from saying that which I now wish to say: to wit, shut your damned mouth, sir! You are in no position to criticise and in hardly any state to oppose. I will, against my better judgement, allow you and Colonel Lushington to remain in this house as my client's guests until such a time as the law deems your presence here indefensible. I will then throw you out, and if I have to put my boot to the seat of your pants, then I most certainly shall do so. In the meantime, Detective Inspector Trounce is welcome to stay here until his investigation is done. As for you two—" he turned to Burton and Swinburne "—you can depart forthwith. Your presence is neither required nor desired."

"Kenealy!" Hawkins yelled. "How dare you! This is an absolute outrage!"

"I am the prosecuting lawyer, Hawkins!" Kenealy roared, his face turning purple and the veins pulsing on his forehead. "I'm well aware that you intend to countersue, but you haven't filed the case yet, and until you do, there's not a damned thing you can do to oppose my client's wishes—and his wishes, at this moment, are that Burton and Swinburne get the hell off his estate!"

Hawkins opened his mouth to reply but was interrupted by Burton: "It's quite all right, Mr. Hawkins. We'll leave. We don't want to contribute to what is obviously already a tense situation."

"Yaaas," the Claimant drawled. "Go now."

Without another word, Burton took Swinburne by the arm and steered him out of the room.

"Sir Richard!" Hawkins called as the two men crossed the threshold. Burton looked back, met the lawyer's eyes, and gave a slight shake of his head.

As they climbed the stairs to their rooms, Swinburne said: "Well, that's that. I'd say our job here is done."

"You really think we just met the real Sir Roger?" Burton asked.

"Don't you?"

"Absolutely not!"

"Really? What on earth is there to be suspicious about?"

"Are you serious, Algy?"

"Yes."

"You don't think it odd that Sir Roger was five foot eight at most, and very slim, whereas the Claimant is pushing seven foot tall and is probably the most obese individual I've ever set eyes on?"

"I suppose life in Australia can change a man, Richard. Anyway, there's no reason for us to stay, is there? Shall we return to London?"

"In due course."

Thirty minutes later, as Burton was packing his portmanteau, Trounce knocked at his bedroom door, entered, and cried: "What the devil are you playing at? Why are you scarpering?"

"We're not. Algy and I are going to get rooms at the Dick Whittington Inn in Alresford," the king's agent replied. "And you? How long do you expect to stay?"

Trounce blew out a breath. "Phew! What can I do? How does a man go about investigating ghosts? No, Captain, I'll return to the Yard this evening and we'll see what Commissioner Mayne has to say about the whole sorry business."

"In that case, would you do me a favour and get a message to Herbert Spencer? I need him to let us back into the house and into the pantry. One way or another, we have to find our way through that secret door. I'm convinced the diamond is beyond it and I want to get to it before the ghost does. Tell him to meet Algy and me by the lake at three in the morning."

Trounce shook Burton's hand. "Very well. Good luck, Captain."

"The bloomin' door is open, Boss!" Herbert Spencer whispered. "But it weren't me what opened it!"

He glanced around nervously. The mist was rolling down the slope again, creeping toward the lake, and he wasn't happy.

The giant swans, as yet unnoticed by Kenealy and his client, were sleeping on the mirror-smooth water, their heads resting on their backs, beaks tucked under their wings.

Spencer, Burton, and Swinburne were crouched under a crooked willow.

"Open?" Burton hissed.

"Yus. I checked it afore comin' out, an' blow me down with a feather if the back wall weren't sunk right into the floor!"

"And what was beyond it?"

"A tunnel."

"Take us there, Herbert. We must hurry!"

Keeping their heads low, the three men ran up the slope to the back of Tichborne House. Despite the hour, lights were burning on the ground floor. They skirted the patio and followed Spencer around the corner to the left side of the building, where the door to a coal cellar stood open.

"We'll have to go down the chute, an' I fear you'll get your togs a bit dirty, gents."

"That's all right," Swinburne whispered. "I'm an expert at this sort of thing."

He was referring to the time he'd spent as an apprentice to Vincent Sneed, the master chimney sweep. The poet had been worked hard and mal-treated by his vicious boss, but his experience had been instrumental in Burton's subsequent exposure and defeat of the cabal of scientists who'd been planning to use the British Empire as a subject for social experimentation.

Swinburne swung himself onto the coal chute and slid down into dark-ness. Burton and Spencer followed him.

They stood, brushed themselves down, and passed through a door into a passage, which they followed past storerooms until they found themselves back at the three pantries. The rightmost one was still empty, its contents stacked in the corridor.

"You go on back to bed, Herbert," Burton said, keeping his voice low, his eyes fixed on the brick tunnel visible at the back of the small room. "If you don't mind, I'd like you to remain in the house for as long as possible. The Claimant and his lawyer don't know you came with us and will take you for a member of staff. That means you're perfectly placed to keep an eye on things. Any time something of interest occurs, make your way to the Alres-ford post office and send a message via parakeet to me at 14 Montagu Place."

"Right you are, Boss!" replied the philosopher. "When you get back to the Smoke, will you tell Miss Mayson that her swans are hale and hearty? She worries about them so."

"I will."

"Good luck, gents!"

Herbert Spencer departed.

"Come on, Algy—let's see where this leads."

The king's agent and his assistant passed through the pantry and entered the tunnel. It was about eight feet in height and the same in width. After a few paces, it angled to the right; then, a few steps beyond, back to the left.

Burton shuddered. He wasn't fond of enclosed spaces, but felt somewhat encouraged when they came to a flaming brand set in a bracket on the wall. By its light, he examined the walls, floor, and ceiling.

"All brick," he whispered to his companion, "and not so very old. I'd put money on this having been constructed during Sir Henry's time. And look— it definitely runs out in the direction of the Crawls."

They moved on until they reached a point where the tunnel's brickwork gave way to plain stone blocks.

"Granite," Burton noted. "We're not under the house anymore. And look how this passage is level, though we know the surface above us slopes upward. It must cut straight through to a structure beneath Lady Mabella's wheat fields."

"Brrr! Don't mention her! I don't want to see that blasted spook again!"

They crept forward. Burning brands were spaced regularly along the walls.

A few minutes later, they came to a junction and had to choose whether to turn left or right.

"We're probably below the bottom edge of the Crawls now," Burton observed.

He examined the floor. There was no dust or debris, no footprints, nothing to suggest that anyone had passed.

"What do you think, Algy?"

"When Sir Alfred took us around the Crawls, we went counterclockwise. I say we follow suit, and go right."

"Jolly good."

They turned into the right-hand passage and proceeded cautiously along it, listening out for any movement ahead.

Swinburne placed a hand on the left wall, stopped, and pressed an ear against the stone.

"What is it?" Burton asked.

"The wall is warm and I can hear water gurgling on the other side of it."

"An underground spring. A hot one, too. I thought so. It explains the mist. Let's keep moving."

As they walked on, Burton measured their progress against his memory of the topography of the surface above. He knew they were following the bottom edge of the Crawls and predicted that the tunnel would turn left a few yards ahead.

It did.

"We're moving deeper underground now," he observed.

Swinburne cast a sidelong glance at his friend. Burton's jaw was set hard and the muscles at its joint were flexing spasmodically. The famous explorer, who'd spent so many of his younger years traversing vast open spaces, was struggling to control his claustrophobia.

"Not so deep, really," the poet said encouragingly. "The surface isn't far above."

Burton nodded and moistened his lips with his tongue, peering into the shadows.

The sound of dripping water punctuated the silence, though they couldn't see any evidence of it. They kept moving until they came to an opening in the left wall.

"We're about halfway along the length of the fields," the king's agent whispered. "This looks like it'll take us into the middle."

They stepped into the opening and followed the passage. After a few paces, it suddenly angled leftward, taking them back in the direction of the house. They kept going, eventually reaching a right turn, and, a good few minutes after that, another.

"Now we're going back up the fields," said Burton, "but this time on their left border."

When they again reached what he estimated was the halfway mark beneath the fields above, Burton expected to find an opening in the wall to his right. There wasn't one. Instead, the passage continued straight up to the topmost border of the fields then turned left. It continued under the highest point of the Crawls then swerved ninety degrees to the right.

"Back in the direction of the house again!" Burton murmured.

"This is getting ridiculous," said Swinburne.

The tunnel led them back down to the middle point beneath the edge of the Crawls, turned right, then a few paces later, right again.

"And now back up to the top. We're slowly spiralling inward, Algy. It makes sense. This place follows the design of a classical labyrinth."

"And here's us without a skein of thread!"

"We don't need one. Labyrinths of this sort are unicursal. Their route to the centre is always unambiguous: just a spiral that folds back in on itself over and over until the middle is reached."

"Where the minotaur awaits."

"I fear so."

Swinburne stopped. "What? What? Not another monster, surely?"

Burton smiled grimly. "No. The same one, I should think."

"Sir Roger?"

"The Claimant."

"Yes, that's what I meant."

Burton looked at the diminutive poet speculatively. "Odd, though, how you keep referring to him as Sir Roger."

"Merely a slip of the tongue."

"Like Colonel Lushington's?"

"No! Let's push on."

The echoing dripping increased as they passed along the stone corridor, which angled back and forth, ever closer to whatever lay at the centre of the structure.

Burton stopped and whispered: "Listen!"

"Water."

"No, there's something else."

Swinburne concentrated. "Yes, I hear it. A sort of low hum."

"B below middle C, Algy. I'll wager it's the diamond, singing like the Choir Stones. That's what sets the piano off—resonance!"

They turned a corner and saw that it was much lighter ahead.

"Careful," Burton breathed.

They started to walk on their toes.

The sound of running water was loud now, and the droning musical note could be easily heard.

Voices came to them.

One, harsh in tone, said: "Check the walls."

"Edward Kenealy," Burton whispered.

"Yaaas, I check," answered another.

"The minotaur," Swinburne hissed.

"Hammer on each stone," Kenealy instructed. "Don't miss an inch. There has to be a cavity concealed here somewhere."

The king's agent tiptoed forward with Swinburne at his heels. They came to a right-angled turn and peeked around its corner.

Ahead, the tunnel opened onto a large tall-ceilinged square chamber. A stream of water, about two feet wide, fell vertically from a slot in the top of the right-hand wall, cascading into a channel built into the floor. It flowed, steaming, across the middle of the room and disappeared into an opening in the brickwork opposite.

"*Tears, that weep within My Lady's round*," quoted Swinburne under his breath.

The humming of the diamond filled the space, seeming to come from everywhere at once, yet the gem was nowhere in sight.

Something pushed through the hair at the nape of the poet's neck. A cold ring of steel touched the top of his spine.

"Hands up!" said a voice.

Swinburne did as he was told.

Burton turned. "Doctor Jankyn," he said, flatly.

"A bullet will drill through this young man's brain if you try anything, and you wouldn't want that, what!"

"Don't try anything, Richard," Swinburne advised earnestly.

They heard Kenealy call: "What's going on?"

"A couple of uninvited guests," Jankyn replied.

"Bring them here!"

"Move into the chamber, gentlemen," the physician ordered. "Keep your hands where I can see them, please."

They obeyed.

"Burton," the Tichborne Claimant grunted as the king's agent stepped into view. "Bad man."

"And a trespasser," Kenealy added. "What are you playing at, sir? I ordered you to leave the estate."

"I had unfinished business to attend to."

"As we observed. Rather stupid of you to leave the contents of the pantry piled up in the kitchen. Bogle brought it to my attention."

"How did you open the door?"

"I found a lever in the left-hand room—a shelf that slides sideways and twists upward."

"I was a fool to miss it."

"You had no right to be nosing around. I should have you arrested."

"Arrested," drawled the mountain of flesh standing in the centre of the chamber. The Claimant surveyed Burton with mindless eyes.

"Try it," the king's agent challenged.

"Why are you meddling?" Kenealy demanded. "You're a geographer, sir! An explorer! A Livingstone! What has this affair to do with you?"

Burton ignored the question, especially the Livingstone reference, and pointed nonchalantly at the Claimant.

"Who—or should I ask *what*—is that, Kenealy?"

"It's Sir Roger Tichborne."

"We both know that's not true, don't we?"

"I insist that it's Sir Roger Tichborne." The lawyer looked past Burton. "Is that not so, Doctor Jankyn?"

"Absolutely!" said the physician.

"And what do you think, Mr. Swinburne?" Kenealy asked.

"Me? I think my arms are aching. May I lower them?"

"Yes. Step away from him, Jankyn, but keep your pistol steady. If our guests misbehave, shoot to kill."

"Thank you," Swinburne said. "And may I say, you're an absolute charmer, Mr. Kenealy."

"Answer my question. Is this, in your opinion, Sir Roger Tichborne?"

Swinburne hesitated.

"I think—"

He raised a hand to his head and winced.

Burton watched his assistant carefully.

"I think—"

The Claimant let loose a bubbling chuckle.

"I think," the poet groaned, "that—he is—is probably—Tichborne."

"Ah. There we have it." Kenealy smiled.

"Are you quite all right, Algy?" Burton asked.

"Yes. No. Yes. I—my head hurts."

"Sir Roger," the lawyer said, turning to the Claimant, "there is an intruder on your property. You have every right to protect your interests."

"Protect!" the Claimant rumbled. He lumbered forward. "Protect!"

"Kenealy!" Burton snapped. "There is no need to—"

The Claimant's elephantine body blocked his view of the chamber. A meaty hand shot out and grasped the lapels of Burton's jacket and shirt. Cloth ripped as the fingers closed.

Burton was hauled off his feet, swung around, and thrown with tremendous force clear across the room. He slammed into a wall, bounced from it, and landed in a loose-limbed heap on the floor.

"Sir Roger!" Swinburne cried. "Don't!"

"Heh heh!" the Claimant gurgled. He shuffled over to the prone man.

"Perfectly legal, of course," Kenealy observed.

"I say! He's a jolly strong bounder, what!" Jankyn exclaimed as Burton was hoisted over the Claimant's head and thrown back across the chamber.

"He is, Doctor," Kenealy agreed. "Life in the colonies does that to a man, even if he was born an aristocrat."

Burton rolled, reached into his jacket pocket, and pulled out his pistol. As the light from the burning torches pushed the Claimant's vast shadow across him, he raised the weapon and pulled the trigger. The shot was deafening in the enclosed space and everyone flinched. A hole appeared in the cloth stretched across his assailant's belly, but no blood flowed and the bullet appeared to have little effect.

"Baaad man," the Claimant moaned, reaching down.

The gun was wrenched from Burton's fingers and flung away.

"Leave him alone!" Swinburne pleaded as Burton was gripped by the neck and jerked to his feet. "Sir Roger! Think of your family's good name! God! My head!"

Burton launched a ferocious uppercut into his opponent's chin. His fist sank into a wobbling mass of fat. In reply, he was shaken like a rat caught in the jaws of a carnivore. His teeth rattled together. Desperately, he loosed a furious tattoo of blows into the gargantuan body, hammering it around the ribs, but he might have been punching a pillow for all the damage he did; the rib cage was buried deep beneath layers of blubber. The Claimant took the assault without so much as a groan.

Squirming out of the creature's grasp, Burton ducked under groping hands and, like a whirlwind, dealt out roundhouse punches that should have rocked his opponent on his heels. It was useless.

The Claimant lunged and swept his arms around Burton's shoulders. The king's agent felt them tighten and tried to slip downward, but the creature held him with the strength of a grizzly bear. Terrible agony shot through the explorer's chest and it felt as if every bone in his torso must splinter.

It was not the embrace of a human being. Beneath the thick jellied padding flexed the tremendous muscles of a predatory beast.

Pain exploded in Burton's back and his lower spine creaked audibly. Blood pounded in his ears as the awful constriction increased. The monotonous tone of the diamond was filling his head. His legs flopped uselessly and, when the Claimant lifted him from the floor, his feet dangled as loosely as a rag doll's.

Swinburne looked on helplessly as his friend was hoisted up over the creature's head, ready to be dashed against the wall once again.

"Tell me, Swinburne!" Kenealy said. "You don't happen to know where Sir Henry concealed that black diamond of his, do you?"

"No," the poet whimpered. "Except that—"

"Yes?"

The Claimant swung Burton back to fling him into the air. As he did so, a spark of vitality flared in the explorer's dimming consciousness and, with a desperate effort of will, he put all the strength he could muster into a jab, hooking his stiffly held fingers down into his opponent's right eye.

The creature let loose a howl and dropped him. Burton hit the ground at the Claimant's feet.

"Except the poem," said Swinburne.

"Poem, sir? What poem is that?"

"Algy, don't," Burton croaked.

"*The tears, that weep within My Lady's round,*" Swinburne proclaimed. "Do you mind if I sit down? I have the most dreadful headache."

"Please, be my guest." Kenealy grinned. His glasses magnified his little red-rimmed eyes.

Jankyn strode over to Burton and looked down at him. "My goodness. He doesn't look at all well!"

"I bow to your expertise, Doctor," Kenealy said. "Sir Roger, be careful!

Don't break him! You may be defending yourself against a ruthless intruder but a charge of manslaughter would be most inconvenient at present. Tears, Mr. Swinburne?"

"I can't help it. It's the pain. My brain is afire!"

"I was referring to the poem."

"Oh, that gobbledygook. The diamond's behind the waterfall, obviously."

The Claimant bent to pick Burton up. The explorer quickly drew in his legs and kicked his booted feet into the fat man's face. His left heel caught one of the seven lumps that circled the bloated thing's skull, ripping open the little line of stitches.

The Claimant's head snapped back.

"Ouch! Hurt me!" he complained, clutching Burton's arm and dragging him upright.

The king's agent caught sight of a black diamond glittering inside his opponent's wound.

"Choir Stone!" he mumbled.

A massive fist crashed into his face.

He looked up at the off-yellow canvas of his tent.

The exhaustion and fevers and diseases and infections and wounds ate into his body.

There was not a single inch of him that didn't hurt.

"Bismillah!"

No more Africa. Never again. Nothing is worth this agony. Leave the source of the Nile for younger men to find. I don't care anymore. All it's brought me is sickness and treachery.

Damn Speke!

Don't step back. They'll think that we're retiring.

How could he possibly have interpreted that order as a personal slight? How could he have so easily used it as an excuse for betrayal?

"Damn him!"

"Are you awake, Richard?"

"Leave me alone, John. I need to rest. We'll try for the lake tomorrow."

"It's not John. It's Algernon."

Algernon.

Algernon Swinburne.

The yellowed canvas was yellowed plaster—a smoke-stained ceiling.

Betrayal. Always betrayal.

"Algy, you told them where to find it."

"Yes."

"Was the diamond there?"

"Yes. Kenealy reached through the waterfall. There was a niche behind it. He pulled out the biggest diamond I've ever seen, black or otherwise. It was the size of a plum."

Betrayal.

To hell with you, Speke! We were supposed to be friends.

Is there shooting to be done?

I rather suppose there is.

Voices outside the tent. War cries. Running footsteps, like a sudden wind. Clubs beating against the canvas.

A world conceived in opposites only creates cycles and ceaseless recurrence. Only equivalence can lead to destruction.

"And final transcendence."

"What? Richard, are you still with me?"

"Be sharp, and arm to defend the camp."

"Richard. Snap out of it! Wake up!"

"Algy?"

"I'm sorry, Richard. Truly, I am. But I couldn't help it. Something got inside my head. I can't explain it. For a few moments, I really believed that monstrosity was Roger Tichborne."

"Get out, Algy. If this blasted tent comes down on us we'll be caught up good and proper!"

"Please, Richard. We're not in Berbera. This is the Dick Whittington Inn. We're in Alresford, near the Tichborne estate."

"Ah. Wait. Yes, I remember. I think the malaria has got me again."

"No, it hasn't. It was the Claimant. That confounded blackguard beat you half to death. You remember the labyrinth?"

"Yes. Gad! He was strong as an ox! How serious?"

"Bruises. Bad ones. You're black-and-blue all over. Nothing broken, except your nose. You need to rest, that's all."

"Water."

"Wait a minute."

The labyrinth. The stream. The Claimant.

The Cambodian Choir Stones!

The Claimant has Brundleweed's stolen diamonds and the two missing Pelletier gems embedded in his scalp. Why? Why? Why?

"Here, drink this."

"Thank you."

"I have no memory of how we got here, Richard. The last thing I recall is seeing Kenealy pass the diamond to the Claimant. The creature looked at it, then he looked at me, and suddenly that low hum that comes from it overwhelmed me. I heard a woman's voice behind me, turned, and saw the ghost of Lady Mabella. I must have passed out. I woke up here a little while ago. The landlord says we were delivered in a state of intoxication by staff from the estate. I found a letter addressed to us on your bed. Listen:

Burton, Swinburne,

Against my client's express instruction, which was issued through me, his lawyer, in front of witnesses, you chose to trespass on the Tichborne estate and you attempted to steal Tichborne property. Were it not for the fact that we are already preparing a complex legal case against Colonel Lushington, I would not hesitate to prosecute you. As it is, my client has agreed to let this matter drop on the condition that you make absolutely no further attempt to intrude upon Tichborne property. I remind you that the law states that trespassers may be shot on sight. If you set foot on the estate again and somehow manage to avoid such a fate, I assure you that you will not avoid the full force of the law.

Doctor Edward Vaughan Hyde Kenealy
On behalf of
Sir Roger Charles Doughty Tichborne

"It bears Kenealy's signature and, believe it or not, what looks to be the Claimant's thumbprint. It's also witnessed by Jankyn and the butler, Andrew Bogle."

"That's that, then."

"What do you mean?"

"I mean there's nothing more we can do here, Algy. Kenealy and the Tichborne Claimant are obviously in league with the ghost of Lady Mabella, and they are now in possession of the South American Eye and the fragments of the Cambodian Eye. So we'll pack up and return to London, we'll investigate the Claimant's background, and we'll watch carefully to see what our enemies intend to do with those peculiar stones."

THE SECOND PART

IN WHICH THE
STEAM WRAITHS RISE

No one can be perfectly free till all are free.
No one can be perfectly moral till all are moral.
No one can be perfectly happy till all are happy.
—HERBERT SPENCER

RIOT AT SPEAKERS' CORNER

USE FORMBY COAL

IT LASTS LONGER AND PRODUCES MORE HEAT!

Each lump is marinated for ten days in Mr. Formby's secret formula, which causes it to burn with greater intensity and for three times longer than common untreated coal.

More Power!

THE FORMBY FORMULA HAS CHANGED THE WORLD!

Rotorchairs could not fly without it!

Velocipedes would become impractical!

Factory production would slow by two-thirds!

USE FORMBY COAL!
It fuels the Empire!

Sir Richard Francis Burton had been in South America for three weeks. He was unshaven and his skin was dark and weather-beaten. He looked untamed and dangerous, like a bandit.

"Difficult times, Captain," said Lord Palmerston softly as the king's agent sat down.

Burton grunted an agreement and studied the prime minister's waxy, eugenically enhanced features. He noticed that the man's mouth seemed to have been stretched a little wider and there were new surgical scars around the angles of his jaw, a couple of inches beneath the ears. They were oddly gill-like.

He looks like a blessed newt!

The two men were in number 10 Downing Street, the headquarters of His Majesty's government.

"How goes the war, sir?" he asked.

"President Lincoln has formidable strategists directing his army," Palmerston responded, "but mine are better, and, unlike his, they aren't defending two fronts. Our Irish troops have already taken Portland and large sections of Maine. In the south, Generals Lee and Jackson have forced the Union out of Virginia. I wouldn't be at all surprised to receive Lincoln's surrender by Christmas."

A great many people, Burton included, held the Eugenicist faction of the Technologist caste responsible for Great Britain's entry into the American conflict. Had the scientists left Ireland alone, it was argued, there would not have been such an overwhelming refugee problem; and if there had not been an overwhelming refugee problem, then Palmerston may have reacted rather less aggressively to the Trent Affair.

The Eugenicists had started sewing seeds in Ireland last March, around the time of the Brundleweed robbery.

It was an attempt to put an end to the Great Famine, which had been devastating the Emerald Isle since 1845. Nearly two decades of disease had obliterated the potato crop before spreading to other flora, leaving the island a virtual desert. The source of the blight remained a mystery, though its failure to cross to mainland Britain suggested a disease of the soil.

The Eugenicists, working with the botanist Richard Spruce, had planted specially adapted seeds at twelve test sites. These germinated within hours and the plants grew with such unexpected rapidity that they were fully mature within a fortnight. By the end of April, they'd blossomed and pollinated. During May, their seeds and spores spread right across the country, and by early July, from shore to shore, Ireland was a jungle.

Inexplicably, the plants confined themselves to the island; their seeds wouldn't germinate anywhere else. This was a stroke of luck, for, as with every other Eugenicist experiment, the benefits were accompanied by an unexpected side effect.

The new flora was carnivorous.

The experiment was an unmitigated disaster.

During June and July, more than fifteen thousand people were killed. Venomous spines were fired into them, or tendrils strangled them, or acidic sap burned away their flesh, or flowery scent gassed them, or roots jabbed into their bodies and sucked out their blood.

The scientists were at a loss.

Ireland became uninhabitable.

Its population fled.

During the middle months of summer, mainland Britain struggled with a massive influx of refugees. Wooden shanty towns were set up to house them in South Wales, along the edges of Dartmoor, in the Scottish Highlands, and on the Yorkshire Moors. They quickly deteriorated into disease-ridden slums—scenes of terrible squalor, violence, and poverty.

Lord Palmerston's solution to the problem was both ingenious and very, very dangerous.

In his mind's eye, Burton could picture the prime minister contemplating two reports, one entitled *The Irish Crisis* and the other *The Trent Affair*, and could imagine the glint in his eyes as a radical and daring scheme occurred to him.

The Trent Affair had begun the previous December, when two Confederate diplomats, John Slidell of Louisiana and James Mason of Virginia, had been dispatched to London to convince Palmerston that an independent Confederacy would establish a mutually beneficial commercial alliance with Great Britain. They'd been travelling on the British mail packet *Trent* when the Union ship USS *San Jacinto* intercepted it. The British vessel was boarded, searched—not without some rough handling—and the envoys taken prisoner.

This was viewed, right across Europe, as an outrageous insult and a blatant act of provocation.

Angrily, Palmerston demanded an apology from the Union.

While he awaited President Lincoln's response, he ordered the army to begin amassing its troops on the Canadian border and the Royal Navy to prepare for attacks on American shipping the world over.

Toward the end of January, Lincoln's secretary of state responded by setting Slidell and Mason free and by explaining, in a letter, that the interception and searching of the *Trent*, while conducted in an unfortunate manner, had, in fact, been perfectly legal according to maritime law.

Palmerston was in no way mollified. He called an emergency cabinet meeting, stamped into the room, slammed his top hat onto the table, and flew into one of his infamous tantrums. "I don't know whether you're going to stand this," he screamed, "but I'll be damned if I do!"

The military buildup continued.

The prime minister ordered the construction of twelve shallow-draught ironclad steam battleships, designed specifically to operate in American coastal waters. Six new dreadnought-class rotorships were also built, all with bomb bays.

On the 4th of July 1862, Palmerston made two declarations. The first stated that Great Britain was now at war with Lincoln's Union. The second promised that any Irishman who agreed to join the British army would receive free transportation for his entire family to one of the Confederate States, plus two hundred pounds with which to purchase a home and start a new life.

In one fell swoop, he solved the immigration problem, relocated a homeless nation, and created one of the strongest and most willing armies the world had ever seen.

Even Napoleon III and Bismarck, both of whom had been threatening British interests in Europe, reluctantly admitted that the prime minister was a genius, an arch manipulator, and a man they'd rather not cross.

Abraham Lincoln sent a lengthy letter of protest, which contained the sentence: *If you are against the Union, you support slavery.*

Palmerston made history with his terse, five-word reply: *To hell with you, sir!*

Sir Richard Francis Burton hated slavery with a passion. He'd seen with his own eyes the wholesale destruction, humiliation, and misery it wrought—had seen the deep wounds that scarred Africa. It prompted him to now ask: "What of the slave trade, Prime Minister?"

Palmerston's right eyelid twitched. He drummed his long manicured fingernails on the mahogany desktop.

"I didn't call you here to examine my policies."

"Nor am I doing so. I'm merely curious to know whether there *is* a policy in this regard."

"I'll not have your impudence!"

"You misunderstand me. There is no challenge or disapproval in my words. I'm aware that Lincoln's Crittenden–Johnson Resolution states that his army is fighting to preserve the Union and not to end slavery. I am also aware that the Confederates mean to continue that filthy trade. So where do you stand?"

Palmerston slapped his hand down and shouted: "Damn you, man! How dare you question me?"

Very quietly, his voice barely above a whisper, Burton replied: "When I was in Arabia back in '53, I could have purchased a little black boy or girl for just one thousand piastres. I could have bought a eunuch for double that sum. Girls from the Galla country cost considerably more due to the fact that their skin remains cool in the hottest weather and is silky to the touch. Female slaves have their genitals mutilated before they are sold to prevent any possibility that they might enjoy sexual union. The theory is that it prevents them from straying. The wounds—"

"Stop! Stop! Your point is made!" Palmerston interrupted. "Very well, I'll tell you. When the Confederates win the war, they'll be in Britain's debt. I'll demand abolition as repayment."

"And if they refuse?"

"I'll block their trade routes."

"It's a big country."

"They may have a big country, sir, but I have a bigger Empire, and if they show one iota of ingratitude, I'll not hesitate to incorporate the old colonies back into it!"

Burton's eyes widened. "Good lord!"

"Empires require resources, Burton, which is why the whole of Europe is scrambling for Africa. With that accursed continent proving so damned intractable, perhaps the Americas are a better option. Much of them were ours in the past. All of them can be ours in the future."

"Surely you're not serious?"

Palmerston's mouth stretched even wider. "Perhaps it hasn't occurred to you that imagination is required in a politician?"

"But how could you possibly justify—"

"Justify? Justify? Justify to whom, sir?"

"To the electorate."

Palmerston threw his head back and made a crackling noise that may have been laughter.

"They already elected me, Burton. While I occupy this seat, I'll do what I think is best, whether they like it or not."

Burton shook his head in amazement. "You politicians are a breed apart."

Palmerston pulled a silver snuff tin from his waistcoat pocket and clicked open its lid. He placed a pinch of powder on the back of his right hand, raised it to his nose, and sniffed.

"Stanley's eight rotorchairs have turned up."

Burton blinked at the sudden change of subject then sat bolt upright. "Where?"

"They were found near the village of Ntobe, to the southwest of Speke's Lake Albert—"

"The Ukerewe Nyanza," Burton corrected.

"Call it what you will. An Arab trader discovered them. He—excuse me—" Palmerston turned his head and let loose a prodigious sneeze. He looked back at Burton with his left eye. The right had slipped out of alignment and was directed at the ceiling. "—he brought word back to Christopher Rigby, the consul at Zanzibar."

"And what of Stanley?"

"No sign. Have you caught up with the newspapers?"

"No. I returned yesterday. The only thing I've been catching up with is lost sleep."

"The *Times*, the *Globe*, and the *Empire* are calling for another expedition. A rescue mission. They all agree that there's only one man qualified to lead it."

"Who?"

"Sir Richard Francis Burton."

Burton's jaw clenched. He cleared his throat and said: "I'll start to make arrangements for—"

"You can't. You're busy."

"But, surely I—"

"I forbid it. You're under commission to the king. Your services are required here. I've spoken to Sir Roderick Murchison and, on his recommendation, the government will offer financial backing to the Baker and Petherick expedition."

Burton glowered ferociously and remained silent.

"Incidentally," Palmerston said, ignoring the explorer's expression, "on the subject of rotorchairs, His Majesty has ordered that a second be delivered to you. It's for Mr. Swinburne. Our monarch was most impressed with the young poet's contribution to your solving of the Spring Heeled Jack mystery."

"Thank you."

"You'll receive it some time this week."

The politician reached into a desk drawer and pulled out a sheaf of documents. With a slight air of embarrassment, he clipped pince-nez spectacles to the bridge of his nose. Behind their smoked-blue lenses, his right eye slid back into place. He peered down at the papers.

"Your dreadful penmanship seems to have improved remarkably," he noted. "I can actually read these reports."

"I've been using a writing machine."

"Really? I didn't know such a thing existed. Well now, you've been busy this summer, haven't you? These accounts are remarkable: *The Case of the Tottenham Court Road Vampire*; *The Men Who Jumped*; *The Secret of the Benevolent Sisters*; *The Problem of the Polite Parakeet*. You're earning your keep, though I rue your tendency to hang such lurid titles on your reports. These are government files, sir, not penny dreadfuls. That aside, I'm much satisfied."

He peered over the top of his lenses.

"But what of the Tichborne matter? Why am I still reading about it in my morning newspapers? Why have you spent the past three weeks overseas?"

Burton fished a cheroot from his jacket pocket. "Do you mind if I smoke, sir?"

"Yes, I do."

The king's agent looked at the Manila wistfully as he considered the Tichborne case. Since April, though working on other assignments, he and Swinburne had contrived to follow Kenealy and the Claimant. Now, at the tail end of September, events appeared to be building a new head of steam.

Steam! By God! He would forever associate the Tichborne case with steam! The entire season, London had been akin to a Turkish bath, enveloped in hot white vapour, quite unlike the usual "London particular" fogs.

It wasn't just the unusually hot weather causing the problem; it was also the frenzy of creativity that had gripped the Technologists. Their Eugenicists had simplified and perfected the process of breeding giant insects, and the Engineers were experimenting with species after species. In May, Isambard Kingdom Brunel had declared himself alive, much to the joy and astonishment of the British public. In his bell-like voice he'd announced: "Though I continue to be confined to this life-maintaining contraption, I have decided to end my seclusion in order to pursue a number of engineering projects. Thanks to the work of my Eugenicist colleagues, a wholly new method of transportation has become possible, and I can confidently predict that the wheel will soon be a thing of the past!"

By July, the number of steam-driven insects on the capital's roads had increased so dramatically that few could disagree with his claim. The city was literally swarming with scuttling, crawling, hopping, and buzzing vehicles, and, just as Detective Inspector Trounce had feared, the consequence was total chaos.

Amid all this, the Tichborne affair dragged on, and even with the capital in crisis and the country at war, it managed to make headlines on a weekly basis.

Burton had, for the time being, kept quiet about the François Garnier Choir Stones, not even telling Detective Inspector Trounce that they were embedded in the Claimant's head. Better to find out *why* they were there than to have the lumbering creature arrested for their possession and never discover what their opponent was up to. So the king's agent maintained his distance and watched as Dr. Edward Kenealy instigated legal action to recover Sir Roger's property.

Midway through May, there arrived at 14 Montagu Place a communiqué from Herbert Spencer, who was still below stairs at Tichborne House. It was delivered by a small blue and yellow parakeet, which landed on the study windowsill and tapped at the glass.

Burton had pulled up the sash and exclaimed: "By James! Surely it's Pox?"

"Shut your trap!" came the squawked response, then: "Message from the beautiful and magnificent Herbert Spencer. The Claimant, Kenealy, Jankyn, Bogle, and moronic Lord Lushington are holdin' weekly séances in the bloody billiard room. They've been summonin' the ghost of Lady Mabella. I haven't been able to overhear their conversations with her. Message bleeding well ends."

"Well now, I wonder what they're up to?" Burton muttered. "And why is Lushington playing along with them?"

"Stinky twisted bum-face!" POX JR5 responded.

"Message for Herbert Spencer," Burton said. "Get out of there. Take the swans home. Message ends."

Pox gave a whistle and flew away.

By early summer, the Tichborne case was such a cause célèbre that legal processes were hastened to bring it to trial as soon as possible. The Claimant was the plaintiff, of course, but, in truth, few people regarded him as such—he was going to have to prove that he was the man he represented himself to be.

The trial had opened in May.

Kenealy began by reviewing Sir Roger Tichborne's youth, which, he claimed, was a thoroughly unhappy affair. James Tichborne, he alleged, was an alcoholic and violent father, while the boy's domineering mother was smothering in the extreme.

Roger had been driven into the company of gamblers and reprobates, and this had eroded his aristocratic nature. It was then further weakened by the terrible ordeal he'd suffered during the many days adrift in a longboat after the sinking of *La Bella*.

"Undoubtedly," said Kenealy, "long exposure to the unremitting sun affected the young man's brain."

Rescued, Roger Tichborne was landed at Melbourne and wandered aimlessly through New South Wales until he eventually settled in the little town of Wagga Wagga. He lived there as Tomas Castro, a name borrowed from a man he'd known in South America, and worked as a humble butcher until the day he opened a newspaper and saw Lady Henriette-Felicité's plea for information.

After the reading of the affidavits, witnesses for the Claimant had been paraded before the court. They included Anthony Wright Biddulph, one of Sir Roger's distant cousins, who'd mumbled his way through an incoherent statement of support; Lord Rivers, a Rakish aristocrat who'd refused to reveal why he was providing money to the Claimant; and Guildford Onslow, a Liberal member of parliament who was very obviously working his own agenda.

A great commotion had then erupted when Colonel Lushington declared himself a firm supporter of "Sir Roger," even though it was he himself against whom the legal case had been brought.

Next, a number of Carabineers, who'd served with Tichborne, had come forward, as had residents from the estate, servants, a tailor, Sir Edward Doughty's former coachman, and, unsurprisingly—at least to Burton— Doctor Jankyn.

When the latter took the stand, he made a point of mentioning that while in the army Roger Tichborne had been tattooed on his left arm by a fellow soldier. The Claimant was asked to remove his jacket and roll up his shirtsleeve. He did so. His left forearm, quite unlike its opposite, was white and slender. On its inner surface, there was tattooed a heart overlaid with an anchor. About four inches above it, a line of rough stitches encircled the arm. The flesh on the other side of it was dark, coarse, and bulged corpulently.

In mid-June, Edward Kenealy sat down, Henry Hawkins stood up, and the cross-examination commenced.

Swinburne, in the gallery with Burton, made the observation that Sir Roger seemed to have grown even fatter.

"Sir Roger?" Burton asked.

Swinburne massaged his temples, winced, and mumbled: "Why do I keep saying that? I meant the Claimant, of course."

The court clerk said: "State your name, please."

"Sir Roger—Charles—Doughty Tichborne," came the drawling reply.

Hawkins tested the Claimant's education, his knowledge of the Tichborne family, and his familiarity with Roger Tichborne's history. To anyone with a modicum of intelligence, the replies were wholly unsatisfactory, yet somehow, opinions of the Claimant's performance differed in the extreme.

One journalist wrote:

In all the fifteen years I have spent reporting court dramas, I have never witnessed such a shambolic performance as that offered by the Tichborne Claimant. That anyone can doubt he is anything other than an audacious confidence trickster fair boggles this writer's mind.

Another countered with:

For shame! For shame! That a man should return home and be subjected to this pitiful circus! What foul plot has Sir Roger Tichborne in its clutches? For none who see him can possibly believe he is anyone other than the person he says he is.

The questioning continued through into July. During those hot, clammy weeks, the Claimant visibly swelled, growing so obese that the witness stand had to be rebuilt to accommodate him. His gums bled constantly, and when three of his back teeth dropped out, his speech became so difficult to follow that an amplifying screen was erected beside him.

Hawkins, by contrast, had been loud, erudite, and devastatingly effective.

"This person who presents himself to you as a lost aristocrat," he'd proclaimed to the jury, "is nothing but a conspirator, a perjurer, a forger, an impostor, a dastard—a villain!"

He'd then brought forth the first of his witnesses and had begun, piece by piece, to tear apart the Claimant's story.

By the third week of July, the jury had heard enough. They stopped the trial and asked the judge to allow them to come to a verdict. He agreed to their request.

The Claimant was found guilty of perjury. He was immediately arrested and incarcerated in Newgate Prison.

It was now a criminal matter.

Scotland Yard began to investigate his background.

So did Sir Richard Francis Burton.

The king's agent had travelled to New Orleans on the troop-carrying rotorship *Pegasus*. There he'd boarded a steamer, which transported him down to Buenos Aires, where he'd fallen in with an Englishman named William Maxwell, who was searching for his missing brother. Burton had helped, and the subsequent adventure—which he intended to log under the title *The Case of the Wayward Wendigo*—had, coincidentally, led to the completion of his mission.

He now reported the result to Lord Palmerston: "I know where Tomas Castro is."

"The man whose name the Claimant borrowed?"

"Yes."

"Where?"

Burton told him.

Lord Palmerston's eyebrows did not shoot upward, but that was only because they were no longer capable of such a movement.

"You need to speak to him," he said.

The king's agent grunted his agreement.

They spoke for a further forty minutes, then the prime minister turned his attention to a pile of parliamentary papers.

"I have to deal with matters of economy and foreign policy now, Captain. You are dismissed."

Burton rose to leave.

"One more thing—"

"Yes, sir?"

"In your report—these Eyes of Nāga stones—"

"Yes?"

"They're not the only black diamonds in existence. Am I correct?"

"You are, sir. There are others. However, the Eyes seem to be the only ones possessed of the peculiar properties that Sir Charles Babbage noted."

"Hmm."

Burton made to move to the door.

"Wait!" Palmerston snapped. "I have—I have a confession to make."

"A confession, sir?"

"I have not been entirely truthful with you. At the end of the Spring Heeled Jack case, I informed you that Edward Oxford's time-jumping suit had been destroyed."

"It hasn't?" asked Burton, with mock surprise. He'd never believed that particular assertion.

"No, it hasn't. I wanted it examined. If you recollect, Oxford wore a circular device attached to the front of it."

"I remember."

"The machinery inside it is baffling. There are no moving parts, for a start. My people have yet to identify a single component of the thing they can understand."

"So?"

"So they found six small black diamonds fitted into the device."

"Do they emit a low, almost inaudible hum, Prime Minister?"

"Yes, as a matter of fact, they do."

"Then in all probability, sometime in the future, they will be cut from one of the Eyes of Nāga."

The rapid clicks and scrapes of a fencing match filled Burton's study. It was *combat à la Florentine*—he and Admiral Lord Nelson were holding long knives in their off-hands, using them as a secondary defence.

Burton was being forced backward around one of his three desks by his valet. As he came abreast a bookcase, the clockwork man "broke time," suddenly changing the tempo of his attack, which caused Burton to miscalculate his parry. It was a classic move, but exercised with such speed and precision that it completely fooled the king's agent, whose foil flew wide. The brass man followed up with a *balestra*—a forward hop—and an *attaque composée*, which skipped lightly past Burton's instinctively raised knife to penetrate his defence before he could regain control.

The famous explorer grunted as the tip of his opponent's foil prodded into his right shoulder.

"Superb!" he cried enthusiastically. "Now do it again. I want to examine your change of balance when you break time. *En garde!*"

The competition continued.

Burton puffed and panted with exertion as his foil met and parried the clockwork man's thrusts. He backed across the hearthrug, avoided a *prise de fer*, and tried to press his opponent's foil aside. His valet responded by sliding his weapon from a high line to a low line, then twisted and lunged. Burton countered but Admiral Lord Nelson's move had been a feint; the brass man broke time again, skipped sideways then forward, and his *attaque composée* flashed past the opposing blade, his point stabbing hard against Burton's sternum.

"Bismillah, but you're good! Again! Again! *En garde!*"

Their foils clicked together.

There came a knock at the door.

"Not now!"

"You have a visitor, Sir Richard."

"I don't want to be disturbed, Mrs. Angell!"

"It's Detective Inspector Honesty!"

Burton sighed. "Disengage," he ordered.

Admiral Lord Nelson lowered his weapon. Burton did the same and pulled off his mask.

"Oh, very well," he called in exasperation. "Send him up!"

He took his valet's foil and placed it, and his own, in a case that lay on one of the desks.

"We'll continue later, Nelson."

The clockwork man saluted, walked across the room, and stood at attention next to the bureau between the two windows.

Moments later, there was a short sharp rap at the door.

"Come!"

It opened and Detective Inspector Honesty stepped in. There were beads of sweat on his brow.

"Hallo! Too hot. Hellish weather."

"Come in, old chap. Take that confounded jacket off if you don't want to cook!"

The Scotland Yard man divested himself of his outer garment, hung it on a coat hook behind the door, rolled up his shirtsleeves, and settled into a chair. He looked around the study with interest, running his eyes over the swords hanging on the walls, the heavily loaded bookcases, the teakwood chests, the pistols displayed in the alcoves on either side of the chimney breast, the huge African spear leaning in a corner, the three big desks, and the many souvenirs of Burton's travels.

Detective Inspector Honesty was a slightly built man and rather fussily dressed, but he had a wiry strength about him and Burton knew that he was a formidable opponent in hand-to-hand combat. His brown mustache was extravagantly wide, waxed, and curled upward at the ends. His hair was parted in the middle and lacquered flat. His eyes were grey. There was a monocle clenched in the right.

"Back yesterday?" he asked, in his characteristically clipped manner.

"The day before," Burton answered. "I spent most of yesterday reporting to the prime minister."

"Any luck in South America?"

"Yes, I know where Tomas Castro is."

"Do you, by crikey!" Honesty exclaimed, sitting upright. "Where?"

"In the Bethlem Royal Hospital."

"Bedlam? Lunatic asylum? Here in London?"

"Yes."

Burton took a cheroot from a box on the mantelpiece, applied a lucifer to it, and sat opposite the detective. He gave a quick nod of permission when Honesty half pulled a pipe from his waistcoat pocket. As the policeman went through the ritual of scraping its bowl and pressing in a plug of tobacco, the king's agent explained.

"I've had rather a high old time of it these weeks past. I shan't bore you with the details. Suffice it to say that I got caught up in an adventure that took me from Buenos Aires across Argentina and into Chile. There, I was able to trace the Castro family to Melipilla, a town on the main road between Valparaiso and Santiago. I met Pedro Castro, the son of Tomas, who revealed that his father went missing almost a decade ago while prospecting in the mountains with a Frenchman. This individual had been staying with the family for some weeks. I showed Pedro a daguerreotype of the Claimant. He recognised the face as the lodger's but was astonished at the size of his body. The Frenchman, apparently, had been very slim."

Honesty put a match to his pipe and muttered, "Impossible to get that fat. Even in ten years."

Burton nodded, and continued, "So Tomas and this Frenchman spent weeks prospecting until one day they never came back. Nothing further was heard until earlier this year, when rumours reached Pedro that a person named Tomas Castro was in an asylum in Santiago. He rode there to make enquiries and was told that, around the time of his father's disappearance, a man had been delivered to the establishment in a state of near insanity. He'd later, during a moment of lucidity, given his name as Castro. Naturally, Pedro wanted to see him, but was informed that the patient had recently been transported to London to be incarcerated in the Bethlem Royal Hospital. Apparently, he'd turned out to be from a rich English family. Pedro therefore concluded that the lunatic in question was neither his father nor the Frenchman."

"English!"

"Yes. So now we have to find out exactly who that man is."

"Roger Tichborne?"

"It seems likely. You'll remember that he was raised by a French mother and had a French accent."

"Which the Claimant doesn't."

"Notably."

Honesty asked, "Who took him from the Santiago asylum?"

"Ah, that's an interesting point."

"It is?"

"He was removed by a rather well-known individual."

"Who?"

"Nurse Florence Nightingale."

"The Lady of the Lamp!"

"The very same. Which, considering I was told she's missing, intrigues me a great deal!"

"Told by whom?"

"Isambard Kingdom Brunel, at the time of the Brundleweed robbery."

"By gum! What's she up to? We must see that man in Bedlam! A police raid, perhaps?"

"Good heavens, no! That would be far too heavy-handed! No, no, softly, softly, catchee monkey. Palmerston's men, Burke and Hare, are preparing false papers. In a couple of days, they and I will enter the asylum in the guise of government inspectors."

Honesty grunted and sucked thoughtfully at his pipe.

Burton pulled a cord at the side of the fireplace. He and his guest sat in contemplative silence until Mrs. Angell answered the summons. Burton requested a pot of coffee. As the old lady left, he turned back to the Yard man and said: "So Commissioner Mayne sent you to Australia to find out more about our faux aristocrat? How went it?"

"Went well. I took Commander Krishnamurthy. Remember him? Fine fellow. Head of Flying Squad now!"

"Yes, so I've heard. What did you two find down there?"

Honesty bent and placed his pipe on the hearth. He licked his lips, interlaced his fingers, and rested his hands in his lap. He eschewed long sentences, but he was now in a position where they might be necessary, and he needed to prepare himself.

The study door creaked open and footsteps padded across the room.

"Hello, Fidget," Burton muttered. He reached down to fondle his basset hound's ears. "I'm afraid you'll have to wait for your walk."

The dog sat at his feet and regarded the man opposite.

"In Wagga Wagga," Honesty began, "no one has heard of Tomas Castro. No one recognised the face in the daguerreotype. They did speak, however, of a man named Arthur Orton, a local butcher. Tremendously fat. Had an insatiable appetite for raw meat. Mysteriously disappeared."

"When?"

"Four weeks before the Claimant arrived in Paris."

"Ah!"

"Orton learned his skill as a butcher in London. He originally hailed from Wapping. Upon my return, I found the family. Interviewed his sisters. They say he moved to Australia some fifteen years ago. Never heard of again. I showed them the daguerreotype. They say it's not him."

The study door swung open and Mrs. Angell entered with the coffee. She poured them each a cup.

"Thank you, my dear," said Detective Inspector Honesty. The housekeeper smiled. There came an impatient hammering at the front door.

"I'll get it," she said, and departed.

"I have the distinct impression, Inspector," said Burton, "that a very tangled web has been woven."

"I should say so. Who's assaulting your door?"

"I'd recognise that knock anywhere. It's our mutual friend William Trounce."

Footsteps thundered up the stairs and the door was flung open. Trounce stamped in, ruddy-faced and puffing. He banged his bowler hat onto a desk.

"He's been released on bail!" he yelled. "Ah! Honesty! There you are! Hallo, Burton! Long time no see! The Claimant was taken to the Old Bailey at nine o'clock this morning and walked out a free man thirty minutes later. There was a crowd of cheering idiots to greet him. How the blazes has that fat monstrosity garnered so much support these past weeks, eh? Tell me that, Captain!"

He dragged an armchair over to them and plonked himself into it, rubbed his short hair vigorously, then punched one hand into the other.

"Blast it!" he shouted.

"Admiral Lord Nelson," Burton said to his valet, "would you fetch a cup for Detective Inspector Trounce, please?"

The clockwork man saluted, walked to the door, and left the room.

"I'll be blowed!" Honesty exclaimed. "Thought it was a suit of armour!"

Burton rubbed his chin thoughtfully. "I don't know, Trounce, old man," he said. "I don't know. But you're absolutely right—the most remarkable aspect of this case is that, from the very start, the Claimant has gained supporters left, right, and centre. Judging by what I've seen so far, I'd say he radiates some sort of powerful mesmeric influence, though why it affects some and not others is quite a mystery."

Burton remembered the people he'd seen in court rubbing their heads as if experiencing discomfort; Colonel Lushington's sudden headache when the Claimant arrived at Tichborne House; and Edwin Brundleweed's strange migraine.

It was the black diamonds, of course. Something was emanating from them. Sir Charles Babbage had said they could store and transmit the electrical fields generated by a human brain. All the evidence suggested they could influence a human brain as well.

"Your average man in the street seems under the impression that there's a conspiracy against the Claimant," Trounce said. "He's become a hero to the working classes."

"An aristocrat who laboured as a butcher," Honesty commented. "They like that."

Trounce grunted his agreement.

Admiral Lord Nelson entered with a cup in his hand.

"Pour Detective Inspector Trounce a coffee, would you?" Burton said.

"Good lord!" Honesty muttered as the clockwork man obeyed.

Strident screams and cries reached them from the street below.

"That sounds like young Swinburne," Trounce observed.

"Arguing with a cabbie, I'll wager," Burton agreed. "He's convinced that any cab ride, whatever the distance, costs a shilling, and he'll argue until he's blue in the face if the cabbie disagrees!"

He smiled. It had been a while since he'd seen his diminutive and highly eccentric assistant, and he'd missed him.

A few minutes later the doorbell jangled and a shout of, "Hallo, sweet angel!" floated up from the hall below. Footsteps sounded, the study door opened, and Mrs. Angell announced: "The eleven-thirty express has just pulled in at platform three, Sir Richard. Will there be much more traffic passing through the station this morning, or can I go and bathe my aching corns?"

"Send him in, Mother." Burton chuckled. "And consider the service suspended until further notice!"

As the landlady turned to leave, Swinburne bounded past her into the room.

"Hallo! Hallo! Hallo!" he cried. "Greetings one and all! Come on! Up and at 'em! Shake a leg! Hats on heads! Let's be off! We don't want to miss it!"

Burton crossed to his friend, shook his hand, slapped his back, and said: "Hello, Algy! Off where? Miss what?"

"I'm delighted to see you too, Richard, but a little less power to your welcome, if you don't mind! Every time you pat my back, I fear bones will break. By George, you look tanned! Was South America fun?"

"Hardly that."

"Hallo, Pouncer! Hallo, Honesty! How are London's crooks these days?"

"Busy," Honesty answered.

"Unusually so," added Trounce, frowning at Swinburne's use of his nickname.

"Maybe they think the steam hides their many sins! Move yourselves! Let's be off!"

"Blast it, Algy!" Burton growled. "Where to? And have you been drinking?"

"To see Kenealy and his corpulent client. They're about to perform at Speakers' Corner! Yes, I have. Quite frankly, I'm sloshed!"

"Speakers' Corner?" Trounce cried. "The Claimant's only just been freed from Newgate!"

"I know! But the streets are abuzz with it; he'll be lecturing the heaving throng within the hour! And I, for one, don't want the throng to heave without me!"

"I'm with you, my boy!" Trounce enthused.

Burton took a leash from the hatstand and clipped it to Fidget's collar. Jackets were buttoned, hats were placed on heads, canes were retrieved, and the four men and dog hurried out of the house into the haze of Montagu Place.

"Let's leg it down Gloucester," Swinburne suggested. "We'll be there in five minutes."

They strolled eastward, and, as they approached the corner, Mr. Grub's barrow came into view.

Burton touched the brim of his topper in greeting.

"Morning, Mr. Grub! How's business?"

"What's it to do with you?" came the snarled reply.

Burton halted and looked at the man in astonishment.

"I beg your pardon?"

"Oh, do yer? Well, you ain't gettin' it, you blasted snob!"

"I say!" Swinburne gasped.

Detective Inspector Honesty turned toward the vendor and stuck out his chest. "Better watch your manners!" he said. "Respect your betters!"

"Betters, is it? Ha! You ain't no better than nuffink, an' that's a fact!"

"Why, what on earth has got into you, Mr. Grub?" asked Burton, and Trounce added: "Come, come, dear fellow. Surely that's no way to talk!"

"Why don'tcha all clear off, hey?" Grub responded.

"Is something troubling you?" Burton enquired. "Has something happened?"

"All that's bleedin' well 'appened is that you're a-standin' on me patch gettin' in the way of them honest workin' folks what wants to buy cockles an' whelks."

"Well, what say I buy a bag?" Swinburne suggested. "I like my cockles with a sprinkling of vinegar, if you please." He hiccupped.

"I don't please, an' you can keep yer bloomin' money, you pipsqueak! Get away from 'ere! Go on! Skedaddle, the lot o' yer!"

The end of a tremendously long, thin leg thumped onto the road beside them as a harvestman of the order *Phalangium opilio* passed. The colossal arachnid—called by some a "daddy-long-legs"—was a one-man delivery vehicle. The carapace of its small oval body, which bobbed along twenty feet in the air as the eight elongated legs propelled it forward, had been carved into a bowl-shaped driver's seat, behind which a steam engine chugged. Beneath the body, a wooden crate dangled, held by netting.

The vehicle's twin funnels pumped a thick plume of steam into the air, and a tendril of the vapour curled down and rolled over the men, momentarily obscuring Mr. Grub. When he came back into view, he was holding his hand to his forehead and his face was twisted with pain.

"Why don't you all bugger off!" he mumbled as the bizarre vehicle vanished around a corner.

"I'm placing you under arrest for—" began Detective Inspector Honesty.

"No," Burton interrupted, gripping the smaller man's upper arm. "Leave him, there's a good chap. Let's move on."

"But—"

"Come!"

Burton guided the Yard man away, followed by Swinburne and Trounce. The latter looked back at the street vendor in puzzlement.

"By Jove! What extraordinary rudeness!" he muttered.

"And entirely out of character," Burton observed. "Perhaps he's having trouble at home."

"Should be arrested!" Honesty grumbled. "Insulting a police officer."

"There are bigger fish to fry," Burton noted.

They walked on down Gloucester Place until the northeastern corner of Hyde Park came into view. A big crowd had gathered there, comprised almost entirely of working-class men, with rolled-up shirtsleeves, suspenders, and cloth caps. A few top-hatted gents were hovering at the outer edges of the gathering. Dr. Kenealy and the Claimant could be seen near a podium. They were encircled by a number of foppishly dressed individuals—obviously Rakes—who appeared to be acting as bodyguards.

"What a crowd!" Trounce observed as they pushed their way into the mob.

"All come to goggle at the freak!" Swinburne said.

A man with pocked skin and bad teeth leaned close and said: "He ain't no bloomin' freak, mister. He's an haristocrat what's been cheated outa what's rightfully 'is by the blasted lawyers!"

"My good sir!" the poet protested.

"Go about your business," Trounce commanded.

The man sneered nastily, turned his back, and hobbled away, swearing under his breath.

They stood and waited.

Ten minutes later, Burton asked, "Is it my imagination or are we on the receiving end of some rather hostile glances?"

"Shhh!" Swinburne responded. "The Claimant's about to speak!" He pulled a silver flask from his jacket pocket and swigged from it.

The grossly obese giant had heaved himself up onto the podium. The crowd spontaneously broke into song:

"I've seen a great deal of gaiety throughout my noisy life,
With all my grand accomplishments I ne'er could get a wife,
The thing I most excel in is the P. R. F. G. game,
A-noise all night, in bed all day, and swimming in Champagne!"

Swinburne laughed, and in a loud, high-pitched voice, joined in with the chorus:

"For Champagne Charlie is my name;
Champagne Charlie is my name,
Good for any game at night, my boys;
Good for any game at night, my boys,
Champagne Charlie is my name;
Champagne Charlie is my name,
Good for any game at night, boys;
Who'll come and join me in a spree?"

"Be quiet, you idiot—you're attracting attention!" Burton hissed.

Dr. Kenealy climbed up beside his client and waved for the crowd to quiet down.

Reluctantly, it did so.

"I'd like to introduce to you," he began, in a loud voice, "a man who is well acquainted with this country's aristocratic families, due to the fact that he is himself one of their number."

"Boo!" hooted someone close to Burton and his colleagues.

"In fact," Kenealy continued, "he is actually a distant cousin of my client!"

"Hurrah!" yelled the man who'd just booed.

"Please spare a little of your time for Mr. Anthony Biddulph!"

Kenealy stepped down and a short, skinny man sporting a mustache and bushy side whiskers took his place at the Claimant's side.

"My friends," Biddulph boomed, in a surprisingly powerful tone, "I could point out several English gentlemen who would not pass muster as English gentlemen any better—" he placed a hand on the Claimant's forearm "—than this man here does."

Laughter and jeers from the crowd.

"For no matter the circumstances of their birth, they are apparently no better than farmers, and I would place Tichborne among that class."

"Cor blimey! You ain't suggestin' that aristos are stupid, are yer?" someone shouted.

The crowd cheered.

"I refer to the accusations that have been levelled at this man which suggest he can't be who he says he is because he seems uneducated. Well, let me tell you, I have heard of persons called English gentlemen who were so illiterate in conversations that you would take them to be nothing better than pig-jobbers!"

"There ain't nuffink wrong wiv a pig-jobber!" cried a voice. "I should know, I be one meself—an' I hain't hilliterate neither!"

More laughter.

"Quite so!" Biddulph cried. "And this man is unique in his class in that he knows what it means to earn his daily crust!"

Long enthusiastic cheers erupted.

Biddulph stepped down.

"Tichbooooorne," the Claimant rumbled, grinning vacantly. A string of drool swung from his lower lip.

Kenealy reappeared beside him. "You have all heard our enemies' protestations!" he cried. "You all know that they refuse to believe that this man is Sir Roger Tichborne."

"It's a conspiracy!" someone shouted.

"Precisely!" Kenealy agreed. "Precisely! I have here a former Carabineer who served at my client's side; slept in the same barracks; spent day after day in his company! Spare a moment, if you will, for Mr. James M'Cann!"

He removed himself from the podium again and was replaced by a burly individual, who, in a melodramatic tone, announced: "There's no doubt in my mind that the man who stands at my side, though rather stouter than previous—"

Loud guffaws all around.

"—is undoubtedly Roger Tichborne, or 'Frenchy,' as we used to call him. I recognised him the instant I saw him by his forehead, head, and ears."

More laughter, cheers, and jeers.

"His ears I knew well by seeing him in bed every morning for two years."

"Stuck out from under the blankets, did they?" came a distant voice.

Burton stood on tiptoe and looked back. The crowd had more than trebled in size since he and his friends had arrived.

"There is nothing extraordinarily particular about the ears that I know of," M'Cann answered. "Only I knew 'em. I don't know if I could have recognised him from his ears if I had seen nothing else."

A fresh outburst of raucous laughter rippled through the crowd. Cloth caps were thrown into the air.

Steam billowed over the gathering, rolling from east to west. The platform was momentarily obscured, and when Burton saw it clearly again, M'Cann had departed and Edward Kenealy was silencing the vast audience.

"Sir Roger Tichborne will now address you directly," he proclaimed.

This was greeted by more cheering, which quickly gave way to an expectant silence.

The Claimant grinned, and drawled, "Cruelly persecuted is what I am. Yesss. There is but—one course I can—seeee, and that is to—to—to adopt the suggestion so many have made to me. Thus, I must a-appeal to you—the British public—for funds for my—my—my defence. Yesss. I appeal to you to help defend the weak against—against—against the strong."

Burton looked down at Fidget in surprise. The hound was growling ferociously and all along his spine the hair was standing on end. The king's agent looked up and around. For the most part, the gathering seemed transfixed by the Claimant. Off to his left, though, it appeared that an argument was developing between a small group of gentlemen and the workers surrounding them. There were also—

Burton blinked and peered into the steam. *Bismillah!*

There were *things* moving in the ever-shifting white vapour!

"Look!" he hissed at his friends.

Unfortunately, Swinburne, Trounce, and Honesty were too short to see over the heads of the men surrounding them, so only Burton was aware that vague, wispy, and transparent figures were materialising among the crowd, dispersing then re-forming, glimpsed then instantly doubted. He could only see them from the corners of his eyes; the moment he directed his gaze full upon them, they seemed to melt away.

He rubbed a hand across his face, squeezed his eyes shut, and opened them again.

A sudden cry of pain came from one of the gentlemen off to the left.

"What was that? What's happening?" Trounce demanded.

"I insist—upon," the Claimant declared, "fair play for—for every maaan!"

"A fight has broken out," Burton answered. He started to shoulder his way toward the scuffle, with Fidget at his heels and Swinburne and the two police detectives following behind.

"I look—to the—the working classes!" the fat orator bellowed, his voice thick and slurred. "That noble part of the—the—the British public!"

The crowd loosed a deafening roar of approval.

Burton saw a top hat knocked from a head.

"Watch where you're bleedin' well goin', you stupid git!" a man spat as the king's agent pushed past.

"Them lawyers call me such baaad names, yesss," the Claimant rumbled.

Burton nearly tripped over a body that lay sprawled on the grass. He looked down and saw a well-dressed youth whose nose had been badly bloodied. A brutish-looking older man, dressed in canvas trousers and a grimy cotton shirt, was in the act of swinging his booted foot into the prone youngster's side.

Burton pushed the assailant away.

"Get off him, man!"

"Oy! What's it to do wiv you?" came the aggressive response.

"Yeah, tell 'im to keep 'is toffee-nose out of it, Jeb!" another of the crowd added.

Swinburne bent to help the young gentleman to his feet but hiccupped, lost his balance, and pitched over on top of him.

"Oops!" he said.

The man pushed him aside, cast him a doubtful look, retrieved his dented top hat, scrambled to his feet, and backed away.

Trounce and Honesty positioned themselves at either side of the king's agent.

The man named Jeb stepped close to Burton until their noses were just inches apart and tried to stare him down.

"Are you an' your pals gonna get in my way, chum?"

"My *pals* are from Scotland Yard," Burton replied quietly, his sullen and intense gaze holding firm.

Jeb looked from Burton to Trounce to Honesty then back at Burton.

"Need the ladies' protection, do yer? Can't take care o' yerself, I suppose?"

"Ow!" Swinburne yelled.

Jeb looked down and saw a small basset hound with its teeth embedded in the little red-haired man's ankle. He looked up and saw Burton's knuckles. The punch caught him square between the eyes and he stumbled backward, with blood spraying from his nose, into one of his cohorts.

Trounce and Honesty swooped and grabbed him by the arms. He struggled, shouting incoherently.

Burton saw madness in the man's eyes and shuddered. Faces in the crowd were turned toward the commotion. There were mutterings and curses. He snapped his head around as something seemed to flit past to his right. He had an impression of a ghostly figure but saw only steam, coiling and curling.

"Get out of here!" a voice hissed. "Scarper while you can, Boss!"

He turned and was surprised to find Herbert Spencer, with a flat cap pulled low over his forehead, standing at his side.

The young gent with the bloodied nose muttered, "Thank you," and pushed past the onlookers to join his friends, three well-dressed young men who were standing nervously nearby. They moved away, with catcalls and hoots of derision following them.

"Be quiet!" Detective Inspector Trounce shouted angrily.

"Make us!" came a challenge.

Honesty twisted Jeb's arm up behind his back, holding it locked there with one hand. With the other, he pulled a truncheon from his belt. Trounce noticed the move and followed suit.

"It's the pri—privileged what decides the—the fate of honest folk!" came the Claimant's voice. "And I have no doubt—that—lawyers can do a great many things, yesss. They freq—freq—frequently make black appear—appear white. But I'm sorry to say, they more freq—frequently make white app—appear black!"

Burton frowned. Everything the Claimant said sounded rehearsed. They were plainly not his own words.

"There's trouble a-brewing!" Spencer whispered. "Can you see the wraiths? They're the same as what I saw down by the lake at Tichborne House. I reckons it's them what's turnin' the crowd ugly!"

"I think you're right," Burton replied, looking around at a sea of angry faces.

Trounce and Honesty began to force their way through the throng, dragging their prisoner after them. They were cursed and insulted as they pushed past men whose faces were contorting with fury and contempt.

"Why, hallo, Herbert!" Swinburne said, noticing the vagrant philosopher for the first time. "Exciting, isn't it? Are you resisting the influence? I am!"

"Algy!" said Burton. "What are you prattling about?"

"They're trying to make me think old flabby guts is Roger Tichborne," his assistant replied. "I can feel them prodding at my head. But this time they can't get in!"

He raised his fists and dodged about, taking wild swipes at the air.

"Bloody spooks! You'll not get me!"

Fidget bit him again.

"Argh!"

"Stop it, you drunken ass," Burton snapped. "Calm down. Let's make ourselves scarce before this lot get any nastier."

Swinburne swayed. "My hat! I'm absolutely blotto," he grumbled, fumbling for his flask.

The three of them and Fidget followed the two policemen. They weathered a worsening storm of abuse from those they passed.

One man, a big bearded fellow, stepped forward and swung a fist at Burton. The king's agent ducked beneath it and rammed his own into the man's stomach.

"Bastard!" someone yelled.

Kenealy's voice rang out over the cloth-capped heads.

"You have heard my client speak! I say again, there is a conspiracy against him! The government is attempting to prosecute a man who they know is innocent of the charges made against him! The object is clear: they wish to keep the large Tichborne estate in the hands of the Arundell and Doughty families— families that we all know possess undue influence in many sections of English society! Catholic families! Catholic, I say! Are we going to stand for it?"

"No!" the onlookers roared.

Trounce and Honesty, heaving the writhing Jeb along, broke through the edge of the crowd, with Burton, Swinburne, Spencer, and Fidget in their wake.

Burton noticed that the four young gents who'd moved away a few minutes earlier were once again enduring rough handling at the hands of thuggish men. Their hats had been knocked to the ground and stamped on, their walking canes broken. As he made to go to their aid, more men separated from the crowd and ran over to Trounce and Honesty, jumping onto them with fists flying. Trounce was struck on the back of the head by a beefily built individual. He went down. Burton ran and dived at the attacker, catching him around the waist. He lifted him clean off his feet and dashed him to the ground.

Jeb, meanwhile, his left arm still locked in Honesty's iron grip, sent his right fist arcing up toward the smaller man's chin. Honesty jerked his head back, the fist flew up past his face, and he replied by ramming his truncheon into Jeb's rib cage. The big man groaned and fell to his knees.

Trounce, struggling to his feet, caught a boot that was swinging at his face and twisted it violently. The man to whose leg it was attached pitched over.

A mean-looking fellow dug his fingers into Honesty's shoulder. Burton caught him by the collar, wrenched him around, and sent him spinning into others who were coming to join the fray. They all went down in a tangled heap.

The king's agent barked a command at Herbert Spencer: "Grab Swinburne and drag him away from here!"

Spencer made a move toward the poet but was sent staggering when a small wiry man swung a metal rod into his forehead. As the vagrant philosopher stumbled into him and they both fell to the grass, Swinburne looked up and saw that the attacker possessed a perfectly enormous nose.

"Bloody hell! It's Vincent Sneed!" he cried, for it was the man who'd been his employer when he'd masqueraded as a sweep during the Spring Heeled Jack case. "It's the Conk!"

Sneed looked down at him with a vicious light in his piggy eyes.

"What didja call me?" he hissed. "The Conk, is it? The Conk? Who the heck are you to—to—" His eyes widened. "Stone me!" he breathed. "It's you! The blinkin' whippersnapper what left me in the lurch!"

"And gladly so, you callous blackguard!" Swinburne declared as he pushed himself to his feet. "What in God's name has prompted you to set foot outside of the East End?"

Sneed stuck out his scrawny chest and said with pride, "I'm a funnel scrubber, ain't I!"

Funnel scrubbers worked on the big Technologist rotorships, cleaning out the pipes and exhausts. The job was a step up for a lowly chimney sweep, and paid enough to get a man out of the slums and into cheap lodgings.

Sneed cast his eyes over the smaller man's smart jacket, waistcoat, and trousers. "What're you a-wearin' them gentleman's togs for?"

"Because, Mr. Conk," Swinburne replied, "it just so happens that I *am*— hic!—a gentleman, and, as such, I feel honour bound to—"

Without bothering to finish his sentence, Swinburne let out a piercing scream and charged forward with his head bent low, driving it straight into Sneed's stomach. The East Ender grunted as the wind was knocked out of him, but managed to fling his arms around the poet's waist and heaved him up, head downward.

"All right, you little rat——" he began.

"Oh no you don't!" Herbert Spencer cried, and kicked Sneed's legs from under him. The sweep fell flat on his back and Swinburne's shoulder buried itself in his groin.

"Oof!" he gasped, and as the poet rolled off him, Sneed curled into a ball and vomited onto the grass.

"Ha!" Swinburne yelled. "That'll teach you, you swine!" The poet adopted what he thought might be a boxer's stance and swayed unsteadily. "Come on! Get up so I can knock you down again!"

"Beggin' your pardin for a-sayin' so," Spencer interrupted, "but you ain't got no chance against the likes o' this scoundrel." He grabbed Swinburne by the wrist. "So just you follow me out o' this here affray."

"What? No! I want to punch him on the blasted nose, Herbert! The fiend treated me foully when I was——" Swinburne's words were lost in the escalating commotion as Spencer dragged him away and off toward the edge of the crowd.

Sneed took a great gulp of air and yelled after them: "I'll get you yet, you pipsqueak! This ain't finished by a long shot! By God, I'll flay you alive!"

Burton, meanwhile, was helping Detective Inspector Trounce up off his knees. "Come on, Trounce. Hey! Honesty! Leave that man! Let's go!"

"He's under arrest!" Honesty protested. His dapper appearance had been considerably dishevelled.

"He's more trouble than he's worth!" Burton shouted above the noise of the angry crowd. He bent and picked up Fidget.

Herbert came abreast of him, dragging Swinburne.

"Naargh!" the poet cried, incoherently. He broke away from the philosopher, swung his fist at nothing in particular, missed, and stumbled. Spencer bent low, scooped him up, and threw him over his shoulder.

Burton and his companions backed away from the crowd.

The workers howled abuse at them and shook their fists.

"What in God's name is happening?" Trounce gasped.

"There's a riot developing," Burton said, "and we have to get out of it immediately. Are you all right? You took a blow to the head."

"I know. It's aching abominably."

"Mine, too," Honesty noted. "But I wasn't hit."

"Me neither, but I have a throbbing at the back of my skull, too," said Burton.

"I'm fine," put in Spencer. "P'raps it's me life on the streets what's given me a stronger constitution."

They hurried out of the crowd, pushing aside swearing, threatening individuals, and hurried away from Speakers' Corner and into Park Lane. Men poured into the streets behind them. There came the sounds of breaking glass, screams, yells, and crashes. Burton glanced back and saw a group pushing a hansom cab onto its side. A velocipede was stopped, its rider pulled off the high saddle and punched in the face.

The king's agent and his companions jogged along the pavement until they came to the corner of Edgware Road. They hastened down the wide thoroughfare. A millipede omnibus—they were now known as "omnipedes"—thundered past and the cloud belching from its sides curled across the street. Two ghostly figures formed within the vapour then faded from sight.

"Put me down," Swinburne groaned.

Spencer placed the poet on his feet and the little man doubled over and clutched his head.

Burton held his assistant by the arm. "Is it the same pain you felt in the labyrinth at Tichborne House?"

"Yes. Pounding at my brain! I tell you, Richard, it's like they're trying to get inside of me!"

Trounce looked at the little poet. "By James, I know what he means!"

"An invisible force of some sort is trying to influence us," Burton answered. "It succeeded before with Algy, but this time it's met with some resistance."

Detective Inspector Honesty turned to his fellow officer. "Better summon reinforcements. Riot in progress. Could be bad."

Trounce ran a hand over his forehead. "Of course. I'm forgetting my duties. By Jove, I can hardly think straight! Captain Burton, Detective Inspector Honesty and I had better get to work. We'll whistle for constables, see if we can get that rabble under control."

Burton put Fidget down, clipped on the lead, then shook the two men's hands. "Very well. Good luck! And be careful."

The Scotland Yard men dashed away, and the king's agent turned to the vagrant philosopher.

"Thank you, Herbert, you helped us out of a tight squeeze. What were you doing there, anyway?"

"Workin' the crowd, Boss."

"You mean begging?"

"Yus."

"But you're gainfully employed now!"

"More or less, but I like to keep me hand in, so to speak. Waste o' time, though. Them what was a-givin' were givin' to the Claimant, not to me!" He looked down at Swinburne, who was leaning heavily on Burton for support. "How you feelin', lad?"

"I need a brandy."

Burton snorted. "I think you've had quite enough!"

"Bloody Vincent Sneed, of all people!" the poet moaned.

"Herbert, you'd better come home with us. I'll dress that wound on your forehead," Burton said.

They moved along Edgware Road then turned into Seymour Place. People ran past, all going in the same direction. Velocipedes and hansoms clattered by, too, pumping steam into the already laden atmosphere as they fled from the disturbance. Burton clearly saw a well-dressed wraith materialise in the vapours and drift across the cobbles to where a chaunter was leaning against a lamppost. The man's eyes were closed and he seemed oblivious to both the approaching phantom and the panic around him as he mournfully sang "Molly Malone:"

"She was a fishmonger,
But sure 'twas no wonder,
For so were her father and mother before,
And they each wheeled their barrow,
Through streets broad and narrow,
Crying, 'Cockles and mussels, alive, alive-o!'"

The wraith hovered around the man. For a moment the apparition became almost completely opaque, taking on the appearance of a tall, stooped bearded man, then it faded from sight. The chaunter paused, winced, shook his head, then continued singing, but his song had changed, though he didn't seem to realise it:

"Give me the man of honest heart,
I like no two-faced dodger,
But one who nobly speaks his part,
Like Kenealy does for Roger!
One honest lawyer's found at last,
Who'll ne'er desert his client,
He knows right well the cause is just,
He stands up like a giant.

"Then say men say,
Be you low or rich born,
And have fair play,
For Kenealy and for Tichborne."

"Aye!" a passing costermonger cried. "Give a cheer for brave Sir Roger!" Various voices answered his call: "Hurrah! Hurrah! Hurrah!"

"Bastard upper-crust bastards!" a milk deliveryman yelled. "Bastard bloomin' bastards!"

He bent, pulled a loose cobble from the road, and threw it through a house window.

Burton and Herbert Spencer, dragging Swinburne and Fidget along, entered Montagu Place and mounted the steps of number 14.

The front door was open. A table had been overturned in the hallway, pictures on the wall were hanging askew, and young Oscar Wilde, the newspaper seller, was picking pieces of a shattered vase up from the floor inside. His face was scratched, as if gouged by fingernails.

Muffled screams and thuds sounded from the cupboard beneath the stairs.

"What's been happening here, Quips?" Burton exclaimed, plonking Swinburne onto a hall chair.

"Oh, there you are, Captain," said Oscar. "I was passing by and heard some sort of brouhaha from your house. As you know, my own business always bores me to death, I prefer other people's, so I poked my nose in. It seems your little maid has lost her mind. She was attacking Mrs. Angell, so she was."

"What? Young Elsie? Is Mrs. Angell all right? Where is she?"

"Don't be worrying yourself, Captain, she's fine and dandy. She took herself downstairs to rest awhile. I said I'd clean up the mess."

"Thank you, Quips. You're a good lad." Burton set the table upright. "You locked Elsie in the cupboard, I take it?"

"To be sure. 'Twas the only way to keep the young madam from wrecking the entire house. Phew! What a wildcat!"

Burton sighed. "Well, she can stay in there until she calms down. I'd ask what the devil got into her, but I suspect the answer would be Tichborne!"

"Aye, something of the sort. She was screaming incoherently, but from what I could make out, she seems to have acquired a bee in her bonnet about the suppression of the working classes."

"Tichborne isn't working class," Swinburne mumbled.

"You're right there, Mr. Swinburne! But the man who *says* he's Sir Roger most certainly is, don't you think?"

"It seems obvious," said Burton, "but a surprising number of people don't see it that way. If what I witnessed today is any indication, three-quarters of the population are supporting a man they know is a liar and charlatan. It's utter lunacy!"

"Ah well, now I know you haven't been affected," Oscar responded. "To disagree with three-fourths of the British public is one of the first requisites of sanity!"

BEDLAM

The Best Cookery Book in the World

Miss Mayson's Book of Household Management

Strongly bound, 12s. 6d. net ; also half-Morocco.
Containing over 2,000 pages of Letterpress, besides hundreds of
Illustrations and many Coloured Plates. Forming a complete guide to:

COOKERY IN ALL ITS BRANCHES, plus

Daily Duties, Hostess and Guest, Menus and Menu Making, Sick Nursing,
Discipline of Servants, Marketing and Accounts,
Problematical Tobacco Stains, Eugenically Enhanced Foods,
Care of Children, Mechanical Aids, Automated Animals, The Home Doctor,
The Home Lawyer, Whisker Trimming.

From all Booksellers, or from the Publishers,

STAGG, BOSCOE & Co., Ltd., Salisbury Square, London, E.C.4.

Algernon Swinburne pulled his legs up onto the saddlebag armchair and crossed them. He accepted a cup of coffee—his second—from Admiral Lord Nelson, rested the saucer on his ankles, and gazed down into the liquid.

"Whatever that headache I had was, it's been replaced by a different one. A hangover. Strange to say, that's actually a relief!"

Herbert Spencer, sitting opposite, his eyes fixed on the clockwork valet, nodded distractedly, and took a sip from his own cup.

Burton, ever the observer, was standing by the window looking down at the street. He saw isolated instances of vandalism and misbehaviour but, in the main, the riot had bypassed Montagu Place, though distant shouts and crashes suggested that it was in full swing elsewhere.

"I daresay the food helped, Algy. It was good of Mrs. Angell to cook for us after her ordeal."

"She's everything her name suggests," Swinburne responded. "I feel much happier now that my stomach is full."

"Here's something else to cheer you up. I meant to tell you earlier but it slipped my mind. There's a second rotorchair in my garage. A gift to you from His Majesty."

"My hat! A present from the king! How splendid!"

"Don't get too excited. We're going to have to be cautious about using the flying machines during this Tichborne business. Our opponent has already demonstrated an uncanny ability to deprive springs of their elasticity, thus disabling clocks, wind-up lanterns, and the hammer mechanisms of gun triggers. Since rotorchair engines employ spring pistons, I think we'll stick with swans for the time being."

"Blast! I have a new toy and I can't play with it!"

"We may have to drop our ideas about John Speke, too. Whatever is going on, it seems less and less likely to me that he's behind it."

"Why so?"

"Because what began as the theft of diamonds has broadened into some sort of political agitation. That's not John's style at all. He's far too selfish a man to care about such matters."

"Then who? Edward Kenealy?"

Herbert Spencer interrupted: "No, lad. Back at the house, after you left, Kenealy was a-holdin' séances to consult with Lady Mabella. If you ask me, the ghost is the one pullin' the strings."

Burton made a sound of agreement, but then the words *the puppeteer is herself a puppet* flashed through his mind.

"The odd thing is," he said, "when Sir Alfred was being dragged through the house to his death, the apparition warned me not to interfere. I heard her voice clearly in my mind and it had a distinct accent. Russian, I'm positive."

"Why is that odd?" asked Swinburne. "Aside from the obvious."

"Because Lady Mabella Tichborne was from Hampshire."

"Hamp—what? She was English?"

"Thoroughly. So whatever's been haunting Tichborne House, it is *not* the ghost of the woman who crawled around the wheat fields. In fact, I doubt that it's really a ghost at all."

"It looked like one to me."

"Then perhaps you can explain why it was rapping its knuckles on walls rather than floating straight through them?"

"You have an explanation?"

"I have never given credence to ghosts, but I've read much about what spiritualists term the projection of the ethereal or astral double. Occultists state that it is perfectly possible to pass through solid objects while in astral form, but it should not be done too often, as it can disrupt the connection between the ethereal and the physical bodies. My supposition is that we witnessed an individual in such a form, and they solidified their knuckles for the purpose of searching the house rather than risk being forever separated from their corporeal body."

Swinburne jerked his limbs spasmodically—a sign of his growing excitement.

"So we're dealing with a spiritualist, a table-tapper?"

"That's my current theory, and one who appears to be using the Cambodian fragments and the South American Eye to somehow transmit and amplify mediumistic projections. I'm almost certain that support for the Claimant—who anyone in their right mind can see is a phony—is, through this method, being artificially generated to stir up the masses. What puzzles me is why the emanations influence some and not others. You are apparently rather sensitive to them, though more resistant when you're drunk. Myself, Trounce, and Honesty feel them only faintly, while Herbert here is not touched at all."

"From what I can see, the working classes are the most susceptible," put in Swinburne. "Though I'd hardly place myself in that category. Whereas Herbert—"

"—is a bloomin' philosopher," the vagrant interjected. He tore his eyes away from the mechanical man and peered at the poet from beneath his bushy grey eyebrows, one of which was raised speculatively.

"Quite so. Quite so," Swinburne conceded. "Forgive me for the observation, though, my dear chap, but you seem to be a singularly unsuccessful one. What exactly is your philosophy? Perhaps the nature of your thoughts bears some relation to your apparent immunity."

"That's an interesting hypothesis," Burton said. He faced his two guests. "Talk to us, Herbert."

"Hmmph!" Spencer grunted. "You'll have to give me a minute or two to prepare meself. It don't come easy to me, I'm afraid."

"Go ahead. Take whatever time you need."

The king's agent and his assistant looked on in interest as the vagrant set his glass aside, propped his elbows on the arms of his chair, steepled his fingers in front of his face, closed his eyes, and laid his head back. He relaxed, and a remarkable tranquillity seemed to wash over him.

Swinburne looked at Burton, who whispered almost soundlessly: "Self-mesmerism!"

The clock on the mantelpiece clicked softly.

Distant shouts and crashes sounded from outside.

Two minutes passed.

Herbert Spencer sniffed, cleared his throat, and began to talk. Astonishingly, he was suddenly possessed of a finely spoken, urbane, and educated voice.

"Well, gentlemen," he said, without shifting position or opening his eyes, "let's see if I can offer you a little food for thought. To illustrate the core of my philosophy, I would ask you to imagine that you are blindfolded and don't know where you are. You stretch out your hands and walk slowly ahead until you encounter a wall. It may be a single wall blocking your way or it could be the side of a room. You don't know. Your only certainty is that the wall is there. So what do you do? I haven't a notion. What I *do* know is this: whatever your next action, it will be done in relation to the fact that you ran into that wall. Maybe you'll climb over it. Maybe you'll try to knock it down. Maybe you'll build a house adjacent to it."

Burton and Swinburne glanced at each other, amazed at their friend's eloquence and perfect intonation; wondering where his words were leading.

"The question now is this: if you weren't the only blindfolded person to have bumped into the wall—let's say, for argument's sake, that twenty others have done so, too—which of you is best able to make the most of your situation? I'm not referring to the strongest or most intelligent or most resourceful; what I mean to ask is, which of you happens to be in possession of the abilities and attitude that can best adapt to the circumstance of encountering a wall? Am I making sense?"

"Manifestly," Swinburne replied. "When we first met, you used the phrase 'survival of the fittest.' You're referring to that, yes?"

Spencer opened his eyes, which were oddly glazed, and jabbed a finger at the poet.

"Exactly! However, don't mistake the 'fittest' for the healthiest or the cleverest or any other specific trait. I use it in the same sense that a square peg 'fits' into a square hole. The fittest man is the one most constitutionally suited to the conditions in which he finds himself. It's a two-way relationship: the particular nature of the individual confronting the particular nature of reality. Or, I should say, what appears to be reality."

"What *appears* to be?" Burton asked.

"That's right, because it isn't possible to know if the reality you perceive is all there is. You can only deal with what you are cognizant of."

Burton frowned and nodded. "Knowledge is phenomenal? It pertains only to appearance—or in the case of your blindfolded individual, to the other material senses?"

Spencer resumed his closed-eyed, steeple-fingered position.

"Something like that, yes, though I don't mean to suggest that it's necessarily deceptive. We might only be aware of a small portion of reality, but it is reality nevertheless, so however we apprehend it, that apprehension has validity.

"Existence, then, is, I posit, a continuous adjustment of internal relations to external relations. Which brings us to the crux of the matter, for if our existence depended not upon such adjustments but rather upon quantifiable attributes such as strength, health, and endurance—and if reality were known in its entirety and measured, mapped, and gauged—then it would be easy to determine one individual's chances of survival against another's. The Eugenicists propose the improvement of the human race on just such a basis. They are in error. What they overlook is that, because one person's reality isn't necessarily the same as another's, so the traits required to best prosper differ from person to person."

Swinburne bounced in his chair excitedly. "I see! I see! A man who perceives a barrier needs the dexterity to climb over it, while the man who sees a foundation would benefit from the talent to design and erect a structure upon it."

The philosopher nodded without reopening his eyes.

"Just so. These differing notions of life and how to best deal with it have caused the human race to tend toward greater heterogeneity. Individuals are becoming more specialised and differentiated as they each adapt to their own perception. To compensate for this diversification, we, as a species, have developed the ability to integrate almost everyone by creating an interdependent society.

"If we allow the Eugenicists to alter the race according to their infinitesimally narrow criteria, I think it almost certain that this interdependence will collapse and extinction will follow."

With eyes fixed on the vagrant philosopher, Burton moved to his saddleback armchair and sat down. "While I find myself in agreement with your notion of interdependent diversity," he said, thoughtfully, "do you not think that it is overwhelmed by a rather more dominant division? I speak of that which we've seen demonstrated today—to wit, the segregation of society into the working and the educated classes."

"Ah, Captain Burton, you have hit the nail on the head. The Eugenicists may be wrong in their approach, but they are correct in their assessment that our society, in its present divided form, must either change or die. It is what prompted me to bring Darwin's theory into the picture."

"How so, Herbert?"

"You see, when the mechanism of natural selection is transposed from the biological to the social arena, we can immediately see that our interdependence has become so extreme that evolution cannot possibly occur. Individuals have become *too* specialised. Consider our prehistoric ancestor. He knew how to create a fire, make a weapon, hunt an animal, fashion clothes and a shelter from its skin, cook it and eat the flesh, carve tools from its bones, and so much more. What man of the nineteenth century can do all those things? None! Instead we have engineers and weapon-smiths and tailors and cooks and craftsmen and builders—each excellent in his own field, each entirely helpless in the others!"

Spencer opened his eyes again and turned them toward Admiral Lord Nelson, who was standing in his usual position by the bureau.

"The idea that the Empire is progressive is an insidious myth. A myth! Look at that brass man! It is our tools that are evolving, not us! If anything, we are going in the opposite direction. While an increasingly exclusive elite are gathering information about ways in which the world might function, the ever-expanding majority are becoming ever more proficient in a single field of endeavour while comprehending less and less about anything else."

Swinburne paraphrased something Burton had said on the evening of the Brundleweed robbery: "The acquisition of knowledge has become too intimidating a prospect for them, so they shun it in favour of faith."

"Sadly so," said Spencer. "There is a principle which is a bar against all information, which is proof against all arguments, and which cannot fail to keep a man in everlasting ignorance—that principle is contempt prior to investigation; contempt carved from the immovable rock of faith.

"Thus it is, gentlemen, that the masses are not only kept from the knowledge that would aid their ability to adapt and evolve, but they also actively reject it. Minds have become trammelled by ingrained social conditions. Working-class parents instill in their children the concept that reality offers nothing but hardship, that poverty always beckons, and that small rewards can be achieved only through strife and labour. Why should they teach differently when, under those same conditions, they themselves have survived? The child takes this as the unquestionable truth of the world. Opportunities are not recognised. The desire for change remains within the realm of dreams. Adaptability is devalued. Evolution is halted."

Spencer's face suddenly dropped into an expression of abject misery.

"I'm runnin' out o' steam," he said. "Me bloomin' brain can't cope with it!"

His arms suddenly dropped and dangled over the sides of his chair, his head nodded forward, and he emitted a loud snore.

"Good lord!" Swinburne exclaimed.

"Asleep," Burton noted. "What an extraordinary man!"

"I say, Richard, what do you make of all that?"

Burton reached for his cigar case. "I think this warrants a two-Manila muse, Algy. Sit quietly, would you, while I give it a ponder."

Sitting quietly didn't come naturally to the diminutive poet but he gritted his teeth and managed to remain silent for ten minutes while Spencer snored and Burton smoked.

"Fascinating!" Burton said, speaking at last.

Herbert Spencer snorted and looked up. "Hallo, Boss! Did I take forty winks?"

"You did, Herbert. Does that always happen after you philosophise?"

"Yus. It exhausts me bloomin' brain. How did I do? I hope I didn't humiliate meself."

"Humiliate?" Swinburne cried. "Good lord, no, Herbert! You did splendidly! You are absolutely remarkable!"

Burton blew out a plume of tobacco smoke and said, "Forgive the question, Herbert—I mean no offence—but why on earth aren't you a sensation? With an intellect like yours, you should be writing books and touring universities!"

Spencer shrugged and tapped the side of his head. "When a man's knowledge ain't in order, the more of it he has, the greater is his confusion." He looked at Admiral Lord Nelson and sighed. "I should be more like him! There's one what's got an ordered mind!"

"But no knowledge, Herbert," Burton said. "No knowledge at all. So do you mean to say that your thinking processes are more usually in disarray?"

"Yus, just that. When I sits down an' talks, it's all fine, but for most o' the time, me brainbox is a right old jumble."

"Hmm. I wonder if that has some bearing on your immunity to the Tichborne influence?"

"Richard, that doesn't make sense," Swinburne objected. "In the main, it's the working classes who've come out in support of the Claimant, which suggests they're most affected by whatever this emanation is. If a disordered mind is immune, then the working classes have ordered minds and most of London's gentry, including yourself, don't!"

"No, Algy, that's not it at all. Let me pose a question: what would you be if you weren't a poet?"

"Dead."

"Seriously."

"I *am* serious. There's nothing else I could be. I was born a poet. I think like a poet. I act like a poet. I look like a poet. I'm a poet."

"Accepted. By contrast, Herbert here, when we first met him, made it quite clear that he wasn't at all sure that he was cut out to be a philosopher."

"It's no way to earn a livin', that's for certain," Spencer muttered.

"As for me," Burton continued, "I've never possessed a clear idea of my function in society. I've been a soldier, a spy, a geographer, an interpreter, an explorer, an author, a surveyor, and now the king's agent, whatever the blazes that is. As for this country's gentry, I think you'll find that they mostly have a sense that life is filled with options; that, in terms of what they actually do with their time, there are few limitations."

"Herbert used the word 'trammelled.' Are you suggesting that the trammelled mind is the susceptible mind?"

"Precisely."

"Funny. I've never considered myself trammelled. Quite the opposite, in fact!"

"It's not that your mind or imagination is in any respect confined, Algy. It's simply that you've never given consideration to the notion of doing anything else. You even offered your services as my assistant because you felt the danger involved would cure your ennui and inspire greater depth in your poetry."

"Which it has. You suspect, then, that the black diamonds somehow break down the mental structures that keep a mind channelled, which is why the working classes are suddenly feeling hard done by—they're realising that they're being cheated out of alternatives?"

"Yes. Remember the line in the poem? *Vexations in the poor enables.* And what about Edwin Brundleweed's story of how, the afternoon before the robbery, he suddenly and inexplicably felt dissatisfied with his lot in life?"

"But what's it all about, Richard? What's the point?"

"Judging by today's events, I'd say the point is chaos; maybe even insurgency—an assault against the very fabric of our society. I would even go so far as to say that the British Empire is under attack."

"My hat! By a foreign power?"

"Or a budding despot. You understand now why John Speke can probably be discounted?"

Swinburne nodded. "Unless it's the Prussians. You did say he'd gone to Prussia. On the other hand, our ghost is Russian."

Burton asked Admiral Lord Nelson to top up their cups from the coffee pot and they sat in silence for a few moments.

"Are we on the brink of a revolution?" Swinburne whispered. "Think of it! A reign of terror could descend on us just as it did on France. We might end up under the rule of an abominable tyrant like Napoleon!"

"Or we might not," Spencer muttered. "Would it be so bad if the workin' man—an' woman, I might add—gained some measure of power? Don't you think it's becomin' a matter of urgency that they do?"

"Maybe so," Burton replied, thinking of Countess Sabina and his subsequent dream: *a transition begins—a melting of one great cycle into another.* "But do we really want such a change to be forced upon us by an external power? I find it inconceivable that they might be doing it for our own good!"

He flicked the stub of his cheroot into the fireplace, stood, and paced back across to the window.

"We must get to the root of this."

His eyes scanned the road below. Two labourers were trailing along behind a gentleman, mocking him relentlessly. Despite this scene, Montagu Place was unusually quiet for the hour.

"In order to strengthen our campaign against the enemy, Algy, we must first strengthen ourselves. I've resisted it in the past, but I think it's time I mesmerised you."

"Really?"

"Really. I want to see whether I can stop you becoming a Tichborne supporter every time the Claimant is nearby. If I can't, the only other option is for you to stay permanently drunk, and I'd rather avoid that."

Swinburne puffed out his cheeks and expelled a breath with a pop. "Oh, it wouldn't be so bad! Besides, you've always refused to exercise your mental magnetism on me before!"

"True," Burton affirmed. "I was concerned that your excitable disposition might react in an unpredictable manner. However, seeing as this affair is making you unpredictable anyway, my former caution seems somewhat misplaced. I shall employ a Sufi technique to fortify my own psychic defences, too. Then I have a task for you."

"Good! What?"

"The Rake connection interests me. We've yet to identify their new leader. I want you to dig around—but keep out of mischief."

"I'll talk to my Libertine chums. I say, though—Rakes and Tichborne—it seems a contradiction, doesn't it? If our mysterious opponent is attempting to stir up the working classes, why employ Rakes, who epitomise the idea of the insouciant aristo?"

"My thought exactly!"

Swinburne suddenly froze and looked at his friend with a puzzled expression.

"That wraith," he said. "The one by the chaunter. You saw it?"

"Clearly!"

"For a moment, it seemed to manifest rather more solidly and took on the appearance of a tall bearded man. I swear he was wearing wire-rimmed spectacles, too. The thing of it is, I feel I've seen him somewhere before."

"You recognised the manifestation as an actual person?"

"Yes. That wisp of steam resembled someone whose path I've crossed at some point, I'm sure of it, but for the life of me I can't recall whom. The name 'Boyle' or 'Foyle' springs to mind."

"Keep thinking on it, Algy—it could be important."

Spencer rubbed a hand over his bald scalp and said, "Is there anythin' I can do to help, Boss?"

"Thank you, Herbert, there is. Your immunity and your—if you don't mind me saying so—disreputable appearance, enable you to wander through the thick of it without being molested. I'd like you to keep an eye on things at street level, see how widespread the apparitions are, and, if possible, find out where they're most numerous."

"Right you are!"

"First, though, I'd like you to return to Miss Mayson's to make a purchase on my behalf."

He explained further and supplied the philosopher with the requisite amount of money.

Swinburne piped up: "It's a quarter to eight, Richard. What say you we toddle on over to the Cannibal Club for a natter with Monckton Milnes? He usually has a better handle on what the Rakes are up to than I do. You can mesmerise me afterward."

"An excellent idea. We'll take the penny-farthings. I don't fancy walking the streets at night, not while the rank and file are up in arms."

Half an hour later, Herbert Spencer descended the steps of 14 Montagu Place and headed off toward SPARTA on Orange Street.

Meanwhile, Burton and Swinburne left the study and went down the stairs to Mrs. Angell's domain. While Swinburne waited by the back door, Burton tapped lightly on the entrance to the old lady's parlour. A voice called from within. He poked his head into the room beyond.

"I thought I'd check to see how you are," he said. "I hope you didn't tire yourself cooking for us. It was very kind of you to do so."

"I'm fine, Sir Richard. No need to worry. A bruised hip, nothing more. How's little Elsie?"

"Doctor Steinhaeuser gave her a sedative. She's asleep in the guest room and certainly won't wake up before morning. I sent a message to her parents and they'll come to pick her up soon. You needn't do anything more this evening. Just rest, my dear, and if you want anything, ring for Admiral Lord Nelson."

"I will. Thank you."

Burton returned to Swinburne and they went out to the garage. A few moments later they steered their penny-farthings into Wyndham Mews and set off toward Leicester Square.

The evening sky was clear, a dark and deepening blue, with three or four stars already twinkling. It was warm. A slight, directionless breeze stirred the air lazily.

At ground level, ribbons of steam twisted slowly across the surface of the road, occasionally rising up like serpents poised to strike. They swirled away from passing traffic then curled back inward.

There were far fewer vehicles on the streets than usual.

"Where is everyone?" Swinburne called over the racket of his penny-farthing's chugging engine.

"Sheltering behind locked doors, I imagine," Burton responded. "Or resting after a hard day's rioting!"

"By golly, what a lot of broken windows! It looks as if a tornado passed through town!"

"Watch where you steer. There might be debris in the road. Hey! Where are you going?"

"This way, it's a short cut!" the poet shrilled, suddenly veering off the main street and into a narrow lane.

"Blast it, Algy, what are you up to?"

"Follow me!"

The steam proved to be much thicker in the backstreets; a dense milky pall, reminiscent of that which rose from the Crawls in the grounds of Tichborne House. The top of the cloud was almost level with the saddles of the velocipedes—about the same height as the top of an average man's head—and the two penny-farthings, as they clattered through it, left a widening wake behind them, exactly as if they were steering through a liquid.

Gas lamps flared, casting sharp shadows on the sides of the buildings and walls on either side of the lane, and making the top of the mist glaringly luminescent.

"Slow down, Algy! I can't see the surface of the road! Are you sure you know where we're going?"

"Yes, don't worry! I've been this way many a time!"

"Why?"

"For Verbena Lodge!"

"The brothel?"

"Yes!"

"I might have—" Burton's teeth clacked together as his vehicle bounced over a pothole "—known!"

They turned right into a less well-lit street, then left into another, and immediately found themselves in the midst of a disturbance. Yells and screams rose out of the cloud, women's shouts and men's protestations.

There came a loud report, almost like a gunshot, and Swinburne suddenly vanished.

The king's agent saw the small rear wheel of his assistant's velocipede fly upward before dropping back into the mist. He heard the machine's engine race, cough, splutter, and die.

He squeezed his brake levers and swung down from his vehicle, plunging into the cloud.

"Algy? Did you hit something? Are you all right?"

"Over here, Richard! I—"

Crack!

"Yow!"

Burton moved toward the raised voices, peering into the murk. Were those figures just ahead?

"Algernon?" he called.

"Gah!" came the response.

A man ran out of the rolling vapour. He was dressed in nothing but a ripped and bloodied shirt, a top hat, and a pair of socks held up by gaiters. "She's bloody insane!" he wailed, and sped past.

Another gentleman followed, barefoot and buttoning up his trousers. "Get out of here! The strumpet is spitting feathers!"

A woman in a floral dressing gown hurried into view and shouted after them: "Oy! Sir George! Mr. Fiddlehampton! Come back! Sirs! Sirs! You ain't paid the bleedin' Governess!"

She looked at Burton. "You a bloody rozzer, or what? 'Cos if you are, you can bleedin' well stuff it."

"I'm not the police. What's all that noise about? Who's screaming?"

Crack!

"Yow! Ow! Ow! Ow! Ha ha!"

That was Algy!

"What's happening? Answer me!"

The girl shrugged and gestured over her shoulder. "It's Betsy, ain't it? She's gone bloody loopy. 'Ere, if ya ain't a rozzer, maybe we could—"

Burton pushed past her and strode forward until he found himself mingling with a small crowd of semi-clad men and girls who'd gathered in a wide ring around a curvaceous brunette. She was heavily made-up, and wore little more than a tight black whalebone bodice, French bloomers, and high-heeled boots.

In her left hand she held a whip, the end of which was coiled around the neck of a man kneeling meekly behind her wearing nothing but underpants. She had a second whip in her right hand, and with this, she was lashing at a small figure that hopped, jerked, and danced before her.

It was Algernon Swinburne.

Crack!

The leather thong coiled around the poet's hindquarters.

"Ouch! Ouch! Hah, yes! But really, Betsy, what do you think—"

Crack!

It slashed at his waist, ripping his shirt and slicing through his belt.

"Woweee! No! Ow! Ow! —do you think you are doing with that—"

Crack!

His trousers slid to his ankles.

"Narrgh! Oof! Ha ha ha! —doing with that poor gentleman?"

Burton glanced at the woman's prisoner. He looked again, and recognised him: it was the chancellor of the Exchequer, William Gladstone.

"Mr. Gladstone!" he called, pushing past prostitutes and angry customers. "What are you doing?"

"Shut up!" snapped the whip-wielding woman, who Swinburne had addressed as Betsy.

"It's all right, Richard!" the poet panted. "I have the situation under control."

"So I see," Burton replied sarcastically.

"Who are you, sir!" the kneeling politician demanded haughtily.

"Sir Richard Burton."

"I said shut up!" Betsy ordered.

"Palmerston's swashbuckler?"

"Well, I wouldn't put it quite like that, but—"

Crack!

Burton cried out and fell to one knee, clutching his head, feeling his scalp open up above the left ear. Blood dripped through his fingers.

Crack!

Leather encircled his forearm and neck, tightened cruelly, ripped his sleeve, and slid away. The explorer toppled to the cobbles and quickly rolled aside as the lash sliced through the air again and smacked loudly against the road beside him.

"Hey! I say!" Swinburne shouted. "Don't flog him! Flog me!"

"Be quiet!" Betsy commanded.

"Yes," said Burton, scrambling to his feet, "be quiet, Algy."

Above the general hubbub, there sounded the clank and rattle of an approaching litter-crab.

The crowd thinned as men slipped away into the mist.

"Burton," called Gladstone. "Do not misjudge what you witness here. I am present simply to rehabilitate these fallen women."

"In you undergarments, sir?"

"They stole my clothes!"

Betsy pulled her lips back over her teeth and hissed: "Oppressor! Hypocrite! Conspirator!"

"Betsy, dear," said Swinburne, soothingly, "the middle of the street is no place for a discussion about—about—by the way, what *is* it we're discussing?"

"Pervert!"

Crack!

"Argh! Yowch! You mean *poet*!"

"For pity's sake," Burton growled impatiently. He took three long strides and grabbed the prostitute by the wrists. She let out a howl of fury and started to struggle, biting and kicking.

"Algy! Pull your bloody pants up and help me!"

Swinburne hoisted his trousers up to his waist, held them with one hand, shuffled over, and pulled the thong from around Gladstone's neck.

"I'm married," the politician told him earnestly. "I've never been guilty of an act of infidelity."

"You may tell that to the marines—" the poet grinned "—but the sailors won't believe you. There. You're free. I suggest you leg it before the police get here."

"The police!" Gladstone exclaimed in horror, and without a backward glance, he jumped to his bare feet and took off.

"I'd love to see how he gets home," said Swinburne.

"Damn it!" Burton yelled as Betsy sank her teeth into his wrist. He pushed her from him and backed away, with Swinburne at his side. The woman, with a whip in either hand, spat and snarled like a wild animal.

The crowd had dispersed—the men running off, the women retreating into the brothel.

Crack!

The tip of a whip flicked through the skin of Burton's forehead. He staggered. Blood dribbled into his eyes.

Betsy circled the two men. "Tichborne is innocent!" she said.

The bulky grey metallic form of the litter-crab loomed out of the mist behind her, its eight legs thumping against the road. From beneath its belly, twenty-four thin arms extended downward, flicking back and forth, picking rubbish from the road and depositing it into the mechanism's flaming maw to be incinerated.

"Move aside, madam," Burton advised.

"Why don't you keep your fat mouth shut?"

"Betsy, there's a litter-crab right behind you," Swinburne shrilled, urgently.

Betsy giggled insanely. "Stupid bloody toffs."

"You're going to be—" Burton began.

The prostitute let out a piercing cry and flicked her whip up to strike. Burton flinched in anticipation, but even as he did so, the tip of the girl's weapon flew back and tangled with one of the collector arms under the lumbering machine. The thong was yanked violently, jerking her off her feet. She went sprawling backward and rolled under the advancing crab. The twenty-four metal arms pummelled and thrashed at her. She screeched and writhed and fainted. Seconds later, the litter-crab froze as the fail-safe system activated, a valve clicked open on its back, and steam whistled out at high pressure. The emergency siren started to wail.

Burton stepped over to the machine, bending to peer at the prone body beneath.

"Is she dead?" asked Swinburne, raising his voice over the noise.

"No, just scrapes and bruises."

The poet gave a sigh of relief. "Thank goodness! She's one of my favourites."

"Still?"

Swinburne nodded, smiled, and gave a shrug.

His trousers dropped.

"Don't shrug again until you have a new belt," Burton advised. "Come on, let's get away from this bloody racket. The girl is already coming round and the crab's siren will attract a constable soon enough. We'll let the police sort this one out. I've had quite enough of it!"

They returned to their penny-farthings, restarted the engines, and steered past the hulking street cleaner.

"Ow! Hah! Yes! Ooh!" Swinburne exclaimed. "My hat, Richard! These boneshakers play the merry devil with freshly striped buttocks!"

"Spare me the details."

They rode out onto a main road.

"It confirms your—ouch!—theory, though," said the poet.

"What does?"

"The girls in Verbena—ah!—Lodge are all victims of the usual—argh!—sad process. You know the routine, they worked as maids, were seduced by—ooh! Ha!—their masters, fell pregnant, and were coldly thrown out onto the streets to fend for themselves."

"Despicable!" Burton snarled.

"Indeed. But sadly—yowch!—all too common."

"You don't feel guilty taking advantage of their misfortune?"

"Please, Richard! I never—ow!—lay a finger on them! I pay them to apply the birch, nothing more!"

"Humph!"

"Anyway, I happen to know that Betsy is an exception. She didn't suffer that cruel fate. She's the only one of them—oy!—who was *born* in a brothel. She's the daughter of—yow!—a madam. In other words, she's never known anything—oof!—different and has probably never harboured any expectations beyond being a—oh!—working girl."

"The trammelled mind."

"Ex—ah!—actly!"

No further incidents interrupted their journey, and they arrived some fifteen minutes later at Bartoloni's Italian restaurant in Leicester Square. It was closed and the window, which had apparently been broken, was boarded up.

Bartoloni responded to Burton's knocking. His eyes widened with surprise when he saw the blood on his visitor's face but he quickly regained his composure and acted as if there was nothing untoward.

"*Vi prego di entrare, signori,*" he said, with a slight bow. "*Il ristorante e' chiuso ma i vostri amici sono al piano di sopra.*"

"*Grazie, signore,*" Burton responded.

Passing through the eatery, he and Swinburne entered a door marked "Private" and ascended a staircase to the rooms above.

In a large, wood-panelled chamber, comfortably furnished and with its own bar, they found fellow members of the Cannibal Club: Captain Henry Murray, Dr. James Hunt, Thomas Bendyshe, Charles Bradlaugh, and, inevitably, Richard Monckton Milnes.

Tall, handsome, enigmatic, and saturnine in aspect, Milnes was one of Sir Richard Francis Burton's best friends and staunchest supporters. Rich and influential, he'd interceded many times in the past when lesser men had tried to undermine the famous explorer. He also owned the largest collection of erotica ever gathered by a private collector. It included everything written by the Marquis de Sade—plus thousands of banned volumes concerning witchcraft and the occult. He was, of course, a Libertine. However, he was also a man who, at an emotional level, separated himself from others, preferring to conduct all his relationships on a purely intellectual basis. Some thought him cold. Others, Burton among them, realised that he was simply one of life's onlookers, a man who studied everything but who never fully engaged with anything. This included the Libertine movement, which suited his temperament but failed to draw him in too deeply. He rarely became involved with its politics or various causes.

Burton and Swinburne entered the room to find Milnes standing in its centre pontificating about the latest Technologist developments.

"—so they take the species *Scarabaeus sacer*," he was saying, "more commonly known as the scarab beetle, and their Eugenicists grow them to the size of a milk wagon!"

"Be damned!" Charles Bradlaugh exclaimed.

"I'm sure the Technologists will be, for once each beetle has matured, the engineers kill the poor creatures, scrape 'em out, and insert a seat and controls in the front and a bench and steam engine in the back. Thus a man can sit in the beetle, with his family behind him, and drive the blessed thing."

"By thunder!" Henry Murray cried. "Yet another new species of vehicle!"

"My good man!" Milnes objected. "You're missing the point entirely. It's not a species of vehicle, it's a species of insect; and not just any insect, but the one held sacred by the ancient Egyptians! They are being grown on farms and summarily executed, without so much as a by-your-leave, for the express purpose of supplying a ready-made shell. And the Technologists have the temerity to name this vehicle the *Folks' Wagon*! It is not a wagon! It's a beetle! It's a living creature, which mankind is mercilessly exploiting for its own ends. It's sacrilege!"

"Interesting that you should rail against the exploitation of insects by scientists when, it seems, the greater percentage of London's population is currently up in arms over the exploitation of the working classes by the aristocracy," Burton declared. "Are labourers no better than insects, in your view?"

"Richard!" Milnes cried, turning to face the newcomers. "How good to see you! How long have you been standing there, and—by George!—why is that bestial face of yours covered in blood? Don't tell me you've been in yet another scrap? Are you drunk? Hallo, Swinburne!"

"We're perfectly sober."

"I'm a little hungover, actually," the poet added.

"You poor things! Hunt, old horse, supply these good fellows with a tipple at once. Large ones! It's a medical emergency! Murray, fetch a basin of water, there's a good chap."

Burton and Swinburne collapsed into big leather armchairs and gratefully accepted the proffered drinks.

"What happened?" Bendyshe asked. "Did you get caught up in the public disorder like Brabrooke?"

"Brabrooke? What happened to him?"

"He was hit over the head with a spade. A crossing cleaner attacked him out of the blue, for no good reason."

"He's all right," said Bradlaugh. "He has a mild concussion and a nasty laceration but he'll be on his feet again in a couple of days."

"Poor old Brabrooke!" Swinburne exclaimed.

"So you were in the thick of it too, hey?" Milnes asked.

"Somewhat," Burton answered. "We were at Speakers' Corner when the fracas began."

"Ah ha!" Bendyshe shouted gleefully. "So you started it, hey? Was young Swinburne giving a public performance? Is that what set them off?"

"The performance wasn't from Algernon. It was from the Tichborne Claimant."

"Gad!" Milnes exclaimed. "That character is certainly stirring up a hornets' nest."

"He is. We managed to extricate ourselves, but then, on the way here, we were set upon by a prostitute."

The men burst out laughing.

"Ha ha!" Bendyshe yelled triumphantly. "Surely beastly Burton hasn't been trounced by a terrible trollop?"

"I can assure you that it was no laughing matter. And less of the 'beastly,' if you don't mind."

"She was half crazed," Swinburne said. "And she was lashing at us with whips!" He grinned and shuddered with pleasure.

"But what on earth did you do to set her off, dear boy?" Milnes asked.

"Took his shilling's worth and the shilling as well, I'll wager!" Bendyshe guffawed.

"Not a bit of it," Burton grumbled. "We were on our way here and got caught up in it through no fault of our own."

"The unwashed masses have gone mad," opined Murray, who'd just reentered the room with a basin of warm water in his hands and white towels draped over his forearms. "It's this Tichborne character."

"Yes, Milnes was just saying," Bradlaugh offered.

"The Claimant's become some sort of figurehead," Murray continued. "To the lower classes, he represents everything that's bad in an aristocrat and everything that's good in a working man, all wrapped up in one extremely bulbous bundle. It's patently absurd. Here, wipe the blood off yourselves. You look perfectly horrific."

"It occurs to me," said Burton, "that a symbol cannot gain such potency unless there's a real desire for it. Another port, if you please, Henry. I appear to have swallowed mine in a single gulp."

He picked up a towel, dipped a corner into the water, and began to rub it over his face. He looked up at Richard Monckton Milnes. "As a matter of fact, the Tichborne situation is what we've come to talk to you about. The Claimant seems to have acquired a bodyguard of Rakes. Do you have any idea why?"

"Has he, indeed? That seems rather peculiar!"

"That's what we thought. What are the Rakes up to these days? Who's their new leader?"

"I'm afraid I can't cast much light on the matter. The veil of secrecy surrounding the faction has never been more impenetrable. The new leader is a Russian, I believe, and arrived in this country early in February. Who he is, where he's staying—those are questions I can't answer."

"He?" said Burton. "Or she?"

"Hmm. I couldn't say. A woman, though? Doesn't that seem rather unlikely? What I *can* tell you is this: since he—or she—took over, the Rakes have been holding séances around the clock."

"Well now, that's interesting! Are they trying to communicate with someone who's died? Laurence Oliphant or Henry Beresford, perhaps?"

"I don't know, Richard, but if they *are* speaking to the departed, then I doubt that it's their former leaders they're conversing with."

"Why so?"

"Simply because the Rakes who were closest to Oliphant and the Mad Marquess have been rather on the out and out these months past. The new regime has been assiduous in sidelining the old."

"So who's close to the new leader? Can you name names?"

Milnes looked thoughtful for a moment but then shrugged and said: "I'd help if I could, but I simply don't know any of the new crowd."

Swinburne piped up: "What about a chap named Boyle or Foyle? A tall, stooped fellow with a big beard and wire-rimmed spectacles."

Milnes shook his head. "Doesn't ring any bells."

"Do you mean Doyle?" Bradlaugh asked.

"I don't know. Do I?"

"He fits the description and he's a Rake, of that I'm sure. He was at a party at my place a few months back. You were there, too. A little before Christmas. You were in your cups at the time. So was I, come to think of it."

Swinburne threw up his hands. "I was at a party at your place?"

Bradlaugh chuckled. "Your absence of memory is no surprise. You'd been at it long before you even arrived. My footman opened your carriage's door and you plopped out face-first onto the street, while your topper rolled away into the gutter. If it's any consolation, Doyle is a much worse drunkard than you ever were."

Bendyshe snorted. "I don't know about that! There was that time when——" He stopped as Burton's hand clamped his arm tightly.

"Sorry, Tom, but this could be important. Bradlaugh, this Doyle fellow—who is he?"

"A storybook artist. From Edinburgh. Charles Altamont Doyle. He's the brother of my friend Richard Doyle, who's also an artist—you've probably seen his work, he's quite successful. Charles, on the other hand—at least from what I know of him—is simply too unworldly to make much of himself. He's an awfully morbid sort—prone to black moods and fits of despair. I think that's what drives him to drink. It's a tragedy, really. He has a young wife and God knows how many children to support, but what little he earns is spent on the demon booze. He has a taste for burgundy and will sink to any depths to get it, and if he can't, he'll resort to anything else he can lay his hands on. Rumour has it that on one particularly desperate occasion he drank a bottle of furniture polish."

"Good lord!" James Hunt exclaimed. "The man should be in an asylum!"

"I have no doubt that he will be soon," Bradlaugh responded. "At the aforementioned party, he certainly appeared to be teetering on the brink of insanity. He has a pet obsession, a delusion, which seems to haunt his every waking hour. He ranted about it interminably that night; didn't stop until he passed out."

"What is it?" Swinburne asked.

"He's convinced that fairies exist and are communicating with him from the unseen world."

Sir Richard Francis Burton felt goosebumps rise on his forearms.

Bismillah! Fairies again!

"You mean he hears voices in his head?" said Swinburne.

"Absolutely. I should say he's damaged his brain through excessive drinking."

"Where is he now?" Burton asked. "Where does he live?"

"Not with his wife. She threw him out after he stole pocket money from his own children. I believe he has lodgings somewhere in the city but I don't know where."

"And his wife's address?"

Bradlaugh gave it, and Burton copied it into his notebook.

The king's agent looked at the bloodstained towel in his hands.

"If you'll excuse us for a moment, I think Algy and I should repair to the washroom to get properly cleaned up. We'll rejoin you in a few minutes."

"Of course! Of course! Is there anything else you need?" Milnes asked.

"I could do with a belt," Swinburne answered, gripping his trousers as he stood.

"'Tis ever the case," Bendyshe opined with a smirk.

The following morning, while Algernon Swinburne went to call on Charles Doyle's wife, Sir Richard Francis Burton received a visit from Burke and Hare.

Palmerston's odd-job men resembled nothing so much as a couple of eighteenth-century gravediggers. Despite the hot weather, they were dressed in their customary black surtouts, with black waistcoats and white shirts underneath. The Gladstone collars of the latter were cheek-scraping, eye-threatening points that looked utterly ridiculous to Burton. The shirts were tucked into high-waisted knee-length breeches. Yellow tights encased the men's calves. Their black shoes were decorated with large silver buckles. They each held a stovepipe hat.

As the two men stepped into Burton's study, they were greeted with: "Slobbering dolts! Bumble thick-wits!"

"My apologies, gentlemen," Burton said, with a grin. "The new member of my household is somewhat lacking in manners." He gestured toward a perch standing near one of the bookcases. "Meet Pox, my messenger parakeet."

"Sod off!" the bird trilled.

"You're a brave man, Captain Burton," Burke said, in his sepulchral voice. "There's not many could stand having one of those little devils in their home."

Damien Burke was tall, slightly hunchbacked, extremely bald, and sported the variety of side whiskers popularly known as "Piccadilly weepers." His face hung in a permanently maudlin expression, with a down-curving mouth, jowly cheeks, and woebegone eyes.

"Have you been in the wars, sir?" he asked. "You appear somewhat bedraggled, if you'll forgive the observation."

"It wasn't a war, it was a riot," the king's agent corrected. "But the cuts are shallow and the bruises are healing."

Burke placed something onto Burton's principal desk.

The king's agent eyed the object, which was wrapped in linen and had the approximate shape and dimensions of a pistol. "I haven't been outside yet. How is it? Are the streets quieter?"

"Somewhat, sir," Gregory Hare responded. "Isn't that so, Mr. Burke?" He was shorter than his companion and immensely broad, with massive shoulders and apish arms. A shock of pure white hair stood upright from his head and grew down around the angle of his heavy square jaw to a tuft beneath his chin. His pale-grey eyes shone from within deep gristly sockets, his nose was splayed, and his mouth was tremendously wide and filled with large, flat, tightly packed teeth.

Both men, in Burton's opinion, were hideous-looking.

"Quite so, Mr. Hare," Burke replied. "I should point out, however, that the Tichborne Claimant intends to address the public from a platform in Saint James's Park at four o'clock."

"You think it will lead to further rioting?" Burton asked.

"Do you, Captain?"

"I consider it highly likely, yes."

"We share your opinion, don't we, Mr. Hare?"

"We do, Mr. Burke."

"Noxious fume-pumpers!" Pox screamed.

Hare ignored the bird and indicated the package. "A gift for you, Captain."

"Really?"

Hare took hold of the linen and unfolded it, revealing the item wrapped inside. It was a green, organic, fleshy-looking thing, with a stubby barrel and a handgrip from the base of which small white roots grew. There were various nodules protruding from the object, one being positioned where the trigger would be on a pistol.

"What on earth is it?"

"It's a cactus," said Burke.

"A cactus?"

"Yes. A cactus. From Ireland."

"It has no spines."

"As a matter of fact, it does, but they grow on the inside. You are aware of a gentleman named Richard Spruce?"

"Yes, of course. He's been much in the public eye of late. He's a member of the RGS. I bump into him from time to time."

"He's become something of a pariah, wouldn't you agree?"

Burton nodded. "As far as the public and the press are concerned, he's solely responsible for the Irish tragedy."

"Indeed, Captain, indeed. Which, in turn, some say, has led us into the American conflict. That's a lot of weight for one man to carry."

"I would think so."

"Which may explain why he and a number of his Eugenicist colleagues met with a German spy named Count Zeppelin last week and attempted to flee to Prussia, taking state secrets with them."

"He did what? The confounded idiot!"

"Monkey gland!" Pox added.

"You call him an idiot, sir. I call him a traitor. The damage he could have done selling secrets like this—" Burke nodded at the object on the desk "—is incalculable."

"A cactus is a state secret?" Burton asked, puzzled.

"This variety most definitely is."

Hare took over from Burke: "Fortunately, we were able to capture Spruce and his cohorts before Zeppelin got them away. The count himself, I regret to say, eluded us. The Eugenicists are currently being held in the Tower of London."

"Why there?"

"We have a special security establishment below the old dungeons. It's where the likes of Darwin and Babbage would have ended up, had you not—um—*dealt* with them as you did. Isn't that right, Mr. Burke?"

"Indeed, indeed, Mr. Hare." Burke tapped the cactus. "Anyway, the point is, we can't allow material of this sort to fall into foreign hands, least of all Prussian ones. The Bismarck Dynasty is attempting to unite the Germanic states in order to establish a European Empire. If that comes to pass, it could lead to a war the likes of which the world has never seen. We don't want them in possession of weapons like this."

"'Tumultuous the change that comes,'" Burton quoted softly. "'A storm shall wipe many of thy soft-skinned kinsfolk from the Earth.'"

"I beg your pardon, Captain?"

"Nothing. Just something I heard once."

The storm will break early and you shall witness the end of a great cycle and the horrifying birth pains of another; the past and the future locked together in a terrible conflict.

He remembered his dream.

He remembered Countess Sabina.

He remembered that John Hanning Speke was currently in Prussia and had taken Eugenicists with him.

He looked down at the cactus. "It's a weapon?"

"Yes," said Hare. "You must be very, very careful with it. Carry it with you at all times and never allow it into the hands of your enemies."

"Allow me to demonstrate," Burke said, picking up the cactus. He held it like a pistol. "Strangely comfortable in the hand," he noted. "Slightly yielding to the grip yet solid and a good weight. You see this nodule here? Give that a tweak and the cactus immediately goes into a defensive state. Inside, juices are coagulating, forming sharp, venomous spines, and doing so in an instant. Now, I'll just—" He aimed the cactus at the opposite wall and pressed the trigger nodule. There came a sound—*phut!*—and a number of spines suddenly appeared in the wall, their arrival announced with a soft thud.

"Great heavens!" Burton exclaimed. He crossed the room and counted the projectiles. They had embedded themselves in the wallpaper perilously close to where a treasured framed miniature of his mother and father hung. There were seven, each about three inches long, each gleaming wetly. He reached up to pull one out.

"Don't touch!" Gregory Hare cried. "They're coated with a tremendously potent resin. One drop of it on your skin and you'll fall unconscious in an instant and won't recover your wits for three hours!"

"Bloody hell!"

"The venom will become harmless in five minutes or so."

"The cactus has reloaded already," Burke said, waving the pistol. "For as long as it's in a defensive state, it'll produce spines continuously. You could fire this thing for hours on end and never run out of ammunition! However—" he pinched the activation nodule "—There. It's dormant now. No chance of accidentally shooting you in the leg. Not that I would. I'm cautious by nature, aren't I, Mr. Hare?"

"Very cautious, Mr. Burke."

"Take it, Captain," Burke said. "It's yours. Be sure to soak this end, with the roots, in water for a couple of hours each week."

Burton returned to his visitors and took the proffered weapon. It felt strange, alive—which, he reminded himself, it was.

"If you'll pardon me raising what I'm sure is a sensitive subject," Burke said, "you've been responsible for a few deaths since taking on your current role. We understand why those deaths occurred and we fully support you."

Gregory Hare nodded his agreement. "Even in the case of Sir Charles Babbage," he said. "An execution which some might say was unprovoked."

Burton swallowed. "I must confess," he said, quietly, "I have asked myself over and over whether my action was justified. Did I commit murder that day?"

"No!" Burke and Hare chorused.

"I was delirious with malaria. I wasn't in a fit state to judge."

"You judged correctly. We'd been following Babbage and his work for some time. He was what we in our business classify as 'a developing threat.'"

"This spine-shooter will ease the moral burden of your role, Captain Burton," Hare added. "You can simply render your opponents insensible, then call us. We will remove them to a place of safekeeping where they'll be interrogated and, ultimately, if possible, rehabilitated."

"That sounds strangely ominous."

Neither of his visitors answered.

The clock began to chime eleven.

"Rabbit-ticklers!" Pox murmured.

Burton slipped the cactus gun into his pocket.

"Thank you, gentlemen," he said. "I daresay this pistol, peculiar as it is, will prove most useful. Now, to business: you have the papers?"

"Yes," Burke answered.

"They will pass examination?"

"Even the most rigorous," Hare replied.

"Then if you'd care to step into my dressing room, I'll make you up and fit you out with clothing more suited to asylum inspectors."

Hare gave an audible gulp and glanced at Burke.

Burke cleared his throat and looked first to the right, then to the left, then at Hare, and finally at Burton.

"I thought—" he mumbled. "I thought we might go like this."

Burton gave a bark of laughter. "Trust me, chaps, if you step into Bedlam dressed like that, there's every chance that you'll never step out again!"

Bethlem Royal Hospital.

First it was a priory, erected by the sisters and brethren of the Order of the Star of Bethlehem in the year 1247.

Then it became a hospital in 1337.

Twenty years later it started to treat the insane, if "treat" is the appropriate word for what amounted to restraint and torture.

In the 1600s it gained the nickname "Bedlam," which was soon a part of everyday language, invoked to suggest uproar, confusion, and madness.

The 1700s saw it opening its doors to the public to allow them to point and laugh at the antics of the lunatics.

By the mid-1800s, measures had been taken to improve conditions at the hospital, the principal one being its transference to new premises.

It didn't take long for the huge new edifice to become a larger version of what it had been before: a dark, brutal, malodorous, deafening, perilous, and squalid hellhole.

Sir Richard Francis Burton was standing in the midst of it.

The director of the hospital was a pale-faced man of average height and build. He possessed widely set brown eyes, closely cropped grey hair, and a small clipped mustache. Every few moments, a nervous tic distorted his mouth and pulled his head down to the right, causing him to grunt loudly. His name was Dr. Henry Monroe.

Accompanied by two male assistants, who wore suspiciously stained leather aprons, he'd guided Burton, Burke, and Hare through the north, east, and south wings of the hospital and they were now proceeding through a sequence of locked doors into the west. The inspection had so far taken four hours. Four hours of screaming, wailing, roaring, moaning, babbling, snarling, hissing, sobbing, blaspheming, begging, threatening, despairing, cacophonous insanity.

Burton felt that his own faculties might break down beneath the foul stench and unending barrage of mania, and when he looked at his companions, he saw that the normally phlegmatic Burke and Hare were both showing signs of distress, too.

"Keep a grip," he whispered into Hare's ear. "The person we're looking for has to be in this wing. We'll not have to endure this pandemonium for too much longer."

Hare looked at him balefully, leaned close, and said in a low tone: "It's not the noise, Captain. It's this—this *suit* you've squeezed me into. Most unbecoming! Were it not for the cravat, which thank goodness you allowed me to wear, I would hardly feel myself at all!"

Monroe unlocked the final door in the gloomy passage leading from the south wing to the west. He turned to face his three visitors and, raising his voice above the clamour from beyond the portal, said, for the umpteenth time: "Quite honestly, gentlemen, I don't comprehend why this inspection is—*ugh!*—necessary. The last was less than a year ago and it found everything to be above board and thoroughly shipshape. In fact, significant improvements in the establishment were noted."

Burton, who was wearing a brown wig and long false beard, answered: "As I said before, it's simply a formality. Paperwork was lost in a small fire and we are obliged to replace it. To do so we have to repeat the inspection. I grant you it's inconvenient, but it's also unavoidable."

"Don't misunderstand—I'm not trying to avoid it," Monroe objected. "There's nothing to hide. As a matter of fact, I'm very proud of the work we do here and am happy to show it off. It's simply that you seem to be rather more needlessly thorough than your predecessors and anything that disturbs the normal routine of the hospital is, well, rather—*ugh!*—unsettling for the inmates."

"We're just following governmental regulations, Doctor."

"Be that as it may, I'd like you to put it on record that I'm scrupulous in my duties, that the hospital offers its patients a very high standard of care, and that such interruptions are potentially damaging."

"I shall be sure to do so."

Somewhat mollified, Monroe smiled, grimaced, jerked his head down to the right, and said: "*Ugh!* You'll find fewer patients in this part of the establishment. However, I should warn you that those unfortunates who reside in these wards are the most seriously disturbed and can be exceedingly violent, so please refrain from making eye contact with them. It's also the reason why we don't have a communal hall here, just individual rooms."

He led his visitors into a filthy cell-lined corridor, where the section's head nurse greeted them with a bob. Monroe's two assistants moved along the passage, sliding open viewing hatches. Burton, Burke, and Hare walked from door to door, peering through into the bare square cubicles, trying hard to ignore the abominations that blasted their eyes and assaulted their ears from within.

This went on for corridor after corridor, each one presenting them with more nurses, more cells, more degradation, and more horrors.

Burton walked with his arms folded tightly across his chest, clamping his hands against his ribs to hide the fact that they were shaking.

They came to corridor nine on floor four.

Doctor Monroe introduced another nurse to Burton: "This is Sister Camberwick. She oversees this section. Sister, these gentlemen are from the Department. Inspectors Cribbins, Faithfull, and—*ugh!*—Skylark."

Sister Camberwick bobbed and said, "Good afternoon, sirs. I think you'll find everything to your satisfaction."

The examination of corridor nine followed the same pattern as those before until, at its end, Burton turned to Monroe and said, "Doctor, I'm aware that we're imposing upon your time. May I suggest that we hasten matters?"

"Certainly. That would be most welcome. How so?"

"In addition to completing this tour of inspection, we need to conduct private interviews with selected members of your staff—"

"That wasn't required last time!" Monroe objected. "I can assure you that working conditions here are absolutely—*ugh!*—"

Burton held up a hand to stop him. "Quite so! Quite so! It's nothing more than a formality, I assure you, but one that must be observed in order to complete the paperwork and leave you in peace."

Bismillah! Peace! Here? In this Jahannam!

Monroe ran his tongue across his lips, shrugged, and gave a curt nod. "Oh, very well, very well. Whatever you say. How should we proceed?"

"I suggest you continue the inspection with Mr. Faithfull and Mr. Skylark. In the meantime, I'll remain here to interview Sister Camberwick and her nurses. It should be enough to fulfill the terms of the inspection. Once done, a sister can escort me to your office. My colleagues and I will then take our leave and, I assure you, we'll draft a most favourable report. I think it fair to predict that you'll not be bothered by us again."

The doctor heaved a sigh, gave a smile, and suffered a facial spasm.

A few minutes later, Burton was seated in a small office, alone with Sister Camberwick. The door was closed, muffling the screams and curses from the cells.

"Would you care for a cup of tea, Mr. Cribbins?"

"No thank you, Sister. Please sit and relax. This is merely a routine procedure, there's nothing to be nervous about."

"I'm not nervous," she said. She sat down and adjusted her bonnet. "After working in an asylum, one ceases to feel nerves."

"I should think that's a great advantage."

"It is."

"When did you start here?"

"At the beginning of the year. Early February."

She glanced into his eyes then looked down at her skirts and straightened them.

"And before that?"

She blinked rapidly. "I served in the Crimea, and, when the war was over, in workhouses."

"The Crimea. You must have seen great suffering."

He moved his chair closer to hers and in a low, melodious, and rhythmic tone, recited:

"Lo! in that house of misery
A lady with a lamp I see
Pass through the glimmering gloom,
And flit from room to room.
And slow, as in a dream of bliss,
The speechless sufferer turns to kiss
Her shadow, as it falls
Upon the darkening walls.
As if a door in heaven should be
Opened, and then closed suddenly,

The vision came and went,

The light shone was spent.

On England's annals, through the long

Hereafter of her speech and song,

That light its rays shall cast

From portals of the past.

A lady with a lamp shall stand

In the great history of the land,

A noble type of good,

Heroic womanhood."

Sister Camberwick's lower lip trembled.

"'Santa Filomena' by Henry Wadsworth Longfellow," Burton murmured. "Look at me, Sister."

She looked. Her eyes slid away, returned, held.

Burton began to rock back and forth very slightly, almost imperceptibly. "It is fine work you have done."

She leaned forward to better hear him.

"And it is fine work you continue to do."

She seemed transfixed by the deep, soothing quality of his voice, and, unaware that she was doing it, she began to sway, keeping in time with his own movement.

"For the purposes of this interview," he said, in almost a whisper, "it is important that you relax. This exercise will help. I want you to breathe with me. Feel the air entering your right lung. In. Out. Now breathe into your left. In. Out. Slowly, slowly."

Gently and patiently he guided her through a Sufi meditation technique, watching as her attention centred on him to the exclusion of all else. He softly issued instructions, taking her from a cycle of two breaths to a cycle of four, subduing her mind through the complexity of the exercise until she was entirely under his control.

"What is your name?" he asked.

"Patricia Camberwick," she answered.

"And behind that? The other name? The one that you've been forbidden to use?"

"Florence Nightingale."

"Tell me about the circumstances that led to your presence here, Miss Nightingale."

"I—I can't—I can't remember."

"I know. The memory has been blocked. What occurred to you happened while you were enslaved by a mesmeric influence. Can you feel that blockage, like a wall in your mind?"

"Yes."

"It is only a wall because you've been made to think so. The truth is, it's a door. Just walk through it, Florence. Open it and pass straight through."

Silently, Burton thanked Herbert Spencer for inspiring this mesmeric technique.

"Yes. I'm through."

"You see how easy that was? The barriers planted in your mind have no power now."

"No power."

"So, tell me. What happened?"

"The woman."

"Woman? Who?"

"The Russian. I don't know how she entered my surgery. I was conducting an experiment and had locked the doors. I didn't want to be disturbed. I heard a footstep behind me. I turned and there was the woman."

"What did she look like?"

"Medium height. Heavy. The maternal type. Horrible black eyes."

"Was she solid? I mean to say, was she an apparition?"

"An apparition? A ghost? No, she was there."

"What happened next?"

"I—I—I fell into her eyes. Those eyes! I fell right into them!"

"She mesmerised you. What did she instruct you to do?"

"She told me to travel to Santiago in South America, to go to the asylum there and use the authority of my name to take charge of a patient named Tomas Castro. I was to escort him back here to Bethlem Royal, but upon entering this hospital I must use the name Patricia Camberwick and forget my true name. Service here had been prearranged for me and my primary duty was to care for and guard Mr. Castro. I must not allow anyone to see him apart from the woman and a man named Edward Kenealy."

"Castro is still here?"

"Yes, on this floor, in the observation chamber."

"Why were we not shown that room?"

"Doctor Monroe and the senior staff have had their memory of the room removed. An aversion to the door that leads to it has been implanted into them. They think it's a broom cupboard."

"So, with the exception of the Russian and Kenealy, are you the only person who visits Castro?"

"Yes."

"Take me to him."

"Yes."

Nightingale stood and, as if sleepwalking, drifted across and out of the room, leading Burton along the corridor to a nondescript door. She pulled a bunch of keys from her apron pocket and unlocked it. Burton followed her across the threshold and down a short passage leading to a heavily bolted portal.

"There," Nightingale said.

"Lead the way," he replied.

Keys were inserted and turned, bolts drawn, a padlock opened, and a chain removed. With the nurse's shoulder pressed against it, the barrier swung aside with a painful creak. She stepped onto a platform that ran around the wall of a tall circular chamber, about fifteen feet up from the floor. The room was fifty feet or so in diameter, fitfully illuminated by four gas lamps, and was sparsely furnished with a bed, table, chair, and a wooden screen, which, Burton guessed, concealed a toilet and basin.

A thin chain, attached to an iron ring set in the middle of the floor, snaked across to where a man lay on the bed. It was joined to a manacle that encircled his left ankle.

He was dressed only in ragged trousers and an undershirt, and was dreadfully thin. His left arm ended in a bandaged stump just below the elbow. His face was encased in an iron mask, featureless but for four horizontal slits, one for each eye, one level with his nostrils, and one for the mouth.

Tomas Castro.

The man struggled to a sitting position and looked up at them.

"*Ce qui maintenant?*" he whispered huskily. "Is there to be more torment? Who is this? I have not seen him before."

He spoke with a French accent.

Burton turned to Nightingale. "Follow me."

He walked along the platform until he came to a ladder and descended to the chamber floor.

Castro rose weakly to his feet as Burton approached.

"Please, don't exert yourself," the king's agent said. "Remain seated. You are Sir Roger Tichborne, I take it?"

"Tichborne? *Mon dieu!* You are the first to call me that in a long time. It has been Castro, only Castro." His voice sounded hollow behind the mask.

Burton took the chair and placed it near the bed. He sat down. Tichborne fell back onto the thin mattress and said: "But you address me as 'Sir.' Is it that I have inherited the baronetcy?"

"No little time ago. I'm afraid your uncle and father both died within a week of each other back in '54, shortly before you were committed. It was reported that you were lost at sea whilst voyaging back to England. Your brother Alfred took the title. I regret to inform you that he, too, is dead. He was murdered by your enemies earlier this year."

"Alfred," Tichborne croaked. "*Mon cher frère!*" He raised his hand and rested the front of his mask against it. "And this year, it is?" came his muffled voice.

"It is now September of 1862."

There was a moment of silence, broken when the prisoner began to quietly weep.

Burton leaned forward and placed a hand on the man's upper arm.

"Sir, there has been a vast and terrible conspiracy against you. I am trying to untangle the web, to discover who has spun it and why. It would help considerably if you could tell me your story. Do you have the strength?"

Tichborne raised his head. "Then you mean to help me?"

"I will do everything in my power. My name is Richard Burton. I am an agent of the king."

"No, wait," said Tichborne. "*Non. Non.* It cannot be. *Non.* This, it is a trick. That—" he pointed at Nightingale "—that *fiend* is one of the conspirators. If she is with you, then you are with *them*!"

"You are mistaken, sir. This woman, who you may know as Sister Camberwick, is, in fact, named Florence Nightingale. She has been operating under a deep mesmeric trance. She knows neither what she has done nor why. She is as much a victim as you are."

"*Ce n'est pas possible!* And now? Why is she not screaming for help?"

"Because I myself have a modicum of talent as a mesmerist and have gained control of her."

Tichborne sat silently, gazing at the nurse. Burton could see his wet, lidless eyes shining through the slits of the mask.

"My story," the baronet whispered. "My story." He looked at Burton. "Very well. I shall tell it. Where would you like me to begin?"

"With your voyage to South America—but we have little time, Sir Roger, so broad strokes, if you please."

"*Bien.* I sailed in '54. I had been wooing a distant cousin, Kattie—"

"Katherine Doughty," Burton interjected.

"*Ah! Oui. Elle vit?*"

"Yes, she lives. She is well."

Tichborne nodded, paused, and asked: "Married?"

"Yes."

"*Oui. Oui. Naturellement.*" He looked down, ran his fingers over the stump of his left arm, looked up, and went on: "Kattie's parents, they were not in favour of me, and I cannot blame them. I was young and irresponsible. I felt I had to prove myself to them, and got it into my head that I would go to Chile to follow in my grandfather's footsteps, for there is a legend in the family that he discovered a fabulous diamond in that country, and though no one has ever seen it—and the legend is no doubt untrue—it fired my imagination. What a fool I was! I arrived in Valparaiso—"

"Which is where they say you received the news that your uncle had passed away."

"*Mais non!* I never did! I stayed in the port for but a day then began my journey inland toward Santiago. I eventually settled in a town named Melipilla, at the foot of the Cerro Patagua Range, which is where I suspected my grandfather had done his prospecting. I lived with the family of a man named Tomas Castro, and in his company made forays into the mountains, sometimes living in tents for many days before returning to his home.

"What happened next, *monsieur*, is difficult for me to explain, for my memories, they are confused. Castro and I had ventured farther into the mountains than ever before, and were both suffering from the altitude and thin air. My friend seemed to be the most affected. He began to experience wild hallucinations and became delirious. He insisted that we had displeased the secret inhabitants of the mountains by our presence, and that the only way to placate them was by sacrifice. I began to fear for my life, for he seemed to me to be losing his mind."

"Secret inhabitants?" Burton asked. "Did he have a name for them?"

"*Oui.* He called them the *Cherufe*. He said they were the ghosts of an ancient race that had once inhabited the Earth."

"What happened?"

"As the days passed, I was stricken by terror, not only of him, but also of the things I began to see hiding amid the rocks and undergrowth."

"What things?"

"I am embarrassed to say. You must understand, *monsieur*, that they were not real. I was suffering from visions caused by an insufficiency of oxygen."

"It's important, Sir Roger. What did you see?"

"I saw fairies, tiny people with the wings of moths, butterflies, and dragonflies. I saw them in broad daylight, and at night they came to me in my dreams. I know now that I was going insane. Certainly, Castro was, for one night, he tried to murder me. He struck me on the head and laid me on a rock. It would serve as an altar, he said. He then took a knife and went to thrust it into my heart. I rolled from the rock and we fought. He was savage, a wild beast, his eyes were filled with madness. I pushed him. He fell and cracked his skull. The blow killed him.

"The little people had gathered to watch our conflict. They terrified me, and I think, *monsieur*, that the fear broke my mind. I remember little else until, one day, I became aware that I was in an asylum. They called me Tomas Castro. It seems I had taken my victim's name. I protested that I was an English gentleman but they would not believe me. I was trapped in a nightmare and my sanity was a frail thing. I am sure it failed me again and again. The time I spent in that hell—it—it—"

Tichborne bent and was wracked by a great sob that shook him from head to toe. Burton held tight to the man's shoulder.

"Sir Roger, your suffering is coming to an end, I give you my word. You must hold yourself together for just a little while longer."

"I—I apologise, Monsieur Burton. I am weak. If you had—if—"

"I understand. Pray finish your account."

"That woman—" he nodded toward Florence Nightingale, where she stood, blank-eyed "—came to the asylum one day, sedated me, and took me away. I was brought to this place. How long I have been here, I do not know. I have seen no one but her, a Russian bitch, and a lunatic named Kenealy."

"And these latter two, what did they want of you?"

"The diamond! Always the diamond! I said to them again and again: 'There is no diamond, it is a myth! The story is as absurd as the legendary Tichborne curse!' So then they wanted to know all about that, and I told them of Roger de Tichborne and Lady Mabella and the Tichborne dole, and then—and then—"

"Yes?"

"Then they took me into a room, strapped me to a table, and sedated me. In my last moments of consciousness, I saw her, the *connasse*—" he jabbed a finger at Nightingale "—lean over me with a scalpel in her hand. When I awoke, she had taken my arm and my face. *Mon dieu! Mon dieu!*"

"I am sorry," Burton said. "They have kept you prisoner here since then?"

"Yes, but that is not all. They visit me frequently and ask always about my life and my habits. They want to know everything! Every detail! On and on! Questions! Questions! Questions!"

"It is because they have a man masquerading as you," Burton revealed.

"They have—what? Why?"

"Their scheme is elaborate and I'm still unsure of the ultimate motive. I shall find out, though, you can be sure of that. I will stop them, Sir Roger, and soon. When I do, you will be liberated from this frightful place. Until then, you must remain here and keep this visit of mine a secret. Can I trust you to do that?"

"Yes. Me, you can trust—but her?"

"I am going to bring Nurse Nightingale out of her trance now. I will reveal the truth to her. I believe she will work with us to secure your freedom. She's a strange woman; her dedication to medical research has driven her into ethically dubious territory in recent years, but no one can forget what she did during and after the Crimea. I believe that, at heart, she desires only the greater good."

"I will trust your judgement, Monsieur Burton. But you cannot take me with you now?"

"If I do so, your enemies will know that I'm moving against them. They may flee before we ever learn their intentions. It's better that they remain in the dark."

"So you wish me to stay? Truly, I don't know that I can! If I allow myself to believe that liberation is close at hand, every extra moment in this hell will seem an eternity. But no, no, I understand your reasoning. Stay, I must—and stay, I shall! What matters a few more days or weeks after all this time?"

"Good man. I must hurry now. I've already been away for too long."

He stood and paced over to Florence Nightingale.

"You have listened to this discussion?"

"Yes," she replied dully.

"I am going to take you through some breathing exercises. They will bring you to full awareness. You will remember everything."

"Ah, Mr. Cribbins, at last. You've taken a deuce of a—*ugh!*—time!"

"My apologies, Doctor Monroe, I became fascinated by one of your unfortunates. Patient 1036 on corridor nine."

"1036? 1036? Which one is that?"

"The gentleman who ate his mother."

"Oh, yes. A fascinating study. We tested an interesting therapy on that one. We—*ugh!*—introduced him to another of our patients. A mother who ate her son."

"And what happened?"

"They had dinner together."

"Are you serious?"

"There were doctors in attendance, of course."

Damien Burke stepped forward. "A most intriguing scenario, Doctor Monroe, but I feel we've already taken up far too much of your valuable time. We should be going, isn't that right, Mr. Skylark?"

"Absolutely correct, Mr. Faithfull. Do you agree, Mr. Cribbins?"

"Indeed! Indeed! My apologies, Doctor Monroe, and thank you very much indeed for allowing us to tour your fine establishment. I think it fair to say that it has made an indelible impression on all three of us."

Monroe smiled and shook Burton's hand, then Burke's, then Hare's.

They proceeded down to the lobby and out onto the front steps. Monroe bade them a final farewell and indicated a horse-drawn carriage waiting on the driveway. "This will take you across the grounds to the main—*Ugh!*"

"Gate," Burton finished.

Monroe blinked at him, pursed his lips, turned, and disappeared back into the hospital.

The king's agent looked at the sky and frowned. The atmosphere was thick and steamy, and through it, ugly smudges of smoke could be seen drifting raggedly overhead. Flakes of ash were falling.

"It's been a while since we had a London particular," he muttered.

They climbed into the carriage and, a couple of minutes later, arrived at the big main gate, in which a smaller door was set.

They thanked the driver and tipped their hats to the guard who opened the door for them.

Sir Richard Francis Burton, Damien Burke, and Gregory Hare stepped out of the mental asylum into—*madness!*

LONDON BURNING

Resistance to aggression is not simply justified, but imperative.
—HERBERT SPENCER

Londona was ablaze.

At ground level, the smoke was suffocating. Hellish red and orange light flared through the swirling clouds.

"What the—"

Burton was cut off by a scream of fury. A man came tearing out of the murk, dressed only in trousers and boots, his naked upper body smeared with blood, sweat, and soot. His face was contorted with animal ferocity, and before they could react, he swung a pitchfork with vicious force into Damien Burke's upper left arm.

Burke fell sideways with a yell of pain.

Gregory Hare jumped onto the back of the attacker, snatched the pitchfork out of his hand and threw it aside, wrapped a huge forearm around the man's neck, and squeezed. Seconds later, he was lowering the limp body to the pavement.

Burton snapped back into himself. The assault had been so sudden and brutal that he'd stood frozen, disassociated.

"Damn it!" he muttered, and joined Hare on his knees at Burke's side.

"It's bad," Burke gasped. "Broken."

"You're losing blood. Hare, give me your cravat. We need to get a tourniquet on him right away. Don't worry, old man," he encouraged Burke. "We'll have you fixed up in no time."

"Mr. Hare will attend to me, Captain," Burke responded weakly. "I recommend you draw your spine-gun and see to our defence." He nodded at the street behind Burton.

The king's agent twisted around and saw five individuals shuffling into view. There were two men and three women. All wore dishevelled clothing and diabolical grins. Their eyes were wide and glazed.

One of the women held a dripping severed arm that had, apparently, been torn from its owner's shoulder.

She seemed to recognise the shock in Burton's eyes and responded to it by shouting: "Meat! Tichborne wants meat!" She then raised the limb to her mouth and clamped her teeth into it with a muffled giggle. The giggle turned into a gurgle as blood bubbled down over her chin.

"Your gun, sir!" Damien Burke groaned.

Burton grunted, stood, and reached into his pocket. He pulled out the cactus pistol and pressed the nodule that activated it.

"Die!" said one of the approaching men. "You—upper—crust—bastards."

The woman with the arm, distracted by the taste of blood, lost interest in Burton and his companions. She squatted on her haunches and began to rip mouthfuls of flesh from the bone, swallowing chunks of raw, bloody human meat.

Burton, sickened, wanted to look away. Instead, he raised his strange pistol and shot her in the forehead.

She collapsed onto her back and lay still with the arm across her throat.

The remaining two men and two women screamed and lurched forward, their arms outstretched, their fingers curled into claws, their eyes rolling aimlessly.

Holding his right wrist with his left hand to keep it steady, Burton shot them each in turn.

He released a shuddering breath, looked at the fallen bodies, and allowed his arms to drop to his sides. He was trembling as if in the grip of another malarial fever.

"What the hell is happening?" he muttered.

Something exploded in the distance.

He stepped back to the hospital gate and hammered upon it.

"Let us in! Hey in there! Open up!"

There was no response. The guard had apparently locked the door before returning to the main building with the carriage driver.

"Help me up with him, if you would, Captain," Hare said.

Burton lifted his hat, yanked off his wig and false beard, shoved them into a pocket, replaced his topper, and assisted Hare.

"The rioters appear to be rather more zealous than they were yesterday," the prime minister's man noted. "Yet, equally, rather more mindless. I need to get Mr. Burke back to Whitehall. I suggest we make our way along the

Lambeth Road to Saint George's Circus, and follow Waterloo Road to the bridge. What say you?"

"I say let's go."

"I can support Mr. Burke now that he's up, Captain. You keep that pistol handy."

Burton nodded and began to move slowly through the eye-watering fumes, with his companions following behind.

Beams of light swept over them from above. A huge police rotorship descended, its turbines roaring, steam belching from its exhausts. The down-draught from its rotors cleared the street of smoke, and Burton saw that debris and bodies were scattered all over.

"This is the police!" an amplified voice announced.

The king's agent looked up and noticed a cluster of speaking trumpets projecting down from the ship's hull.

"This is the police. Return to your homes. Stay inside and bar your doors and windows. Do not venture onto the streets. A state of emergency has been declared. Return to your homes. This is the police. Return to your homes. Remain inside."

The mammoth flying machine slowly slid away over the rooftops. As it passed, ash-laden smoke rolled back over Burton and his colleagues.

A horse bolted past, trailing the broken shafts of a wagon behind it.

Somewhere nearby, glass smashed and rained onto the pavement.

Incoherent shouts echoed from the near and far distance.

Cautiously, they moved on.

Ahead, a male voice pleaded: "Help me! Oh, sweet Lord, help me! No! Please! Though I walk in the valley of death I shall—"

It was cut off.

A broken walking stick came whirling out of the miasma and clattered onto the cobbles inches from Burton's feet.

Moments later, through the gloom, they saw the other half of it. One end was held in the hand of a snarling street pedlar. The other end—the broken end—had been thrust up into the base of an elderly clergyman's chin and was projecting from the top of his skull. The pedlar was holding his victim upright but released him as he saw the trio approaching. The dead man crumpled to the pavement. His murderer laughed. Froth sprayed from his mouth. He wiped his bloodied hand on his thigh.

Without hesitation, Burton shot cactus spines into the pedlar's neck and winced at the sound the man's skull made as it hit the road.

"We should proceed with greater haste," he advised Palmerston's men. "Can you manage?"

"Yes, Captain," Hare replied. "Though Mr. Burke seems to be uncon— *Look out!*"

Burton gasped and stepped back as a wraith materialised right in front of him. He saw the figure clearly. It was dressed in a long frock coat, wore a top hat, and its mouth was hidden behind a soup-strainer mustache. Then it dissolved and blew away, nothing but a ribbon of dirty particles.

"What *are* those things?" Hare whispered.

"I don't know, but each time I see one it appears a little more solid, more opaque. I think they're gaining in strength, and they're inciting this violence."

They pressed on and reached Saint George's Circus. A man ran out of a shop, stopped in front of them, and raised an antiquated blunderbuss.

"Die for Tichborne, you posh sods!" he shouted. He pulled the trigger and the weapon exploded in his face, blowing off his right ear.

"Christ!" he screamed. "My bloody head!"

Burton shot him and the man crumpled.

The rumble of approaching wheels came out of the smoke.

"Let that be an empty cab!" Burton pleaded.

It was.

A steam-horse erupted from the fumes, pelting along at full speed, its crankshafts clanking. It was dragging behind it an old-fashioned landau, engulfed in flames. The vehicle careened past them, bounced onto the pavement, and ran smack into the front of a tavern. Glass burst noisily and an angry clamour of voices came from within the building. The vehicle's boiler detonated, hot metal flying in all directions. The front of the building collapsed into the street, sending bricks, glass, and masonry spinning into the air.

Gregory Hare yelled in pain.

Burton turned and saw that a chunk of metal had embedded itself in his colleague's left arm. He slipped under the semiconscious Burke's shoulder to keep him upright and gave a steadying hand to the other man.

"Oof!" Hare grunted. "This isn't good! Ouch! Ouch! Not good at all, Captain!"

The king's agent looked at the wound.

"Wait," he snapped.

He lowered the two men to the ground then shrugged out of his jacket, dropped it, gripped the sleeve of his shirt, and ripped it off.

"How many tourniquets am I to tie today, hey, Hare? Must you and Burke do everything together? You both have wounds in exactly the same blessed place!"

"I apologise, sir," Hare groaned. "A terrible inconvenience. Is it serious?"

"Three men, two out of action, one weapon between them, in the midst of a riot? Yes, I should judge that to be fairly serious. As for the wound, it would be as severe as Mr. Burke's were it not for the fact that your biceps are the size of thigh muscles. The bone is intact."

"As I say, sir, I'm terribly sorry."

"Don't be a fool," Burton growled, tugging the tourniquet tight. "You hardly leaped into the path of that projectile."

In the distance, the police announced: "Get off the streets. Remain inside."

Tongues of flame licked from the ruined tavern. Screams came from within.

Burton retrieved his jacket and put it back on. "Mr. Burke is out cold. Stay with him. Hold this." He pushed the cactus gun into Hare's hand. "I'll be back in a jiffy."

He dived into the murk. Something had caught his eye moments ago. It had possibilities.

"We have to keep moving, Captain!" Hare called after him.

Burton ran back the way they'd come until he reached the edge of the square. He peered to his right, through the swirling haze.

It was still there.

He returned to Burke and Hare.

"There's an abandoned omnipede," he reported, taking back the pistol. "I suggest we hijack the blighter. It'll get us over Waterloo Bridge in no time."

"You can drive the contraption?" Hare asked.

"I can try. I don't think the controls are much different from those on a rotorchair. Come on."

He helped Hare with Burke, dragging him along until they reached the giant mechanised millipede. It was slumped across the road, empty but for the driver, whose corpse hung over the edge of the control seat.

"Looks like he was bludgeoned," Hare muttered.

They hauled Burke up the steps in the side of the vehicle's carapace and laid him on a bench. He stirred and moaned.

"Help me to shift the driver," Burton said. "Try not to use your injured arm—I don't want you bleeding any more than you already are."

"Me neither, Sir Richard."

They descended and moved to what used to be the head of the gigantic insect. As they dragged the dead body down and across to the side of the road, Hare noted that there weren't many people about. "It seems like a wave of rioters has come and gone through this part of town," he ruminated. "I wonder where they are now? Do you think they're still at it, Captain?"

"From the various cries and screams we're hearing, it appears that passions are still running high," Burton replied. "But whether the riot is dying down or has just moved past this district remains to be seen. There were certainly a fair few unfortunates in that tavern when the landau hit it."

He suddenly pointed the pistol at the other man and pressed the trigger. With a soft *phut!* seven spines flew past Hare's ear and embedded themselves in the throat of the woman who'd loomed out of the smoke behind him. The length of pipe she held poised to crack down onto his head fell from numb fingers and clanged onto the road. She dropped on top of it.

"Much obliged," said Hare.

"Take the cactus gun again. I'll drive. You shoot."

Hare grasped the proffered weapon and clambered back onto the omnipede. He stood by the bench upon which Burke lay and braced himself against the canopy, clamping his injured arm against his side, holding the spine-shooter ready.

Burton slipped into the driver's seat and examined the controls. A gauge indicated that the furnace was still burning and another that boiler pressure was high. He settled his feet onto a plate which operated in the same way as the one in his rotorchair: press it forward with the toes to accelerate and backward with the heels to slow and brake. There were two levers to facilitate steering.

"Simple enough," he breathed. "Let's be off."

He pushed gently on the footplate. The insect shuddered and rattled, steam whistling from the vents between its many legs. It jerked ahead, stopped, the engines spluttered, snarled, and the vehicle began to rumble forward.

Burton struggled with the controls. The machine was so long that, as he exited the square and guided it onto Waterloo Road, its middle strayed onto the pavement and scraped against the corner of a bakery, grinding horribly on the brickwork and causing red dust to plume into the already dense atmosphere.

Some of the millipede's legs cracked and snapped against the building. The shop's display window shattered.

"Careful! Careful!" Hare shouted.

Burton jammed down his heels.

"Steer out into the centre of the street, else we'll lose all the limbs along this side!"

"Sorry," the king's agent mumbled. He looked back along the length of the vehicle, trying to judge distances. "Whose bloody stupid idea was it to turn an insect into a confounded 'bus?" he growled.

A yank at the right-hand lever followed by a slow pull back on the left sent the machine away from the corner and out into the middle of the road.

He accelerated along the thoroughfare, fighting to maintain control as the omnipede snaked wildly from side to side, hurtling into abandoned carts, overturned braziers, and all manner of debris, smashing everything aside or crushing it flat beneath its numerous short, powerful legs.

Burton tried to slow it down—he could barely see where he was going—but the footplate was far too responsive and his clumsy efforts caused a jolting motion that had his teeth clicking together and Hare yelling at him.

"Stop or go, if you please, Captain, but for pity's sake try not to do both at once!"

The king's agent glanced again at the gauges.

Perhaps if—

He reached to a small wheel beside the pressure indicator and turned it counterclockwise. Immediately, all along the great length of the omnibus, plumes of steam screamed out of the vents.

The vehicle stabilised.

"The pressure was too high!" he called. "I've got her in hand now!"

Phut! Phut! Phut!

He looked back.

Gregory Hare was shooting at a brougham that had emerged from the swirling smoke and was racing alongside, its steam-horse panting, its driver hollering incoherently. A man was hanging loosely out of the passenger cabin, his arms dangling, cactus spines projecting from the side of his head. Behind him, using him as cover, another man was brandishing a pair of pistols and taking potshots at Hare.

"Shoot the blessed driver!" Burton yelled.

"I'm trying! Perhaps you could pilot this contraption a little more steadily?"

"God-damned stupid machine!" ground out Burton through gritted teeth. "Why in the name of all that's holy did I *ever* leave Africa?"

He wrenched at the left steering lever, sending the omnipede thundering around a motionless and badly dented litter-crab.

A bullet whined past his ear.

"Lions I can bloody well cope with. Mosquitoes I can bloody well cope with. Even traitorous bloody partners, I can bloody well cope with. But giant steam-operated insects I can quite—"

The 'bus slammed into a beer wagon, sending splintered wood exploding outward.

"—happily—"

The vehicle bucked and shook as it trampled over the shattered cart.

"—do without!"

"I'm hit!" Hare cried.

Burton looked back and saw that Palmerston's man had slumped down, clutching his hip, his wide mouth contorted with pain.

The brougham drew closer to the head of the racing insect.

"Stupid stuck-up ponce!" bawled the driver. "You think you can cheat Tichborne?"

Bullets thudded into the carapace at Burton's side.

The stench of the Thames wafted over the king's agent as the omnipede streaked past empty tollbooths and out onto Waterloo Bridge. He caught a glimpse of Big Ben through the stifling atmosphere. Orange light reflected from the side of the tower. The Houses of Parliament were burning.

A shot clipped his ear.

"Upper-class pig bastard!"

"Snooty pisspot!" yelled the brougham's passenger. "Tichborne forever!"

"You two are worse than parakeets," Burton shouted. "And I've had quite enough of it!"

He tugged at the right steering lever, sending the omnibus swerving sideways until it collided with the pursuers. The driver shrieked as his vehicle was rammed into the bridge's parapet.

"Sweet Jesus!" screamed the man inside the cabin as it crunched against the stone barrier. With shocking rapidity, the entire box suddenly flew to pieces and was thrown into the air. The steam-horse overturned and the disintegrating brougham somersaulted over it, smashed against the railing, and disappeared over the side of the bridge.

"There you are, gents," Burton muttered. "A little river water for you. Wash your mouths out." He called over his shoulder: "Are you all right, Hare?"

"Just keep going, Captain! I seem to be immobilised but I daresay I'll live!"

A group of wraiths hove into view at the side of the bridge then wafted away.

A man walked into the path of the omnipede. He was carrying the headless corpse of a woman slung over his shoulder. As Burton jammed his heels down, the man looked up and grinned. Blood oozed from the corners of his mouth.

The millipede hit him square on and he vanished beneath its stampeding legs.

"Idiot!" Burton spat.

The machine ran on, slowed to a scuttle, and came to a stop. The explorer hoisted himself out and moved back to Hare.

"I just caught sight of a police cordon at the end of the bridge. It looks like they've blocked off the Strand. We can get help."

Damien Burke groaned and his eyes fluttered open. "You appear to be injured, Mr. Hare," he mumbled.

"I am, Mr. Burke. As are you. Don't worry, we haven't far to go."

He looked at Burton, held out the spine-shooter, and said: "Your gun, Captain."

"No, you keep hold of it while I run ahead."

"But—"

The king's agent jumped to the ground, scooped up a sharp-ended length of wood, and stalked forward, holding it like a spear, his eyes stinging as particles of ash and soot drifted into them.

"Oy! You there!" came a shout. "Go home! Get off the streets or you'll find yourself under arrest!"

"Police?" Burton called.

"Yes."

"I am Captain Sir Richard Burton."

"The Livingstone chap? You're joking!"

"I'm perfectly serious, Constable, and please don't ever refer to me as 'the Livingstone chap' again!"

A uniformed man emerged from the smoke. "Sorry, sir. No offence intended. And it's sergeant, actually. There's a police cordon behind me. I'm afraid I can't allow you to pass."

Burton threw his makeshift weapon aside, dug a hand into his pocket, and pulled out his wallet. From it, he took a card which, approaching the policeman, he held out for inspection.

The sergeant examined it. "Stone the crows!" he exclaimed. "You're rather important!"

"It would seem so," responded Burton dryly. "I have two injured men with me, Sergeant—?"

"Slaughter, sir."

"Slaughter? Really? How grimly appropriate."

"Yes, sir. Sergeant Sidney Slaughter at your service."

"My colleagues are Lord Palmerston's men and they need to get to Whitehall without delay. Can you rustle up an escort?"

"Certainly. Are they back there?"

"Yes. In an omnipede."

"I'll give you a hand with them. We'll get them to the tollbooths—they mark the edge of the cordon—then I'll arrange transportation."

"Thank you."

They hurried back to the giant insect where they found Damien Burke propped weakly against one of its canopies, brandishing the spine-shooter.

"Thank goodness, Captain," he gasped. "I appear to have regained my wits just as Mr. Hare lost his. However, I fear I may revisit oblivion at any moment. I'm in quite dreadful pain."

Burton took the gun from him and helped him down to the road.

"This is Slaughter," he said.

"I wouldn't go that far, Captain."

"The sergeant. It's his name."

"Oh dear."

The policeman slipped his shoulder under Burke's healthy arm. "Don't worry, I've got a hold of you. Let's be off."

They staggered away, while Burton climbed onto the omnipede and, employing his great strength, lifted the prone form of Gregory Hare from the floor. He dragged him down the steps then followed after the policeman.

A couple of minutes later there came a hail.

"Hey! Sergeant! Over here! I say! Is that you, Captain Burton?"

"Yes, who's that? Come and give me a hand!"

The haze parted as Constable Bhatti stepped out of it.

"Ah! Hallo there!" Burton said.

"Hello, Captain. Strewth! Who're these two?"

"Palmerston's men."

Slaughter lowered Burke and said to Burton: "Lay your man against the booth here." He called to a nearby colleague: "Constable Peters, dash off and fetch a carriage, would you?" Then he turned to Burke: "I'll run you both to a hospital."

"No," Burke responded hoarsely. "We need to get to Whitehall. I'll give you the address."

"But you need your wounds seen to, man!"

"We'll get medical assistance there. Please, do as I say."

Slaughter shrugged. "Very well, sir."

Constable Bhatti muttered, in a low voice: "Captain, I saw Mr. Swinburne a little while ago and managed to snatch a quick word with him. He was with Herbert Spencer—and disguised as an urchin. They were on the trail of a fellow named Doyle."

"How long ago? Any idea where they were headed?"

"Perhaps an hour, and to the Cheshire Cheese tavern on Fleet Street."

"Good. Maybe they're still there."

"If you're going to follow, I recommend you take the same route they did—along the Embankment and up Farringdon Street. It's a little less direct but whatever you do, don't try to pass through the Strand. There are monsters running rampant and no one who's gone in has come out again."

"Monsters? What do you mean?"

"I don't know what they are. One has been glimpsed through the smoke. Huge, apparently. We tried to do a recce by air but our rotorchairs dropped like stones. We lost four men. Then we tried to fly swans over the area but they panicked as soon as they got near and flapped off in the other direction, taking their drivers with them. Only our runners and parakeets can get in and out, but, of course, that's not doing us much good. Now we're waiting until morning before we try to clear the area. By the way, what's wrong with Mr. Swinburne?"

"Wrong? What do you mean?"

"He seems, um—how shall I put it?—even more incomprehensible than usual."

"Ah. Yes. My fault. I mesmerised him. I'm sure the side effects will wear off in due course."

"Mesmerised! Why?"

"I believe this rioting is being instigated by some sort of mediumistic transmission. I was trying to shield him against it."

"Phew!" Bhatti exclaimed. "I wish you'd stay and give my colleagues the same treatment. We've had men going off half-cocked about Roger Tichborne, men running into the Strand and not returning, men collapsing with headaches—it's been bloody mayhem!"

"And you, Constable? How are you faring?"

"I've had a throbbing skull since this chaos began but I'll survive. Is that the carriage I hear?"

"I believe so. Will Burke and Hare be taken care of?"

"Yes, Captain, Sergeant Slaughter will get them to where they need to go."

Burton turned to Palmerston's men, both of whom were conscious now, both slumped against the side of a tollbooth.

"I'm going to leave you in Sergeant Slaughter and Constable Bhatti's capable hands, fellows."

"Right you are, sir," Damien Burke said. "Incidentally, we never got the chance to ask: was our mission successful?"

"It was. My thanks to you both."

"Good luck, Captain."

Burton gave a nod of his head, slapped Bhatti's shoulder, nodded to Slaughter, and ran off into the swirling haze. He sprinted to the end of the bridge, past constables who, having learned of his presence, allowed him through the cordon, then descended the steps to the Albert Embankment, which he followed eastward.

The foul stench of the Thames enveloped him as he ran, the exertion causing him to gulp lungfuls of the poisonous, particle-laden air. He started to cough, his eyes and nose streamed, and when he reached the end of Middle Temple Lane, he stopped, bent double, and spewed black vomit into the gutter.

His head was spinning and his chest wheezed horribly, reminding him of Isambard Kingdom Brunel's creaking bellows. He spat, trying to rid his mouth of the foul taste of ash, bile, and pollutants.

He pushed on.

Time and again he saw wraiths but only two actual men tried to accost him and both went down in an instant with cactus spines in their thighs.

He reached Farringdon and moved in a northerly direction along the thoroughfare, away from the reek of the river. There were fewer buildings ablaze here and the smoke cleared somewhat, allowing him a better view of the abandoned street.

A runner went past him, a blur of grey. He saw more of the dogs speeding back and forth. He guessed they were carrying messages between police stations; the force made extensive use of the postal system.

There were just a few people stumbling about, looking dazed and bewildered, barely conscious of their surroundings. He shot a man who lurched at him, but the others left him alone. Then it dawned on him that every tavern he'd passed appeared full, each producing the sounds of merriment and arguments, songs, shouts, and laughter. Obviously, now that the evening was drawing in, the rioters were taking shelter and refreshment, preparing to see the night through with copious amounts of alcohol. He wondered whether it would loosen the grip of whatever was influencing them, as it had with Swinburne.

He entered Fleet Street and had progressed but a few yards when he spotted Herbert Spencer standing in the shelter of a doorway.

"Boss!" the vagrant philosopher exclaimed. "I weren't expectin' to see you!"

"Hallo, Herbert. Where's Algernon?"

"In there," Spencer replied, pointing at an ancient tavern. The sign above the door read *Ye Olde Cheshire Cheese*. "He found out from Mrs. Doyle that her ne'er-do-well husband was livin' in a flat above a public house what's called the Frog and Squirrel. He went there disguised as a street waif an' sure enough found the man himself proppin' up the bar. Drunk as a skunk, he was. Doyle has some sort of appointment later on, and Master Swinburne has tagged along with him as far as this here pub. I saw 'em headin' down to the Embankment, to give the Strand a wide berth, so I followed and managed to exchange a few words with the lad on the sly. Incidentally, the Strand is where the wraiths are thickest—an' there are crowds of Rakes wanderin' about in it, too, but the thing is—" He stopped and shuddered.

"What is it, Herbert?"

"Them Rakes what I glimpsed—"

"Yes?"

"I think they was dead."

Burton frowned. "How can they be wandering about if they're dead?"

"I know. It ain't possible, but that's what I saw. They're dead, but they ain't realised it yet!"

"Walking dead? By God! And what's this about huge monsters? Constable Bhatti said something of the sort had been seen."

"Yus, but it's just one and it's the Tichborne Claimant, Boss, grown fatter than a whale! I tells you, if'n you go into the Strand, the wraiths will confuse your mind, the dead Rakes will beat you senseless, an' the Claimant will bloomin' well eat you!"

"Eat you?"

"Yus. He's got a taste for human flesh—an' those what are riotin' are followin' his lead!"

"I saw as much. What the hell is happening, Herbert?"

"Dunno, Boss, but it ain't nuthin' good. An' to think back in March we thought it were just a simple diamond robbery!"

"I wonder if Algy has discovered anything useful from that Doyle fellow. Do you think I can get into the tavern without having the living daylights kicked out of me?"

"If you muss yourself up a bit more and go in your shirtsleeves, you'll pass muster, what with your face all sooty, as it is."

Burton slipped out of his jacket and waistcoat, handed them to the vagrant, and looked ruefully at his one-armed shirt.

"I suppose this will be regarded as a qualification," he muttered. "At least I look like I've been in a scrap!"

"Yus. An' if you don't mind me a-sayin' so, you have the face of a pugilist, too."

"Forgive me if I don't thank you for that comment. So, do I look the part?"

"Muss up your hair a little bit more, Boss."

Burton did so.

"Perfect."

"Wait here, Herbert. I hope this won't take too long. It depends how drunk my wayward assistant is."

He crossed the street, paused outside the tavern, pushed the door open, and entered.

The low-ceilinged interior was quite literally packed to the rafters with working men and women of the very lowest order, with, no doubt, thieves, murderers, and whores mixed liberally among them. They were drunk and boisterous, and many appeared glassy-eyed with something beyond alcoholic intoxication. A few were so far gone they were practically catatonic, standing motionless amid the cacophony with slack faces and eyes rolled up into their sockets.

He pushed his way through the laughing, shouting, singing, squabbling mob, feeling that, at any moment, a knife might be thrust between his ribs or a broken bottle mashed into his face.

"To hell with soddin' aristocrats!" someone bellowed.

A roar of approval went up and Burton joined in, so as not to stand out.

"Ari-sto-craaats—" rasped a man beside him.

"Three cheers for Sir Roger!"

Burton cheered with them.

"Up with the working man!"

"Aye!" they yelled.

"Aye!" Burton shouted.

As he shoved through what looked to be a group of poorhouse workers, they broke out in song:

> "When the Jury said I was not Roger,
> Oh! How they made me stagger,
> The pretty girls they'll always think
> Of poor Roger's wagga wagga!"

A wave of maniacal laughter greeted the verse. One man's guffawing turned into a loud, incoherent wail then cut off abruptly. He stood grinning stupidly, with spittle oozing down his chin.

"Pour more booze down the silly bugger's neck," someone called. "That'll get 'is engine runnin' again!"

"Aye!" shouted another. "Them what's not quaffin' will end up in a coffin!"

This was greeted with more mirth and raised glasses.

Burton registered the paradox that those who were most inebriated were apparently also the ones who retained most of their wits. It confirmed that alcohol did, indeed, go some way to counter the effect of the Tichborne emanations.

He saw Swinburne, looking every inch the guttersnipe, squashed into a corner with a hollow-eyed, bespectacled, long-bearded individual.

"Oy! Nipper!" he roared. "Get yer arse over 'ere, yer little brat!"

"You tell 'im, mister!" A dirty-faced strumpet giggled, nudging him in the side. "Put the scamp over yer knee and give 'im a bloody good spankin'— an' after that, you can do the same to me!"

Raucous laughter erupted around him. He joined in, and bawled, "Aye! An' the flat of me hand ain't all you'll be a-hankerin' after, is it? I has it in mind that you'll be a-wantin' a bloody good roger, too—an' I don't mean his nibs Tichborne!"

A deafening cheer greeted his gibe and, under cover of the clamour, raised tankards, and gleeful scoffing, he signalled Swinburne to join him.

The poet said something to his companion, stood, and pushed his way through to Burton's side. The king's agent thumbed toward the door, mouthing, "Let's get out of here!" then grabbed his assistant by the ear and dragged him through the pub and out onto the street.

"My ear!" the poet squeaked.

"Dramatic necessity," Burton grunted.

They crossed the road and joined Spencer.

"How are you holding up, Algy?" the explorer asked.

Swinburne rubbed his ear and said, "Fine. Fine. What about that spanking?"

"You got quite enough of that outside Verbena Lodge. What's Doyle up to?"

"Drinking, drinking, and more drinking. He can really knock it back. I'm astonished he's still standing, and, as you know, I'm a past master in such endeavours. I really am very impressed. If it came down to a challenge, I'd—"

"Stop babbling, please."

Burton wondered whether mesmerising the poet had been such a good idea. As he'd suspected, the consequential behaviour was proving unpredictable, Swinburne's verbosity being the most obvious symptom.

"He's on his way to a séance, Richard. It's at ten o'clock at 5 Gallows Tree Lane, on the outskirts of Clerkenwell, very close to the Literary Gentlemen's Unpublishables Club. You know the place—I believe you once went there with old Monckton Milnes. If I remember rightly, you wanted to consult their copy of *The Seven Perilous Postures of Love* by one of your obscure—or do I mean 'obscene'?—Arabian poets. It's the club with the supposedly secret scroll of—"

"I know! I know!" Burton interrupted.

"My hat! Do you think they chose Gallows Tree Lane because of its name? Nice and morbid for summoning spirits!"

"Be quiet a moment, Algy. I need to think."

"Very well. I shan't say another word. My lips are—"

Burton grabbed his assistant, whirled him around, pulled him close, clapped a hand over his mouth, and held him tightly.

"Herbert, would you say Doyle is my height?"

"Yus, more or less, but thinner."

"Reach into the left pocket of my jacket, would you?"

Spencer, who had Burton's jacket draped over his arm, did as directed and pulled out the brown wig and false beard the king's agent had worn to Bedlam.

"A decent match, do you think?"

"I'd say so, Boss. P'raps his is a touch lighter in colour, but not by much."

"Mmmph!" Swinburne added.

"Good. When Doyle comes out of that tavern, we're going to jump on him and exchange his jacket and hat for mine. Then I want you and Algy to drag him back to Montagu Place. Keep him there and under no circumstances let him go. Is that understood?"

"To the hilt."

"Question him. He's intoxicated, so maybe he'll blab something of interest. Ask him about fairies."

Swinburne squirmed wildly and managed to wriggle out of his grasp. The poet hopped up and down excitedly.

"Fairies? Fairies?" he squealed. "Fairies? What's his pet obsession got to do with anything?"

"Just ask him, Algy. See what he says."

Spencer eyed Swinburne. "If he can get a word in edgeways."

"Richard! Surely you don't intend to—"

"Yes, Algy. I'm going to that séance in the guise of Charles Altamont Doyle."

THE SÉANCE

Sir Richard Francis Burton was a master of disguise, but even he couldn't masquerade as another man so convincingly that his subject's friends and acquaintances would be fooled.

He stood on the doorstep of 5 Gallows Tree Lane, an approximation of Charles Doyle. The foppish jacket he wore was too tight, and while makeup from his pocket kit had hidden his scars and given his eyes and cheeks the appropriately gaunt cast of an addict, his pupils were almost black, whereas Doyle's were a pale and watery blue.

He was, therefore, feeling rather nervous when he knocked on the door.

It was dark now and the streets were quiet. The throbbing of a police rotorship pulsed through the air from afar.

The door opened and a man stood silhouetted by gaslight.

"Yes?"

"Am I late?"

"Yes. We've been waiting."

"The riot—"

"I know. Come in. Leave your hat and cane on the stand."

Burton stepped inside.

"Put this on. No names. You know the rules."

Burton was handed a black crepe mask. He placed it over his eyes, knotting the ribbons behind his head. Inwardly, he sighed with relief. Now his disguise was more secure.

The man closed the door and turned, revealing that he, too, was masked. "Follow me."

The king's agent was led through a reception room and into a large parlour. A dense stratum of blue tobacco smoke floated just above eye level. There was a big round table in the middle of the room with seven chairs arranged around it. Two men stood by a bureau, three by a fireplace. All were dressed in the Rakish manner. All wore masks. They turned as he entered.

"Gentlemen, we can start," the man who'd answered the door announced. "Please lay your drinks aside, extinguish your cigars, and take your places at the table."

Each man did as directed, while the host turned down the gas lamps until the room was in near darkness. His guests moved to the chairs, seeming to sit in preselected positions. Burton hung back until it became clear where he should place himself. He sat.

There was a moment of silence, broken only by the ticking of a grandfather clock.

"I shall begin this meeting as I have begun every meeting," the host intoned, adopting a low and rhythmic manner of speech, as if beginning a ritual, "with a statement of purpose, for we are undertaking a great work. Those who would flinch from it must remind themselves that what we do, in the fullness of time, shall be for the greater good of mankind."

"The greater good of mankind," the gathering echoed.

Burton's jaw muscle flexed. He was going to have to anticipate these repetitions and join in.

Don't get it wrong!

"Our watchword is freedom."

"Freedom!"

"Our object is liberation."

"Liberation!"

"Our future is anarchy."

"Anarchy!"

"Join hands, please."

Burton reached out and felt his hands gripped by his neighbours.

"True freedom comes not from rights granted in the courts of law but from the complete absence of law. True freedom cannot be imposed from without but must flower from within. True freedom is not the prerogative to do something but the right to do anything. True freedom knows no bounds, no reason, no moral centre, no belief, no time, no place, no status, no god."

"No god," they chorused.

"Gentlemen, rules must be broken."

"Rules must be broken."

"Propriety must be challenged."

"Propriety must be challenged."

"The status quo must be unbalanced."

"The status quo must be unbalanced."

"Though each of us here occupies a privileged position, we must each be willing to sacrifice it that the human species may progress, for the cycle of ages turns and a time of transition is upon us."

Burton stifled an exclamation. Again, those words!

"Each has a part to play in the great upheaval that is to come. Each part is essential to the whole. Do not waver. Do not doubt. Do not question."

The room was suddenly heavy with a presence, sensed but not seen.

The clock stopped.

A strange tone entered the host's voice; it was as if another person—female—was beginning to force her own words through his vocal cords.

"We shall go forth this night, as we have done before. We shall carry the vibrations of change to the people. We shall guide them to true liberty."

"True liberty!" the group chanted.

"*Urk!*" the host said.

Burton stared at him. The man had suddenly thrown his head back and opened his mouth. A bubbling, shifting, globular substance was rising into the air from deep within his throat—the king's agent could see the sides of the man's esophagus undulating as the matter rose up through it.

Ectoplasm!

Possessing the qualities of both a liquid and a gas, the strange material rolled and twisted upward into the cloud of tobacco smoke. Burton squinted, unsure how to interpret the scene that unfolded before him. It appeared that the layer of smoke was glowing slightly and bulging downward over the centre of the table.

The female voice now filled the room. It wasn't coming from the man any longer, but reverberated, it seemed, in the very atmosphere itself.

"Send forth your astral bodies, my sons. Undertake our great work. Walk abroad and touch the souls of the unenlightened."

The bulge in the smoke rapidly congealed into the shape of a woman's head and shoulders, hanging upside down from the cloud. A swirling, wispy arm reached out and a vague finger touched one of the Rakes on the forehead. Burton watched in amazement as a ghostly form detached itself from the man's seated figure. It hovered behind him for a moment before blowing away on an unfelt breeze, dissolving into the gloom of the chamber.

"Go forth, apostles, and liberate the downtrodden and the oppressed."

She had a Russian accent.

The woman's finger touched a second man and a wraith emerged from him and vanished.

She turned until she was facing the Rake sitting on Burton's left. Her eyes were jet black, glinting in the smoke like gemstones.

Lady Mabella. The murderer of Sir Alfred Tichborne.

"Travel through the astral plane, my child, and—"

She paused.

Her eyes swivelled to Burton and fixed upon him.

"You!"

He jerked back in his chair and gasped, tried to stand but couldn't. Pain gripped the back of his head as if a cold hand had clamped down on his brain.

"Intruder! Spy!"

She had not spoken aloud. Her voice was now inside his skull.

The host twitched and choked as the ectoplasm continued to flow from his mouth. The two men whose astral bodies had departed sat blank-eyed and motionless. The three other men turned their heads and regarded Burton. One of them said something but no sound emerged. There was no sound in the room at all; a profound, unnatural silence had fallen.

Everything slowed and became motionless. Only the ghostly woman moved.

Something wormed its way into Burton's mind.

"Who are you?" she hissed.

He flinched and fought against her intrusive probing. *Get out of my head!*

"My! How resistant! I am impressed! You have willpower! No matter, your defences are nothing to me. Your name is Richard Burton. Ah. I see you have a reputation. A scholar, an explorer, and—an irritant!"

Withdrawing into himself, the king's agent visualised the mental chambers and structures he'd established through self-mesmerism. His knowledge of Edward Oxford—and of a future that had been destined but which was now cut loose and replaced—he set aside. He devalued all the routes to it and made them seem so entirely insignificant that they would, he hoped, be overlooked. At the same time, he strengthened the mental walls surrounding his more personal and sensitive memories and tried to make them impenetrable.

He was using his own insecurities to entice her away from the information he needed to protect.

It worked.

"No, no, malchik moi! *There is no hiding!"*

The words were like a blade, running him through.

Who the hell are you? Don't try to fool me with that Lady Mabella nonsense!

A cruel chuckle echoed in his skull.

"*Ah yes, the unfortunate Tichborne clan and their silly curse! How convenient that was!*"

His walls were breached.

Stop!

"*My, a complicated little thing, aren't you? What is this? You are in the employ of the king himself! So I was right! You* are *a spy!*"

The beady black eyes bored into his. He struggled and failed to look away.

He tried to distract her: *For all your hokum, you're nothing but a murderer and thief. You killed Jean Pelletier, didn't you?*

"*Pah! I simply appeared before him and he dropped dead from fright, the weak fool.*"

You took his diamonds. And then the François Garnier Choir Stones.

"*Yes, yes. I lifted them through the solid metal of a safe just as I could pull your brain from your skull without breaking the skin of your scalp.*"

And replaced them with onyx crystals. Why? Did you think to delay investigations into the matter?

"*Yes. I see that it didn't work. How did you discover my little deception? Let us find out.*"

He felt her burrowing deeper and deeper, and he allowed the intrusion, for as she penetrated his mind, he found that he was able to stealthily enter hers.

"*Bozhe moi! Brunel and Babbage! So, the detestable Technologists have an interest in the diamonds, too!*"

Babbage had plans for the stones. Your intentions, though, seem rather more nefarious, and to achieve those ends, you've made unwitting pawns of the Rakes, have you not?

"*Unwitting? More like witless. The vacant-headed fools! Becoming the leader of their pathetic clique was child's play to one such as I.*"

The woman's weakness was obvious: she possessed overweening vanity. She was supremely confident in her abilities and, having no knowledge of his Sufi training, vastly underestimated him. However, in order to inveigle information from her, he had to keep her occupied, and the only way to do that was to sacrifice the deeper reaches of his own mind—to give her access to his insecurities, sorrows, and regrets.

It was agony.

Burton felt his heart tighten as she infiltrated the grief he associated with the Berbera expedition—but he pushed through the pain and surprised her with a question: *Who is Arthur Orton?*

His unexpected probe was so forceful that the answer flared in her mind before she could stop it. Burton saw confirmation that the Tichborne creature and Orton the butcher were one and the same. The man had been chosen for her scheme because he possessed a peculiarly well-developed ability to project coercive mental energy, though he was oblivious to this talent. He'd been using it unknowingly in Wagga Wagga to attract customers to his shop, and they had come, despite fearing and loathing him due to his disgusting appetite for raw meat. Implanting the Choir Stones beneath his scalp had greatly enhanced the ability.

The woman's invasive presence assaulted Burton with greater intensity.

"Very clever, Gaspadin Burton! But I shall get far more from you than you can get from me! Already I am deep inside your memories. I see poor Lieutenant Stroyan there. You killed him. How careless of you!"

Still she misjudged him, and while she dug her claws into his painful memories, she also exposed much more of herself than she realised. He felt a sense of triumph blazing through the woman. She gloried in the fact that Britain's labourers were falling under the spell of her great deception, eagerly swallowing the story of a lost aristocrat who'd returned home to find himself snubbed by the society that produced him simply because he'd worked as a commoner. It was the perfect means to rouse their sleeping passions.

How valuable the Tichbornes had been! Her faux prodigal not only gave her the means to disseminate her evil influence among the working classes, but had also secured for her the South American diamond.

Burton, gathering information, struggled to resist her taunts. He remembered his friend's courage, and told her: *Stroyan died as he would have wished—a brave man performing his duty.*

"Nonsense! You killed him! The guilt eats away at you!"

Again, he tried to surprise her into revealing more: *Tell me, madam, where did you find out about the Eyes of Nāga?*

He felt her reel at the question.

"Dorogoi!" she exclaimed. *"You know too much!"*

This time, however, an answer did not inadvertently enter her thoughts. Instead, Burton detected the presence of an impassable barrier, as if part of the woman was—was—

He couldn't define what he sensed.

"How I learned of the Eyes is of no consequence. All that matters is that I employ them to open the minds of the poor and the downtrodden. You see how I clear the blinkers from their eyes?"

You speak as if you are performing some manner of social service, but that is not your intention, is it? Tell me the truth. What do you hope to achieve?

"Revolution."

You want to overthrow the British Empire?

"*I want to demolish it.*"

Why?

"*Because I am a seer,* malchik moi. *I have cast my mind into the future and I know the destiny of my beloved country. I have watched Mother Russia brought to her knees. I have watched her wither and die!*"

What the hell has this to do with Britain?

"*Everything! See what I have seen!*"

White-hot pain seared into Burton's head. He screamed his anguish as the woman's clairvoyant vision flooded into his brain—too much information, too fast, blasting down the channel that joined their minds, overwhelming his senses, telling him far more even than she'd intended, and driving him into a near stupor.

Paralysed in thought as well as body, he watched helplessly as her prophecy slowly unfolded in his mind's eye.

Blood.

Light.

A first taste of air.

A child is born in Russia, the son of peasants.

Grigori Yefimovich Rasputin.

He is blessed—or perhaps cursed—with clairvoyant powers.

His childhood is unhappy. Everyone knows there is something different—strange—about him. He is shunned. Only his siblings give him the attention he craves. He adores them. Then his sister drowns in a river, and his brother, saved from the same fate, is taken by pneumonia.

Rasputin knows that one day he will also die in water. The knowledge terrifies him—unhinges him. He becomes erratic and violent. His parents banish him to a monastery deep in the Ural Mountains, unaware that the establishment has been overrun by the banned Khlysty sect; flagellants, whose orgiastic rituals end in physical exhaustion, and, for Rasputin, in ecstatic mediumistic hallucinations.

Two years later, now a lanky, straggle-haired youth, he emerges from the mountains, intoxicated with a sense of his own importance and in no doubt that he will gain control of his country and make of it a great power. He has seen it. It has been prophesied. It is the future.

Before his twentieth birthday, he marries and comes to hate his wife, has children and is repelled by them, and indulges in affairs—many affairs—

before walking out of his home, never to return. He travels back and forth across Russia, and, after three years, makes his way to Saint Petersburg.

Soon the whole city knows him. They call him the "Mad Monk." He is the holy man who heals the sick, who sees the future, and who gets drunk and seduces married women and their daughters.

The tsaritsa comes to him, drawn by his reputation as a miracle worker. Her son is dying. Rasputin eases the boy's suffering. He gains the royal family's trust. By now he is an alcoholic and a sexual deviant, but he has the tsar's ear.

A new century dawns.

For years, Britain and Prussia—now United Germany—have been engaging in skirmishes in Central Africa. The tensions deepen, and Britain's Technologists begin an arms race with Germany's Eugenicists. The British government is nervous. It has come to regard eugenics as an insidious evil, a menace to civilisation, an antithesis to freedom and the rights of man.

The prime minister seeks to publicly downplay the growing threat from the foreign power. After all, the British Empire is massive. It counts North America, India, the Caribbean, Australia, and huge chunks of Africa among its many territories. What can a comparatively small nation like Germany do against such a global power?

Then Britain's reclusive monarch, King Albert, dies, aged ninety. Lord Palmerston's masterful manipulation of the constitution had given Albert the throne after the assassination of Queen Victoria, but has now left it with no obvious successor.

The republican movement gains popular support. The country is thrown into crisis. The government is distracted.

Germany invades France.

Germany invades Belgium.

Germany invades Denmark.

Germany invades Austria–Hungary.

Germany invades Serbia.

They all fall.

The Greater German Empire is born.

Britain declares war.

Emperor Herbert von Bismarck sends his chancellor, Friedrich Nietzsche, to Russia to win the backing of the tsar.

Secretly, Nietzsche also meets with Grigori Rasputin. It's the first time they've encountered each other in the flesh, but for many months they've been in mediumistic contact, for Nietzsche, like Rasputin, is profoundly clairvoyant. He is also a profligate, drug-addict, and sadomasochist.

They have a plan.

Rasputin will manipulate the tsar into allying Russia with Germany. When the British are defeated and their Empire is carved up, assassinations will be arranged. The Bismarck and Romanov dynasties will be destroyed. Together, Nietzsche and Rasputin will become the supreme rulers of the entire Western world. They convince themselves that they will be strict but benign.

It begins.

Tsar Nicholas has no resistance to Rasputin's mesmeric influence. Russia declares war against Britain.

For three appalling years, the conflict rages, spreading across the whole world, with the British Technologists' steam machines on one side and the German Eugenicists' adapted flora and fauna on the other.

An entire generation of men is slaughtered.

Europe is battered until it is little more than one gigantic, muddy, blood-soaked field.

Britain falters, but fights on, and when the British American States join the conflict, Germany is bruised and, for the first time, retreats.

Russian troops arrive in the nick of time. There is another great push forward. For two more years, the battles seethe back and forth over Europe's devastated territories, until finally, the biggest empire the world has ever seen topples and falls.

The war ends. The spoils are divided. The treachery follows.

Tsar Nicholas and his entire family are rounded up and shot in the head. Bismarck is garrotted. His family and supporters are executed.

Friedrich Nietzsche rises to power, receives life-prolongation treatments, and begins a near-century-long reign of terror that will earn him the sobriquet *The Devil's Dictator*.

Britain, from its deathbed, makes one final gesture of defiance. Two days before Rasputin is to be named president of Russia, three members of the palace staff surround him. They are British spies. They produce pistols and, at point-blank range, pull the triggers. All three guns jam. Rasputin has long feared assassination, and projects around himself a permanent mediumistic energy field that alters the structure of springs, robbing them of their power. No trigger mechanism will function anywhere near him.

He laughs in the faces of the would-be killers, and, with a careless gesture, causes their brains to boil in their skulls.

The following day, he is poisoned with cyanide. Realising that he's the subject of a second assassination attempt, he slows down his metabolism and begins to consciously secrete the poison out through his pores. Four men corner him and hack at him with an axe. They bludgeon him into submission, bind him hand and foot, and wrap him in a carpet. Rasputin is carried to the ice-bound Neva River and thrown in.

Despite his terrible wounds, it is—as he's known it would be all his life—the water that kills him.

He dies believing the British have had their revenge.

He is wrong.

The assassins are German.

The year is 1916, and Nietzsche, now the most powerful man in the world, considers himself well rid of the Mad Monk. Russia, without a visionary in control, will never pose a threat. It is left isolated, friendless, ungoverned, and poverty-stricken.

With millions of its sons killed in the war, the sprawling country's agricultural infrastructure collapses. Famine decimates the population. A harsh winter does the rest.

Russia's death is lonely, lingering, and catastrophic.

"There!"

The woman's voice hissed through Burton's skull.

He gulped in air and a tremor shook his body as consciousness returned.

"There!" she repeated. *"That is why I do what I do! I have seen Mother Russia die, and I will not allow it! No! I shall change history! I shall ensure that Britain is in no condition to oppose Germany! I shall see to it that the World War is over in months rather than years! I shall cause your workers to bring this country to its knees! And when the terrible war comes—for there is no stopping it—Germany will wipe your weakened, filthy Empire from the Earth without need of Russia's aid. And while it is doing so, Rasputin will be making the homeland strong, and when the war is done and Germany is weakened, he will strike! There will be a new Empire—not Britain's, not Germany's, but Russia's!"*

You're insane.

"No. I am a prophet. I am the saviour of my country. I am the protector of Rasputin, the death of Britain, and the destroyer of Germany. I am Helena Petrovna Blavatsky, and Destiny is mine to manipulate!"

She pushed deeper into his mind. Burton opened his mouth to scream but could make no sound. It felt as if his cranium was filling with maggots.

"Dorogoi!" she exclaimed. *"You killed Babbage! How gratifying! But what is this? Even more guilt? My, my, Gaspadin Burton, what a brilliant mind you have, but so filled with fears and insecurities—and so many regrets! I see now that killing you is not enough, for there is something you fear more, and that shall be your punishment: I will cause your own weaknesses to deprive you of your reason!"*

Her mesmeric power intensified. It overwhelmed his crumbling resistance. His capacity for independent thought was summarily crushed and immobilised.

A fracture opened. Burton's subtle and corporeal bodies lost cohesion. His mind began to splinter. His viewpoint suddenly changed and he found himself hovering outside his own body. He watched the intelligence fade from his own eyes.

The odd disassociation gave him his one slender chance.

RESCUE

An insuperable obstacle to rapid transit in Africa is the want of
carriers, and as speed was the main object of the Expedition
under my command, my duty was to lessen this difficulty as
much as possible. Rotorchairs were the obvious solution.
—HENRY MORTON STANLEY

Algernon Swinburne was in no fit state to conduct an interrogation.
He'd been drinking with Charles Doyle, first in the Frog and Squirrel,
then in Ye Olde Cheshire Cheese, and, in Herbert Spencer's opinion, he'd
taken another step closer to becoming a chronic alcoholic. The philosopher
hoped the pitiful state of Doyle would teach the young poet a lesson.

The Rake had not put up much resistance when they and Burton had shang-
haied him. As a matter of fact, when informed that the séance had been post-
poned—which was a lie, of course—and invited for drinks at Montagu Place,
he'd expressed relief, hooked his arms in theirs, and cried: "Lead on, Macduff!"

They had led on, after first indulging in a comedic charade of jacket and
hat swapping which baffled the already befuddled Doyle and had Swinburne
in fits of giggles.

Burton headed off toward Gallows Tree Lane, while Swinburne and
Spencer ushered Doyle north along Gray's Inn Road, then west along the
Euston and Marylebone Roads. Rioters were still on the rampage but they
paid scant attention to the trio, who weaved through and around the
wreckage and fights and fires, appearing to be nothing but an urchin, a
vagabond, and a hopeless drunk.

They were twice stopped and questioned by the police. Fortunately,
Swinburne was familiar with both the constables and, after he surreptitiously
lifted his wig to reveal the carroty red hair beneath and whispered words of
explanation, they allowed him and his companions to pass.

The next hurdle was rather more intimidating. Mrs. Iris Angell responded to their hammering on the front door by opening it and placing herself on the threshold, with hands on hips and a scowl on her face.

"If you think you're setting foot in this house while three sheets to the wind you must be even more intoxicated than you smell. How many times must I put up with it, Master Swinburne?"

Unable to reveal his mission while Doyle was beside him, Swinburne charmed, flattered, wheedled, demanded, apologised, and almost begged, all to no avail.

In the distance, Big Ben chimed ten. In his mind's eye, the poet pictured Richard Burton joining the séance, and he jumped up and down in frustration.

Then he remembered that the agent and his housekeeper had shared with him a password to use when on king's business.

"My hat, Mother Angell, it completely slipped my mind! Abdullah."

"Now then, you'll not be using that word carelessly, I hope. Sir Richard will not stand for that, you know!"

"I promise you, dear lady, that I employ it fully cognisant of the consequences should your suspicions, which I insist are entirely unfounded, prove to be true. Abdullah, Mrs. A. Abdullah, Abdullah, and, once more, Abdullah! By George, I'll even throw in an extra one for a spot of blessed luck! Abdull—"

"Oh, stop your yammering and come in. But I'm warning you, gentlemen: any monkey business and I'll have Admiral Lord Nelson ejecting you from the premises with a metal boot to your posteriors!"

She allowed them to pass through.

"Master Swinburne, a message arrived by runner for Sir Richard. I left it on his mantelpiece."

They climbed the stairs and entered the study.

"Buttock face! Strumpet breeders!"

POX JR5 fluttered across the room and landed on Herbert Spencer's shoulder.

"Gorgeous lover boy!" the parakeet cackled.

Doyle collapsed into an armchair.

Swinburne read the message mentioned by the housekeeper:

Miss Nightingale communicated with me the moment you left Bedlam. Situation understood. Thank you, Sir Richard. I am in your debt. If you require assistance, my not inconsiderable resources are at your disposal. I can be contacted at Battersea Power Station.

Isambard Kingdom Brunel

The poet raised his brows and muttered: "An old enemy may have just become a new friend."

He took a decanter of brandy from Burton's bureau and joined Doyle. They set about emptying it.

Spencer abstained from drinking. He felt obliged to remain sober enough to record any useful information Swinburne might extract from Doyle. By contrast, Burton's assistant felt it incumbent upon himself to make their guest—who was too far gone to realise that he was actually their prisoner—feel that he was among friends; that he could talk freely. He therefore matched the Rake drink for drink.

The subsequent conversation, if it could qualify as such, was, to Spencer's ears, verging on gibberish.

Doyle, who didn't seem to care that he was drinking with a child—for that's what Swinburne, in his disguise, appeared to be—was regaling the "boy" with "facts" about fairies. His voice was thick and slurred and his eyes rolled around in a disconcerting manner.

"Sh—see, they—they fiss-fick-fixate on a person, like they've fig-fixated on me, then they play merry miz-mischief. It's peek-a-boo when ye least ess-expect it; diz-distraction when ye least—*urp!*—need it; wizz-whisperings when ye least want 'em. Aye, aye, aye, they're not the joyful little sprites I dep-depict for the pish-picture books, ye know. Och no. I have to paint 'em that w-w-way, y'zee-shee-see, just so I can sell ma work." He groaned, swigged from his glass, and muttered: "Damn and—*urp!*—blast 'em!"

"But where do they come from, Mr. Doyle? What do they want? Why are they tormenting you? What do they look like? Do they speak? Have they intelligence?"

"Och! One q-question at a time, laddie! They are eff-etheric beings, and they latched onto ma ash-ash-ass-astral body while I was shhh-sharing the eman-eman-emanations."

Swinburne started to say something but Spencer jumped in with: "Sharin' the emanations? What's that mean?"

Doyle belched, drained his glass, wiped his mouth with his sleeve, and held the tumbler out for a refill. His hand trembled.

Swinburne took aim and poured the brandy. Half of it hit the tabletop.

"The Ray-Rakes want a better sh-sss-society but no one listens to us, do they? They do-don't take us sh-say-seriously. Ye've sheen our dec-declarations?"

"Posted on walls and lampposts." Swinburne nodded, and quoted: "'We will not define ourselves by the ideals you enforce. We scorn the social attitudes that you perpetuate. We neither respect nor—*hic!*—conform with the views of our elders. We think and act against the tides of popular opinion.

We sneer at your dogma. We laugh at your rules. We are anarchy. We are chaos. We are individuals. We are the Rakes.'"

"Codswallop!" Pox squawked from Spencer's shoulder.

"Aye, w-well, it was a waysh-waste of good ink and paper. Sh-so our new leader—"

His voice trailed off and his eyes lost focus. The glass slipped from his hand, spilling brandy into his lap. He slumped forward.

"Damn, blast, and botheration!" Swinburne shrilled. "The bally fool has passed out on us just as he was getting to the good bit!"

"Yus, and he's out for the count by the look of it, lad," Spencer observed. "He won't be openin' his eyes again until tomorrow, mark my words. What shall we do with him?"

"We'll carry the bounder upstairs and lay him out on the sofa in the spare bedroom. I'll sleep on the bed in there. You can kip here, if an armchair's not too uncomfortable for you."

"I've slept in so many blinkin' doorways that an armchair is the lap o' bloomin' luxury!"

"My sweetie pie," Pox whispered.

Swinburne stood and swayed unsteadily. He stamped his foot.

"What the dickens is all this fairy nonsense about, Herbert?"

"It beats me."

By midnight, Algernon Swinburne was staring at the spare bedroom's ceiling, wishing he could be rid of the sharp tang of brandy that burned at the back of his throat.

He couldn't sleep and the room seemed to be slowly revolving.

He felt strange—and it was something more than mere drunkenness.

He'd been feeling strange ever since Burton had mesmerised him.

Tonight, though, the strangeness felt . . . stranger.

He shifted restlessly.

Doyle, draped over the sofa, was breathing deeply and rhythmically, a sound not too far removed from that made by waves lapping at a pebble beach.

The house whispered as the day's heat dissipated, emitting soft creaks and knocks from the floorboards, a gentle tap at the window as its frame contracted, a low groan from the ceiling rafters.

"Bloody racket," Swinburne murmured.

From afar came the paradiddle of rotors and the muffled blare of the police warning.

"And you can shut up, too!"

He wondered how much damage the riot had caused. There had been a great many acts of arson and vandalism, and beatings and murders, too.

"London," he hissed. "The bastion of civilisation!"

He could hardly believe that the supposed return of a lost heir had developed into such mayhem.

He looked at the curtained window.

"What was that?"

Had he heard something?

It came again, a barely audible tap.

"Not a parakeet, surely! Not unless its beak is swathed in cotton wool! Good lord, what's the matter with me? I feel positively spooked!"

Tap tap tap.

"Go away!"

He experienced the horrible sensation that someone other than Doyle and himself was present in the room. It didn't frighten him—Swinburne was entirely unfamiliar with that emotion—but it certainly made him uneasy, and he knew he'd never sleep until he confronted it head-on.

"Who's there?" he called. "Are you standing behind the curtains? If so, I should warn you that I'm none too keen on cheap melodrama!"

Tap tap.

He sighed and threw the bed sheets back, sat up, and pushed his feet into the too-big Arabian slippers that he'd borrowed from Burton's room. He stood and lifted a dressing gown from the bedside chair, wrapped it around himself, and shuffled to the window. He yanked open the curtains.

Smoke and steam, illuminated by a streetlamp, were seething against the glass.

"Hasn't it cleared up yet?" the poet muttered. "What this city needs is a good blast of wind. I say! What's that?"

The fumes were thickening, forming a shape.

"A wraith? Here? What on earth is it up to?"

He pulled up the sash and leaned out of the window.

"What's the meaning of this? Bugger off, will you! I'm thoroughly fed up with phantoms! Go and haunt somebody else! I'm trying to sleep! Wait! Wait! What? My hat! Is that—is that you, Richard?"

The ghostly features forming just inches from his own were, undoubtedly, those of Sir Richard Francis Burton.

"No!" the poet cried. "You can't be dead, surely!"

His friend's faintly visible lips moved. There was no sound, but it seemed to Swinburne that the defensive walls Burton had implanted in his mind suddenly crumbled, and the noise of their destruction was like a whispered voice: *Help me, Algy!*

"Help you? Help you? What? I—*My God!*"

He stumbled backward away from the window and fell onto the bed.

The ghostly form of Burton had melted away.

He sat for a moment with his mouth hanging open, then sprang up, grabbed his clothes, and raced from the room. He thundered down the stairs and into the study.

"Herbert! Herbert! Wake up, man!"

"Eh?"

"Richard's in trouble! We have to find him!"

"Trouble? What trouble? How do you know?"

"I had a vision!"

The vagrant philosopher eyed the younger man. "Now then, lad, that brandy—"

"No, I'm suddenly sober as a judge, I swear! Get dressed! Move, man! We have to get going! I'll meet you in the backyard!

Spencer threw up his hands. "All right, all right!"

Swinburne somehow combined putting on his clothes with descending the stairs. In the main hallway, he snatched a leash from the hatstand, and continued on to the basement and out of the back door.

The poet crossed the yard and squatted down in front of Fidget's kennel.

"Wake up, old thing," he urged, in a low voice. "I know you and I have our differences but there's work to be done. Your master needs us!"

There came the sound of a wheezy yawn followed by a rustling movement. The basset hound's head emerged. The dog stared mournfully at the poet.

"Your nose is required, Fidget. Here, let me get the lead onto you, there's a good dog."

Swinburne clipped the leather strap onto the hound's collar then stood and said, "Come on, exercise time!"

Fidget dived at his ankle and nipped it.

"Ow! You rotter! Stop it! We don't have time for games!"

Spencer stepped out of the house, wearing his baggy coat and cap.

"Take this little monster!" Swinburne screeched.

"So where are we off to, lad?" the philosopher asked, grabbing Fidget's lead.

"Gallows Tree Lane."

"It's past midnight the night of a riot! How do you expect us to get to bloomin' Clerkenwell? Weren't it difficult enough gettin' here from Fleet Street?"

"Follow me—and keep that mongrel away from my ankles!"

Swinburne walked to the back of the yard, opened the door to the garage, and passed through. "We'll take these," he said, as Herbert stepped in behind him.

"Rotorchairs? I can't drive a blinkin' rotorchair!"

"Yes you can. It's easy! Don't worry, I'll show you how. It's just a matter of coordination, which means if I can do it, anyone can."

"An' what about the dog?"

"Fidget will sit on your lap."

"Oh, heck!"

Swinburne opened the main doors and they dragged the machines out into the mews. Despite his protestations, Spencer absorbed the poet's instructions without difficulty and was soon familiar with the principles of flying. It was only experience he lacked.

"Swans I'm happy with," he grumbled. "They was born to it. But takin' to the air in a lump o' metal and wood? That's plain preposterous. How the blazes do these things fly?"

Swinburne nodded and grinned. "I felt the same the first time. It's the Formby coal, you see. It produces so much energy that even these ungainly contraptions can take to the air. I should warn you, though, Herbert, that there's a chance our enemy will cause them to cease working. We could plummet from the sky. All set, then?"

Spencer stared at his companion. "Was that a joke?"

"There's no time for larking about, man! Richard may be in dire peril!"

"Um. Yus, well, er—the basset hound won't jump off, will he?"

"No. Fidget has flown with Richard before. He positively delights in the experience."

Swinburne went to the back of Spencer's machine and started the engine, then crossed to his own and did the same. He clambered into the leather armchair and buckled himself in. After fitting a pair of goggles over his eyes, he gripped the steering rods and pushed forward on the footplate.

Above his head, six wings unfolded as the flight shaft began to revolve. They snapped out horizontally, turned slowly, picked up speed, and vanished into a blurry circle. The engine coughed and roared and steam surged out from the exhaust funnel, flattening against the ground as the rotors blew it down and away.

The machine's runners scraped forward a couple of feet then lifted. Swinburne yanked back the middle lever and shot vertically into the air.

He rose until he was high above the smoke-swathed city. Above him, the stars twinkled. Below him, fires flickered.

The riot seemed to have confined itself to the centre of London, and had been concentrated, in particular, around Soho and the West End.

Far off to the east, the Cauldron—the terrible East End—showed no signs of disturbances.

"But, then, why should it?" Swinburne said to himself. "You'll not find a single representative of High Society for them to rail against in that part of town. By crikey, though, imagine if that sleeping dragon awoke!"

Spencer shot up past him, slowed his vehicle, and sank back down until he was hovering level with the poet.

Swinburne gave him a thumbs-up, and guided his craft toward the Clerkenwell district.

Their flight was short and uneventful, though they saw many police fliers skimming low over the rooftops.

When they reached Coram's Fields, they reduced altitude and steered their machines through the drifting tatters of smoke from street to street until, below, they spotted a constable on his beat.

Swinburne landed near the policeman and stopped his rotorchair's engine.

"I say! Constable!"

"I shouldn't park here, sir, if I—Hallo! Here comes another one!"

Spencer's vehicle angled down onto the road, hit it with a thump, and skidded to a halt with sparks showering from its runners.

Fidget barked.

"Gents," the policeman said as the engine noise died down, "this is no time and no night to be out and about in expensive vehicles!"

"We're on the king's business!" Swinburne proclaimed. "I'd like you to guard these chairs and have them returned to 14 Montagu Place at the first opportunity."

The constable removed his helmet and scratched his head. "Forgive me for saying so, sir, but I don't know that you're in any position to give me orders, 'specially ones that'll take me from my duties."

"My good man, I am Sir Richard Francis Burton's personal assistant," Swinburne countered haughtily. He pulled a card from his pocket and waved it in the man's face. "And Sir Richard Francis Burton is the king's agent. And the king, God bless him, is the ruler of the land. It also happens that I claim Detective Inspector Trounce and Detective Inspector Honesty of Scotland Yard as close personal friends. Then there's Commander Krishnamurthy, Constable Bhatti—"

"Stop! I surrender!" the policeman said, taking the card. He read it, handed it back, put on his helmet, saluted, and said: "Right you are, sir. My apologies. I'll see that your machines are returned in good time. How about if I have them shifted to the Yard for the night? For safekeeping?"

"Thank you. That will be most satisfactory, my man. I shall be sure to mention—*Ow!* Herbert! I told you to keep that little devil away from me! Goodbye, Constable. Thank you for your assistance!"

The policeman nodded, and Swinburne, Spencer, and Fidget crossed the road and approached the corner of Gallows Tree Lane.

Swinburne whispered, "If you see any Rakes, walk straight past them! Act normally."

"That I can do," Spencer mumbled inaudibly. "Dunno 'bout you, though!"

They entered the dimly lit street and stopped outside number 5. The house was in darkness.

Swinburne hissed, "Keep a tight rein on the dog, Herbert. I have to squat down to speak to him and I'd rather not have my nose bitten!"

"Right ho."

"Now then, you vicious little toerag," Swinburne said to the basset hound, "where's your master, hey? Seek, Fidget! Seek! Where's your master? I know the air is full of ash, but I'm sure those blessed nostrils of yours can sort the wheat from the chaff. Seek!"

Fidget's deep brown eyes, which had been regarding him with disdain, slowly lost focus.

"Find your master!" Swinburne encouraged.

Fidget blinked, looked to the right, then to the left, then at Swinburne, then at Herbert Spencer.

"Wuff!"

He lowered his nose to the pavement and began to snuffle back and forth.

All of a sudden, he raised his head, bayed wildly, and set off at a terrific pace, almost yanking Spencer off his feet.

"He's got it!" Swinburne enthused, racing after the pair.

They ran out onto Gray's Inn Road, turned left, raced up to King's Cross Railway Station, then swerved left again onto the Euston Road.

"He seems mighty sure of himself!" Spencer puffed as they galloped along.

"That nose never fails!" Swinburne panted. "It saved my life last year. It's just a shame it's attached to the rest of the beast!"

At the junction with Russell Square, they encountered two constables who were grappling with a mad-eyed individual dressed in a bloodstained butcher's apron.

"What the devil do you think you're doing out and about at this time of night?" one of the policemen yelled at them.

"Government business!" Swinburne declared.

"Pull the other one, it's got bells on it!"

"Aargh!" the butcher howled. "Look at the little one! The red-haired git! He's a bloody toff! Kill 'im! Kill 'im!"

"Shut up," the second policeman snapped. He grunted as the man's knee thudded into his stomach, and groaned to his companion: "Bash the blighter on the head, Bill!"

The poet, philosopher, and basset hound ran past the brawling trio and kept going.

Fidget led the two men onward until the bottom end of Regent's Park hove into view. The trail led past it and onto Marylebone Road. They had run about a mile so far.

"I never thought I'd be thankful for a riot!" Swinburne gasped.

"What do you mean, lad?"

"Isn't it obvious? Whoever's got Richard couldn't find transport! They're on foot!"

They hurried on for another mile. The road, one of the city's main highways, was empty of people but filled with rubble and wreckage. Fires still blazed and they found themselves plunging through clouds of black smoke. Many gas lamps had been vandalised, too, and lengths of the thoroughfare were pitch dark.

"Whoops!" Spencer cried as Fidget made an unexpected left turn.

"Bishop's Bridge Road," Swinburne noted.

Just ahead of them, the lights of Paddington Railway Station flared out from within an enormous cloud of white steam. Fidget plunged straight into it.

The terminal was a scene of out-and-out chaos. A locomotive had derailed while entering the station, ploughing into one of the platforms. It was lying on its side with its boiler split open, vapour shooting out of the ripped metal.

Policemen and station workers milled about, and the moment Swinburne and Spencer stepped into the building, a constable, whose features were dominated by a truly enormous mustache, pounced on them.

"Stop right there! What are you two up to?" He looked at Swinburne curiously. "Hello hello. Haven't I seen you somewhere before? Hey up! I know! It was back when that brass man was left in Trafalgar Square! Constable Hoare is the name, sir. Samuel Hoare."

"Hello, Hoare. We're on official business! Have a squint at this."

Burton's assistant presented his credentials to the uniformed man, who examined them and raised his bushy eyebrows.

Fidget whined and tugged desperately at his lead. Hoare shook his head.

"This is too much for me," he said. "I'll call my supervisor over, if you don't mind." He cupped his hands around his mouth and yelled into the cloud: "Commander! Commander!"

Swinburne breathed a sigh of relief as the steam parted and Commander Krishnamurthy strode into view. He was wearing the new Flying Squad uniform of a long brown leather coat and a flat peaked officer's hat. A pair of flying goggles dangled around his neck.

"What ho! What ho! What ho!" the poet cried happily. "Krishnamurthy, old horse! Why, I haven't seen you since the Battle of Old Ford! Aren't you sweltering in all that leather?"

"Hallo, Swinburne, old chap!" Krishnamurthy exclaimed, with an unrestrained grin. He grabbed his friend's hand and shook it. "Yes I am! Regulations, a hex on 'em! What on earth are you doing here, and at this time of night? Wait a minute—" he looked at Spencer "—aren't you Herbert Spencer, the philosopher chap? My cousin—Shyamji Bhatti—is always talking about you. Singing your praises, in fact."

"That's very kind of him; he's a good fellow!" Spencer replied. "You look like him."

"Dashingly handsome, you mean? Thanks very much. So what's the story, Mr. Swinburne?"

"Fidget's nose has led us here. We're tracking Richard. He's in trouble!"

Krishnamurthy looked down at the basset hound. "Well, this isn't the end of the trail by the looks of it. Let him lead on, we'll see where he takes us. You can tell me all about it on the way. Stay with us, Constable Hoare!"

"Yes, sir," the mustachioed policeman answered.

In the event, Fidget didn't take them very far at all. The trail ended at the edge of platform three.

"They got on a train," Krishnamurthy said. "So when do you think, Mr. Swinburne? It's just past half-two now and there've been no locomotives in or out of the station since rioters threw something onto the line and caused that one to derail a little over an hour ago."

"Richard had an appointment at ten o'clock," Swinburne answered. "His—um—his—er—his message reached me around midnight. So I guess whatever train left here with him aboard did so during the hour before the crash."

Krishnamurthy turned to his subordinate. "Hoare, run and get a Bradshaw, would you? We'll look up the train times and destinations."

The constable hurried away and, while he was gone, Swinburne gave the commander a brief outline of the events leading up to Burton's plea for help.

"So he got a message to you, did he? The resourceful so-and-so! What was it, a parakeet?"

Swinburne cleared his throat. "Um. I heard a tapping at the window, yes."

"So what's all this séance malarkey about? What are the Rakes up to? I've been receiving preposterous reports from the West End. Some of my colleagues claim that dead Rakes are shuffling about in the Strand!"

"It's true," Spencer said.

"As to what's going on," Swinburne added, "hopefully Richard will be able to tell us, if we can snatch him out of their hands!"

Hoare returned with a portly gentleman in tow.

"I went one better than a Bradshaw and brought the stationmaster, sir."

"Ah, good show. Hello, Mr. Arkwright. I presume you know the station's timetable better than the back of your hand?"

"I certainly do," confessed the uniformed man. "I could sing it to you in my sleep, if I ever sleep again, which after this disaster I probably won't. Just look at the state of my station!"

"No serenades are required, thank you, but perhaps you could tell us what trains left this platform prior to the crash, after, say, half-twelve?"

"Just the one, sir, on account of it being the night timetable and us having a reduced service due to the public disorder."

"And that was?"

"An offence against the king, if you ask me, sir."

"I meant the train, Mr. Arkwright. When did it leave and where was it bound?"

"It was the twelve forty-five atmospheric service, sir, to Weymouth via Reading, stopping at Basingstoke, Winchester, Eastleigh, Southampton, Bournemouth, and Poole. Due in at—"

"Winchester!" Swinburne interrupted. "That's where they've taken him, I'd bet my life on it."

"Yus," Spencer agreed. "Then by carriage to Alresford and on to Tichborne House!"

"Bloody hell!" the little poet cursed, flapping his arms wildly. "Our rotorchairs are somewhere between Clerkenwell and Scotland Yard by now! I say! Krishnamurthy, old bean, I don't suppose we could commandeer a couple of your police fliers?"

The commander shook his head regretfully. "I'd say yes, of course, but they're all in the air, what with tonight's disturbances. We're monitoring the edge of the riot zone as it expands outward. The bigger it gets, the closer we're pushed to our limit."

"If it's police business, you could requisition an atmospheric carriage," the stationmaster said quietly.

"Confound it! I suppose we'll have to make our way to Miss Mayson's place, though we can ill afford the delay, and I daresay she's sick of us making off with her swans—" Swinburne stopped and looked at Mr. Arkwright. "What was that?"

"I said, if it's police business, you could requisition an atmospheric carriage. We've been moving them to the sidings since the crash, so there are plenty available. And there'll be no more trains on the line until daylight. If I wire ahead to the pump stations and signal boxes, you'll get a clear run. It's only sixty miles, and one carriage alone will do you a good fifty-five-miles-per-hour minimum."

"You can supply a driver?"

"You won't need one, sir, which is just as well, since some of the beggars seem to have lost their heads and others have been taken ill. But no, it's all automated."

Krishnamurthy punched a fist into his palm. "I'm in on this!" he snapped.

"Me too, if that's all right, sir," Constable Hoare interjected.

Swinburne slapped his hands together. "Then let's get this rescue party moving!"

The atmospheric railway system was one of Isambard Kingdom Brunel's inventions. Between its wide-gauge tracks ran a fifteen-inch-diameter pipe, its top cut through lengthwise by a slot which was sealed with a leather flap-valve. Beneath the train carriages, a thin shaft ran down through the slot and was affixed to a dumbbell-shaped piston, which fitted snugly inside the pipe. Every three miles, pump stations sucked air out in front of the trains and forced it back into the pipe behind. The pressure differential shot the carriages along the tracks at great speed.

The run down to Winchester was fast and uneventful. They arrived at half-past four in the morning. The carriage drew to a halt and its passengers jumped down onto the station platform. The night guard greeted them.

"The police special from London," he said, unnecessarily. "Commander?"

"Me," Krishnamurthy answered. "Did passengers leave the previous train?"

"Just a small group, sir. A black fellow brought a steam-horse and wagon to meet them. Some sort of medical case. They were escorting the patient."

"Richard!" Swinburne exclaimed. "And that must have been Bogle driving the wagon."

"I don't know what you intend now, gentlemen, but there won't be any cabs available at this time of morning."

"How far is it to Tichborne House, Mr. Swinburne?" Krishnamurthy asked.

"Four miles or so. I should think we can leg it across country."

"Then let's do so!"

By virtue of its famous cathedral, Winchester was a city, but in size it was little more than a small town, and it wasn't long before the four men and one dog were beyond its bounds.

The land to the east was heavily farmed; a patchwork of wheat and corn-fields separated by high hedgerows and well-trodden dirt paths; a rippled terrain of low hills and shallow valleys, with scarecrows darkly silhouetted against the starry sky.

They traversed it silently.

Swinburne was beside himself with anxiety, and his nervous energy infected the rest of the party, so that none of them felt the effects of their sleepless night. A grim mood overtook the group, and they walked with jaws set and fists clenched, expecting a battle and determined to win it.

Finally, they reached the brow of a hill and looked down at the Tichborne estate just as a vague hint of orange smudged the eastern horizon.

It occurred to Swinburne, when he looked at that first glimmering of dawn, that he was also looking in the direction of burning London, and he realised that whatever the enemy's plans were, they were coming to fruition now, and the one person who might be able to oppose them was either their prisoner—or dead.

The party was descending at an angle into the shallow valley at the back of the manor house, drawing closer to the willow-lined lake, when Constable Hoare pointed and asked: "Is that a man?"

It was.

A dead man.

For a dreadful moment, Swinburne thought it was Burton, but as they reached the body, which lay facedown beside a crooked tree, and turned it over, he recognised Guilfoyle the groundsman.

"What happened to him?" Krishnamurthy gasped.

All the capillaries beneath the skin of Guilfoyle's face had burst, and blood, still wet, had leaked from his eyes, nose, mouth, and ears. His lips were drawn back over his teeth and frozen in an appalling expression of agony.

Herbert Spencer sighed. "Poor blighter. Nice chap, he was. Kept an eye on Miss Mayson's swans when I was a-stayin' here afore. Saw to it that they had plenty to eat."

A double-barrelled shotgun lay beside the corpse. Krishnamurthy picked it up and examined it.

"It's been fired. One barrel."

"No lights showing in the house, sir," Hoare noted.

"Oof!" Spencer grunted as Fidget yanked at his lead. "Looks like the dog has picked up the scent again!"

"Allow him to show us the way, Mr. Spencer," Krishnamurthy ordered. "And voices low, please, gentlemen!"

Following behind the basset hound, they ran up the slope to the back of Tichborne House, crossed the patio, and entered cautiously through the open doors to the gunroom.

The house was silent.

Hoare touched his superior's arm and pointed to the floor. Krishnamurthy looked down and, in the dim light, saw black spots trailing across it. He bent and touched one, raised his finger to his nose, and whispered: "Blood. Someone's hurt."

"Not Richard, I hope!" Swinburne hissed.

They moved across the chamber and out into the hallway, tiptoed along it, and passed into the large ballroom.

Fidget's nose, and the trail of blood, took them straight across the dance floor, out through another door, and along a passage toward the smoking room. Before they got there, the dog pulled them into an off-branching corridor.

"I thought so," Swinburne muttered. "There are stairs ahead that lead down to the servants' quarters, the kitchen, and the entrance to the labyrinth."

"You think they have him under the Crawls, lad?" Spencer asked.

"I think it likely."

Commander Krishnamurthy pulled his truncheon from his belt and nodded to Hoare to do the same.

"Move behind us, please, gentlemen," he said. The poet and philosopher obeyed.

They crept on, reached the stairs, descended, and became aware of a low-pitched repetitive rumbling.

"It's Mrs. Picklethorpe's bloomin' snorin'!" Spencer whispered.

A few steps later, voices came to them from the kitchen.

"Shhh," Swinburne breathed. "Listen!"

"—knows the finances of the estate, so we need to keep the fool alive for the time being."

The poet recognised the brash tones at once. It was Edward Kenealy.

"But can we make him cooperate?" came an unfamiliar voice. "He's a stubborn old sod."

"He'll crack as soon as we get him near the diamonds again, don't you worry. He's very susceptible. No resistance at all. How's the doctor, Bogle?"

"He's bleeding badly, sir."

A fourth man spoke, his voice tremulous: "I'll be all right."

Swinburne recognised the tones.

"We need you for the séance, Jankyn," Kenealy said.

"Just bandage me up tightly," came the response. "Bogle can run me to the Alresford doctor later. I'll be fine for the séance."

"I should dig out the pellets, sir."

"No, Bogle," Kenealy snapped. "There's no time. We have to contact the mistress as soon as we can. She wants to check on Burton's condition. Waite, help me find a table and chairs. We'll carry them to the central chamber. We have to conduct the séance in the presence of our prisoners."

Krishnamurthy turned to his companions and whispered, "Four of 'em, and one disabled. Come on!"

He and Constable Hoare dashed forward, with Swinburne, Herbert Spencer, and Fidget at their heels. They hurtled into the kitchen and all hell broke loose.

Swinburne caught a glimpse of Jankyn, shirtless and bloodied, lying on a table with Bogle standing beside him. Edward Kenealy and a Rake—the man named Waite—were near the pantries.

"Stop! Police!" Krishnamurthy bellowed.

"Don't move!" Hoare shouted.

"Damnation!" Kenealy barked, swinging around and raising his right arm.

Swinburne dived aside as a bolt of blue lightning crackled out of the lawyer's hand and whipped across the room to envelop the policemen's heads.

Krishnamurthy covered his eyes and collapsed to his knees.

Hoare, though, took the full brunt of the attack. His body snapped rigid and rose six inches from the ground, floating within a dancing, sizzling aura of blue energy. He shook wildly and let loose a high-pitched howl of pain. His face turned red, then blue, and blood spurted from his nose and eyes.

"Bleedin' heck!" yelled Spencer, who'd fallen against a cupboard. "Stop it!"

Swinburne looked around, saw a frying pan, and before he knew what he was doing, he'd grabbed and thrown it.

The pan hit Kenealy's forehead with a tremendous clang. The lawyer staggered, tripped, and fell onto his back. The energy shooting from his hand left Hoare, fizzled across the ceiling, and vanished.

The constable dropped.

Waite leaped over to a work surface, seized a wooden chopping board, and launched it at Swinburne. The poet ducked. It spun past his head and smacked against the wall behind him.

Krishnamurthy moaned and fell forward onto his hands.

Bogle picked up a dinner plate and pitched it in Spencer's direction.

Fidget barked and ran out of the room.

Kitchen implements were suddenly flying back and forth; pans, crockery, and cutlery, crashing and smashing with a deafening racket.

Constable Hoare's truncheon rolled to Spencer's feet. The philosopher grabbed it and sent it spinning through the air. It hit Waite in the throat, and the Rake doubled over, choking.

Krishnamurthy crawled forward, moaning with the effort. He'd almost reached Kenealy when the lawyer rolled over, turned, and looked up. Blood was streaming down his face from a wound in his forehead. He jerked a hand toward the policeman. Blue flame grew around his fingers.

"None of that!" the Flying Squad man groaned, and whacked his truncheon down onto the hand.

Kenealy screamed as his finger bones crunched.

Krishnamurthy slumped forward and passed out.

"What's the meaning of this!" demanded a voice from the doorway. It was Mrs. Picklethorpe, resplendent in her nightgown and hair curlers. A pan, launched by Bogle, hit her square between the eyes. She toppled back against the corridor wall and slid to the floor.

Swinburne flung a full bottle of wine at Bogle and whooped with satisfaction as it bounced off the Jamaican's head and exploded against a cupboard behind him. The butler swayed and buckled, dropping onto Kenealy.

The lawyer pushed his uninjured hand out in Swinburne's direction.

"I'll kill you!" he snarled.

Spencer bounded across the room and sent a thick hardbound cookery book thudding down onto Kenealy's head, knocking him cold. The heavy volume fell open at the title page: *Miss Mayson's Book of Household Management*.

"Well, I'll be blowed!" Herbert muttered. He bent and retrieved the volume then sent it slapping into the side of Waite's head. The Rake collapsed, out for the count.

Jankyn sat up and moaned. He held both his hands flat against his left side. Blood leaked between his fingers.

"Bastards!" he said huskily.

"You're hardly in a position to insult us," Swinburne observed. "I assume Guilfoyle shot you?"

Spencer knelt and helped the recovering Krishnamurthy to his feet.

"Yes," Jankyn groaned. "He tried to take Burton from us. Kenealy killed him but the man's shotgun went off as he died. The only working gun on the whole bloody estate, and I have to get it!"

"What was that lightning Kenealy fired from his hand?"

"Get me to a hospital. I'm bleeding to death."

"Answer my questions and I'll consider it," the poet answered, and Spencer had never heard the little man sound so grim.

"It's etheric energy. Kenealy has a talent for channelling it, which the mistress has enhanced."

"The mistress? Who's she?"

"She's the leader of—Ah! It hurts! I need treatment, man!"

"The leader of the Rakes? I know. And she's a Russian. But what's her name?"

"I haven't the foggiest, I swear! Enough! Enough! Look at this blood! Help me, damn it!"

"Is Burton alive?" Swinburne demanded.

"Possibly. He's in the centre of the labyrinth."

"How many are in there, guarding him?"

"None."

"You're lying."

"I'm not."

"If that's the way you want to play it, fine. Physician, heal thyself, and if you bleed to death, I'll not mind one little bit, you damned blackguard."

"All right! All right! There's just one man, I swear. His name is Smithers. He and Waite took Burton from a séance to Paddington Station. They were—" he groaned and whimpered, then continued in a whisper "—they were joined by Kenealy there and all rode a train to Winchester. Bogle met them at the station with a carriage, but just outside Alresford the steam-horse broke down. They had to continue on foot, dragging Burton between them. As they crossed the grounds, Guilfoyle interfered and paid the price. Please, get me to the doctor now. I don't want to die."

Krishnamurthy, who was being supported by Herbert Spencer, swore vociferously. "Neither did Sam Hoare, but he's lying there dead, you swine!"

Jankyn fell onto his side on the table and said faintly: "It wasn't me. Kenealy killed him."

"Gentlemen," Krishnamurthy said hoarsely, "if you'd be so kind as to help me bind and gag these three rogues—he indicated the unconscious Kenealy, Bogle, and Waite—I'll then remain here and see what I can do for the cook. Maybe, if the mood takes me, I'll attend to Jankyn, too. On the other hand, I might just let him die like the diseased dog he is."

"Will you be all right? You look done in," Swinburne said.

The commander was, indeed, in a bad way. There was blood oozing from his eyes, nose, and ears, and he was trembling uncontrollably.

"I'm afraid I'm not much up to running through tunnels at present but I'll be fine. I'll rest here once these bounders are secured, then I'll rustle up the local constabulary to sort this mess out while you get your man back to London."

It took a few minutes to tie the men's hands and feet, after which Swinburne and the vagrant philosopher entered the pantry containing the door to the labyrinth. Fidget looked into the kitchen, saw that the violence had ended, and scampered after them.

They stepped into the tunnel and took off along it, passing under the house, beneath the carriageway, and toward the Crawls. The passages were well lit and nothing occurred to hamper their progress through the folding-back-on-itself spiral until they were close to the central chamber, when Swinburne, who was barrelling along as fast as his short legs would allow, skidded around one of the turns and ran slap bang into the Rake, Smithers, who'd been walking in the other direction. The two men went down in a tangle and started to punch, kick, and wrestle frantically until Spencer caught up with them. The philosopher calmly bent, grasped a handful of Smithers's hair, lifted the man's head, and slammed it hard against the stone floor. The Rake's arms flopped down and he lay still.

"Let's pull him along with us to the central chamber," Swinburne panted.

They took an ankle each and dragged the prone form the last few yards until they exited the tunnel into the inner room.

"Is that you, um—um—um?" came a familiar voice.

"Algernon Swinburne. Hello, Colonel."

"Bally good show! That is to say, I'm very pleased to see you."

Lushington was sitting against the wall, hands bound behind his back, looking bedraggled, with his extravagant side whiskers drooping miserably.

"Burton's a goner, I fear," he announced, nodding toward the small waterfall. "Lost his mind, the poor chap."

The king's agent was slumped lifelessly in the water channel with his arms spread wide, wrists shackled to the wall on either side of the falling stream. Flowing out of the slot above, the hot water was descending straight down onto his head.

Swinburne let loose a shriek of rage and bounded across to his friend.

"Herbert, help me unbolt these bloody manacles!"

While he and the philosopher got to work, Lushington gave an account of himself.

"Not entirely certain how I came to be here, to be frank. These past months have been rather hazy. Bit of a nightmare, really. Was I supporting that fat fake? Rather think I was. Couldn't help myself. Every time he was anywhere near me, I was convinced he was Sir Roger. By Gad, I even spoke for the bounder in court! Didn't come to my senses, regain my wits, start to think straight, until I found myself being held captive here, wherever here is."

"You're under the Crawls," Swinburne revealed.

"Am I, indeed? Am I? Closer to home than I thought, then! Barely seen a soul for—how long? Days? Weeks?—apart from that scoundrel Bogle, who's been keeping me fed, and Kenealy, damn him for the rogue he is."

"That's got it, lad," Spencer muttered, yanking the manacles off Burton's wrists. He and Swinburne pulled the limp explorer across the floor, away from the water, and laid him down. His eyes opened and rolled aimlessly. He mumbled something. The poet bent closer.

"What was that, Richard?"

"Al-Masloub," Burton whispered.

"What?"

"Al-Masloub."

"What's he sayin'?" Spencer asked.

"Something in Arabic. Al-Masloub," Swinburne replied.

"What's a bloomin' Al-Masloub?"

"I don't know, Herbert."

"He's been mumbling it over and over," Lushington revealed. "Hasn't said another blessed word. Place in Arabia, perhaps?"

Spencer crossed to the colonel and began to pull at the cords that held the man's wrists.

Swinburne stared helplessly at the king's agent.

"What's happened to him?" he cried, aghast at his friend's vacant eyes. He took Burton by the shoulders and shook him. "Pull yourself together, Richard! You're safe now!"

"It's no use," Lushington offered. "I'm afraid he's utterly loopy."

"Al-Masloub," Burton whispered.

Swinburne sat back on his heels. He turned to Herbert Spencer. A tear trickled down his cheek.

"What'll we do, Herbert? I can't get any sense out of him. I don't know what this Al-Masloub thing is!"

"First things first, lad. We should get him home."

Burton suddenly sat up, threw his head back, and screamed. Then, a far more horrifying sound—he gave a mindless giggle. "Al-Masloub," he moaned quietly. His eyes moved aimlessly. His mouth hung slackly. He slowly toppled onto his side.

Swinburne looked at him and sucked in a juddery breath. He couldn't help but think that the enemy had won. London, the heart of the Empire, was in chaos, and Burton, the only man who could possibly save it, looked like he might return to Bedlam—permanently!

IN WHICH A
GREAT DECEPTION IS EXPOSED

The Technologists tell us not to worry about the machines.
They assure us that no harm can come from them.
They admit that their inventions are changing society.
But it is a measured change; it is controllable and safe.
Everything, they say, is running smoothly, like clockwork.
In my experience, clockwork always rings alarm bells.
            —William Holman Hunt

"MY NAME IS ARTHUR ORTON!"

WANTED

FOR TREASON AGAINST
THE BRITISH EMPIRE

Richard Spruce

A Botanist, described as 5' 9" tall,
Slim Build, with Dark Receding Hair,
and a Greying Beard and Mustache.

A REWARD of £100

for Information Leading to his Capture.

Contact SCOTLAND YARD

Midmorning the following Saturday—two days after Burton's rescue—an extraordinary carriage thundered into Montagu Place. It was a huge box constructed from iron plate and mounted on six thick wheels. There were no windows in it—just a two-inch-high horizontal slot in each of its sides—and its doors looked better suited to bank vaults than to a conveyance. The driver, rather than being situated on top in the normal manner, was seated inside a wedge-shaped cabin at its front. He, like the passenger, was entirely hidden from prying eyes. From the four corners of the vehicle, crenellated metal bartizans projected, and in each one stood a soldier with a rifle in his hands.

It was nothing less than a small metal castle drawn by two large steam-horses. Accompanied by four outriders from the King's Cavalry, it rumbled, creaked, sizzled, and moaned to a standstill before number 14.

Inside the house, Mrs. Angell, all petticoats and pinafore, tore into the study and shrieked: "The king's here! The king's here!" She jabbed her finger at the window. "Lord Almighty! His Majesty King Albert himself has come to the house!"

Algernon Swinburne, who'd been sitting in quiet conversation with Herbert Spencer and Detective Inspector Trounce, looked up wearily. There were dark circles under his eyes.

"That's very unlikely, Mrs. A," he said.

"It's impossible," Trounce put in. "My dear woman, the king, God bless him, is under siege in Buckingham Palace. He can't get out and no one can get in, and it'll stay that way until our riffraff revolutionaries calm down and stop demanding that we become a damned republic! Pardon my language."

Spencer grunted and murmured: "The republican form of government is the highest blinkin' form of government, but, because of this, it requires the highest type of human nature—a type nowhere at present existin' in London, that's for bloomin' certain!"

"Stop your blessed chinwagging and look out of the window!" the house-keeper cried.

Trounce raised his eyebrows.

Swinburne sighed, stood, and crossed the room. He stepped past Admiral Lord Nelson, who was standing in his customary position, and peered out of the window. The doorbell jangled.

Mrs. Angell lifted her pinafore and slapped it over her mouth to stifle a squeal.

"My hat!" the poet exclaimed, staring out at the mighty armoured carriage.

"What shall I do? What shall I do?" the old woman panicked.

"Bed-wetter," Pox the parakeet opined, with a cheery whistle.

"Calm yourself, Mother. Stay here. I'll go," Swinburne answered. He left the room.

Trounce and Spencer stood and brushed down their clothing. Mrs. Angell bustled anxiously around the room, straightening pictures, adjusting ornaments and curios, dusting and fussing at top speed.

"Nelson!" she barked. "Put these gentlemen's glasses away in the bureau and wipe the tabletop, then come here so I can give you a quick polish."

The clockwork man saluted and moved to obey.

"I'm sure that ain't necess—" Spencer began.

"Quiet!" Trounce whispered. "Never interrupt her when there's housework involved! You'll get your head bitten off!"

Multiple footsteps sounded on the stairs. Swinburne entered, followed by Damien Burke and Gregory Hare, who were both back in their usual outlandish and outdated clothes. Palmerston's men each had their left arm in a sling.

They stood aside.

A tall man stepped into the room between them. He was dressed in a dark blue velvet suit with a long black cape draped over his shoulders. A black veil hung from the brim of his top hat, concealing his face completely.

"Your Highness," Mrs. Angell said, lowering herself into a deep curtsy.

"Hardly that, madam," the visitor replied, pulling off his hat and veil. "I am Henry John Temple, the Third Viscount Palmerston."

"Oh! It's only the prime minister!" the housekeeper exclaimed. She clutched at a chair and hauled herself back upright.

"Sorry to disappoint," Palmerston muttered ruefully.

"No!" Mrs. Angell gulped. "I mean—that is to say—ooh er!" She turned a deep shade of red.

"Gentlemen, good lady," Swinburne announced, "some of you have met, some of you haven't, so a quick who's who: this is Mrs. Iris Angell, Sir Richard's esteemed housekeeper; Detective Inspector William Trounce, one of Scotland Yard's finest; Mr. Herbert Spencer, our friendly neighbourhood philosopher; Lord Admiral Nelson, Richard's rather extraordinary valet; and Mr. Damien Burke and Mr. Gregory Hare, agents for the prime minister!"

A loud warble interrupted him: "Cross-eyed nitwits!"

"My apologies—and that is Pox, Sir Richard's newly acquired parakeet."

Palmerston looked disdainfully at the colourful little bird, gazed in awe at the clockwork man, then turned to Swinburne and said: "You sent me a message. You said Captain Burton is out of action. Explain. Where is he?"

"Ah," the poet answered. "You'd better come upstairs, Prime Minister. If the rest of you wouldn't mind waiting here, I'm sure Mrs. Angell will see to it that you're supplied with whatever refreshments take your fancy."

"Of course, sir," the housekeeper simpered, curtseying again in the prime minister's direction. She winced and held her hip.

Swinburne glanced at her and, despite his fatigue, managed a cheeky wink.

He ushered Lord Palmerston from the room and up two flights of stairs to the library. As they approached the door, Palmerston asked: "Is that music I hear?"

"Yes," Swinburne said, laying his fingers on the door handle. "We rescued Richard two days ago. He was practically catatonic and repeated just one thing, over and over: Al-Masloub."

"Which means?"

"We didn't know until we got him home. Mrs. Angell recognised it straightaway as the name of a musician Richard has over from time to time. We summoned the man, who arrived, spent a few minutes looking at our patient, went away again, and returned with two more musicians in tow. Since then, and without a moment's cease, this—"

He pushed open the door.

The library was filled with the swirling melodies and rhythms of an Arabian flute and drums. All the furniture had been shoved against the book-lined walls, and, in the middle of the floor, Sir Richard Francis Burton, dressed in a belted white robe and white pantaloons, his feet bare, and a tall fez upon his head, was spinning deliriously on the spot.

His arms were held out, the forearms poised vertically, the palm of his right hand directed at the ceiling, the palm of his left at the floor. His head was thrown back and his mouth and eyes were shut, as if in peaceful contemplation. There were droplets of sweat on his face—and he whirled and whirled!

Around and around, gyrating at considerable speed, in time with the drumbeat, he appeared entirely oblivious to their presence.

"Do you mean to tell me that His Majesty's agent has been spinning in circles for two days?" Palmerston huffed.

"Yes, Prime Minister, he has. It's the dance of the Dervish, of the Sufi mystic. I believe he's attempting to repair the damage our enemies did to him."

Palmerston, his face as expressionless as ever, watched Burton for a few moments.

"Well," he muttered. "He'd better pull himself together soon. He might be the only person in the country who can tell me exactly why our normally industrious labouring classes have decided to go the way of the damned French. In the meantime—"

Footsteps sounded as Burke and Hare pounded up the stairs.

"Prime Minister, please excuse the interruption," Burke said, speaking rapidly and with his voice raised above the music. He turned to the poet: "Mr. Swinburne, when you recovered Sir Richard, did he have an odd-looking pistol in his possession?"

"The green thing?" the poet asked. "Yes, I found it in his jacket pocket. Is it a pistol? It doesn't look like one!"

"Where is it now?"

"In the top drawer of his main desk, by the windows."

Burke turned to Hare. "If you would, Mr. Hare?"

With a nod, his colleague turned and headed back to the study.

"What's happening?" Palmerston snapped.

"A minute, if you please, sir," Burke responded briskly. He leaned across and pulled the library door shut, muffling the melodic noise. He then indicated another door, just along the hall, and addressed Swinburne again: "What's in there?"

"It's Richard's storeroom."

With a swift nod, Burke pushed past them, opened the door, and looked inside. He saw a room piled high with wooden boxes.

"Excellent. In you go, please, Prime Minister."

"What the devil—!" Palmerston began.

Gregory Hare reappeared, with Burton's spine-shooter in his hand. He passed it to his colleague.

"Sir!" Burke's voice was filled with urgency. "If you recall, I advised you in the strongest possible terms that coming here was a grievous miscalculation. Sir Richard and his colleagues have made themselves known to the enemy forces. They are targets. You have knowingly placed yourself in the line of fire for no good reason except to satisfy your curiosity—"

"How dare you speak to me like th—"

Burke continued, raising his voice and speaking over the prime minister's objection. "What I feared most is now occurring. The street outside has just filled with wraiths. They caused your guards to shoot your outriders dead then turn their rifles upon themselves. We can only assume that this house is about to be attacked, isn't that so, Mr. Hare?"

"Quite right, Mr. Burke," Gregory Hare answered.

"We must barricade ourselves inside," Burke continued. "If it becomes necessary, Mr. Hare and I will act as your last line of defence."

"I—" Palmerston said, but a thick arm was suddenly wrapped around his waist and Hare hoisted him off his feet, carried him past Burke and Swinburne, and plonked him into the storeroom.

"Unhand me, sir!" came his receding protest.

Burke turned to the poet: "I'm sorry, Mr. Swinburne, but Lord Palmerston's safety is my and Mr. Hare's primary duty. I have no choice but to leave you and your companions to defend this house as best you can. Besides which, we are somewhat hampered by our injuries. If our attackers make it past you, hopefully you will have weakened them enough for us to be able to deal with them."

"You mean to make of us a forlorn hope?" Swinburne asked. "Ruthless bugger, aren't you?"

"You object?"

Swinburne grinned. "Not at all! This is just my cup of tea! Go! Barricade yourselves in. I'll rally the troops."

"Thank you, sir. Um—" Burke looked at the cactus pistol in his hand "—I should keep hold of this but Mr. Hare and I are armed with revolvers and, under the circumstances—"

He passed the strange weapon to the poet, quickly explained its use, then turned away, entered the storeroom, and closed the door.

Swinburne let loose a breath and whispered: "Tally-ho!" He descended the stairs. As he reached the landing, he saw Mrs. Angell in the hallway below, carrying a coffee pot and cups on a tray.

There was a knock at the front door.

The housekeeper immediately put the tray down on the hall table and reached for the door handle.

"Don't!" Swinburne yelled.

It was too late. Even as she turned to look up at him, Mrs. Angell's fingers had twisted the doorknob.

The portal swung inward, pushed by a big bloated hand.

The old woman staggered backward and screamed.

A bulging mass of clothing blocked the threshold. Swinburne recognised it at once: the Tichborne Claimant!

The hideous head came ducking under the lintel and, as the hulking mass of blubbery flesh pushed through after it, Mrs. Angell dropped in a dead faint.

Swinburne raised the cactus pistol and pressed the trigger nodule. He missed. Spines thudded into the doorframe. The Claimant raised his repulsive face, looked at the poet, and smiled sweetly.

"You must be Algy."

His voice was female, with a Russian accent.

"Forgive me for not visiting you in person, *kotyonok*, but I am a little stretched at the moment." The Claimant glanced down at his corpulent belly. He looked back up at the poet and chuckled. "He he he! Horribly stretched! But as a matter of fact, I was referring to the uprising. It goes well, does it not? Your capital burns! Ha ha! How your poor King Albert must tremble!"

"Who the hell are you?" Swinburne snarled.

The door beside him opened and Detective Inspector Trounce stepped out. "What's going—*Bloody hell!*"

"Ah, is that William Trounce? How gratifying. I do hope you have Herbert Spencer with you, too. It would be so convenient if my emissary can kill you all at once before he retrieves Sir Richard. Really, it was very rude of you to take him from me before I'd finished ruining that extraordinary mind of his. I would have come for him sooner but I have so much to do. I am quite dreadfully busy. Ah well, let us proceed. Time for you to die! As we say in Russia: *Bare derutsya—u kholopov chuby treschat!* Farewell!"

The Claimant's eyes suddenly dulled. He emitted a loud bellow, in his own voice, and started up the stairs. His girth was such that the banister and its balusters cracked, splintered, and fell away from the staircase as he heaved himself up.

Trounce went to draw his police revolver. It snagged in his pocket.

"Confound it!" he cursed.

Swinburne raised the spine-shooter and fired again, hitting the advancing monstrosity in the chest. The spines had no effect other than to elicit another roar.

The poet and policeman retreated into the study.

"What's happenin'?" Herbert Spencer asked.

"Big trouble," Trounce grunted. "Very big indeed!"

The Claimant blocked the doorway, wedged his vast body into it, and began to shove himself through. The door frame split.

"Cover your ears," Trounce muttered. Swinburne and Spencer did so. The Scotland Yard man had finally freed his revolver. He fired a shot into one of the unwelcome visitor's beefy thighs.

The Claimant yelled incoherently, grabbed the side and top of the door, and ripped it from its hinges. He threw it at Trounce.

The slab of wood smashed into the detective inspector and sent him stumbling backward. He fell to his knees, dazed.

"Repulsive toad!" Pox squawked, and sought refuge on top of a bookcase.

Herbert Spencer grabbed a brass poker from the hearth and brandished it like a sword.

"What'll we do, lad?" he mumbled, gaping at the slowly advancing mountain of flesh.

Swinburne, standing beside the vagrant philosopher, became conscious that the mantelpiece was at his back. No retreat. He glanced to the left. Both the study windows were closed. No escape there, not that anyone could survive the jump. He grimaced. His head had started aching and his thoughts were becoming turgid and confused. He was feeling the baleful influence of the Choir Stones, which were still embedded in the Claimant's scalp. He felt an urge to welcome Sir Roger Tichborne to the house and to help him fight his enemies.

He gritted his teeth.

He looked to the right and saw Admiral Lord Nelson standing immobile by the door to the dressing room.

The faux aristocrat lumbered closer.

A fat hand reached out.

Swinburne, without thinking, screeched: "Nelson! Throw this obese bastard out of the house the fastest way possible! At once!"

The clockwork man bent his upper torso forward and accelerated away from the wall, a blur of gleaming metal.

The Claimant turned toward the movement.

Nelson collided with the giant's belly, snapped his mechanical arms out straight, and pushed with all his spring-loaded might.

Neither Swinburne nor Herbert Spencer had any inkling that the clockwork man possessed the power that, in a shocking instant, now became evident.

The whalelike mass of the Tichborne Claimant was thrown into the air and right across the study. He hit the window and went out through it, taking the glass, the frame, and a considerable chunk of the wall on either side of it with him.

The shattering crash was tremendous, and was followed by the clatter and bangs of falling masonry as the front part of 14 Montagu Place suffered his unexpected exit.

Detective Inspector Trounce, shaking his head to clear it, staggered to his feet and peered around at the room. It looked as if a bomb had exploded in it. The Claimant's passage had wrecked furniture, brick dust swirled around, and Burton's papers were raining down like autumn leaves.

"Bloody hell!" he gasped.

Admiral Lord Nelson turned to the poet and saluted.

"Yes, thank you, old chap," Swinburne responded meekly. "Very effective, though not quite as neat as the trick they worked on Sir Alfred. My hat! Mrs. Angell is going to kill me."

Herbert Spencer gingerly approached the gaping hole in the wall and squinted out at the street below. It was enshrouded by steam, billowing about in a slight breeze. He saw movement in the cloud.

"Gents," he said quietly. "Do you happen to have a spare pistol I could borrow? That thing ain't dead."

"You're not serious?" Trounce exclaimed.

"It's layin' on the pavement but it looks to me like it's just winded."

The Scotland Yard man retrieved his revolver from the floor.

Swinburne stepped up to one of Burton's desks and pulled a pistol from its drawer. He handed it to Spencer.

Trounce growled: "Let's get out there and finish that abomination off!"

He set his jaw and marched out of the study. Spencer and Swinburne followed. The poet looked back over his shoulder at Nelson.

"Come on, Admiral."

The three men and the clockwork device descended to the hallway. Trounce quickly checked Mrs. Angell, who was sitting dazed against the wall.

"Go down to your rooms, dear. We'll come and tell you when it's safe."

Swinburne picked Burton's silver-handled swordstick from the elephant-foot umbrella stand by the front door. He handed it to Nelson.

"Here, unsheathe it and don't hesitate to use it. If you can manage it, slice the lumps off the fat man's head."

The mechanical valet saluted.

"What's that?" Trounce exclaimed. "Why play silly beggars? Wouldn't it be better to run the damned beast through the heart?"

"The François Garnier diamonds are sewn into those lumps, Detective Inspector."

"Brundleweed's stones!" Trounce cried. "And you've only just thought to tell me?"

"Richard had his reasons for keeping it quiet. All you need to know for now is that if we can free the fiend from their influence, we might be able to get some information out of him."

Trounce grunted and shook his head. "Perhaps, but I'll tell you, lad: if that brute looks to be getting the upper hand, I'll not hesitate to put a bullet through his brain!"

They went outside. Palmerston's guards were slumped in the mobile castle's bartizans, their heads shattered by their own bullets. The four cavalrymen lay dead in the road.

Wraiths moved through the haze.

As Swinburne led his companions out onto the pavement, the mist parted, and the Claimant came charging out of it like an enraged hippopotamus. Before any of them could raise a weapon, they were sent flying. Swinburne and Spencer both ended up on their backs in the gutter, while Nelson clanged noisily against one of Palmerston's steam-horses. Trounce was grabbed by the collar, yanked off his feet, and thrown high into the air and clear across the road. He thumped down headfirst onto the opposite pavement, rolled, and lay still.

Nelson ducked under the Claimant's swinging fist and scuttled away to retrieve the rapier, which had been knocked out of his hand. Swinburne rolled under the steam-horse and out the other side. He jumped up then back-pedalled rapidly when he found himself looking a wraith full in the face.

"Argh!" he cried, and clutched the sides of his head. He felt a terrible pressure on his brain. "No!" he gasped. "I'll not let you inside! Not ever again!"

A gunshot echoed as Herbert Spencer put a bullet into the Claimant's side. The philosopher scrambled to his feet, turned, and ran to the back of the prime minister's carriage. A ghostly hand clutched at his arm. He struggled in the grip of a wraith.

The Claimant flew into a berserk rage. Stamping his feet and waving his arms, he hollered and howled, screamed and hissed, and threw himself into the side of the foremost of the two steam-horses. It must have weighed well over a ton, but under his onslaught, the machine keeled over, narrowly missed crushing Swinburne, and skidded across the cobbles on its side, showering sparks and emitting a plume of white vapour as one of its pipes tore open.

"Mother!" a muffled voice cried from inside the mobile castle's front cabin. "Help me!"

It was Palmerston's driver, who'd been quaking inside the box ever since the wraiths had appeared and caused the deaths of the guards.

The piggy eyes of the Claimant flicked to the source of the sound. In one stride he was beside it, grabbing the edges of the wedge-shaped compartment. He began to heave it back and forth. The man inside wailed piteously.

Swinburne heard himself mutter: "Tichborne! The bloody toffs are—are—are trying to do away with Tichborne!"

He shook his head.

"No!" he growled. "No! No! No! That is *not* Sir Roger bloody Tichborne!"

He stepped straight through the drifting wraith, levelled the cactus gun, and fired. As he touched the trigger nodule, his arm jerked aside, and the spines flew wide.

"Bloody conspiracy!" he gasped, fighting the words as they forced themselves out of his mouth. As fierce as the battle in the street was, the fight in the poet's head was even more intense.

Admiral Lord Nelson bounded over to the Claimant and lunged in. His rapier danced. He skipped away. Wraiths swooped around him, grabbing at his arms, but they couldn't hold him.

The corpulent creature screamed as two of the lumps on its scalp disappeared, sliced off by the sword blade. Blood gushed from the wounds. Black gems bounced into the gutter.

Swinburne felt a sudden lessening of the pressure on his brain.

"Herbert!" he cried. "Collect the diamonds! We mustn't lose them!"

The Claimant twisted and lumbered after Nelson, who now stood a short distance away in the *en garde* pose. He reached the clockwork man and there commenced a flurry of arms and blade as Nelson jabbed and sliced at the fat behemoth, while the latter attempted to deflect or catch the flashing rapier.

Herbert Spencer tore himself away from the tormenting wraith and darted forward. He retrieved the two fallen Choir Stones. As he did so, another one fell.

The Claimant let loose a terrific shriek and clutched his head.

"I remember!" he shouted. "I remember!"

Nelson backed away from his opponent, who once again lurched after him. The sleeves of the Claimant's jacket, and the shirt beneath, hung in tatters. When he raised his hands to grab the rapier, his mismatched forearms were fully exposed. They were terribly lacerated, but the creature appeared to be entirely immune to pain.

The rapier danced away from the clutching fingers.

The Claimant roared with frustration.

Herbert crept up behind him and picked up the third stone, then two more as the fourth and fifth flew from the swollen man's head.

Swinburne started to shoot spines into the creature's back, hoping that the accumulating venom would at least slow the juggernaut down.

"I want meat!" the Claimant raged. His face was covered with blood. Every few moments, his tongue snaked from between his lips and licked at the red liquid.

The sixth diamond dropped.

Admiral Lord Nelson started to duck and dodge more intently. The remaining stone was located at the back of his opponent's head, so he needed to somehow manoeuvre himself into a position from which it could be extracted.

As the two combatants moved back and forth over the cobbles, Spencer followed cautiously, slipping the sixth stone into his pocket.

The clockwork man stepped in close, bent under a lashing fist, sprang forward, whirled, and sent his rapier's tip digging into the remaining fleshy protuberance on the back of his adversary's skull. A small chunk of flesh dropped away. Blood spurted. A black diamond sparkled. It landed at Spencer's feet. He snatched it up. He now had the complete François Garnier Collection in his pocket.

"Aaaaargh!" the Claimant cried. "Hurts! It hurts! Give me meat! I want meat!"

He turned to face Nelson and backed away a couple of steps, peering through the blood streaming over his eyes.

His fury seemed to leave him for a moment.

He blinked.

Swinburne felt a profound sense of release, as if he was fully himself again. He lowered the spine-shooter and watched.

"No," the fat man uttered. "No. I am not—I am not—"

He lifted the larger of his two hands up to his face.

"I am not Roger—"

He dug his blunt fingernails into his forehead and cheeks.

"I am not Roger Tichborne!"

With a stomach-churning tearing noise, he ripped his face from the front of his skull and held it out triumphantly.

"My name is Arthur Orton! And I want meat!"

He pushed the drooping skin and tissue into his mouth and started to chew.

"Ah," Swinburne whispered. "So there we have it at last."

Arthur Orton considered Admiral Lord Nelson.

"You," he rumbled, "are not meat."

His gory countenance, all raw muscle and throbbing veins, turned until he was looking directly at Herbert Spencer.

"But you——"

With startling agility for one so gargantuan, Orton lunged at the vagrant philosopher.

Spencer turned to run.

Admiral Lord Nelson sprang into action. He took two great strides, raised the rapier, sent it plunging toward the back of Orton's spine, suddenly slowed—and froze.

The clockwork man had wound down.

Corpulent fingers closed around Spencer's neck.

Swinburne started shooting, pressing the trigger nodule again and again.

"Trounce!" he shrilled. "Your pistol! Your pistol!"

There was no response. The detective was either out cold or dead.

Spencer yelled as he was yanked off his feet.

"Meat!" bellowed Orton triumphantly and sank his teeth into the back of the philosopher's neck. His victim's scream of agony was cut short as vertebrae crunched and shattered, and a gobbet of pulsating flesh was wrenched free.

Orton twisted Herbert Spencer's head off and threw it to one side. It bounced away across the cobbles. Blood pumped from the severed neck, and the monstrous butcher laughed as it sprayed over his face.

"No," Swinburne sobbed. "Oh Jesus, please no."

Holding Spencer's twitching corpse with the larger of his hands, Orton plunged the other into the neck, pushing it deep into the body.

"Aaah," he sighed, and when he pulled the dripping red arm back out, the philosopher's still-beating heart was gripped in his fingers. He tore it free of stretching arteries and flesh, raised it to his mouth, and licked it.

"Why won't you fucking die?" Swinburne raged, tears streaming down his cheeks.

The Claimant turned and regarded the poet. He grinned and chewed on the twitching organ.

Swinburne raised the cactus gun and, without aiming, touched the trigger nodule.

Spines sank into Orton's right eye.

The butcher flinched, shook his head, and waddled slowly toward the tiny man.

"More meat! I like meat!"

Swinburne turned to run but suddenly found himself gripped by vaporous hands. Two wraiths had swooped upon him and now, just as they had dragged Sir Alfred Tichborne through Tichborne House to his doom, so they began to pull Swinburne to his.

"Get off me! Get off me!"

Orton gave a bloody smile and said: "Come to me. I eat you up!"

Closer and closer Swinburne was drawn, until the gigantic butcher towered over him, dripping blood onto his flame-red hair.

"Yum yum," Orton drawled, through a mouthful of Herbert Spencer's heart.

He reached out and caught the poet by the lapels. He lifted him into the air. The wraiths floated beside Swinburne, holding his arms, preventing him from using the cactus pistol.

Orton spat the lump of flesh from his mouth. His lips peeled back from the big green incisor teeth. His jaws opened. He leaned forward, his mouth approaching the poet's skinny neck.

Swinburne suddenly felt completely calm.

"Two things," he said, looking straight into the little piggy eyes. "Firstly, I concede defeat."

Orton stopped and regarded the small man.

"You've won. So why not rein yourself in a little? After all, London is on its knees. The Houses of Parliament are half destroyed. Buckingham Palace is under siege. The working classes are in control. My friends have been beaten into submission or killed. I mean to say, there's no need to dine on an insignificant little poet like me just to prove a point, is there?"

Orton gave a bubbling chuckle and licked his lips.

"Meat!" he hissed.

"Yes," the poet continued. "I thought you might say that, which brings me to my second point, which is this: your manners are truly appalling. Have you not read *A Manual of Etiquette for Young Ladies?*"

Emitting an animal growl, the Claimant opened his mouth wide and placed his teeth against Swinburne's throat.

There was a sound—*thunk!*—and the poet suddenly fell to the ground, the wraiths swirling away from him.

He looked up.

Arthur Orton's head was transfixed by a huge African spear, which had pierced his skull above the right ear and exited beneath the left. Blood and grey brain matter oozed from its point.

The man who'd called himself Roger Tichborne toppled backward, hit the road with a tremendous thud, and lay still.

Algernon Swinburne sat bemused. Then he looked to his left at number 14 Montagu Place. In the gaping hole where the study window had once been, Sir Richard Francis Burton stood, his Dervish robes fluttering slightly in the breeze.

COUNCIL OF WAR

I see a tremendously bright future. I see plants and flowers everywhere. They will fulfill their natural functions, of course. They will add colour and beauty to our cities and landscapes, of course. They will freshen and perfume the air, of course. But, by god, they will do so much more.
—RICHARD SPRUCE

"**M**ay Allah bless thee and grant thee peace," Al-Masloub murmured.

"And peace and blessings upon thee," Burton replied. "You are certain you do not require an escort?"

"Allah is our escort."

"Then I am assured of your safety. Until next time, my friend."

Al-Masloub smiled and bowed and he and his fellow musicians departed, slipping into the thickening atmosphere of Montagu Place.

"You, on the other hand," Burton said, turning to Mrs. Angell, "most definitely will be escorted."

"I should stay, Sir Richard," his housekeeper protested. "Look at the state of the house! It's a terrible mess!"

"And one that I shall see to. Your carriage awaits, Mother Angell. A constable will drive you to the station and stay with you on the train all the way to Herne Bay. A few days in a bed and breakfast enjoying some fresh sea air will work wonders on your nerves."

"There's nothing wrong with my nerves."

"Well, there jolly well ought to be after what you've been through today! Now off with you, and I promise to have this place as good as new by the time you get back."

Reluctantly, the old lady descended the front steps, accepted a helping hand from a policeman, and climbed into the brougham parked just in front of the prime minister's mobile castle. With a quick blast of its steam-horse's whistle, the carriage chugged away, heading to the Queen Victoria Memorial Railway Station.

Detective Inspector Trounce emerged from the mist.

"Your local postmaster is a stubborn ass!" he complained. "He absolutely refused to open up shop. I had to threaten him with arrest."

"Can you blame him, after this?" Burton responded, indicating the debris-filled road.

"Humph! I suppose not. Anyway, I sent off a parakeet to Scotland Yard. More men will be here in due course." He hesitated. "And a mortuary van is on its way."

Burton gave a curt jerk of his head in acknowledgement and the two men entered the house.

The king's agent said: "Pox found Constable Bhatti, who says he's on his way. The bird has since been racing back and forth between here and Battersea Power Station. Brunel has agreed to assist us."

Trounce reached up and gingerly felt the big bump on his head. "Ouch! So the Steam Man will fight alongside us rather than against us on this occasion?"

"Yes, although not literally. There are a lot of springs in that lumbering life-maintaining contraption of his. If the mechanism ceased to function, he'd die. Best to keep him out of the enemy's range."

They passed Admiral Lord Nelson, who, rewound, and with the cactus pistol in one hand and a rapier in the other, was standing guard in the hallway.

"Same applies to him, then," Trounce said, indicating the valet.

"No," Burton replied.

"No? But he's chock-a-block full of springs!"

"Yes."

"So our opponent will stop him with ease."

"I'm counting on it."

"What? By Jove, what the blazes are you up to?"

"All in due course, Trounce, old man. All in due course."

Algernon Swinburne came down the stairs. His eyes were hooded and his jaw set hard. Herbert Spencer's death had affected the poet greatly.

"I've locked the Choir Stones in the safe in your library, Richard. They were giving us headaches."

"Thank you, Algy."

The three of them entered the seldom-used dining room. Lord Palmerston, Burke and Hare, and the prime minister's driver were seated around the large table.

"Gentlemen, we have very little time to spare," Burton announced. He, Swinburne, and Trounce sat down. "Our riposte must be immediate and devastating. Before we put the wheels into motion, though, I feel I should apologise to you all. Our enemy incapacitated me. She exploited a certain flaw in my character, causing it to echo back on itself over and over until it became amplified beyond all endurance. Fortunately, I retained enough of my wits to put myself through the Dervish meditation ritual. It enabled me to transfer my mind's focus from guilt, disappointments, and regrets to something I said to Charles Babbage right at the start of this whole affair, to wit: *'The mistakes we make give us the impetus to change, to improve, to evolve.'* I should have been regarding my own errors of judgement in that light all along, but I wasn't. Now I am. It's a statement, I believe, that can be applied not only to individuals but also to wider society, and is the philosophy that must guide us now, for whatever the rights or wrongs of a workers' revolution, the crisis currently afflicting London does not have its origin in lessons we, as a nation, have learned. Rather, it has been forced upon us by an external agency, and in relation to a mediumistic divination. We cannot allow it. The woman must be stopped."

"Our enemy is female?" Palmerston asked.

"Yes. Her name is Helena Petrovna Blavatsky. She is a Russian, and she intends nothing less than the wholesale destruction of the British Empire."

"The devil she does!" the prime minister exclaimed. "What's her motive? What's this about divination?"

"She claims to be clairvoyant. She has seen a future where Britain engages in a great war against a united German Empire allied with Russia."

He went on to describe the prophecy Blavatsky had shared with him. As he talked, Palmerston's pale, inexpressive face seemed to grow even whiter, his manicured fingers gripped the edge of the table, and his eyes became fixed, as if he'd gone into shock.

"Her intention," Burton finished, "is to cause such internal strife that Britain is severely weakened in the lead-up to the war. She wants Germany to defeat us without Russia's assistance, so that, once the victory is won, Russia might swoop upon the conquering nation."

"But why make us the target?" Palmerston protested. "Why doesn't she work her voodoo against the Germans directly?"

"If she does that, she will ensure the continuation of the British Empire. She wants all the Western powers on their knees so that Russia might subjugate them in their entirety."

"Gad!" Trounce murmured. "Another lunatic interfering with time! Only on this occasion, instead of someone from the future interfering with the present, it's the reverse!"

"Perhaps," Burton murmured, noncommittally.

Trounce looked at him quizzically. "Is there something you're not telling us?"

Burton ignored the question and lit one of his Manila cheroots. He glanced at Palmerston. The prime minister was sitting stock-still, staring straight ahead.

"We came into this affair, gentlemen," the king's agent continued, "at the point when Blavatsky gained possession of the Choir Stones, which are fragments of a larger diamond, one of the three legendary Eyes of Nāga. She then took advantage of the Tichbornes, both to wrest control of a second, unbroken diamond from them, and to use them as a means to disseminate her call to insurrection."

Detective Inspector Trounce frowned and scratched his head. "Theft and impersonation I can understand," he said, "but this black diamond business has me flummoxed. What's the connection between the stones and the public disorder?"

"The Eyes project a subtle electrical field that can influence a person's mind, causing, in certain types, a profound sense of dissatisfaction. They can also magnify a mesmeric directive. Blavatsky used the Choir Stones to control Arthur Orton, to enhance his natural ability to sway opinion, and to entrance people into believing that he was Roger Tichborne. Once the crowds who came to see him were captivated, she used the greater power of the unbroken diamond to incite them to riot."

"And the wraiths?" asked Trounce.

"A stroke of genius on her part. You know how obsessed the Rakes are with spiritualism and the occult. With her credentials, there was no difficulty in gaining leadership of the faction. She took control and soon had them all walking abroad in their etheric bodies."

Palmerston took a deep breath, as if coming out of a trance, and said: "Their what?"

"The etheric body, Prime Minister, is that part of you which exactly matches your physical dimensions and characteristics but is comprised of rarefied matter. It connects your corporeal self to the spiritual realm."

"The soul?"

"No, it is more a component of material existence. It exactly duplicates your bodily self-perception, even down to the clothes you are wearing."

"Twaddle!"

"Many, especially those of a scientific bent, believe so. Nevertheless, there are wraiths roaming London, and they are doing so because through them Blavatsky can amplify the black diamond's emanations."

There came a knock at the door and Constable Bhatti stepped in. He gaped when he saw Palmerston, and gave a clumsy salute.

"I—I understand you requested my presence, sir?" he stuttered, looking first at Trounce, then at the famous explorer.

"Yes, come in, Constable," Burton said.

"Thank you, but—um—there's a rather extraordinary-looking chap outside. A Technologist. He says he's here on behalf of Isambard Kingdom Brunel."

"Ah, good! That was quick! Would you usher him in, please?"

Bhatti nodded, stepped out of sight, and returned moments later with a short, plump, blond-haired individual who introduced himself as Daniel Gooch.

"Ah ha!" Bhatti cried. "I thought I recognised you! You're the rotorship engineer!"

Gooch bowed his head in acknowledgment. Though dressed conservatively in pale-brown trousers, white shirt, dark waistcoat, and a top hat—which he'd removed and was holding—he was also wearing a bizarre contraption slung around his shoulders and buckled over his chest and around his waist. It was nothing less than an extra pair of arms, mechanical and intricate, multijointed and with a number of different tools arranged at their ends—very similar, in fact, to Brunel's limbs. Two thin cables ran from the harness up to either side of Gooch's neck and were plugged directly into his skull, just behind his ears.

The metal arms moved as naturally as his fleshy ones.

"Mr. Brunel sends his regards, gentlemen," he said. His voice was deep and gravelly. "He apologises for not attending in person, but his size rather limits his access to dwellings such as this. Besides, he's overseeing the manufacture of the item you requested, so felt it best to send me as his lieutenant."

"You're very welcome, Mr. Gooch," the king's agent said. "And thank you for getting here so swiftly. Please, pull up a chair and join us. You too, Constable."

As the new arrivals settled, Burton gave a brief recap.

Palmerston then said: "So our enemy's motive is to change the course of the future war, and she shared with you a vision of the conflict. Just how clear was the—er—hallucination, Captain Burton?"

"If anything, it was *too* clear, sir. My brain is still struggling to process all the information. It was as if I saw events from the perspective of a person who'd lived through them."

"And you say the war will be fought with Technologist weapons on our side and Eugenicist weapons on the other?"

"Yes."

"Hmm. And this Blavatsky woman has the ability to pull one solid object through another?"

"That's correct. She did it with Brundleweed's diamonds and with Sir Alfred Tichborne. What have you in mind, sir?"

Palmerston's hands curled into fists. "The night before last, the traitor Richard Spruce vanished from his prison cell. Its door was still locked. Its one small, barred window—which was too small for him to crawl through anyway—had not been tampered with. There were no escape tunnels or any other means of egress. He simply vanished."

"You suggest that Blavatsky yanked him out through the wall?"

"It's likely, don't you think? If the Germans are going to employ eugenically altered plants as weapons, then, in light of the current situation in Ireland, Spruce seems the obvious source of their future scientific knowledge."

Burton ground his cheroot into an ashtray. He nodded.

"Yes, you're probably right. Do you think he's made it out of the country?"

"I fear so," the prime minister grumbled.

"We have Eugenicists disappearing left, right, and centre, too," Gooch added. "There seems to be an exodus under way. The Technologists have lost a lot of extremely skilled scientists."

"Then it's begun," Palmerston hissed. "Christ almighty, the war against Lincoln's Union we can just about deal with, but a war against the Germans and Russians—!" The prime minister held a hand to his forehead and sighed. "Anyway, one thing at a time. The country is on the brink. Our labourers are running rampant and the dissent is spreading fast. I've called in the army to protect the palace and Whitehall, but a large number of troops are absconding or becoming openly mutinous."

"It's the same at the Yard," Trounce murmured. "Lord knows how many men are AWOL at the moment."

"So what are we going to do about it, Captain Burton?" Palmerston asked. "How do we nip this atrocity in the bud?"

Burton rested his elbows on the table and interlaced his fingers. He tapped his knuckles against his chin and said nothing for a beat. Then: "As dire as they may be, I think we can take advantage of our current circumstances. Firstly, Trounce, take one of my velocipedes and race it over to Scotland Yard. Speak to the chief commissioner and muster as many men as you're able. They need to be in place by midnight—"

He spoke for a few minutes more. Trounce nodded, gave Palmerston a halfhearted salute, and departed.

After Burton heard the front door slam shut, he turned to Burke and Hare.

"I require something that you two have in your possession. I need you to fetch it now, without delay."

He told them what it was.

Burke turned to Palmerston and said: "With your permission, sir?"

"Absolutely. Go."

"And bring back another carriage for the prime minister," Burton called after the two men as they departed.

He turned to Palmerston's driver, who'd been sitting through the discussion with a bemused expression on his face.

"What's your name, sir?"

"John Phelps."

"Tell me, Mr. Phelps, can the mobile castle outside be driven with just one steam-horse?"

"Aye, sir. No trouble, she'll just eat up coal twice as fast."

"Then, if your employer permits it, I'd like you to drive Mr. Swinburne, Constable Bhatti, my valet, and I to Battersea Power Station this evening."

Phelps looked at Palmerston, who nodded.

"Very well, sir."

Burton next addressed the Technologist: "Presumably, you have your own vehicle, Mr. Gooch?"

"I drove here in my Folks' Wagon. I'll return the same way."

"Very well. Before you depart, can I call upon you to assist Constable Bhatti?"

"Surely. With what?"

Burton gave a lengthy explanation—during which Swinburne started whooping with delight—and finished by turning to Bhatti: "Do you think you can do it, Constable?"

"I'll give it my best," the young policeman answered. "It's a case of removal and replacement rather than dismantlement, so we should be able to avoid the dangers. As for the rest of it, I'm sure Mr. Gooch will spot any errors I might make."

"It's not exactly my field of expertise," Gooch said, "but I'll do what I can, and Isambard can check the work over when you get to the power station."

"And what of the task I've set Mr. Brunel?" Burton asked. "Do you think he can supply what I need?"

"Your request was certainly unusual, Captain—especially when communicated through a foul-mouthed parakeet—but it's not a difficult thing to design and Mr. Brunel is the best engineer in the world. He'd prefer to power it by steam, of course, but every single valve in a steam engine employs a spring, so that rules it out. Your alternative is—shall we say—*eccentric*? But it's feasible, and Isambard had already finished a blueprint when I left him. He has all the manufacturing power of the station at his disposal, so I assure you he'll provide what you need in good time."

"Excellent," the king's agent responded. He turned to his assistant. "Algy, tonight we're making our peace with the Steam Man."

The poet, who'd spent the past few minutes with a huge grin on his face, now scowled. "After the way he treated me last time we met I'd rather kick the blighter right up the exhaust funnel!"

"Quite so." Burton smiled. "But let the past be the past. For now we have to concentrate on saving the present!" He stood and paced up and down restlessly. "We have to hurry. I want to move against Blavatsky in the small hours of the morning."

"Why then?" Palmerston asked.

"Because the human mind is at its lowest ebb during that period, sir. We know the woman is at full stretch. I want her exhausted. On which point: Algy, run up to my bedroom. You'll find a vial of Saltzmann's Tincture in my bedside drawer. Bring it down. We're all dog-tired, but if you, Bhatti, and I take five drops each, it will keep us alert for another twelve hours or so."

"Smashing!" the poet exclaimed excitedly and scampered out of the room.

Palmerston drummed his fingers impatiently. "I'll not sit here in the dark! What in the devil's name are you playing at, Burton?" he demanded. "Explain your intentions!"

"There's no time, Prime Minister. As soon as Burke and Hare return, I recommend that you make a swift departure. Mr. Gooch and Constable Bhatti will be fully occupied with their project, while Mr. Swinburne and I have a great deal to arrange."

"In other words, I'm surplus to requirements and in your way?"

"I wouldn't have put it quite like that, sir. I would point out, however, that you are the prime minister, the country is both at war and in the midst of a crisis, yet you are sitting in my dining room."

Palmerston shot to his feet with such suddenness that his chair toppled backward to the floor. He glared at Burton and said slowly, in an icy tone: "There are limits to my patience, Captain. You are developing an unfortunate habit of addressing me with a marked lack of respect. I was warned before I employed you that you're an impertinent rogue. I'll not take it!"

Phelps, Bhatti, and Gooch glanced at each other uncomfortably.

"You gave me a job to do," Burton said. "I intend to do it. If you are displeased with my conduct, you can release me from my duties immediately and I'll get back to writing my books while the country becomes a republic, Germany gathers her strength, and Russia waits in the wings."

A tense silence filled the room.

No one moved.

Palmerston cleared his throat. "Get on with it."

"Yes, sir."

The door opened and Swinburne bounded in.

"I say!" he shrilled. "I'm much more resistant to that Russian cow's emanations when I'm drunk. Do you think I should down a few brandies before we proceed?"

THE BATTLE OF THE STRAND

> The Rakes maintain that there is no inorganic or dead matter in
> nature, the distinction between the two made by Technologists
> being as unfounded as it is arbitrary and devoid of reason.
> —HELENA BLAVATSKY

Charles Altamont Doyle was extremely confused. Two—or was it three?—days ago, he'd awoken slightly before dawn in a strange house and had stumbled down the stairs and out of the front door.

He'd walked aimlessly, enveloped by chaos. People were overturning vehicles and smashing windows, setting fire to shops and attacking one another, chanting something about the upper classes and a conspiracy of some kind.

His memory failed him. The past few hours were nothing but an alcohol-fueled blur.

He wandered through the mayhem and the rioters left him alone.

The fairies, however, did not.

They danced at the periphery of his vision, whispered in his ear, and followed him wherever he went. He cried and screamed for them to stop hounding him. He reasoned and demanded and begged.

They ignored his pleas.

He staggered into the Bricklayer's Arms on Bedford Street, intent on imbibing his tormentors into oblivion. Drink, when taken in copious quantities, always worked. Fairies, he'd discovered, were particularly allergic to burgundy.

The pub was heaving with all manner of lowly types but that didn't matter because in recent weeks the working classes had looked with great favour upon the Rakes. As one man had said to him: "You hoity-toity types need teachin' a blimmin' lesson, mate, but since you be one o' them Rake geezers, the only fing what I'm gonna teach yer is 'ow ter git legless!"

Glass after glass was purchased for him. Doyle emptied them assiduously, and the next thing he knew he was waking up in a doorway halfway down a dark, mist-swathed alley.

How much time had passed? He didn't know. He could hear shouts and screams and violence in the near distance.

He went back to sleep.

The fairies came skipping into his dreams.

"It is in thy blood to see us," they told him. "It was in thy father's and it is in thy sons'."

He awoke again. Hauled himself upright. Staggered onward.

"God in heaven," he slurred. "Are they going to plague my boys, too?"

Young Innes already showed signs of levelheadedness. Perhaps he would resist his tormentors, but little Arthur—dear little imaginative Arthur!— how would he cope?

The memory of his children and his wife and his inability to keep them brought the tears to his eyes. He began to weep and couldn't stop.

Time, chopped and jumbled, went by. Streets tumbled past. Smoke. Steam. Turmoil.

Doyle found himself in another grubby backstreet and another filthy tavern. As before, a boisterous crowd willingly financed his raging alcoholism.

Despite the wine, the fairies started to skip around his feet again. Either they were getting stronger or he was getting weaker.

He drank and walked and drank and cried and drank and ranted and, quite suddenly, Big Ben was chiming midnight and he was aware of his surroundings.

Clarity!

There was something he had to do, a place he had to be, an urge he couldn't defy.

Doyle found himself on the outskirts of the Strand. It was closed off and secured by a police cordon. Access and egress were impossible from Trafalgar Square in the west all the way to Fleet Street in the east.

He had no idea why he wanted to get onto the famous thoroughfare but the determination to do so was all-consuming.

Kingsway and Aldwych were blocked, as were the various roads abutting the main street from the north and those leading up to it from the Thames, to the south. Only Bridewell Alley had been overlooked, due, perhaps, to its extreme narrowness and the fact that it was clogged with rubbish.

Doyle slipped into it, tottered along its length, and lurched out into the wide street beyond. The Strand had once been among London's most glamorous playgrounds but now broken glass crunched underfoot and many of its buildings were gutted, blackened, and windowless.

It was teeming with thousands of Rakes and wraiths. The latter, Doyle was used to. He himself had ventured out in spirit form on countless occasions in recent months. The corporeal bodies, though, unnerved him. Their milky eyes, bluish-grey skin, and dragging walk spoke of the grave. Indeed, the air was heavy with the cloying odour of putrefying flesh.

He kept his eyes downcast and shoved his way past them until he reached a grand old edifice, undamaged by the rioting. Only vaguely aware of what he was doing, he stumbled into the opulent structure and ascended five flights of stairs. He banged on a door and entered.

Fairies darted between and around his ankles.

He sat at a table.

His hands were gripped.

Someone said, in a dry, husky voice, something about the greater good of mankind.

"The greater good of mankind," he chanted, like an automaton. Then: "Freedom! Liberation! Anarchy! No God!"

"Thy shackles are unbreakable, soft skin," a fairy whispered.

"Leave me alone," he hissed, then aloud: "Rules must be broken! Propriety must be challenged! The status quo must be unbalanced! True liberty!"

"Slave to oppositions!" the fairy mocked. "There are but two eyes in thy head! Will the third not open for thee?"

The Russian woman materialised, just as she'd done many times before.

"Go forth, apostles," she said. "Liberate the downtrodden and the oppressed."

She reached out to touch him.

He knew what would happen, and he knew it had happened too many times before. This time would be the last. After so many separations, he was too exhausted for the rejoining.

He tried to say no.

He failed.

Her nebulous finger brushed his forehead.

Time distorted and space warped out of shape.

Somehow, impossibly, he was in two places at once.

He shuffled along the Strand, feeling heavy and sodden and empty and lonely and mindless and lost.

He also drifted, amorphously, elsewhere on the thoroughfare, and the Russian woman's force of will resonated like a church bell through what little substance this aspect of him possessed.

A fairy floated before his two sets of eyes—the corporeal ones and the formless ones.

"Thou hast fulfilled the role assigned to thee. Recurrence, not transcendence, shall come," it tinkled.

"Leave me alone, you bloody lizard!" he snarled.

He wondered at his own words.

Lizard?

At the Trafalgar Square end of the Strand, Commander Krishnamurthy, his entire face mottled with bruises after his ordeal at Tichborne House, squinted through the dense atmosphere and addressed a gathering of constables.

"Now then, lads," he said, "who's got a headache?"

More than half the men raised their hands.

"Me too. And let me tell you, I've had quite enough of it. So tonight we're going to sort it out. However, I'm afraid that, for some of you, the headache is going to get worse before it gets better. We're close to the source of the public disorder that's been disrupting the city these days past, and, whatever it is, it's going to wheedle its way into your brains to try to make a defector of you. You all know fellow constables who've gone absent without leave to join the rioters—"

The men muttered an acknowledgment, and one of them growled: "Bloody deserters!"

"No," Krishnamurthy objected. "Their minds are being controlled—and, as I say, over the next few hours, it's likely that the same thing will happen to some of us."

"No, sir!" the men protested.

"We have to be prepared for it. We don't want to be adding ourselves to the enemy forces, hey? So here are my orders, lads, and I pray I never have to tell you to do anything like this ever again: in the event that you notice one of your fellows supporting, or beginning to support, the opposition, take out your truncheon and clock him over the head with it!"

The constables looked at each other, perplexed.

"I mean it!" Krishnamurthy said. "If needs must, render your colleague unconscious. Knock him out! Do you understand?"

"Yes, sir!" came the hesitant responses.

Krishnamurthy knew that not far away, at the top of Kingsway, Detective Inspector Honesty was giving the same speech to another gathering of constables, though probably in a rather more concise fashion, while in Fleet Street, Detective Inspector Trounce was doing the same.

The three groups of policemen were each about a hundred and fifty men strong. Much smaller teams were guarding the various minor routes into the Strand.

Krishnamurthy estimated that a force of a little over six hundred constables had congregated around the area. From what he'd seen so far, he suspected that at least four times that number of Rakes lurked inside the police cordon.

"Is this really all we can muster?" he muttered to himself. "I knew the force was haemorrhaging men but I'd no idea it was this bad!"

He peered into the rolling ground-level cloud. There was a full moon somewhere above, and its light gave the mist a weird and deceptively bright silvery glow. However, the shadows were dense, and, with most of the street's gas lamps destroyed, visibility was far worse than it seemed.

Sergeant Slaughter approached, stood beside him, and noted: "If it's not one thing, it's another, Commander."

"What do you mean?"

"This murk, sir. There's been a lot fewer vehicles on the streets what with the rioting, so where's the bally steam coming from?"

"Hmm, that's a very good question!"

"Then, of course, the steam got mixed up with the smoke from the fires, so we got this dirty grey soup. But most of the fires in this area burned themselves out a good while ago. So, again, Commander: where's it coming from?"

Krishnamurthy suddenly became aware that his breath was clouding in front of his face.

"By jingo!" he exclaimed. "I hadn't realised! The weather's on the turn!"

"Crept up on us, didn't it!" Slaughter said. "The end of the heatwave, and about time, too. Except, it looks like the change has brought on a London particular."

"Fog!" Krishnamurthy spat. "Curse it! That's exactly what we don't need!"

He heard the chopping of an approaching rotorchair.

"One of your squad, Commander?" Slaughter asked. "He's taking a risk, isn't he?"

"He'll be all right as long as he stays this side of the cordon. We're at the edge of the danger zone. If he flies past us and over the Strand—" He made a gesture with his hand, indicating something plunging downward.

"Hallo! He's landing!" Slaughter cried.

The miasma parted and men ran out of the way as the rotorchair descended, dropping like a stone and only slowing at the very last moment before lightly touching the cobbles and coming to rest. A man, wearing the Flying Squad uniform and with goggles covering his eyes, clambered out of the contraption and ran over to Krishnamurthy.

"Hello, sir!" he said, with a salute.

"Hallo, Milligan. What's the news?"

"Not good, I'm afraid. The rioting is most intense to the east of here, especially around the Bank of England, which is up in flames. As if that's not bad enough, the circle of disorder is fast approaching the East End."

"Blast it!" Krishnamurthy whispered. He removed his peaked cap and massaged his temples. Once the madness touched the overcrowded Cauldron, all hell would break loose. If the East Enders began rioting, London would be lost.

"Milligan, gather together the patrols in the north and west and have them join you in the east. If it becomes necessary, fly low and use your pistols to fire warning shots at the rioters. Shoot a few men in the leg if you have to! Anything that might hold them at bay for a while."

"Yes, sir!"

Milligan ran back to his machine, strapped himself in, and, with a roar of the engine, rose on a cone of steam and vanished into the fog. Seconds later, the chopping of the rotorchair's wings suddenly stopped, there was an instant of absolute silence, then the machine dropped straight back down out of the cloud and smashed into the road.

Krishnamurthy clutched Sergeant Slaughter's arm and looked at him with an expression of shock.

They ran to the wreckage. Constables joined them. The flying machine had turned upside down before hitting the ground. Milligan lay beneath it, mangled and dead.

Wordlessly, Krishnamurthy squatted and closed the man's eyes.

"What happened?" Slaughter asked.

"It seems our enemy has expanded the no-flying zone."

"By the Lord Harry," the sergeant muttered. "They must realise we're here."

Krishnamurthy glanced back toward the Strand. "Damnation!" he said under his breath. "Come on, Swinburne! Hurry up!"

Charles Doyle was dead and he knew it.

Only the Russian bitch's force of will was keeping his carcass moving, his spirit self-aware.

Her words vibrated and throbbed in his mind: "Break free! Cast off your chains! Rise up and overthrow!"

They cut into him, were magnified through him as if he were a lens, then radiated outward, receding into the far distance, where they touched other astral bodies and were bounced farther on.

If only he could press his hands over his ears, block out that voice!

A tiny man with moth wings fluttered in front of his face and sang: "Prepare thyself!"

He tried to bat the fairy away but his hands were either without substance or too heavy and slow, it wasn't clear to him which.

A part of him coiled and writhed through the atmosphere near the Fleet Street end of the Strand, while the other part dragged itself along the pavement of Kingsway.

He was overwhelmed by a voracious hunger. It was not for food, nor even for alcohol. No. This rapacious craving was for the fulfillment of life!

For how long had he been tormented by this lack? His entire existence, it seemed. The opportunities he'd missed or wasted! He'd been so cautious, so afraid of making a mistake, that he hadn't *done* anything—instead, he'd escaped into the bottle, and now it was too late!

"I had life but I didn't live it!" he wept. "I want it back! Please, don't let me die like this!"

Something registered in his consciousness. There was a figure ahead, moving in the thickening fog. He could sense its warmth, its vitality. There were others beyond it, but this one was close.

A beating heart! Pulsating blood! Life!

He must have it! He must have it!

His corpse lurched forward, the arms reached out, the fingers curled into claws.

There came a distant shout: "Constable Tamworth! Come back! Don't wander from the group, man!"

Detective Inspector Honesty looked at his pocket watch. It was ten to three in the morning.

He felt weary.

He loved police work, mainly because he was very good at it, but at times like this his mind tended to drift to what he considered his true vocation: gardening. In his youth, he'd dreamed of becoming a landscape gardener, but his father, one of the original Peelers, had insisted that his boy follow him into the force and wouldn't hear otherwise. Honesty didn't begrudge the old man's stubbornness; policing had, after all, gained him respect, a secure job with prospects, and a loving young wife whom he'd met while on a murder case. He'd been able to buy a house with a large garden, too, and it was the envy of the neighbourhood, with its bright displays of flowers and finely trimmed lawn.

What, though, would his life have been like had he defied his father?

He remembered something Sir Richard Francis Burton had told him: that when Edward Oxford, the man they called Spring Heeled Jack, had altered time, original future history had become disconnected. It still existed—in the same way that, if you find yourself at a junction, taking road A won't cause road B to vanish—but it was inaccessible; there was no way back to the junction without a time-travelling device.

Did that mean that somewhere, some*when*, there was a *Thomas Manfred Honesty, Landscape Gardener*?

He hoped so. It was a strangely comforting thought.

It was ten to three.

His watch had stopped.

He shook it and tut-tutted.

Only a couple of minutes had passed, he was sure. The signal wouldn't come for at least another hour.

His men were restless and he was feeling the same way.

In front of the police cordon, Kingsway had faded from sight, obscured by the fog, which was obviously returning to London with a vengeance. The shambling figures, visible earlier, were now hidden, which made them seem even more uncanny and threatening.

"Dead Rakes," he muttered, for the umpteenth time. "Damned peculiar."

A constable approached and pointed wordlessly back at the men. Honesty looked and saw three wraiths swirling among them. The policemen were swiping at the ghosts with their truncheons, to no effect.

"Stop that!" he ordered. "Waste of time! Save your strength!"

They desisted, but one of the men looked at him, his face suddenly contorting with fury, and screamed: "Don't bloody well tell me what to do!"

"Constable Tamworth! At ease!"

"At ease yourself, you little jumped-up poseur! Who are you to give me orders?"

"Your commanding officer!"

"No, mate. I'll follow no one but Tichborne!"

Honesty sighed and turned to another man. "Sergeant Piper," he ordered. "Your truncheon. Back of Tamworth's head. Now!"

Piper nodded and unhooked his truncheon from his belt.

"Not bloody likely!" Tamworth said. He took to his heels and vanished into the fog.

The detective inspector yelled after him: "Constable Tamworth! Don't wander from the group, man!"

A bubbling wail of terror answered him.

Three policemen broke away from the cordon and ran toward the sound.

"No! Menders! Carlyle! Patterson! Come back!"

"He's in trouble, sir!" Carlyle protested before plunging into the pall.

Honesty turned to the main group and bellowed: "Stay here! Move and I'll have your guts for garters! Come with me, Piper."

He gritted his teeth and, with the sergeant, hurried after his men.

As they came into view, he saw Menders raise his arm, point his pistol at something, pull the trigger, and curse: "Jammed, damn the thing!"

He looked to where the constable had aimed and saw Tamworth sprawled on the ground. The man's jacket and shirt had been ripped aside and his stomach torn open. Squatting over him, hands buried in the policeman's intestines, was a thin, bearded, bespectacled dead man. The corpse looked up, moaned, and stood. Entrails oozed from his hands and fell to the cobbles. "My apologies," he said. "I need life."

"Mary, mother of God!" exclaimed Menders. He threw his pistol and it bounced off the bearded man's forehead.

Sergeant Piper whispered, "Useless. You can't kill a bloody stiff!"

"Piper, stay with me," Honesty commanded. "The rest of you, behind the cordon, now. That's an order."

Menders swallowed, gave a hesitant nod, and started to back away from the bearded man, who stood swaying, as if uncertain whether or not to collapse to the ground and admit his demise.

"A bloody stiff," Piper repeated. "But still bleedin' well movin'."

A top-hatted, well-dressed cadaver suddenly emerged from the cloud beside them, grabbed Menders by the shoulders, and sank his teeth into the constable's throat before dragging him out of sight.

Constable Carlyle saw his colleague die, let loose a high-pitched scream, panicked, fumbled for his police whistle, raised it to his lips, and started blowing long, loud, repetitive blasts.

"That's the signal!" a constable named Lampwick announced.

"Impossible!" Trounce snapped. "It's too early."

He and his men were close to the smoldering skeleton of Ye Olde Cheshire Cheese, which had burned to the ground the day before. The rioters enjoyed setting fire to taverns as much as they enjoyed drinking in them. Judging by the stench, on this occasion they'd made the fatal misjudgement of combining the two activities.

"But listen to that whistle, sir! That can't be a mistake!"

"Constable Lampwick, we're expecting Mr. Swinburne to arrive via Waterloo Bridge, so the signal should more or less come from straight ahead. It sounds to me like the whistle-blower is with Detective Inspector Honesty's team on Kingsway."

Trounce shifted from one foot to the other uneasily. He took off his bowler and gave it a hard slap.

Something wasn't right.

He shoved his hat back onto his head.

A decision had to be made.

What if he got it wrong?

The distant whistling stopped.

"Hell's bells," he hissed under his breath.

What to do? What to do?

Trounce became very still for a moment.

He blinked.

The Scotland Yard man suddenly wheeled to face his men and bellowed: "Arm yourselves, lads. We're moving forward. Proceed with utmost caution. Do not, under any circumstances, mistake this for the Charge of the blessed Light Brigade, is that understood?"

There came a great many, "Yes, sirs."

A hundred and fifty uniformed men took out their police-issue Adams revolvers, unhooked their truncheons, and, following Trounce, advanced slowly into the fog.

"Did you hear that, Commander?" Sergeant Slaughter asked.

"Yes, but it was ahead of time, farther away than it should be, and from the wrong direction, to boot!" Krishnamurthy replied, puzzled.

"It's the fog, sir. You know how it distorts things."

"Humph!"

The commander of the Flying Squad couldn't stop thinking about Milligan. The man was a personal friend and had a wife and child. Witnessing his life terminated so abruptly and so senselessly had been shocking.

He sighed and forced the flier's death to the back of his mind. Duty first!

"Something must have happened," he muttered. "So do we proceed into the Strand now or do we wait until the planned-for moment?"

"Maybe this *is* the planned-for moment, sir," Slaughter suggested. "It's just come earlier than originally intended."

Krishnamurthy clicked his tongue and considered a moment. He addressed his men: "We're going to wait. Ready yourselves. I want absolute silence. Keep your ears to the ground. Be prepared to move at a moment's notice!"

"Stop blowing that bloody whistle!"

Constable Carlyle stopped.

"You blithering idiot!" Detective Inspector Honesty growled. He stamped over to his subordinate. "You just ruined the whole—" He was brought up short by the sight of a sword blade projecting from the constable's chest. It slid back into the man's uniform and disappeared.

Blood spurted.

The whistle fell from Carlyle's mouth and tinked onto the road. The policeman followed it down.

From behind the body, a man shuffled out of the mist. He was a Rake, plainly, but he was also at least three days dead. His lower limbs were saturated with fluids and bulged horribly against his clothing. The swollen hands holding the sword, and the cane from which it had been unsheathed, possessed the sickening appearance of old uncooked sausages. His skin was the colour of earthworms, his sagging bottom lip dangled against his chin, and his eyes were turned up and sunken into their sockets.

"Awfully thorry," he lisped. "That mutht be a terrible inconvenienth!"

There and then, Thomas Manfred Honesty decided he wanted to spend a great deal more of his time tending to his garden.

"More pink dahlias," he muttered to himself, thinking about the state of his little plot's bottom border.

He drew his revolver.

"Yellow marigolds, perhaps."

He aimed at the dead man's head.

"Blue geraniums."

He squeezed the trigger. The gun jammed. He sighed, pocketed it, and hefted his truncheon.

"Perhaps marigolds."

He stepped forward, knocked the sword blade aside, and bludgeoned the corpse's head once, twice, thrice, four times, until it flew apart in a spray of white bone, black clotted blood, and grey brain tissue. The cadaver crumpled and lay twitching.

"Good mulch!" Honesty muttered. "That's the secret."

"Sir!" cried a voice behind him. He turned and saw Piper and Patterson backing away as more bodies loomed out of the miasma.

"Everyone advance!" he shouted to his team behind the cordon. "Guns don't work. Use your truncheons! On their heads. As hard as you can. Crush their skulls!"

Detective Inspector Honesty and Detective Inspector Trounce cautiously led their men toward the centre of the Strand, one team proceeding from the north, the other from the east.

As they penetrated the thickening fog, the walking dead, with sword-sticks drawn, came staggering out of it to meet them. They were well dressed, debonair, and faultlessly polite.

"I'm mortified," one of them confessed as he jammed his fingers into a constable's eye sockets. "This really is despicable behaviour and I offer my sincerest apologies."

"I say!" another exclaimed, plunging his blade into a man's abdomen. "What a terrible to-do!"

"It's all rather unseemly," noted a third, urbanely, after spitting a chunk of flesh from his mouth. He looked at the throatless uniformed man he held slumped in his arms. "I do hope you won't consider me boorish."

The constables swiped their truncheons, crunched skulls, and splattered lifeless brains, but they were badly outnumbered and, furthermore, were distracted by swooping wraiths.

The seeming ghosts wafted in and out of sight, sometimes almost solid, other times a mere suggestion, and every time one appeared, policemen nearby slumped and clutched their heads. More than a few suddenly turned, with the word "Tichborne" blurting out of their lips, and attacked their colleagues.

Police truncheons smacked down onto police heads. The Rakes weren't the only ones apologising.

The battle intensified.

"Don't hold back, lads!" Trounce shouted. "Have at 'em!"

He stepped aside as a svelte and fashionable but sagging and bluish corpse minced out of the pall and said: "What ho! Would you mind awfully if I took your life, old thing? I seem to have mislaid my own. Jolly careless of me, what!"

"Oh, bugger off, you ridiculous ass," the detective snarled. He dodged the Rake's blade and swung his truncheon into the side of the man's head.

The dandy staggered and protested: "Rotten show, old man!"

The detective hit him again, sending him to his knees.

"Really! This isn't at all cricket!"

"Shut the hell up," Trounce hissed, and bashed his attacker's skull in. The Rake folded onto the cobbles and twitched weakly.

Detective Inspector Honesty emerged from the fog and nodded a greeting. Trounce returned it and warned: "Watch behind you!"

Honesty twisted and ducked under a blade. The Rake holding it was a badly moldering cadaver, perhaps one of the first to die. It stank, and when the Scotland Yard man punched it hard on the chin, its head simply fell off and split on the cobbles like an overripe melon. The body toppled after it.

Honesty turned away, his nose wrinkled in disgust.

"Where's Swinburne?" Trounce asked.

"I don't know."

"Was the signal given early?"

"Yes. One of my men panicked."

"Blast!"

"My fault."

"I doubt it. Don't blame yourself. Can we hold them off until he arrives?"

"No choice. Burton's depending on it."

Trounce grunted his agreement, stepped away from his fellow officer, gripped the handle of his truncheon with both hands, and swiped it into the ear of an attacking Rake. The corpse stumbled and fell. The detective stepped onto its chest, heaved himself over, and swung his weapon upward into the chin of another dead man. The head snapped back, came forward, and was met by a crushing blow to the forehead. The Rake grabbed at the detective's arm but missed, and the truncheon came arcing back and impacted against the carcass again. Bone shattered.

"Lie—" Trounce grunted, putting his full strength into a fourth blow "—down!"

The Rake tottered, swayed, and fell.

There was a loud smack and fragments of flesh, bone, and hair showered over the Scotland Yard man. He looked back in time to see a headless body fall. Constable Lampwick stood beyond it, bloodied truncheon in his hand.

"Sorry, sir," he said. "It was about to jump on you."

"Much obliged. I'll send you the laundry bill in the morning."

The constable smiled, grimaced, clutched his head, raised his weapon, and yelled: "Not guilty! Tichborne has been cheated, you bastard!"

He swung his club at Trounce's head. The detective yelled, dodged backward, fell over the corpse he'd just downed, rolled, jumped to his feet, and threw his truncheon. It hit Lampwick square between the eyes and the man collapsed, unconscious.

"I'm sorry, son."

Honesty, meanwhile, had scooped up a second weapon, and, with a truncheon in each hand, was ducking under clutching hands, swiping at kneecaps, and crippling his opponents. Five of his men, staying close to him, were then finishing the job by flattening heads.

It became a routine, almost rhythmic: dodge—duck—*Smack! Smack!*—pulverise. Dodge—duck—*Smack! Smack!*—pulverise.

"Winter jasmine," Honesty declared. "Very cheerful."

Dodge—duck—*Smack! Smack!*—pulverise.

"And maybe wisteria. A good climber for the back fence."

Charles Altemont Doyle's astral body drifted through the fog and mingled with Commander Krishnamurthy's men. Some took a swing at him, which didn't affect him at all, while others seemed to hear the voice that reverberated through what little essence he possessed. "Rebel!" it urged them. "Turn against your oppressors!" They put their hands to their heads, winced, and assaulted their fellows. Fights broke out.

The other part of Doyle was at the junction of the Strand, Aldwych, and Lancaster Place, at the end of Waterloo Bridge. Despite having a dent in his cheek where a truncheon had caught him, he still moved and he still hungered. He could not resist his appetite; others had life, and he wanted it!

A policeman charged at him and slashed at his forehead. Doyle shifted and the weapon thudded down onto his shoulder. He felt nothing, though he heard his collarbone crack. He clutched his attacker's wrist and slammed his other hand into the man's elbow, which snapped with a nasty crunch. The policeman let loose a scream. Doyle released the arm and wrapped his fingers around the man's neck. He started to squeeze. The scream gurgled into silence.

"Give me your life!" Doyle moaned. "Please!"

At the edge of Trafalgar Square, Commander Krishnamurthy listened to the growing sounds of battle and made a decision. He ordered his men to advance.

From the north and south sides of the Strand, smaller police teams also responded to the intensifying conflict and moved into the fog.

Tock!

Krishnamurthy's truncheon bounced from the back of a constable's skull. It was the fifth of his men he'd had to personally render unconscious.

There were wraiths everywhere, and the Flying Squad man could feel them digging into his mind, trying to wheedle their way inside to take control. His headache was almost overpowering.

"Do your duty, old son!" he advised himself. "Don't give in to these bloody spooks."

Despite the steady loss of men, he still had a reasonably sized force at his command, and he was leading them at a steady pace toward the end of Lancaster Place.

Now Rakes, as well as wraiths, began to appear out of the miasma, and combat became rather more deadly. Five men went down before the Flying Squad commander realized that not a single pistol was functioning. The only way to beat the walking corpses was to obliterate their heads. He yelled the order, and a few moments later gore was spraying everywhere.

Krishnamurthy forgot his headache as he started to exact vengeance for Milligan's death.

Amid the carnage, as his team penetrated deeper into the battle zone, he caught sight of Trounce, who was laying about himself like a wild man, and Honesty, who was industriously crippling the shambling monstrosities.

Krishnamurthy realised that the three main groups of policemen had made it to the rendezvous point as planned. However, unlike Honesty and Trounce, he didn't know that the signal whistle had been sounded by mistake or that the advance had been made some considerable time ahead of schedule. Now, as the police teams merged, it dawned on him that something had gone badly wrong.

Swinburne was supposed to be here. The opposition should be on its back foot by now. The police were meant to be in control of the situation.

They weren't.

"Hold fast," he breathed. "Just hope the poet shows up." He lashed out at a Rake and muttered: "A poet, by crikey! A blessed poet!"

Detective Inspector Honesty strode past, brandishing his weapons.

Krishnamurthy clearly heard his superior bark: "Petunias."

"Did you say Tichborne, sir?" he asked.

"No, Commander. Are you all right?"

"Yes, sir."

"Give them hell."

Krishnamurthy nodded and winced. His head was filled with pain.

"Excuse me," said a refined voice. He turned. A Rake stood beside him. "How does it work, old bean?"

The commander stepped back. "What?"

The Rake, not long deceased by the look of him, said: "The thing of it is, you have life. Unfortunately, I don't. Regrettably, that means I have to take yours. What I can't bally well work out is where to look for it after I've run you through." He showed Krishnamurthy his rapier. "Can you advise?"

The Flying Squad man eyed the sword point, which was poised about three inches from his face.

"Um—"

The Rake's head flew apart, the rapier dropped, and the body folded.

"This isn't a bloody debating society, Commander!" Trounce growled, standing over the prone corpse. He wheeled and stalked off into the mist, shouting orders and encouragement to his men.

Krishnamurthy watched him go. "Snooty bastard," he muttered.

Dodge—duck—*Smack! Smack!*—nothing.

Honesty straightened and looked around. His five-strong team of head-pulverisers had been set upon by a large group of Rakes. The constables were fighting for their lives.

"Not very sporting!" exclaimed the corpse at his feet. "Hitting me in the knees like that. How am I supposed to toddle about?"

Honesty ignored the question and took a step toward his men. The fallen Rake grabbed his ankle and unbalanced him. He hit the ground face-first.

"I demand an apology!" said the Rake.

The detective sat up, twisted around, and thumped a truncheon onto the cadaver's head.

"Ouch! Good grief, man! What sort of an apology is that?"

The weapon descended again, harder.

"You should go," said the Rake, in a slurred voice. "I'll just lie here for a bit."

His head caved in under the third blow and he lay still.

"Purple flowering laburnum," said Honesty. "Very hardy. Grows anywhere." He got to his feet.

An arm wrapped around his neck and yanked him backward. One of his truncheons was wrenched from his hand and thrown into the fog. He felt teeth sink into his left shoulder and tried to yell in pain but his throat was too constricted. He struggled, his vision blurring. Bells began to chime insistently in his ears.

He pitched sideways and hit the ground. His assailant's grip broke and Honesty rolled free, lay on his back, and gulped at the dirty air.

A foot slammed down onto his hand. He cried out as his fingers broke around the grip of his remaining truncheon. A body thumped onto his chest, its knees on his shoulders. Hands seized his neck and tightened around it like a band of metal.

The ringing in his ears increased, yet, somewhere behind the cacophony, he heard an approaching rhythmic thunder, too.

The ground started to tremble beneath his back.

Through a red haze of pain, Honesty looked up and saw that his assailant was the bearded man with the dent in his cheek.

Detective Inspector Trounce was covered from head to foot in gore. His truncheon dripped brain tissue. His mouth had frozen into a ferocious snarl and his eyes were blazing. He stood on a pile of motionless Rakes and waited for the next one to come. It was not a long wait. A man lurched into view and ran toward him. He was dressed in evening attire and there was a monocle jammed into his right eye socket. He'd obviously already been in battle, for his jaw was broken and hung loosely with the tongue flapping over it. It didn't matter to him; he was already dead.

The Rake scrambled over his fallen fellows. Trounce sprang to meet him and swept his weapon down, double-handed, onto the bare head. The skull broke with a horrible noise. Trounce hit it again and again and again.

The Rake went limp and still.

There was a moment of respite.

The Scotland Yard man wiped his sleeve over his eyes and peered around. Through the dense murk, he could see shadowy figures locked in combat. A great many constables lay dead or wounded in the road. Rakes milled about.

"How many heads have I smashed in tonight?" he rasped. "And still the bloody stiffs keep coming!"

He turned his head and saw Detective Inspector Honesty sprawled in the road, his face turning blue as a Rake, kneeling on his chest, throttled the life out of him.

Trounce took a step, lost his footing, slipped, and slid across corpses to the cobbles. He scrambled to his feet and made to run to his friend, but he'd taken no more than a single stride before two wraiths suddenly wafted into view and grabbed him by the arms.

"No!" he croaked, as, struggling furiously, he was dragged into the fog, borne away from his dying friend.

The wraiths came to a halt as Krishnamurthy emerged from the haze. The ghostly figure of a top-hatted man loomed behind the commander.

"Watch out!" Trounce cried. "And save Honesty! He's back there being strangled to death!"

"I'm sorry!" the Flying Squad man gasped. "I—I can't—can't—" Lifting his truncheon high, he approached his superior. "Tichborne is—is innocent!"

"Krishnamurthy!" Trounce yelled. "Pull yourself together, man!"

"The op-oppressors must—must die!"

He swung his weapon back, ready to sweep it down onto Trounce's head.

Thunder sounded: *Ba-da-da-doom! Ba-da-da-doom! Ba-da-da-doom!*

The ground vibrated.

A police whistle shrieked repeatedly.

A powerful gust of wind suddenly swept over Trounce, and the two wraiths lost hold of him. They were ripped apart and blown away. Behind Krishnamurthy, the top-hatted apparition disintegrated.

The commander looked over Trounce's shoulder, his eyes wide with astonishment, his mouth gaping.

The detective turned.

"Bloody hell!" he gasped. "I'm seeing things!"

It came pounding across Waterloo Bridge, and when it entered the Strand, the cobbles cracked and powdered beneath its hammering hooves.

Ba-da-da-doom! Ba-da-da-doom! Ba-da-da-doom!

It was a colossal horse, a mega-dray, and on its back, looking as tiny as a child's doll, sat Algernon Swinburne, a Pre-Raphaelite knight, his fiery red hair streaming behind his head, a tremendously long, thin lance gripped in his right hand.

He was blowing enthusiastic blasts on a police whistle, and, perched on his shoulder, a little blue and yellow parakeet was gaily screeching insults at the top of its voice.

As the enormous steed came charging out of the fog, the base of a pantechnicon, to which it was harnessed, followed. The wagon presented the incredulous spectators with an even more fantastic vision, for mounted vertically upon it was a huge spinning wheel. It was similar to a waterwheel in construction, though built from lightweight materials, and it was revolving at a tremendous speed on well-oiled bearings, driven by the twenty greyhounds that raced flat out on its inner surface. Miss Isabella Mayson stood beside the contraption and encouraged the runners with claps and whoops and morsels of food.

From the wheel, a series of simple but extremely well-designed gears and crankshafts drove a mammoth pair of bellows up and down, and snaking away from the nozzle, a tube ran up to the top of a tower at the rear of the wagon and into the back of a cannon-shaped barrel. This was mounted on a swivel and was being aimed at wraiths by Constable Bhatti.

The whole contrivance was a masterpiece of engineering, for it depended upon neither springs nor complex machinery, and was so simple in design that Isambard Kingdom Brunel had been able to build it in a matter of hours.

As the mega-dray pulled the wagon onto the wide thoroughfare, Bhatti directed the jets of air hither and thither, and, though his range was extremely limited, the wraiths caught by the strong blasts were ripped out of existence.

A great cheer went up from constables as they scattered out of the horse's path.

Detective Inspector Trounce and Commander Krishnamurthy looked on in amazement as Algernon Swinburne lowered his lance and aimed its tip at the back of a Rake's head.

Charles Altamont Doyle pressed his dead fingers into Detective Inspector Honesty's neck.

"Squeeze!" he said. "Squeeze the life out of you and into me!"

A fairy pranced at the periphery of his consciousness.

"Recurrence comes!" it sang.

"No! Life comes!" Doyle whispered. "Start again. Get it right. Mend my mistakes."

He felt something touch the back of his neck. From the perspective of his astral body, which drifted through the fog nearby, he could see that it was a long lance held by a small man on a big horse.

His head burst into flames.

"Now!" said the fairy.

The fire ate into his face and scalp, clawed hungrily into the bone and tissue beneath.

He rolled off the police officer and collapsed onto the ground, thrashing wildly as the flames gouged deeper and deeper into his dead flesh.

The lance touched him again, on the chest, and his entire body ignited.

He felt himself being consumed, found that he could struggle no more, lay still, and allowed the conflagration to suck him into oblivion.

Nearby, swirling through the fog, he watched and felt himself burn.

"No!" he thought. "What about all the things I still have to do?"

A powerful gust of air tore into him and ripped him apart.

Charles Altemont Doyle dispersed into the atmosphere and ceased to exist.

Trounce and Krishnamurthy saw the Rake erupt into flames and roll off Honesty. Their friend crawled weakly away from the blazing corpse.

They hurried forward and dragged him to safety.

Trounce looked up and noticed that four cylinders were slung over the mega-dray's haunches. From them, tubes ran up into the hilt of the lance.

"Inflammable gas," he suggested.

"I would venture so," Krishnamurthy replied. "Some sort of flame-throwing weapon. Detective Inspector, I don't know how to apologise. They got into my head. I couldn't control myself."

"Accepted, lad. Say no more about it. Detective Inspector Honesty is injured—let's get him onto the back of that wagon."

They helped their colleague to his feet and guided him toward the pantechnicon.

"Lily of the valley," Honesty wheezed. "The flower of the poets."

A Rake approached them, waving his rapier. His eyes had retreated far into their sockets and his skin was horribly loose, as if the flesh were sloughing off the bones beneath.

He attempted to address them, but his tongue and lips were too slack and only a horrible moan emerged.

"I'll get this," Trounce said.

"Allow me," came Swinburne's voice from above.

The lance touched the decaying, sword-wielding corpse, which combusted, fell to its knees, and toppled onto its face, burning fiercely.

"What ho, fellows!" Burton's assistant shouted enthusiastically.

"Hallo, Swinburne!" said Trounce. "Honesty is injured!"

"Oafish knuckle-dragger!" Pox squawked.

"Hoist the old fellow onto the wagon. Miss Mayson will keep him comfortable until we can get him to safety."

Trounce and Krishnamurthy lifted their comrade and carried him to the pantechnicon.

"His throat," said Trounce to Isabella Mayson, as they laid him on the flatbed.

"I think his fingers are broken, too," Krishnamurthy noted.

The young woman nodded. "Don't worry, I'll make sure he's comfortable."

Up on the horse, Swinburne whispered something to Pox and watched as the brightly plumaged bird launched itself from his shoulder and disappeared into the fog. He looked down at his friends and called: "In the absence of litter-crabs, what say you we clean up this street ourselves, hey, chaps?"

The two police officers brandished their truncheons.

"Ready when you are," Trounce grunted.

CHAPTER 14

THE EYE

If coming events are said to cast their shadows before, past events cannot fail to leave their impress behind them.
—HELENA BLAVATSKY

High above the fog, glinting silver in the moonlight, an ornithopter flapped, circling the Strand at a distance of two miles. A long, irregular ribbon of white steam curved away behind it, marking its course through the sky.

It was controlled by the clockwork man of Trafalgar Square, and, in the saddle at his back, sat Sir Richard Francis Burton.

The flying machine soared northward over the Thames, banked to the left as the Cauldron slipped past beneath it, and headed east until it was over King's Cross.

A parakeet suddenly fluttered out of the cloud below and caught up with the machine. It landed on Burton's shoulder.

"Hello, Pox."

"Lice-infested chump!" the bird whistled. Then: "Message from Algernon Fuddlewit Swinburne. The game has commenced. Message ends."

Burton addressed his companion: "It's time. Take us down."

His valet yanked at a lever, sending the ornithopter skewing through the air as it veered sharply to the south. He switched off the engine and the trail of steam ended abruptly. The machine's wings straightened, and it began to glide down toward the blanket of cloud.

"Here we go," Burton muttered. He placed a hand on the brass man's shoulder. "Now we shake things up. This time, the police are the decoy and you are the main event!"

They sank through the chilly night air.

"Whatever might happen to me," Burton said, "you must complete this mission. However, I have to tell you, I'm acting more on intuition than intellect. Many would think it madness to place so much faith in a dream and I might be completely wrong in my reading of the situation. Do you at least understand my reasoning?"

The brass man nodded his canister-shaped head.

Cloud enveloped them.

Burton sent Pox back to Swinburne.

He checked his harness. He was tightly strapped in.

"I hope your calculations are accurate," he said.

Another lever was pulled. All along the back edges of the wings, wide but thin metal feathers emerged. The machine's nose rose and its silent, powerless descent slowed dramatically.

The king's agent was shaken by a thrill of fear. He could see nothing but thick vapour. For all he knew, they were seconds away from smashing into the ground.

He reached down and released four grappling hooks from the fuselage. They were attached to it by means of long, thin chains. He held two hooks in each hand and waited.

In front of him, a mechanical arm rose. At its end, three fingers and a thumb were extended.

The thumb curled in.

Four.

A finger folded.

Three.

Another.

Two.

The last.

One.

The roof of a large edifice rose up out of the miasma. With bone-jarring suddenness, the ornithopter thumped onto it and skidded across its surface, metal squealing, sparks showering outward.

Feeling as if he was being shaken half to death, Burton threw a grapple; then the second; then the third.

The right wing collided with a chimney stack, sending the machine slewing sideways as bricks exploded and bounced around it.

He flung the last grapple overboard, hung on tight, and called upon Allah.

The vehicle grated across the roof, hit the parapet, went straight through it, and plummeted over the edge.

There was a moment of weightless terror, a shriek of stressed metal, and a tremendous jolt that caused Burton's face to slap into the back of his valet's head.

He blacked out.

Disorientation.

Eyes coming back into focus.

The harness was digging into his chest. He sucked in a shuddering breath, shook his head to clear it, and looked to his left and right. The ornithopter was hanging against the side of the building, between the big, flat, white letters "A" and "R" of the sign, *VENETIA ROYAL HOTEL*. The machine's wings were buckled, and the left one had broken through a window.

Screams and shouts echoed up through the fog. There was obviously a battle occurring in the Strand below.

"Good show!" the king's agent muttered.

He braced his feet against moldings in the fuselage, gripped the lip of the saddle, checked that his cane was still securely thrust through a loop in the waistband of his trousers, and unbuckled his harness.

"Are you all right?" he asked the man of brass.

He received a nodded response.

"I'm going up. Follow."

Transferring his grasp to one of the taut chains from which the flying machine hung, he swung free and pulled himself up hand-over-hand until he reached the roof. With a sense of relief, he hauled himself onto its flat surface.

Moments later, the clockwork man joined him.

Burton saw that three of the four grapples had caught fast amid brickwork. The fourth had crashed through a skylight and jammed against its frame.

"That's our means of entry," he said, pacing over and looking down through the broken glass into an unlit room. "It's some sort of presentation hall. Slightly too long a drop for me, but you'll make it. Get down there and drag over a table for me to land on."

This was done, and from the large room, Burton and his clockwork companion passed through a door into a hallway.

The Venetia Royal Hotel was dark and silent, and the top floor, which consisted entirely of offices, meeting rooms, and storerooms, was entirely abandoned.

They came to a wide staircase and descended to the next floor. Burton looked up at the ceiling. There was something clinging to it. It reminded him of the thick jungle vines he'd seen in Africa, except that it was pulsing and writhing and, somehow, no matter how hard he peered at it, it evaded proper focus, as if it wasn't entirely a substance of this world.

It was ectoplasm. It exuded through the top of the double doors leading to the corridors and rooms, snaked across the ceiling, and disappeared into the stairwell.

"Is it coming up the stairs or going down, I wonder?" he murmured.

He stepped over to the doors and pushed them open. Gas lamps, in brackets on the walls, illuminated the hallway beyond.

There were eight residential rooms on each side of this particular passage. Their doors were open. Ectoplasm twisted out of each one and joined the thick limb of stuff on the ceiling.

Burton clenched his jaw nervously, crept up to the first chamber, and peered in. Its furniture had been pushed aside but for a large table. Seven chairs stood around it. Only one was occupied. The remains of a man sat in it. He was mummified, his skin shrunken and desiccated, his sharp cheekbones poking through. His head was thrown back and ectoplasm was issuing from his mouth and rising up to the ceiling.

"Bismillah!" Burton whispered, entering. "There was a séance, and it doesn't look like this fellow survived it!"

He bent and looked at the man's face, then jerked back with a cry of shock, bumping into his companion, as the mummy's eyes flicked open and rolled sightlessly.

"Alive, by God! How long has the poor devil been here?"

He turned to his valet. "I have a horrible feeling it's going to be the same story in the other rooms."

It was. On the seventh floor of the Venetia, in every room, there was a table at which a séance had been performed, and at every table there sat one shrunken, dried-out man, with head back and ectoplasm streaming out of him up to the ceiling and out into the corridor.

When they descended to the sixth floor, they found the same, though the ectoplasm was more abundant.

On the fifth, it was even thicker and glowed slightly with a greenish-hued light. It had crawled down the walls, forming strange organic shapes reminiscent of ribs and veins and quivering organs.

The fourth floor was worse: walls, ceilings, fixtures, and fittings were so completely buried beneath the pulsating substance that it seemed to Burton as if he and his valet were making their way through the arteries of a living organism.

Cautiously, the king's agent led the way to the stairwell. The route down to the third floor resembled the gullet of a mythical beast.

"Stepping into the dragon's maw," Burton muttered.

He took the step.

Something touched his mind.

"*You should be dead!*" a voice hissed inside his skull.

He felt the devastating force of Madam Blavatsky's presence.

"My apologies," he said, aloud. "Alive and kicking. I thought I'd find you here."

"*And pray tell me,* malchik moi, *what led you to me?*"

"I was told, some months ago, that this hotel had been fully booked by a private party. It's a big place, so the party must have been very substantial indeed; and since the Venetia is slap bang in the middle of the Strand, and the Strand is at the centre of the disturbances—well, you can see why I concluded that the Rakes were here with their elusive new leader."

"*Not all the Rakes, but a great many, yes. Come, stand in my presence. Bring your preposterous toy with you.*"

Burton moved down the stairs. The steps were almost entirely concealed by the thick mediumistic substance, which felt spongy and unstable beneath his boots. He gingerly placed one foot after the other, struggling to maintain his balance. The clockwork man followed.

Blavatsky poked and prodded at his mind.

"*My my! You are so much stronger,* lyubimiy moi!"

"Beware of the brains you invade, bitch. Do you not think I learned just as much about you as you did of me the last time?"

"*Then you know that I lack your vulnerability.*"

"You have your own flaws."

"*Is that so? Then it's to be a duel, is it, Gaspadin Burton?*"

"If you wish."

"*If I wish? I relish the prospect!* Idi ko mne, moi miliy! *You will find me in the library on this floor.*"

At the bottom of the stairs, Burton turned to the left, the direction from which Blavatsky's power was emanating, and passed through open double doors into a hallway. The ectoplasm had made the passage almost tubular, and, as he and his mechanical attendant progressed along it, it constricted to such a degree that they had to proceed on their hands and knees.

The temperature plummeted. A weird silence pressed against his ears, as if he'd suddenly become deaf, and an odd sense of timelessness muddled his senses.

The tunnel tapered. It felt fleshy and damp and it glowed a sickly green. Burton squirmed forward on his stomach, cursing under his breath.

"Do you mean to crush me, woman?"

"*No,* malchik moi. *Let me help you.*"

The ectoplasm started to exude a clear slimy substance.

Burton felt his companion tangling against his legs as the tunnel behind them suddenly contracted. They were both pushed forward, sliding along the clammy pipe, picking up speed, helplessly out of control. Ahead, a sphincter-like opening dilated. Burton shot through it and splatted onto the floor in a high-ceilinged room. The brass man thudded onto his back.

They lay sprawled in a heap, dripping slime.

"Damnation," Burton grumbled. "That wasn't very dignified."

"Dabro pazhalavat, *Gaspadin Burton. What is this device you have brought with you?*"

"He's my valet," the king's agent responded, clambering to his feet and surveying the chamber.

A liquid chuckle gurgled in his head. "*It is good that you have him. The staff here has been very unreliable of late. I cannot remember when I last saw a concierge or even a maid!*"

The library was completely buried beneath huge ribs of glowing ecto-plasm. They curved down from a big tangle of material in the centre of the ceiling, over the walls, across the floor, and melded together in its middle, where they rose up to form a slender three-foot-high plinth. At its top, deli-cate fingers of the material held a plum-sized black diamond—the Tichborne stone. The South American Eye of Nāga.

It hummed faintly.

"*You realise, of course, that I have allowed your companion to approach merely to satisfy my curiosity.*"

"I was counting on it."

"*Mechanisms of that sort do not normally function in my presence.*"

"You are far too confident in your abilities."

"*I am?*"

The king's agent turned to his valet and snapped: "Get the diamond!"

The brass man bounded across to the plinth, reached for the stone, and stopped dead.

A peal of laughter sounded from the ceiling.

Burton looked up.

"Fool!" Madam Blavatsky crowed, her voice deep and resonant. "You think you can defy me with clockwork?"

She was enmeshed in a snarled knot of ectoplasmic tubes, naked; a middle-aged thick-bodied woman, suspended upside down above the plinth, with her arms stretched out horizontally. Her skull had cracked and broken open like an eggshell pushed apart from the inside, and bits of it hung loose. Her swollen brain bulged horribly out of the fissures. Thin ribbons of grey wrinkled tissue dangled down, entwining with her long brown hair and brushing against the diamond below.

Her fathomless black eyes seemed to suck at Burton's very soul, so dreadfully intense were they; they stabbed him like pins transfixing a captured moth.

"You are defeated, Gaspadin Burton. Soon the king will fall, the poor will flood out of your East End, and London will belong to the working classes. The disorder will spread from the capital like a disease. It will infect the entire country! Think of all those downtrodden, exploited, destitute workers in Britain's great manufacturing cities—Manchester, Sheffield, Birmingham, Leeds—where civilised man is lured from his peaceful labours in the countryside and turned back almost into an animal! What barbarous indifference they have suffered! How passionate shall be their revolt!"

Burton snorted in disdain. "Don't try to hide your agenda behind false philanthropy, madam! You care naught for Britain's workers. You regard them as a means to a nefarious end, and nothing more. You've made your intentions quite clear!"

"I do it to save Mother Russia."

The king's agent took three long strides and reached for the Eye of Nāga.

"You do it because you're a demented meddler and you have no control over yourself!" he barked.

"Keep back!"

Blue lightning crackled from Blavatsky's hands, hit Burton in the chest, and knocked him off his feet. He thumped down onto his back. For a second, it felt as if the flesh was boiling off his bones, but the torment passed in an instant, and, with an involuntary groan, he pushed himself up and faced his opponent again.

Her voice echoed in his skull: *"Pah! There is no satisfaction in wounding your body, but your mind,* malchik moi—*ah!—what great value you place upon it, and how fragile it is!"*

She drove a pitiless spike of shame into that part of his memory where regrets and disappointments dwelt, expecting to cripple him as she had in their previous encounter.

Burton reeled and groaned, but then steadied himself and turned his awareness inward. His Dervish meditation had fortified and strengthened his mind to such a degree that her assault did no damage, but rather gave him a route through which to respond. He thrust mortification along the mediumistic channel that linked them, stabbing it deeply into her preening arrogance.

She recoiled and cried out, shocked at the power of his riposte.

"*Oh* bozhe*! You bite back!"*

"Stay out of my head!"

"I will do as I please, *rebenok*. And conceit?" She laughed. "You think that is my weakness? *Nyet! Eto vlast!* It is strength!"

The king's agent shook his head. "No, madam. The love of one's own excellence serves only to obscure one's own mistakes."

"I have made no mistakes!"

Burton looked into the woman's eyes and treated her to one of his characteristically savage smiles.

"Haven't you?"

She attacked again, digging fear into his insecurities, but his qualms had been modified by the conception that weaknesses are, in fact, the seeds of future strength. She was easily repelled, and his response—doubt driven into her confidence—was devastatingly effective.

She moaned and twisted in her web of ectoplasm.

"This self-assurance of yours was not there before!" she gasped, and there was a hint of anxiety in her tone.

He felt her poking around his mind, preparing for another thrust. He pounced, locked her into position, and pierced her with a sharp edge of fear.

She screamed.

"That was *breaking time* followed by a *prise de fer*," he said. "I learned it from an expert."

Blavatsky hung silently and he saw that she was trembling.

"Good," he said. "Perhaps now we can talk?"

"Speak," she whispered.

"Your plan, madam, is defective for two reasons. The first is that you regard Russia's future as predestined; something fixed in time; a fate it is sure to suffer unless you interfere."

"I watched it happen."

"You watched a possibility, but there are many, many possible futures."

"You are wrong! I have seen what I have seen."

"Does your certainty not seem a little peculiar to you? Destiny is far more malleable than you think!"

"You cannot know this!"

"But I do—and I shall show you how!"

He guided the writhing, invasive tendrils of her consciousness to a seemingly insignificant path in his own mind and pushed them along it into his recollections of Spring Heeled Jack.

Blavatsky absorbed the memories, and he felt her astonishment.

"*Oh* bozhe*! A man who jumped through time! How can this be possible?*"

"The point is this, madam: the time we are living in is not the time that was meant to be. Maybe, before Edward Oxford came back to change his past, Russia's prospects were far less tragic. We shall never know. His actions altered the course of future history for the entire world, and now you are seeking to do the same. If he can do it, and you can do it, then surely it's entirely possible that someone else will do it, too. In fact, I contend not only that *anyone* can do it, but that we *all do*! Destiny is not fixed. It is the ever-changing consequence of uncountable actions—actions undertaken by every single person on the face of the planet, each with a unique understanding of reality and of how to deal with it. Even the most obscure, uneducated, unimaginative nobody can, and does, make a difference."

"Burton," came a faint hiss from above, "I have to save Mother Russia."

He looked at the suspended woman and shrugged. "Then you have to use your clairvoyance to predict every single action taken by every single person every minute of every day from now until whatever future date you decide that her fate has been fulfilled to your satisfaction. If you don't, then someone, some-where, will do something that will modify the results you seek. It is inevitable. No single person can make future history entirely what he or she wishes."

Blavatsky hung silently. Her black eyes flicked nervously from Burton, to the motionless clockwork man, to the quietly singing diamond, and back to Burton.

"All this for nothing?" she mouthed.

"As I said, your plan is defective for two reasons."

"What is the second?"

Burton sighed and braced himself. "The second fault, Madam Blavatsky, is that it's not even your plan."

"What?"

"No one—not even a lunatic like you—could possibly believe them-selves exclusively capable of shaping future history. Not unless, that is, the history they're trying to manipulate is actually their own past."

Bolts of etheric energy started to crackle around the woman's body. The library filled with the tang of ozone.

"I do not understand," she whispered.

The king's agent paused, severed his mediumistic connection to her, and said: "I mean simply this. You consider yourself the puppeteer. The truth is: you're the puppet."

Blavatsky suddenly arched her back and shrieked. Etheric energy crackled over her entire body. Blood sprang from her eyes, ears, and nose. It oozed out from her brain tissue and dribbled down onto the Eye of Nāga.

She twisted and struggled and her scream rose in pitch then died to a bubbling gasp.

She hung limply, and for a moment, there was complete silence.

Her mouth opened.

A man's voice, deep and gurgling, heavily accented, and saturated with evil, came from it: "Very clever, *tovarishch*. You are correct. Man from future know history and can change history to make *new* future. *Kukolnyi*—you say *puppet, da?*—very useful!"

The king's agent gave a grim smile. "About time," he said. "I was beginning to think you'd never stop hiding behind the woman, Grigori. She didn't even know you were there, did she?"

"*Nyet.*"

"All this while, thinking she was acting under her own volition, she's been doing your bidding. Tell me, how does it feel to have foreseen so clearly the manner of your own death?"

"I see assassination. See death. I think it . . . disappointing."

"How soon? From your perspective, I mean."

"Two years from now."

"Then you are speaking from the year 1914?"

"*Da.* But I must tell you: I am to make different—umm—schedule for us both. My death, I vill delay; yours vill be much more soon, *nyet?*"

"*Nyet*," Burton replied.

Grigori Rasputin chuckled maliciously.

The rivulets of blood that had been trickling from Madam Blavatsky slowed to irregular drips. Burton could see that the woman was close to death.

"So let me venture a guess," he said. "Your clairvoyance revealed to you the circumstances of your future betrayal and demise, and the subsequent fate of your country. You could have saved yourself by simply avoiding the assassins, but still there would be Germany, still Nietzsche, and, in all probability, still more assassins. So you traced the history of the war back to its origins, seeking a way to alter its course, intending to prevent your own murder and the disaster that would befall Russia afterward."

"Entirely correct, *tovarishch.*"

"It just so happened that while you were looking back through time, Madam Blavatsky was peering forward."

"*Da.* We touch."

"And you projected your astral body into her mind."

"*Da.* It vas easy for such as Rasputin. In future, I have Eye of Nāga. I use it to transfer into woman."

"And to your good fortune, it just so happened that she existed at exactly the point in history where the seeds of the war were planted, if you'll forgive the unintentional pun."

"Pun? Vot is that?"

"I refer to Richard Spruce's eugenically altered plant life, the devastation of Ireland, and his and the Eugenicists' subsequent defection to Germany."

"Ah. So."

"And the Nāga diamonds, Grigori—you say you have one?"

"Cambodian and African stones are, in war, used to—*povyshenia?*"

"Enhance."

"—minds. I have African. Germany has others. Of South American diamond, *nyet*, it is not found in my time. I make Blavatsky find it in yours."

"Leading her to the Tichbornes. So, the African Eye will be found, will it? Interesting."

"Found by you."

"What?"

"No matter. I change that. You die today."

"I think not."

Rasputin laughed, a nasty sound. "I congratulate you, *tovarishch*," he said. "You are—umm—impressive. Speech you give Blavatsky—very interesting. No person can make future entirely vot they vish. *Da. Da.* This maybe is true. But I, Grigori Rasputin, am already in future. I speak to you now from future. Votever I change in past, still, future I am in. You die. You do not find African Eye. Yet here I have African Eye. It is—umm—big paradox, *nyet?*"

"An intriguing situation," Burton mused. "Whereas Edward Oxford travelled to his past and accidentally wiped himself out of the future, you are seeking to change the past *from* the future. You know that whatever your interference here, the consequences will never threaten your existence there, for if it did, how can you be interfering?"

The king's agent stepped closer to the black diamond.

"You must feel indestructible," he said.

"No man can stop me."

"Really?"

Burton extended his hand toward the stone and was instantly stricken with paralysis.

"*Nyet*, my enemy. Not even you. Now life of Blavatsky woman is finished, you I vill possess. You are close to prime minister, *da?* This is very good. Through you, I vill assassinate Palmerston."

A glowing, shapeless wraith oozed out of Blavatsky's shattered skull and began to slide down the strands of brain tissue and hair.

Burton managed to move his mouth: "Maybe I can't stop you, Grigori, but I can warn you. Stay away from the Eye!"

The Russian's voice sounded inside his head: "*I think not. The diamond vill be*—moct?"

"A bridge."

"*Da. It allow me to cross into you.*"

The wraith flowed over the diamond and seemed to soak into it. A long feeler of energy coiled out toward the famous explorer. Cold fingers closed around his brain.

Straining, the king's agent managed to turn his head until he was looking at his valet.

"Now would be a good time."

The clockwork man of Trafalgar Square gave up the charade of immobility, nodded its canister-shaped head, reached out with its mechanical arm, and plucked the Eye of Nāga from its ectoplasmic plinth.

"*Vot? The toy moves?*"

Rasputin's reaction was accompanied by a blaze of ectoplasmic energy. It sizzled across the room, and a bolt of it lashed at Burton and writhed over his body. He cried out with pain and dropped to his knees.

The storm lessened but continued to splutter and jump around the library walls.

"*Vhy cannot I stop it? Things such as this, they not vork close to Rasputin unless I allow!*"

Burton pulled himself upright and said: "Yes, that was rather a giveaway, Grigori. When Blavatsky shared with me her vision of your future, it included details of your parlour trick; of how the guns of the British spies failed when they attacked you. I asked myself: why would the woman be afraid of assassins? The answer was that there was no reason for her to be. I therefore concluded that she wasn't responsible for all the stopped clocks, slack springs, and jammed trigger mechanisms."

"*But this machine clockvork, da? How working now?*"

"Willpower. Allow me to introduce to you the philosopher Herbert Spencer. One of the most remarkable intellects I have ever encountered."

"*Man? This is not man!*"

"In body, no, but Herbert Spencer died with the seven fragments of the Cambodian Eye in his possession. His intellect was imprinted upon them. Those fragments are now fitted into a babbage device designed specifically to process the kind of information they hold. In other words, what you took to be a machine is sentient. It possesses willpower enough to resist your attempts to interfere with its functioning, and it can do a great deal more. Are you aware of the legend of Kumari Kandam?"

"Nyet! *No more talk! Put stone down!*"

"The Eye was shattered by a man who possessed a perfectly ordered brain. When that happened, the intelligences previously bound together through means of the diamond were destroyed."

"Tovarishch! *Vot is this nonsense?*"

"The Choir Stones still have that event imprinted upon them like a memory. If a sufficiently powerful mind—say, for instance, that of a philosopher whose thoughts are ordered by a babbage—could focus that memory upon another Eye, well, I suppose you're aware of the phenomenon of resonance?"

"*Nyet! Nyet!*"

"Where these stones are concerned, I believe only equivalence can lead to destruction. Let us see if that's the case. Proceed, please, Herbert."

The clockwork philosopher didn't move, but the glow from the room's ectoplasmic walls, floor, and ceiling suddenly dimmed, seeming to concentrate itself around the diamond held in his metal hand, and the bolts of energy that had been playing across the walls now arced inward and danced over the stone's facets. Simultaneously, the diamond's soft humming increased in volume and deepened in tone until it passed below the range of human hearing. To Burton, it felt as if invisible hands were pushing hard against his ears.

Rasputin's voice hammered furiously against the inside of his cranium: "Nyet! *Do not do this thing! Let me go! Let me go,* tovarishch*! I vill return to my time!*"

"Too late. But look on the bright side, Grigori, you've achieved your aim—you've avoided your assassins. It will not be water that kills you."

Tiny fractures zigzagged across the Eye, and, as each appeared with a faint *tink*, it seemed to Burton that a small entity was expelled, yet as hard as he might look, he couldn't quite bring the things into focus. At the very periphery of his vision, he could see that the library was rapidly filling with them, but when he turned his head, he saw nothing.

"*Vot are these lizards? Get them avay from me! Get them avay! They put their claws into me!* Nyet! Nyet!"

Etheric energy banged and clapped around the gem, increasing in intensity, whipping out and sizzling up the walls and across the ceiling and floor.

"Most people see them as fairies," Burton told the dying Russian. "They're remnants of an ancient race—nothing but preserved memories. Rather too difficult in nature for us humans to comprehend, so we tend to impose a more palatable myth on top of them. But, of course, you don't have any fairy stories in Russia, do you? They aren't a part of your folklore."

Rasputin screamed. "*They are tearing me apart!*"

"Really? I suggest you fight back. If there's one thing I've learned from you, it's that damaging memories can be overcome. After all, Grigori, it's all in the past, isn't it?"

"*Nyet! Nyet!*"

Rasputin let loose an appalling howl of agony. It pierced Burton's head like a spear. The explorer staggered and gritted his teeth. Blood spurted from his nose.

Spencer turned his brass head.

"No!" Burton managed to gasp. "Don't stop!"

A jagged line of bright blue fire lashed out from a splintering facet of the Eye and enveloped him. It yanked him into the air and held him there. He convulsed helplessly. Capillaries haemorrhaged beneath his skin. The etheric lightning jerked and he was thrown up and slammed into the ceiling then dropped to the floor, where he lay in the grip of a seizure as the fizzling energy snapped away from him.

Pushed beyond the threshold of endurance, his mind seemed to disassociate, and awareness of his physical pain left him. It was no relief. His consciousness was rent by a mortal shriek of anguish—the Mad Monk's death throes as the fracturing diamond tore him to pieces.

It was too much for the king's agent. The world overturned, slid away, grew dark, and was gone.

Sir Richard Francis Burton was dead.

He knew it because he could feel nothing.

There was no world, there were no sensations, there was nothing required, there was nothing desired, there was no past, there was no future.

There was only peace.

A metal finger poked him in the ribs.

He opened his eyes expecting to see, as ever, orange light flickering over a canvas roof.

He saw snow.

He sat up.

No, not snow—flakes of dead ectoplasm falling from the library ceiling, vanishing before they touched the floor.

He pushed himself to his feet, pulled a handkerchief from his pocket, and wiped the blood from his face.

With a loud crack, Madam Blavatsky's corpse dropped. It crashed onto the plinth, which disappeared in a cloud of dust.

Burton turned away from the sight of her crushed skull and horribly folded carcass and found that Herbert Spencer was standing at his side. The brass man held out his cupped hands. The king's agent looked into them and counted.

"Seven fragments. Is that all of them?"

Spencer nodded.

"Good. Hold on to them, will you? The bloody things give me a headache. Let's get out of here. And Herbert—"

The brass head regarded him.

"Thank you."

Burton recovered a chair from a crumbling and fast-disappearing mound of ectoplasm and used it to smash his way through the calcifying substance blocking the door and corridor beyond. The mediumistic material was fading from existence with increasing rapidity, and by the time he and his mechanical companion had descended to the Venetia's ground floor, nothing of it remained to be seen.

They stepped out into the fogbound Strand. It was strangely silent.

Burton swayed, struck by a wave of dizziness, and clutched at his companion's arm for support.

"Give me a moment," he muttered.

The next thing he knew, he was looking up at the anxious faces of Algernon Swinburne and Detective Inspector Trounce.

"Did I pass out?"

"Pillock!" screeched Pox from the poet's shoulder.

"Evidently," Trounce said. "Lord Nelson carried you out of the fog. How's our enemy?"

"Dead. The show is over. And he's not Lord Nelson. Give me a hand, would you?"

Looking perplexed, Trounce reached down and hauled Burton to his feet.

"Not Nelson? Is it a different device?"

Pox hopped from Swinburne to the clockwork man's head and whistled: "Beautiful sweetheart!"

"No," Burton said. "It's our mutual friend Mr. Herbert Spencer."

Trounce frowned. "What?"

"There's no time to explain, old man. Suffice it to say that Sir Charles Babbage was a genius."

"No time? I thought you said Blavatsky is dead?"

"She is, and so is Rasputin. I have to go. There's someone I need to see before I collapse onto my bed to sleep for a week."

"Shall I come with you, Richard?" Swinburne asked, with a trace of anxiety in his voice.

"No, Algy. I have to do this alone."

He turned to the brass philosopher. "Hand me a couple of the diamonds, would you?"

Spencer dropped two stones into the explorer's waiting palm.

Burton slipped them into his waistcoat pocket, turned, and staggered off into the fog.

"Hey!" called Trounce after the fading figure. "Who the dickens is Rasputin?"

"Give Herbert a pen and paper," came the receding reply. "He'll write you an explanation!"

Trounce scratched his head and mumbled: "By Jove! If he's just defeated the Blavatsky woman and brought all this nonsense to an end, you'd think he'd look a mite happier about it!"

The fog thickened.

Burton picked his way through corpses and debris, gave a curt greeting to the constables he encountered, left the Strand, made his way along Haymarket, and passed through Piccadilly Square.

It was maybe five or six in the morning—he was waiting for Big Ben to chime—and there was a faint glow overhead as dawn struggled to penetrate the murk. The city was absolutely silent.

He walked along Regent Street, passing broken windows and gutted shops. He couldn't shake the feeling that the world was crumbling around him.

The riot was over. Blavatsky was dead. Rasputin's mind had been shredded and the present was free of his sinister influence.

Yet something was deeply, deeply wrong.

The vapour swirled around him, muffling his footsteps, as he entered Oxford Circus and turned left.

A weighty despondency was settling over him, exactly like that he'd experienced in Aden after returning from Africa's Lake Regions. It was the notion that, despite his every effort, a job had not been completed.

"What is it?" he muttered. "Why do I feel that I've failed?"

He came to Vere Street and stopped outside a narrow building sandwiched between a hardware shop and the Museum of Anatomy. It had a bright yellow door and a bay window, behind which a deep blue curtain hung.

Taped against the inside of the window there was a notice that read:

The astonishing COUNTESS SABINA, seventh daughter, CHEIROMANTIST, PROGNOSTICATOR, tells your past, present, and future, gives full names, tells exact thought or question on your mind without one word spoken; reunites the separated; removes evil influences; truthful predictions and satisfaction guaranteed. Consultations from 11 A.M. until 2 P.M. and from 6 P.M. to 9 P.M. Please enter and wait until called.

Burton looked at his reflection in the glass. His fierce countenance was a patchwork of red and purple bruises.

"None of this is your doing," he said, "but Chance has put you in the thick of it. Now you have to play the game to the finish."

His eyes moved to the notice.

Prognosticator.

He leaned forward and rested his forehead against the cold glass.

The African Eye will be found.

He was suddenly short of breath and started gulping in mouthfuls of air.

Found by you.

"Bismillah," he gasped. "Bismillah. It's all gone to hell."

An early-morning café had opened across the street. Burton took a moment to even out his breathing then walked over to it, entered, and asked for a coffee.

"You're the first bloomin' customer I've had in days," the proprietor grumbled, glancing curiously at the explorer's battered features. "You fancy a round of buttered toast? It's on the house, mate."

"That would be very welcome," Burton answered. "Thank you."

He sat quietly, sipping coffee and eating toast until a light came on and glowed through the fog from the upper window of the building opposite. He gave it forty minutes or so, then left the café, crossed the road, and knocked on the door.

He waited, and, after a few moments, knocked again.

The countess opened the door. She wore a long, shapeless midnight-blue gown.

"Countess Sabina," he said. "My apologies. I know it's early."

"Captain Burton. My goodness, what has happened to you? Were you run over by one of those dreadful omnipede things?"

He managed a wry grin. "Something like that, yes. I require your talents. It's a matter of great importance."

She gazed at him silently for a moment, her eyes unfathomable, then nodded and stepped aside.

He entered and followed her along a short passageway, through a doorway hung with a thick velvet curtain, and into the room beyond. It smelled of sandalwood. Wooden chairs stood against its undecorated walls.

They stepped into a smaller room. It was sparsely furnished, though its shelves and mantelpiece were crowded with esoteric trinkets and baubles. A camphor lamp hung low over a round table in the middle of the chamber. The countess put a match to its wick.

She sat down.

Burton settled opposite.

He moistened his lips and said: "I'm—I'm afraid."

She nodded silently. Her eyes shifted focus. She seemed to be looking right through him. In a barely audible voice, she whispered: "The cycle is complete. The time of change is upon us. War is coming."

"And I have a role to play."

"Yes."

"I feel . . . displaced."

"You are. This is not your intended path."

"Is it anybody's?"

"No. We live in a strange world, Captain, but soon, it will be even stranger for both of you."

"Both of us? Are you referring to my assistant?"

"Both of *you*, Captain Burton."

"Explain."

"I—I can't. I don't know how. I'm sorry. I feel—I feel that you are divided."

"It's odd," Burton replied. "That's something I have often sensed myself, especially while in a malarial fever. I don't know what it means."

"Neither do I, but—but, somehow, I know that everything depends on it!"

Burton leaned back in his chair, his eyebrows shooting up.

"*What?*"

The countess shook her head and shrugged. "I can say no more."

A silence settled over them and they sat gazing questioningly at each other until the prognosticator murmured: "Why did you come to see me, Captain?"

Burton rubbed his gritty eyes. God, he was tired! He rested his scarred hands on the table, looked down at them, and answered: "Countess, the future should be shaped by the past and the present. The past and the present should not be shaped by the future. Yet on two occasions now—or at least two that I'm aware of—men have reached back and interfered with the course of events. Just how much damage have they done? We must answer this question. I want you to look into the future that was meant to be."

"Original history? That is impossible."

"Is it? When you take route A over route B, does route B cease to exist?"

"No—but though I can sense the other path, I cannot see along it. We are too far past the junction. It is beyond my ability."

Burton reached into his pocket. "I have something that will augment your talent."

He placed two black diamonds onto the table.

They hummed quietly.

THE FUTURE IS NOT
WHAT IT USED TO BE

ANNOUNCEMENT

The Technologist Caste hereby declares the immediate cessation of its association with those members of the Eugenicist faction who have chosen to accept sponsorship from the

Prussian Government.

**Technologists condemn the scientists and researchers who have taken this course.
The Eugenicists who remain faithful to Britain renounce their former colleagues and wish to now be known as**

GENETICISTS

We reaffirm the words of our visionary leader,

Isambard Kingdom Brunel:
"The Technologists Remain Loyal to the Great British Empire!"

—Technologist Propaganda

"Mediumistic powers do not exist."

Sir Richard Francis Burton let his statement hang in the air for a moment.

He continued: "In Victorian Britain—by which I mean our time as it would have been had Edward Oxford not interfered—astral bodies, mind reading, etheric energy, and spiritualism are, from a scientific standpoint, proven to be at best highly implausible and, in all probability, utter balderdash."

The king's agent sat at the head of a long table in a grand hall in Buckingham Palace. There were nine others in attendance: the eugenically enhanced prime minister, Lord Palmerston; the vulture-faced secretary for war, Sir George Cornewall Lewis; the evasive-eyed chancellor of the Exchequer, William Gladstone; the grey-bearded foreign secretary, Lord John Russell; the miserable-looking first lord of the Admiralty, Edward Seymour; the deviant red-headed poet, Algernon Charles Swinburne; the aloof chief commissioner of Scotland Yard, Sir Richard Mayne; the clockwork philosopher, Herbert Spencer; and the steam-powered engineer, Isambard Kingdom Brunel.

Without any shadow of a doubt, it was the oddest gathering the royal residence had ever seen.

There was one further presence: King Albert's eyes and ears hung above the table like a bizarre chandelier—an apparatus comprised of hearing trumpets and lenses, which swivelled this way and that to follow the men as they spoke. The monarch was notoriously reclusive. Of those present, only Palmerston had met him face-to-face.

Brunel chimed: "You do not make sense, Sir Richard. Changing the course of history cannot alter the laws of physics. Whatever etheric energy might be, it plainly does exist."

"As you know to your cost," Swinburne offered, eyeing his friend's yellowing bruises.

"It exists here," Burton responded. "But in Victorian times, it does not."

"Your witch saw with such clarity?" Palmerston demanded.

"She's a seer, not a witch, and yes, Prime Minister, with the aid of two of the black diamonds, Countess Sabina's clairvoyance was accentuated to an extraordinary degree."

"And the reason for the discrepancy?"

"The aforementioned gemstones. The Eyes of Nāga."

"How so?"

"As you know, the South American stone was discovered in Chile by Sir Henry Tichborne in 1796. He secreted it beneath the Crawls at Tichborne House. If time had not been altered, the diamond would have remained there until the building was demolished in the year 2068. About a hundred and thirty years later, Edward Oxford cut shards from it and used them in the mechanism of his time-jumping suit."

"By George!" Sir Richard Mayne exclaimed. "How far into the future did your countess look?"

"Into the *alternative*—that is to say *original*—future, she saw clearly to the end of this century. After that, her vision became increasingly murky. There were certain points of interest that she focused on, the black diamonds being one of them, and she was able to follow those developments much farther through time, to the detriment of other matters. I should point out that she did so at great cost to herself and afterward collapsed with mental exhaustion. I suggest some sort of compensation from the government might be appropriate."

"Be damned!" Palmerston exclaimed. "I'm going to employ the bloody sorceress! Pray continue, Captain."

Burton cleared his throat and glanced at the contraption on the ceiling as it rotated to face him. "So Oxford journeyed back to 1840 and from there was thrown farther, to 1837, where he created an immediate paradox, for now the splinters of the South American stone existed twice in the same time. They were in his suit and they were also beneath the Tichborne estate. This caused them to resonate with each other, and because all three Eyes of Nāga are chunks of the same aerolite, the Cambodian fragments started to resonate, too, producing the hum that led to their discovery. I'd wager the African diamond, wherever it is, also began to 'sing.'

"Being underground, Tichborne's treasure couldn't be heard, but the reverberation caused the equivalent string in the family piano—B below middle C—to let loose frequent twangs."

"Astonishing," Cornewall Lewis grunted. "A man appears in London and, in Hampshire, Cambodia, and probably Africa, diamonds serenade his arrival!"

Burton nodded. "Yes, Mr. Secretary, astonishing indeed. But it's only half the story. I've spent the past few days in the British Library researching clairvoyance. Do you know when the first clear, incontrovertible evidence of mediumistic energies emerged?"

"When?"

"In 1837. Over the ensuing six years there were many recorded instances. They all coincided with periods when Spring Heeled Jack was active in our world. Then there were no more authenticated occurrences until last year. We now know that he jumped directly from 1843 to 1861. The diamonds in his suit have been here ever since, and genuine clairvoyant powers have been demonstrated with increasing frequency this past twelve months."

Brunel clanged: "Then your hypothesis is that the diamonds' resonance has awakened in the human brain some power that would otherwise have remained dormant?"

"That is for your scientists to explore," Burton replied. "But in my opinion, etheric energy and all that goes with it is a product of the human organism and, yes, the resonance stimulates it."

Spencer scribbled in a notebook and held it up, displaying a single word: *Evolution?*

Burton shrugged.

"Damnation!" Palmerston shouted. "If all that you say is true, bloody Rasputin would never have had the wherewithal to stick his confounded nose into our business had Oxford not done so first! Are we now so vulnerable to meddlers and madmen from the future?"

"It would seem so."

An uneasy silence fell over the meeting. It ended with two words from Edward Seymour: "And Prussia?"

"Yes," Burton said. "The countess saw."

Another pause.

"Tell us," said Palmerston, quietly.

"The World War was originally set to begin some fifty years from now. Oxford's actions have brought it forward by at least a decade."

"Christ!"

"The countess described the sequence of events. This is what we can expect—"

For the next hour, Sir Richard Francis Burton described future history. He told the king, the politicians, and his companions how the Eugenicist exodus to Prussia would give that kingdom the means to gain dominance over the German Confederation, incorporating it into a greater union of the Germanic people. How Bismarck, to consolidate the southern borders of his new country, would declare war on France and defeat Napoleon III using biological weaponry developed from the plant life currently infesting Ireland.

He outlined the arms race between the Technologists of the British Empire and the Eugenicists of the Germans; the emergence of Friedrich Nietzsche as a visionary politician who would eventually overthrow Bismarck; and Germany's aggressive expansionist policies that would, inevitably, lead to conflict on a massive scale.

When he finished, the room sank into a deep silence and stayed there.

The politicians could not keep the horror from their faces. Even Palmerston's inexpressive façade had somehow become dominated by the shock in his eyes.

A minute ticked by, and then a voice came from the ceiling, amplified through a speaking trumpet in the mechanism above the table.

It said: "Make me a different future."

The men looked at each other.

"I shall put my people to work at once," Brunel clanged. "We can strengthen our navy; build an air force; design new weapons."

"Good idea," said Cornewall Lewis.

"Excellent," said Edward Seymour.

"Absolutely not!" shouted Gladstone, who'd been assiduously avoiding Burton and Swinburne's eyes for the entire meeting. "How in blue blazes are we supposed to finance it?"

"Impractical and impossible," Lord John Russell agreed. "We've only just avoided a revolution by the skin of our teeth. If we raise taxes we won't need Russian lunatics to start another one!"

"Besides which," Palmerston added, "the whole damned world will say I'm warmongering. Starting an arms race now might precipitate the conflict even earlier!"

Herbert wrote something and held it up: *Diplomacy.*

Cornewall Lewis snorted: "With Germans?"

"I have an idea," Swinburne said.

Palmerston jumped to his feet and kicked his chair backward. He clenched his hands together behind his back and paced up and down.

"What about allies, Burton?" he barked. "Did your sorceress suggest whom we might trust?"

"No, she didn't. I think we're on our own. Prime Minister, Algy can be quite insightful. I strongly suggest—"

"No! No! No! This is unacceptable! I will not go down in history as the man who lost the Empire!"

"Assuming you're still prime minister when it happens," Sir Richard Mayne hissed quietly.

"—that you listen to what he has to say," Burton finished.

His words were lost, for Palmerston had flown into one of his infamous rages. He kicked his chair across the floor, slapped a glass from the table, and yelled incoherently. His eyes were wild, yet through it all, his masklike face remained weirdly impassive.

The men waited for his tantrum to pass. It took three minutes before the prime minister seemed to suddenly deflate. He stood panting, glancing from man to man, his normally white features flushed.

"Madam Blavatsky used the diamonds to enhance her mediumistic talent," Swinburne murmured. "And Richard used them to strengthen Countess Sabina's abilities."

Palmerston gazed blankly at the diminutive poet. "What?"

"I'm merely suggesting that, if we ensure we possess all three Eyes of Nāga, then perhaps we can gain the upper hand. We could recruit talented mediums and use the stones to accentuate their powers. We could divine the enemy's strategy. We could interfere with our opponents' minds. We could wage a war of infiltration and enchantment. We could start now, and our enemies wouldn't even know that war was being waged upon them."

Palmerston's mouth dropped open.

Burton said: "I told you he's worth listening to."

The prime minister blinked rapidly, forced a breath out between his teeth, and pulled his snuffbox from his pocket. He went through his usual ritual, which ended, as always, with a prodigious sneeze, and peered at the poet with one straight eye, while the other slid upward disconcertingly.

"Mr. Swinburne," he said. "You are a god-damned bloody genius." He addressed Burton: "The African stone?"

"You might have problems securing it," the explorer warned. "Quite apart from the difficulties Africa itself presents, we know that nothing can fly over the region where the diamond is undoubtedly located. That suggests to me that some force of mind is at work, interfering with machinery in much the same way that Rasputin was able to jam guns."

"So someone is guarding the Eye?"

"Someone or something, yes. And there's another problem."

"What?"

"I think it highly probable that Lieutenant John Speke is preparing a Prussian expedition to the region."

With his top hat set at a jaunty angle and his cane swinging, Sir Richard Francis Burton strode along Gloucester Place.

A Folks' Wagon beetle scuttled past, belching vapour. A little boy, sitting on its rear bench, looked at Burton as the vehicle went past and poked out his tongue. The king's agent glared at him, snarled, then crossed his eyes, puffed out his cheeks, and blew a raspberry. The youngster laughed delightedly and waved.

A horse shied away from the steam-powered insect and overturned a vegetable stall. Onions and potatoes spilled onto the road and bounced across the cobbles. Shouts and curses followed the giant beetle as it rounded a corner and scurried out of sight.

"Wotcha, 'andsome," crooned a streetwalker from a doorway. "Fancy a bit of 'ow's yer father?"

Burton winked at her, flipped her a tuppenny bit, but kept walking.

Up ahead, a steam-horse emitted a clangourous racket, veered to the right, and crashed into the side of a tavern. An elderly man emerged from the cab behind the engine and shouted: "Great heavens, man! You knocked the stuffing out of me!"

"It's the bleedin' back axle, guv'nor!" the driver explained. "Third time it's broken this week!"

Burton turned into Montagu Place.

"Hey up, Cap'n! How's it diddlin'?" came a hail.

"It's diddling very well, thank you, Mr. Grub. How's business?"

"Awful!"

"The chestnut season is almost upon us. I'm sure that'll improve matters."

"P'raps, Cap'n. P'raps. You been to see his nibs again?"

"The prime minister? Yes, I was summoned."

"Well, I 'ope you told 'im that the lot o' the common man ain't no bed o' roses."

"I always mention it, Mr. Grub."

"An' he does bugger all about it! Bloody politicians!"

"A breed apart," Burton noted.

"That's it in a nutshell, Cap'n!"

They paused while a rotorship roared noisily overhead. Mr. Grub shaded his eyes and looked up at the enormous vessel. "What's that what's wrote on the bottom of it?" he shouted.

Burton, who knew the street vendor was illiterate, said: "It is rather hard to make out, isn't it? I think it says: *Make a new life in India. Space, spice, sunshine, and all the tea you can drink!*"

The mighty ship slid away over the rooftops.

"You've been to India, ain'tcha, Cap'n? Would you recommend it?"

"It has its attractions."

"But not for the likes o' me, I suppose. I reckons I'm better off 'ere on me own little corner of good old Blighty! Got me own patch, ain't I! What more can a man arsk for?"

"Quite so, Mr. Grub. Good day to you!"

"An' to you, Cap'n!" said Grub, touching the peak of his cap.

Burton strode on.

As he neared his front door, he heard: "Read all about it! Lincoln declares slaves free in Confederate States! Read all about it! Emancipation for slaves in America!"

The king's agent whistled in wonder. He spotted little Oscar Wilde and called him over.

"Big news, eh, Quips?"

"Aye, that it is, sir!" The boy exchanged a newspaper for coins.

Burton read out the headline: "*Lincoln's Emancipation Proclamation.* Well, well! That'll make things difficult for Pam! It looks to me as if America's president is every bit as cunning as our own prime minister!"

"We have really everything in common with America nowadays," said Quips. "Except, of course, language."

The king's agent chuckled. "Emancipation!" he announced triumphantly. "I can't say I'll be one whit sad to see that dreadful trade banished. If America is intent on becoming civilised, then Lincoln's proclamation has just taken it a good deal closer to achieving that goal!"

Three harvesters stalked past on their tall legs, each with crated goods swinging in netting below their bodies. The second of them had somehow developed a limp, and as it thudded past, its damaged leg made a rhythmic complaint: *creak—ker-chang, creak—ker-chang, creak—ker-chang.*

Burton recalled Sir Charles Babbage's hatred of noise.

"The fact is, Captain," said Quips, "that civilisation requires slaves. The Greeks were quite right there. Unless there are slaves to do the ugly, horrible, uninteresting work, culture and contemplation become almost impossible. Human slavery is wrong, insecure, and demoralising. On mechanical slavery, on the slavery of the machine, the future of the world depends."

The famous explorer watched the three huge mechanised insects striding away. People scattered from their path. Voices were raised in anger, fists shaken.

"Maybe so, young 'un. Maybe so."

He bade the urchin farewell and mounted the steps of his home, glancing up at the boards that covered the hole where his study window used to be. The builders were due tomorrow to effect repairs.

"William Trounce is upstairs," Mrs. Angell informed him as he entered the hallway.

"You're back!"

"I am, Sir Richard. And a good thing, too. I don't know why, but I've been under the impression that you promised to have the place clean and tidy. I suppose all the sea air must have gone to my head and filled me with funny notions."

"I'm sorry, Mother. There's been a great deal happening. I haven't stopped!"

"Have you made us safe?"

"Yes. The Tichborne business is over and done with."

"Good. Get yourself upstairs, then. I'll fetch some cold cuts and pickles for you and your flat-footed friend."

Burton leaned forward and pecked her on the cheek. "Angell by name, angel by nature. What would I do without you?"

He bounded up the stairs, past the wrecked study, and on to the library.

"Trounce, old man!" he declared as he entered. "It is undoubtedly a splendid day!"

"Gibber-mouth!" Pox squawked from his perch.

The Scotland Yard man rose from a chair, put a book aside, and shook Burton's hand in greeting.

"Thank goodness you're here!" he exclaimed. "I've had to bear the brunt of it all by myself. I don't think I've ever been insulted so assiduously—and that's saying something for a policeman!"

"Sit down. Take a brandy. Smoke a cigar," said Burton, throwing himself into an armchair.

Trounce sat and squinted at him suspiciously. "By Jove, you almost look happy! I didn't know that infernal face of yours was capable of such an expression!"

"I'm full of good tidings! Brunel has designed a new and more efficient voice-producing instrument—no more of that awful ding-donging—and, at this very moment, he's fitting one to Herbert Spencer. Our clockwork philosopher will be speaking by the end of the day!"

Trounce clapped his hands together. "That's tremendous! What's he going to do with himself? It must be rather awkward, being mechanical!"

Burton produced a cheroot and applied a lucifer to it. "He wants Admiral Nelson's old job—wants to be my valet. Says he doesn't trust anyone else to keep him fully wound. And he wants to write; says he's never had such clarity of thought and already has three volumes completed in his head—he just needs to scribble 'em down. If he uses my autoscribe, he'll be knocking them out at ten to the dozen!"

"A wind-up author!" exclaimed Trounce. "That really takes the biscuit!"

"It's a publisher's dream," Burton declared.

"Flap-tongued baboon!" sang Pox.

The king's agent drew in smoke, put his head back, and blew out a perfectly formed ring.

"Good news regarding Sir Roger, too. The Arundell family has taken him in, and Brunel is fitting him with power-driven arms, the same as those worn by Daniel Gooch. That'll certainly compensate for his missing limb. Nothing doing with the face, though; I fear the poor soul will be behind that iron mask for the rest of his life."

"Will he take up residence at Tichborne House?"

"Yes, and he's adamant that the dole will continue to be paid every year. He still believes in Lady Mabella's curse."

"I don't blame him. His family has had nothing but trouble since Sir Henry broke his ancestor's vow."

Burton jumped up and said: "What about that brandy, then?"

He crossed to the chest of drawers by the door and returned with a decanter and a couple of glasses. He poured generous measures and handed one to his friend.

"How's Honesty?" he asked as he returned to his armchair. "Has he recovered from his injuries?"

"More or less. He'll not have use of his hand for a while. He's taking a month's leave. I think the sight of all those animated corpses pushed him to the brink. I've never seen him so unnerved. I daresay time spent with his wife and garden will put him to rights. He's a tough little beggar." The Scotland Yard man raised his eyebrows. "I'm still waiting," he said. "It's all good news but none of it explains your—what is it?—*ebullience*. Is that a word?"

"It is," Burton smiled. "And the correct one."

"So let's have it. Tell all."

The famous explorer took a gulp of brandy, put his glass aside, and said: "Acting on a recommendation from my extraordinarily talented and brilliant assistant—"

"And perverted," Trounce added.

"And perverted—the government has purchased the seven François Garnier Choir Stones from Edwin Brundleweed. They will, I'm happy to report, continue to reside in Herbert Spencer's babbage brain. The government has also bought the seven South American fragments from Sir Roger. Palmerston wants to ensure that all the Eyes of Nāga are in British hands. It's a matter of state security."

"So now they are. What of it?"

"Two of them are, Trounce. Two of them."

The detective inspector frowned and shook his head. "There are only two. The third has never been discovered. It's somewhere in—Oh."

Burton's eyes glinted. "Africa!" he said.

"You mean—?"

"Yes, my friend. Tomorrow I shall start putting together an expedition. I'm off to search for the third stone, and, while I'm at it, I mean to locate once and for all the source of the River Nile!"

"You're going to put yourself through all that again?"

"Don't worry, old man. With the government funding the expedition and Brunel supplying vehicles for the initial stages of the safari, I think I can safely predict that this attempt will be a great deal less traumatic than the last!"

Pox let loose a terrific shriek: "Bollocks!"

MEANWHILE, IN THE VICTORIAN AGE...

SIR RICHARD FRANCIS BURTON (1821–1890)

1862 was a particularly bad year for Burton. Newly married to Isabel Arundell, he was separated from her for almost the entire twelve months. As consul on the disease-ridden island of Fernando Po, he spent much time exploring West Africa and was exposed to areas that had been decimated by the slave trade. As ever, he managed to commit his astute observations and sometimes extremely harsh opinions to paper, resulting in three books: *Wanderings in West Africa*, *Abeokuta and the Cameroons Mountains*, and *A Mission to Gelele, King of Dahomé*.

ALGERNON CHARLES SWINBURNE (1837–1909)

Due in no small part to the efforts of Richard Monckton Milnes, 1862 was the year that Swinburne's maturing poetry gained greater critical recognition. It was not, however, an easy year for him personally. His great friend Lizzie Rossetti (née Siddal) died, and his one and only marriage proposal was rejected—the recipient, whose identity remains a mystery, laughed in his face. His alcoholism was also reaching epic proportions by now, making his behaviour erratic in the extreme.

Wouldst thou not know whom England, whom the world, Mourns? . . .

is from the poem *Elegy*, which appeared in *Astrophel and Other Poems* in 1904. It does not refer to Sir Richard Francis Burton.

If you were queen of pleasure . . .

is from the poem *A Match*, which appeared in *Poems and Ballads* in 1866.

CHARLES BABBAGE (1791–1871)

The man who is regarded as the father of computing was a complex person-ality, haunted by personal tragedies (including the death of five of his eight children) and ongoing funding problems. Some of his most groundbreaking designs, such as his Difference Engine, were never built during his lifetime. The unfinished status of so many of his projects can, in part, be blamed on financial woes, but Babbage's eccentric character certainly didn't help mat-ters. Among his many quirks, he possessed a distaste for "common people" and an aversion to the noise they produced. His ire was particularly directed at street musicians.

Babbage was never knighted.

In 1862, he was busy writing his autobiographical *Passages from the Life of a Philosopher*.

THE MEASUREMENT OF BRAINWAVES

The understanding and measurement of the brain's electrical activity prop-erly began with a British physician, Richard Caton (1842–1926), who pre-sented his findings to the *British Medical Journal* in 1875.

THE TICHBORNE AFFAIR

The sensation of the age, the Tichborne affair commenced in 1866, when the Dowager Lady Tichborne received a letter from a man purporting to be her long-lost son, Roger. This man, who was in all probability Arthur Orton, a morbidly obese butcher from Wapping, had relocated to Australia some years before. When he arrived back in England to claim the Tichborne estates, he was strongly opposed by the establishment but fervently supported by the working classes. Two trials followed. During the first, which lasted 102 days, the Claimant failed to prove his identity and the Tichborne inheritance was denied him. The second trial—a criminal prosecution—lasted 188 days.

Arthur Orton was found guilty of perjury and sentenced to fourteen years of hard labour (he served ten).

Despite the overwhelming evidence against him (not least being the fact that he looked nothing like Sir Roger Tichborne), the Claimant became a great favourite among the lower classes, and was the subject of humour, songs, and plays. His trial exposed the weaknesses of the aristocracy and led many ordinary men and women to the conviction that he was the victim of a conspiracy.

The Tichborne/Doughty/Arundell family weathered the storm, though they became doubly vigilant that the annual Tichborne dole should never be missed.

HERBERT SPENCER (1820–1903)

One of the most influential, accomplished, and misunderstood philosophers in British history, Herbert Spencer melded Darwinism with sociology. He originated the phrase "survival of the fittest," which was then taken up by Darwin himself. It was also adopted, misinterpreted, and misused by a number of governments, who employed it to justify their eugenics programs, culminating in the Holocaust of the 1940s. Spencer, unfortunately, thus became associated with one of the darkest periods in modern history.

Bizarrely, he is also credited with the invention of the paperclip.

He said:

"The wise man must remember that while he is a descendant of the past, he is a parent of the future."

"When a man's knowledge is not in order, the more of it he has, the greater his confusion."

"There is a principle which is a bar against all information, which is proof against all arguments, and which cannot fail to keep a man in everlasting ignorance—that principle is contempt prior to investigation."

"The republican form of government is the highest form of government, but, because of this, it requires the highest type of human nature—a type nowhere at present existing."

ISABELLA MARY MAYSON (1836–1865)

In 1856, Isabella Mayson married Samuel Orchart Beeton. As Mrs. Beeton, she became famous as the author of *Mrs. Beeton's Book of Household Management*, and was arguably the very first celebrity chef. She died from puerperal fever, aged just twenty-eight.

OSCAR WILDE (1854–1900)

As an adult, Oscar Wilde, who in his childhood was neither a refugee nor a paperboy, said:

"Whenever people agree with me I always feel I must be wrong."

"The only way to get rid of a temptation is to yield to it."

"The difference between literature and journalism is that journalism is unreadable, and literature is not read."

"My own business always bores me to death; I prefer other people's."
—From *Lady Windermere's Fan*

"To disagree with three-fourths of the British public is one of the first requisites of sanity."

"We have really everything in common with America nowadays except, of course, language."

"The fact is that civilisation requires slaves. The Greeks were quite right there. Unless there are slaves to do the ugly, horrible, uninteresting work, culture and contemplation become almost impossible. Human slavery is wrong, insecure, and demoralising. On mechanical slavery, on the slavery of the machine, the future of the world depends."

DOCTOR EDWARD VAUGHAN HYDE KENEALY (1819–1880)

Most famous for his role as counsel for the Tichborne Claimant, Kenealy's scandalous conduct during the trial earned him widespread notoriety. In the aftermath, he published a newspaper through which to harangue the judges and jury. He was subsequently disbenched and disbarred. Entering politics, he sought to employ his position in parliament to further the Tichborne cause. He failed, and though always a controversial and extremely eccentric figure, he gradually faded from the public arena.

ANDREW BOGLE (APPROX. 1801–1877)

Formerly a slave, Bogle was taken from Jamaica to England by Edward Tichborne (who became Sir Edward Doughty) to work as his valet. In 1830, he married the family's household nurse and they had two sons.

In 1853, after Sir Edward's death, Bogle, whose first wife had died, retired with a small pension, married a teacher, and moved to Australia where, in 1866, Arthur Orton approached him. Convinced that Orton was the long-lost Sir Roger Tichborne, Bogle travelled with him to England and supported him through the course of the two trials. Afterward, though the Tichborne family restored his pension, the old Jamaican lived in near poverty until his death.

MARIE JOSEPH FRANÇOIS GARNIER (1839–1873)

Garnier was a French military officer and explorer who became famous for his exploration of the Mekong River in Southeast Asia. He did not discover any black diamonds in Cambodia.

RICHARD SPRUCE (1817–1893)

One of the foremost botanists of the Victorian era, Spruce was the first man to successfully cultivate bitter bark quinine, making its antimalarial qualities widely available. During his wide-ranging, fifteen-year-long exploration of the Amazon, he visited many places hitherto unseen by Europeans, and returned with many thousands of specimens. A quiet, solitary, and studious man, he was loyal to the British Empire and was involved with neither Eugenicists nor Germans.

He was elected a member of the Royal Geographical Society in 1866.

Spruce never said: "I see a tremendously bright future . . ."

THE TRENT AFFAIR

Also known as the Mason and Slidell Affair, this was a major diplomatic incident that, in 1861, came close to pulling Great Britain into the American Civil War. Fortunately, President Lincoln was able to calm Lord Palmerston down somewhat, and the prime minister resisted the temptation to align his country with the Confederate forces.

CHARLES ALTAMONT DOYLE (1832–1893)

The father of Sir Arthur Conan Doyle, Charles suffered from severe alcoholism and was also a depressive. Overshadowed by his more successful brother, Richard, he earned a pittance as a book illustrator and became best known for his increasingly macabre paintings of fairies. He was eventually committed to an asylum, and remained incarcerated until the end of his life.

Sir Arthur also became obsessed with fairies, most famously those supposedly photographed at Cottingley. It almost ruined his reputation.

HELENA BLAVATSKY (1831–1891)

A psychic medium and occultist, Madam Blavatsky rode a wave of interest in spiritualism and became one of its foremost proponents, founding Theosophy and the Theosophical Society. She claimed to have many psychic abilities, such as the power of levitation, clairvoyance, astral projection, and telepathy. For much of her life, she toured the world to promote her beliefs. Unsurprisingly, her work attracted a great deal of criticism, and she was accused of fraud, racism, and even of being a Russian spy. She died in England, aged sixty.

Madam Blavatsky said:

"Therefore, the Esotericists maintain that there is no inorganic or dead matter in nature, the distinction between the two made by Science being as unfounded as it is arbitrary and devoid of reason."

"If coming events are said to cast their shadows before, past events cannot fail to leave their impress behind them."

It is not known whether she ever used the Russian proverb: *"Bare derutsya—u kholopov chuby treshchat,"* which translates as, "When masters are fighting, their servants' forelocks are creaking," suggesting that the common people suffer when powerful people fight.

SIR DANIEL GOOCH (1816–1889)

Sir Daniel Gooch was a railway engineer who worked with such luminaries as Robert Stephenson and Isambard Kingdom Brunel. He was the first chief mechanical engineer of the Great Western Railway and was later its chairman. Gooch was also involved in the laying of the first successful Transatlantic telegraph cable and became the chairman of the Telegraph Construction Company. Later in life he was elected to office as a parliamentary minister. He was knighted in 1866.

WILLIAM HOLMAN HUNT (1827–1910)

Holman Hunt, one of the Pre-Raphaelite artists, did not say: "The Technologists tell us not to worry about the machines . . ."

WILLIAM GLADSTONE (1809–1898)

One of Britain's longest serving politicians, Gladstone, a Liberal, was four times prime minister and four times chancellor of the Exchequer. He served under Robert Peel, Lord Aberdeen, and Lord Palmerston. He is credited with the creation of many modern political campaigning techniques. One of the most famous quirks of his personality was his dedication to the rehabilitation of prostitutes. Even while prime minister, he used to walk the streets late at night, approaching "fallen women" to try to persuade them to mend their ways. This, obviously, led to rumours. In 1927, long after his death, claims that he'd had improper relationships with these women led to a court case during which the jury, upon examining the evidence, vindicated Gladstone, confirming his high moral character.

HENRY MORTON STANLEY (1841–1904)

Stanley said:

> *"An insuperable obstacle to rapid transit in Africa is the want of carriers, and as speed was the main object of the Expedition under my command, my duty was to lessen this difficulty as much as possible."*

He did not add:

> *"Rotorchairs were the obvious solution."*

BATTERSEA POWER STATION

Battersea Power Station was not built until the 1920s.

. . . and the Eyes of Nāga, if they exist, remain undiscovered.

ABOUT THE AUTHOR

MARK HODDER is descended from John Angell, a pirate who sailed with Captain Kidd. According to family legend, Angell invested most of his ill-gotten gains in land, particularly in Angell Town near Brixton in London. Anyone who can provide irrefutable legal evidence that they are descended from Angell will inherit the land, which is estimated to be worth at least £64,000,000. Over the course of generations, members of the family have lost a fortune trying to prove the link, and many people who have no connection with the family at all have adopted the name in order to make a claim. As a result, the family tree is extremely tangled and a legal connection to the pirate's treasure is almost certainly impossible to establish.

Mark's great-grandfather was Doctor Albert Leigh, who went to medical school with Sir Arthur Conan Doyle. The two men were great friends—they joined the Freemasons together—and Sir Arthur presented Albert with a complete set of Sherlock Holmes first editions, all inscribed: *To dear Leigh, from your friend Doyle.* They would fetch a fortune at auction today. Unfortunately, upon Leigh's death in 1944, his housekeeper, an actress, made off with the volumes.

Thus it is that two great fortunes have eluded Mark Hodder.

Denied money-for-nothing and the luxury, idleness, and indulgences it would bring, Mark lives in Spain, teaches English as a foreign language, and writes novels. His first Burton & Swinburne adventure—*The Strange Affair of Spring Heeled Jack*—was published in 2010.